FORESKINHEADS

A NOVEL

BY

WARREN STREISAND, MD

GMK WRITING
& EDITING

Published by GMK Writing & Editing, Inc

Produced by GMK Writing and Editing, Inc.
Managing Editor: Katie Benoit
Copyedited by Kelly Nutter Clody
Proofread by Amy Paradysz
Text design by Libby Kingsbury
Composition by Joanna Beyer
Cover design by Libby Kingsbury
Printed by IngramSpark

Print ISBN: 978-1-966981-09-1
Ebook EISN: 978-1-966981-10-7

Note: This publication is a work of fiction. Names, characters, places, and incidents either are the product of the author's imagination or are used fictitiously, and any resemblance to persons, living or dead, businesses, companies, events, or locales is purely coincidental.

I would like to dedicate this book to my wife Isabel, whose life was consistently interrupted by my frequent computer and psychological questions. She graciously tolerated changes in plans and even mealtimes based on "brainstorms," which, I thought, required my immediate attention. With the book completed, I plan to accompany her in catching up on all her beloved TV shows ... and then, with a storyline already in mind, begin my next novel.

ACKNOWLEDGMENTS

I would like to acknowledge and thank my beta readers who did not budge when I disagreed with their recommended changes—and I'm glad they didn't. They are Joan Gerowitz, Stephen Rubin, PhD, and Shelly Strickler.

As my computer skills are marginal, 1 relied heavily on others—getting my story from lined yellow paper onto a computer took a lot of doing. My thanks to Nancy Feldman for taking on this task. Additional technical support came from Scott Streisand, Ashley Streisand, and Randi Streisand Tercyak.

Forensic support was offered by Steven J. Alper, police officer on the Brooklyn Staff Task Force. Legal support was offered by Attorney David H. Greenberg. Oncological support was offered by Alfred M. Kalman, MD. Cardiological support was offered by William Sheinbaum, MD. Psychological support was offered by Isabel Streisand, PhD.

CHAPTER 1

WHAT'S GOING ON HERE?

"Good morning, Aretha," said brown-mustachioed Dr. Jamie Bloom. The thirty-one-year-old board-certified urologist walked into his office with a mild limp, carrying a bag containing bagels and vegetable cream cheese and putting them in the refrigerated eating area. "The bagels are warm."

"Good morning and thank you, Dr. Bloom," replied Aretha. His thirty-three-year-old receptionist entered the Current Procedural Technology code for the surgical insertion of a self-contained penile prosthesis into a computerized insurance form. "Your first patient is here, and his slide is on the microscope."

"Do we have the result of his PSA?" asked Bloom, who was also the vice chief of surgery at University Hospital in Tamarac, Southeast Florida.

"It's in his chart," she replied, entering the CPT code for circumcision into the insurance form for Alvin Lewis's recent surgery. She had been with the doctor since he started practicing four years ago in 1999. "Alvin Lewis has already called three times this morning," she added.

"Is he having a problem?"

"I can't make sense out of what he wants. I'll get him on the phone, and you can speak with him."

"Okay, after I see our first patient."

Bloom finished up with his patient and got on the line with Alvin Lewis.

"Hi, Mr. Lewis, how are you doing?" he asked, remembering the circumcision he did on him a few days ago.

"I'm fine," replied Lewis.

"That's good. What can I do for you? Did you want to make an appointment?"

"I want to schedule my surgery. Can you do it this Friday?"

"You mean you want to follow up your surgery with an office visit? Sure."

"No, not that. I want to *have* my surgery. Don't you remember? Someone from your office called and told me you had an emergency and you had to cancel my surgery last Friday."

"Someone from my office?"

"That's what they said."

"Hold on a second, Mr. Lewis," said Bloom putting him on hold.

Bloom walked over to Aretha's desk and asked her to show him last Friday's schedule.

"That's his name scheduled at one o'clock last Friday at University Hospital," said Aretha touching his name.

"Something is screwy," said Bloom, shaking his head. "Do me a favor. Call outpatient surgery at the hospital and ask them the name of our patient who had surgery last Friday."

CHAPTER 2

HIJACKING

Bloom sat at his desk and stared at the Lucite model of a penile prosthesis. It had been seven hours since outpatient surgery had confirmed he had indeed performed a circumcision on someone named Alvin Lewis last Friday. He had already seen his day's patients and had returned his patients' calls. He was about to make afternoon rounds when Aretha buzzed him.

"Your wife called a little while ago to remind you to get food for Flyer. We start tomorrow at 9:30. See you then."

"Bye."

Still very confused and not able to make sense about what happened last Friday, he left the office, walked over to the hospital, made hospital rounds, and drove to the Pet Supermarket on University Drive and Commercial Boulevard. As he headed toward the bird section, a white stretch limousine pulled in front of the store and waited. He scooped out two pounds of mixed cockatiel feed and sunflower seeds at $1.99 a pound. After waiting twenty minutes at checkout and not seeing or finding any store employees, he put four singles and a quarter on the checkout counter, wrote a note on a shopping bag stating what he had done and how he could be reached, and left the store.

"Dr. Bloom," came a voice from out of the back of the limo's rolled-down window. As he walked toward the voice, the chauffeur opened the back door. Two and a quarter hours later Bloom emerged from the limo and got into his car.

CHAPTER 3

A TON OF BENNIES

earing "The Godfather's Theme" ringtone, Bloom reflexively reached into his trouser pocket, pulled out his BlackBerry, and saw that the University ER was looking for him. He pushed the speaker button and was greeted by Janice at the nurses' desk.

"Dr. Bloom, we've got a patient for you," she said. "The ER doc thinks you'll need to come in for this one."

"What's the story?"

"Some guy with a twisted testicle. He's in a lot of pain."

"I don't think I'm on call."

"He requested you."

"How old is he?"

"He's in his forties."

"Testicular torsion is rare over forty. I doubt he's got that. But I'm close by. I'll be there in a few minutes."

"Good. He's in room 3."

Ten minutes later Bloom entered room 3 and greeted the patient.

"Can you make sure the door is closed?" said the hospital-garbed male.

"Sure," said Bloom, stepping backward and seeing he'd already closed it. "How old are you?" Bloom asked.

"Forty-four."

"What seems to be the problem?"

"There's no problem," replied the patient handing Bloom a package. "It explains why I'm here."

Bloom took the package, opened it, and saw a huge number of hundred-dollar bills.

"You don't have medical insurance?" quipped Bloom, realizing it was probably payment for the circumcision that was done on the person substituted for Alvin Lewis and the one he was just forced to do at gunpoint in the limousine.

"My client thanks you for your surgical skills," said the patient.

"Who's your client?"

When there was no response, Bloom added, "His satisfaction is good enough for me," and handed him back the package.

"You've earned it," said the patient handing it back to Bloom.

"Hardly," said Bloom refusing to take it.

"Don't refuse me," said the patient impatiently.

"I'm sorry, I can't take it," replied Bloom, starting to walk away.

"Doc!" shouted the patient, taking a gun out of his pants.

"Look, I can't take it!" said Bloom, not yet seeing the firearm.

"No, you look!" answered the patient pointing the gun at Bloom. "Tomorrow at 7:15 a.m. your son Peter gets on his bus. Right?"

"Who are you?"

"Someone you're never going to fuck with."

Bloom took some deep breaths, patted his thigh twice, took the package, and put it in his lab coat. The patient put his gun away, finished getting dressed, and left the ER. Bloom sat down on a nearby chair, closed his eyes, and rested his chin in his palms, remaining there until Nurse Janice walked in.

"You cured him, Dr. Bloom," said Janice. "He could hardly walk when he came in."

"That's why I get the big bucks," replied Bloom, patting his lab coat. "What the hell is going on here?" he muttered to himself when the nurse left the room. "What the hell is going on?"

CHAPTER 4

MEANWHILE BACK AT THE RANCHES

The ride home—University Drive to Commercial Boulevard to Sawgrass Expressway then I-75 and finally Arvida Parkway—took Bloom twenty-two minutes, plus another four minutes from the gatehouse at Weston's Windmill Ranches to his house.

"Dadee home!" shouted his two-and-a-half-year-old, pajama-clad daughter, Lisa. She ran to him, her *Cinderella* book in one hand, a frozen juice bar in the other.

"How's the little princess doing?" asked Bloom, picking her up, hugging her, and trying to take a bite of the bar.

"No biy!" she yelled pulling her hand away.

"Okay, no bite," said Bloom laughing, hugging her again, and putting her down.

"Wead Dindawella, dadee," she pleaded.

"Did Lisa have supper?"

"They couldn't wait," said his twenty-nine-year-old psychologist wife Missy, certified sex therapist, as she walked in from the family room, giving him a kiss and a hug. "You and I will eat in twenty minutes. Okay?"

"Good. Where's Peter?" he asked.

"Petaw do puhl," said Lisa.

"Whaaa?" asked Bloom pulling back from the hug, looking to Missy for interpretive guidance.

"Petaw do puhl," repeated Lisa.

"Peter's doing what?"

"Petaw do puhl!" repeated Lisa raising her voice.

"He's doing his puzzle," whispered Missy.

"Oh, his Sesame Street puzzle!" said Bloom. "Did you help Peter with his puzzle?"

"Me hel Petaw."

"Let's see Peter's puzzle," said Bloom, picking her up and carrying her down the hallway.

"No biy," she said holding the pop stick away from him.

Bloom laughed again.

"Hi, Petaw!" shouted Lisa upon entering Peter's room.

"Can I have some of your bar?" asked Peter looking up.

"Dehr," she replied, reaching down with her arm extended.

"Thank you," said the seven-year-old, taking a bite then looking back down at the puzzle.

"Hey, what about me?" asked Bloom.

"Give daddy a bite," said Peter without looking up.

"Peter, I meant you saying hello to me!"

"Hello, daddy," said Peter, briefly looking up.

"I'm waiting."

Peter groaned, got up, gave Bloom a kiss, and sat back down.

Bloom spent the next ten minutes helping Peter with the puzzle. Then he helped Lisa brush her teeth, read *Cinderella* to her for the second time that day, and got ready for dinner.

"Do you have a puzzle for me to figure out?" asked Peter, following Bloom down the hallway.

"Here's one," said Bloom. "A two-hundred-pound man wants to ferry himself and his two children, each weighing a hundred pounds and each capable of operating the boat to and from the other side of the lake, but the boat cannot hold more than two hundred pounds at one time. How does he do it? Tell me after I finish dinner."

"Is this a variation of the farmer, chicken, fox, and corn puzzle?"

"Sort of."

CHAPTER 5

FLORIDA, WE HAVE A PROBLEM

"Did you see his face?" asked Missy, rinsing off the salad bowls and putting them into the dishwasher.

"Just his penis," replied Bloom, putting the salad dressing into the refrigerator and taking out a bottle of caffeine-free Diet Coke and a bottle of Orange Diet Slice along with two insulated mugs from the freezer.

"Would you recognize him if you saw it again?"

"Five penises in a lineup?" asked Bloom pouring the soda into the mugs.

"I mean, don't you have a style?"

"Do you mean do they all pee to the left?"

"You can usually tell the plastic surgeon by the nose," said Missy, opening the oven and turning over the veal chops.

"My jobs are all the same. I don't take off too much or too little. And they all pee straight down the middle."

"Do you want me to defrost a hot dog?"

"I don't think I'll ever be eating another one of those," replied Bloom with a smile, showing her the package he was given. "Have you ever seen a picture of Salmon Chase?"

"Do you mean Salmon P. Chase?"

"How do you know about him?"

"It was on *Jeopardy*. He's on the ten-thousand-dollar bill. Why are you asking?"

"I got paid today for the two circumcisions I did—the one in the hospital last Friday on the person who was substituted for my patient and the one today at gunpoint in the limousine. The amount I received could have been paid with two Salmon P. Chase bills if this was 1945," added Bloom, having counted the number of hundred-dollar bills once he got into his car.

"Twenty thousand dollars is a lot of money."

"That's 200 Bennies. I guess that included the tip."

"Don't urologists work for tips?"

"Ha ha. With the new Medicare fee schedule, we more likely work for peanuts."

"I saw a ten-thousand-dollar bill just last week," said Missy.

"Where'd you see one?"

"Our landscaper had one—and he gave it to me! It was a ten-thousand-dollar bill for the landscaping work they did," she added, putting the chops on the table.

"You're on a roll," cried Bloom, enjoying Missy's repartee.

Missy smiled. "What are you going to do with all the Bennies?"

"It has to be documented."

"By whom?"

"By someone."

"Call Mac."

"I'm not sure I want anyone else to know about it."

"How much does Aretha know about Lewis?"

"She knows he didn't have his surgery."

"Does she think you operated on someone else?"

"I don't know. I would think she does."

"The chops are ready," said Missy, shutting off the broiler and plating them.

As Bloom reached for his fork, he grimaced and held his shoulder, remembering the short-acting barbiturate that had been injected there when he was forced into the limousine.

"They didn't use an alcohol sponge," he said, forking a chop and putting it into his plate.

"What about what *you* used? The instruments? Sutures? Prep? The dressing?"

"I'd have to say it was a pretty sterile circumcision. I used a scrub brush and wore a gown and mask. I double gloved and was very careful not to stick myself. I sure hope the needle used on me was sterile."

"I'm sure it was," said Missy, cutting the meat away from the bone.

"Spoken like a true psychologist."

"No. Spoken like someone who's just been given the facts. That reminds me," she added. "I saw your patient Ida Stern today."

"Good try," said Bloom, regarding the subject change. "I call her Foak."

"I'm sure it was sterile," said Missy, continuing on subject. "Let's eat."

They ate pretty much in silence, both wanting to speak but reluctant to—Missy about the need for an AIDS test down the road, Bloom about the gun and the implied threat to Peter.

CHAPTER 6

THE LAST OF A TRIO

"Where are you going?" asked Missy seeing Bloom grab his keys and wallet.

"I left Flyer's food in the limo," he replied heading toward the garage. I'm going to see if I can find the limo."

"You're an idiot, you know that?" replied Missy, unable to keep herself from laughing out loud over his decision to find the limo rather than doing the easier thing of buying more pet food.

"And funny," said Bloom also laughing.

"Why don't I just pop some popcorn? That should tide the buzzard over until tomorrow."

"Good thinking," said Bloom putting his keys and wallet back into the dish on the pass-through as the phone rang.

"I'll get it," said Missy reaching for the portable phone. "It's for you," she added, handing him the phone.

He spoke for a few seconds, then regrabbed his keys and wallet and handed her back the phone.

"Foak, or rather, Ida Stern, has been shot!"

"Oh God! Is she alive?"

"Barely," replied Bloom from the utility room.

"Was it an attempted suicide?" asked Missy anxiously.

"I don't know," yelled Bloom from the garage.

Four minutes later Bloom was on I-75. As he sped north, he thought about his first encounter with Foak, or rather hers with him. He had just lacerated his buttocks on a diving board during some Father's Day festivities and was fully exposed on the ER table waiting to be sutured. Suddenly he heard someone open the curtain, hesitate for a few seconds, and then close it again. A few hours later, when he was called to the ER to see a patient with urinary bleeding, he remembered introducing himself to the patient.

"I'm Dr. Bloom," he said extending his hand.

"I know," replied the svelte, elderly patient who presented with significantly developed upper body musculature, the result of serving three four-year stints in the Israeli Army from 1948 to 1952, 1954 to 1958, and 1960 to 1964, which she maintained through tri-weekly visits from her trainer and running five miles on Mondays, Wednesdays, and Fridays.

"Do we know each other?"

"We met this afternoon."

"Are you sure?" asked Bloom giving a quizzical look.

"I never forget a face, or a tush."

"Huh?"

"You've got a great tush, doc."

"That was you at the curtain?"

"Do you need someone to take out your stitches?"

"How old are you?" asked the physician.

"Old enough to be your something or other."

"Ninety," said Bloom glancing at her chart.

"Eighty-nine!" she replied correcting him. "I'm all talk, doc. I'm Ida Stern. My friends call me Foak. F-O-A-K."

Bloom remembered finding a large stone in her only kidney, requiring him to perform a percutaneous nephrolitholapaxy, which consisted of ultrasonically disintegrating a stone through a small hole in her back made by the interventional radiologist three weeks later.

As he paid the Sawgrass toll and read the name of the toll collector SISTINE, he chuckled and recalled that her very hard and rare kidney stone was made of an amino acid called cystine. He also remembered her postsurgical depression and his subsequent referral for her to see Missy. So Bloom could understand Missy's concern about a possible suicide. When he arrived at the hospital, Foak was in the OR. Her chest had been cracked open by thoracic surgeon Dr. Ed Causey, and she was on her tenth unit of blood.

"Is she going to make it?" asked Bloom, who had changed into green scrubs, peering over the assistant surgeon's left shoulder.

"Look where my finger is," replied Causey moving a few inches to his left, showing Bloom the anatomy. "I've closed the partial tear in her ventricle and taken out the bullet. Now I'm closing the pericardium," he added taking the needle holder and suture from the scrub nurse.

Bloom watched as Causey then closed the chest and followed the patient into recovery.

"A little more exciting than a prostatectomy, eh?" said the Canadian surgeon sitting down to write the post-op orders.

"Do we know what happened?" asked Bloom.

"She was shot about here," said Causey standing up, turning Bloom around and sticking his index finger between Bloom's ribs.

Pretty much rules out suicide, Bloom thought to himself.

He noted the blood in her Foley catheter tubing—the reason for the urologic consultation—and reviewed the papers constituting her chart, dictated his own note, and wrote some orders. He then changed and drove home, forgetting to stop for food for the family's Quaker parakeet.

CHAPTER 7

HEAD COUNSELOR

"Let's start from the beginning," said William McGuirk, who went by Mac, a sixty-year-old transplanted Louisianan with a Southern drawl, who was senior law partner of McGuirk, Williams, Cohen, and Esposito.

"Last Friday," began Bloom, "I saw my patient in the holding area, then changed into scrubs and did a circumcision. An hour and a half later, outpatient surgery called to let me know they were discharging him."

"You didn't see or speak to him during the surgery?"

"It was done under general anesthesia. The patient's eyes were covered for safety purposes. The ether screen was already up by the time I got into the room."

"What's an ether screen?"

"A partition separating the patient's head and anesthesiologist from the surgical field."

"The patient's head is behind it, right?"

Bloom nodded.

"What about in recovery?"

"The patient was still out from the anesthetic, and I was in a hurry to get back to the office."

"So, you never actually saw him after the operation?"

"No. I usually either see them or speak with them, but Friday the office was crazy. When outpatient called to discharge him, they told me he was still very groggy and couldn't come to the phone. They told me there were two people who were ready to take him home, so I said he could be discharged and told them to give him my instruction sheet and have him call my office on Monday."

"Did you call him that night or over the weekend?"

"I was away for the weekend. I told the doctor who was covering for me the names of my patients who were in the hospital, those who were outpatients, and those who were having problems at home."

"Tell me about your other patient—I know, I shouldn't really be calling either of them your patient," added Mac smiling.

Bloom smiled as well and continued. "When I got into the limo..."

"Start from the beginning," interjected Mac.

Before he could begin, "The Godfather Theme" ringtone stopped him. He reached across his waist, grabbed his phone from his pocket, and saw University Hospital's ICU number displayed. Unable to reach anyone in the ICU or his office, he told Mac there might be something wrong with his ICU patient and he needed to leave.

He hurried out of Mac's office, taking the stairs to the first floor and exiting the building. As he limped down the ramp of the adjoining parking garage, he briefly thought about the time sixteen years before when he lost his leg to a ten-foot alligator while fishing and realized he could have already been on his way had he parked in a handicapped spot, but since he hadn't considered his disability a handicap, he never used those spaces. Yes, his prosthesis was inconvenient, but now it was part of him. He considered his life to be normal. He still swam and played basketball and years ago had played for his college golf team.

He got into his car, headed west on McNab, and turned into the main hospital complex, parking in the physicians' covered parking area and taking the stairs to the second floor, two at a time. Foak, he had learned, had been the third and latest victim in the random Sawgrass Expressway shootings. A few minutes ago in Mac's office, he thought Foak might have had a cardiac arrest. He rushed into the ICU hoping to find a flurry of activity.

"Shit!" he exclaimed. Finding a relative quiet, he assumed the worst.

He walked over to bed 11 and found Foak just as he had left her two hours before.

"Can someone tell me what's going on?"

"It was a malfunctioning ventilator," answered the charge nurse walking toward him. "We noticed it right after you hung up. I tried reaching you, but your office was busy. She's fine."

"That's okay," replied Bloom taking a deep breath. "As long as she's alright."

"Dr. Bloom, before you leave, please give us your phone number so we'll have it," said the nurse.

"The medical staff office should be the keeper of all physicians' private numbers," suggested Bloom. "Once the nursing staff can't reach the physician's office, they should have additional means to contact the physician."

"Dr. Bloom, bring it up tomorrow when you're at the medical staff meeting."

"Good idea."

"It was your idea!"

CHAPTER 8

IN THE LINCOLN

"Good morning, Dr. Bloom's office, Aretha speaking. May I help you? He's with a patient right now, Mr. Jones. Hold on please."

Aretha put Mr. Jones on hold and buzzed Bloom via the intercom. A minute later Bloom walked out of the exam room, went into his office, closed the door, and picked up the phone.

"This is Dr. Bloom."

"Dr. Bloom, this is Mr. Jones. You treated me at the ER two nights ago."

"Yes, Mr. Jones."

"I just wanted to let you know that I'm doing well."

"Yes, Mr. Jones."

"So are your other two patients."

"Yes, Mr. Jones."

"You don't seem very pleased."

"I'm not happy about what's happened!"

"Dr. Bloom, I wish you'd be a bit more appreciative, considering all the patients we're referring to you."

"You can stop right now."

"You've been compensated."

"You can have the money."

"I forgot to tell you how cute Peter looked at the bus stop this morning in his cowboy hat and boots."

Bloom took a deep breath, counted to ten, then hung up. A few seconds later, Aretha put Jones through again.

"Don't fuck with me," said Jones.

"I'm hanging up," said Bloom, terminating the call.

A few seconds later, Jones was back again.

"I'll decide when the conversation is over, you got me?"

"I've got you. Is that all?"

"That's all. Now you may hang up."

Bloom hung up for the third time, sat back in his chair, and took some deep breaths.

"Get me Mac," said Bloom through the intercom, getting up and going back into the exam room.

By the time Mac called back, Bloom had seen two more patients and had done a vasectomy.

"Mac, I don't know what to do," said Bloom leaning forward in his chair, doodling on the appointment schedule sheet.

"What do they want you to do?"

"Right this second? Nothing. I'm never told anything beforehand. The person who called me intimated that there might be others. He also mentioned Peter in a quasi-threatening way. What should I do?"

"I'd make sure Peter was better looked after, especially at the bus stop."

"What about Missy and Lisa?"

"Just some general precautions."

"I shouldn't go to the police?"

"No. You don't have a name or a number other than what was on the ER sheet, right?"

"Right, and the number on the ER sheet was a disconnected number."

"Can you tell me something about the limo?"

"It was white. I think it was a Lincoln."

"What about the inside?"

"I don't remember. It was dark and I was sedated."

"How?"

"Via injection," replied Bloom rubbing his shoulder.

"You were gone for two hours?"

"A little more."

"Where did you do the surgery?"

"I did it in the limo."

"In the limo! You said it was dark!"

"A spotlight was put on the surgical site."

"Was there someone to help you with the surgery?"

"No. The person was pretty much heavily sedated. I added some additional local anesthetic as needed."

"Did you see or speak with the patient, er, I mean, victim?"

"No. I only saw his genitals."

"Anything else you want to tell me?"

"My problem will come from the one that was done in the hospital. The hospital will be sending my patient, Mr. Lewis, the one that did not have the surgery, bills and asking him for money. He's already asked me to reschedule his 'canceled' surgery. Theoretically, I could do his surgery in my office under local anesthesia and pay for the one that was done in the hospital. I was given a fair amount of money the other day by someone connected to the incident."

"Really?" asked Mac.

"Yes," said Bloom. "He came to the hospital a short time after I did the second surgery, faking pain in his testicle and asking to be seen by me in order to pay me for the two surgeries I had already done."

"This is crazy, Jamie."

"Tell me about it."

CHAPTER 9

MORE WITH MAC

"I don't have to be in 'til 9:30," said Bloom, filling Flyer's food cup and putting it back in his cage.

"Good," replied Missy, filling the detergent cup, closing the dishwasher, and turning it on. "Maybe you can take Peter to the bus stop. I have a dental appointment at 7:30 this morning."

"I can take him. Aren't most dental appointments scheduled at tooth-hurty?"

"Tooth-hurty. Very good! Anything happening at the office today?"

"It was yesterday! I was starting to tell you last night, but you fell asleep, and I wasn't even talking about one of my surgeries!"

"I'm up now!" replied Missy laughing. "What happened?"

"I got a call from the University ICU while I was in Mac's office. I lost the connection and was unable to get them or my office on the phone. I thought Foak might have arrested!"

"She's alright though, right?"

"Yes. She's fine. But I didn't know that then. So I quickly got out of his office and ran to the hospital."

"Didn't you have your car? Sorry. Please go on. What was it?"

"It was a ventilator malfunction," said Bloom, rolling his eyes and chuckling about Missy's not having your car joke. Comical banter was a major component of their relationship.

"A ventilator malfunction? Isn't that dangerous?"

"You would think so."

"Have you ever heard of anything like that?"

"No, not that I can remember. In any event, she was fine, and she'll be extubated this afternoon."

"Do you think I should see her?"

"Yes. I'll put in a consult for you."

"What'd Mac have to say?"

"Essentially what he said before. There's nothing we should do right now other than watch you and the kids, especially Peter at his bus stop. He agreed Jones's comments and behavior is threatening. But he also said that since I'm the one doing the surgeries and don't know who's making me do them, I shouldn't involve the police at this time. In addition, he said since we don't know how unstable Jones is, and since I didn't think he was the one calling the shots, I may have already done all that someone may have needed me to do, which in Jones's mind, might mean I am now dispensable, so I need to be careful with him, especially since he's already waved his gun in my face once."

"Three sentences rolled into one. Nice."

"I told Mac I felt helpless. He said he'd feel the same way if he was in my situation. Then he asked me why I thought the circumcisions were being done, but I told him I had no idea."

"What *do* you think is going on?" asked Missy.

"Beats me."

"Do you think either of the people wanted their surgery?"

"I would think more likely they didn't want their surgery."

"You mean someone forced them to have it?"

"That would make more sense."

"Hopefully we won't find out."

"I'm going to make sure we don't."

"How?"

"Like I told Mac, the hospital is going to bill Mr. Lewis, the one who was on the schedule, not the one who had the surgery. I can take care of his entire bill with the money I got from Jones. I could then do Lewis in the office under local anesthesia plus some mild IV sedation. The switch with Lewis was probably made as he was being brought into the OR. Most likely that's when he was given the short-acting barbiturate."

"Wouldn't someone have checked his ID bracelet before they started surgery?"

"You'd think so. Maybe they took it off Lewis and put it on the other guy."

"I guess they could have."

"At this point, anything is possible."

CHAPTER 10

THE NEO-NAZI PASKUDNIK

"Let me help you," said Bloom, adjusting the height of Foak's tray table and pushing it toward her.

"I'm trying to figure out which one's the entree," replied Foak, clearing her throat and spitting into a tissue.

"I don't think there is one," answered Bloom, looking over the tray of apple juice, broth, Jello, and tea.

"When am I getting out of here?"

"You were almost out of here yesterday, but not in the way you'd have wanted."

"So I heard. Seriously."

"I imagine you'll be here at least a week. What did Dr. Causey say?"

"He hasn't been in yet."

"He's the one to ask. Did anyone ever tell you that you have beautiful blue eyes?"

Suddenly, Foak screamed, "You mamzer!" She was sitting straight up and staring at the image on the small TV screen suspended above her bed. "You mamzer!" She cleared her throat and expectorated on the screen. "You mamzer! We should have killed you when we had the chance!"

"Who's he?" asked Bloom, stunned by her outburst.

"You're a Jew and you don't know who this abomination is?"

"I'm not Jewish."

"Bloom?"

"Take my word for it."

"Bloom?"

"I can show you my baptism certificate."

"Hitler is alive!"

"What are you talking about?"

"You've never heard of Hitler?"

"Of course I've heard of Hitler!"

"But you've never heard of William Stine?"

"No. Who is he?"

"I can't believe you've never heard of William Stine! He's one of the leaders of the Nordics Against Zionistic Inhabitation Party. He's Hitler all over again. Do you know what he stands for?"

"I could imagine."

"They're thinking of having a march in Tamarac!" exclaimed Foak, paraphrasing what was just said on the CNN telecast.

"It sounds like you know him personally."

"We met briefly in Chicago in 1977, quite by accident. He was in his thirties and had all the earmarks of a future *fuhrer*. I happened to know he would be in town that week to meet with other neo-Nazis about planning a march in Skokie for later that year. I remember the date, January 19, 1977, the only day in recent history it snowed in South Florida. The thirteen-minute snowstorm—9:04 a.m. to 9:17 a.m.— prompted teachers to take their students out of their classrooms to witness the flurry. It was later that day that I went to Dunkin' Donuts in Ft. Lauderdale to get something warm to drink. I was wearing my blue Dodger hat and a red scarf over my blue Dodger jacket. A nice-looking man held the door for me. I thanked him as I passed in front of him and got in line. He got in line behind me."

"'You're ahead of me,' I said turning around and looking up at the young man who was smiling, motioning him to get in front of me. He looked familiar, but I was unable to place him.

'I'm not in any rush,' he answered flashing a smile and waving me on ahead of him.

'A hot chocolate, please, with extra whipped cream,' I said to the server. As I paid and left the counter, I heard that man say, 'I'll have the same as that pretty young lady.'

'Thank you, but I'm not so young,' I replied turning around and smiling.

'And a Brooklyn Dodger fan, too,' he added.

'Since 19 ... .. whenever,' I answered, turning back around and heading for the table facing the street, the only table that was not occupied. I removed my gloves, hat, and scarf; unzipped and took off my jacket; and sat down at one of the two empty chairs. I got up again, looked at the man who now had his mug and spoon and was standing scanning the coffee shop for an empty seat. I whistled and smiled and pointed to the vacant seat next to me. He walked to the table, put down his mug, removed his gloves and topcoat, and sat down. We introduced ourselves using our first names and chatted as we sipped and spooned our whipped cream concoctions, occasionally looking at the heavy street traffic in front of us. His name was Bill, and he was quite charming.

I gazed out the window and across the street and remember seeing a boy and thinking that he shouldn't be crossing the street at the corner even if he was walking his bike. Then, suddenly, I saw a speeding bus coming from the right. I jumped up, knocking over my mug, splashing chocolate over the man's shirt and pants. 'No, no, no!' I screamed, seeing and hearing the crash and watching the boy being separated from his bike and hurled into the air, landing on the hood of a car. 'Bill, grab your coat and gloves,' I yelled, oblivious to the mess I had caused. We grabbed our things, I screamed for someone in the restaurant to call 911, and we raced out the front door. I spotted what appeared to be a limp rag doll of a boy and ran over to spread my coat on the hood beside him, carefully putting it under him while moving him as little as possible. He had multiple broken bones, and blood was pouring out of his left leg just below his knee. I slipped the scarf under his thigh and made it into a tourniquet. 'Bill!' I yelled. He had been standing right next to me a second ago. I looked around. He was nowhere to be seen. Then I saw the Star of David hanging from a thin gold chain on the boy's neck, and with a jolt, I realized why I had recognized Bill. This man was William Stine. That Nazi bastard wasn't going help this injured kid, because the kid was a Jew."

"Did he ever find out who you were?" asked Bloom after Ida calmed down.

"I don't think so. But if he ever learned my name, then he knew all about me."

"What do you mean?"

"I was an executive of the ADL and was …"

"I'm sorry. The ADL?"

"We and the Anti-Defamation League were trying to prevent a march in Skokie, Illinois. You've heard of Skokie, haven't you, where 20 percent of the population were Holocaust survivors?"

"The neo-Nazis were trying to march, right?"

"This guy Stine was a paskudnik."

"What's a paskudnik?"

"A paskudnik is a nasty, evil person."

"Let me wipe this off before it drips on the bed," she added leaning forward and stretching her solid five-foot-eight-inch frame and wiping the screen with a tissue.

"His name's been linked to more than a dozen acts of terrorism, and he's taken credit for the murder of at least twenty-five Jews."

"How come he hasn't been arrested?"

"Arrested! How come he hasn't been assassinated? Not that we haven't tried. Why am I'm telling you all this?"

"Believe me, it's safe with me."

"I'd give up my life in a second to get rid of this mamzer!"

"What's a mamzer?"

"It's Yiddish for a bastard."

"I'm getting an education."

"Whoever killed this man would be performing the supreme mitzvah—you know what a mitzvah is?"

"Isn't a mitzvah supposed to be an act of kindness?"

"Exactly."

"You'd actually kill him if you had the chance?"

"Without blinking an eye."

"Here I thought you were a nice old, uh, not so old Jewish lady."

"You're right. I am a nice, uh, not so old Jewish lady."

CHAPTER 11

THE TRYST

"'ve got a pile of paperwork to take care of," said Bloom the next day, kissing Missy goodbye, going into the garage, and getting into his powder-blue MGB. He made rounds at two hospitals and saw a half dozen patients in the office. It was Wednesday, only half a workday today, not only for his office, but for most of the Broward County medical offices. At 12:20 p.m. he wished Aretha a good afternoon and took a pile of charts with him into his office.

"I'll be out of here in ten minutes," said Aretha, putting the phones on service and waving goodbye to Bloom. He locked the door to his private office, urinated, washed his penis and hands, and brushed his teeth. At 12:25 there was a single knock on the door that led to the building's corridor, and Bloom let in an attractive blonde woman in a white lab coat.

"Hi sweetheart," he whispered, kissing her after closing the door behind her.

"Why the whispering?" she asked not whispering.

"Shush," he whispered, touching his lips with his index finger. "Aretha's still in the office."

"Should I go?" she asked, now whispering.

"Aretha should be gone in a few minutes."

"We haven't done it with someone in the office. What do you want to do?"

"She's already put service on call. How much time do you have?"

"I have to leave at 1:15," she said glancing at the wall clock. "Do you think we can do it quietly?"

""That doesn't give us a whole lot of time, but I'm already aroused. I just heard the front door close. She left."

"I'm already wet. Is your door locked?"

Bloom nodded and began taking off his labcoat and loosening his tie.

"You'll get your money's worth," she answered taking off her lab coat and unbuttoning her blouse.

"Where are you supposed to be right now?" he asked sitting down at the point of his desk, undoing the bra hook at her intermammary cleft and catching her abundant mounds of flesh in his awaiting palms.

"Under you," she replied arching her back, pushing her crotch against his.

"If I was your husband, I'd fuck you three times a day, at the very least."

"At the very least. That's why I'm here," she added, burying his face in her breasts, then pushing his hands away and rimming his ears with her firm half-inch nipples.

"My pants are starting to get tight," said Bloom trying to reposition his penis so it wasn't tethered by the slit in his briefs.

"Don't tell me you're already out of your underwear?"

"Almost."

"Jamie, you're such a pushover," she said undoing his belt, reaching into his underwear and carefully putting his fully erect organ back in its proper place.

"Who's touching whom?"

"I knew someone was the pushover," she replied still holding onto his penis. "Where's your cock sock?"

"I thought today we'd have some unsafe sex."

"No skin, no in."

"It's here," replied Bloom touching his back left pocket.

"Fetch it," she said.

While waiting for him to take out and unwrap the condom, she let go of his penis, took a throw pillow from the office couch, put it on the floor, removed the rest of his clothing, placed her knees on top of the pillow, and put her mouth tightly around his organ.

"Does this hurt?" she mumbled, feeling his mid-section starting to rock. "Does this hurt," she repeated this time opening her mouth.

"Don't stop," moaned Bloom, starting to gyrate.

"But I don't know whether or not I'm hurting you," she mumbled teasingly.

"Shut up," he moaned, pulling her head into his crotch.

For the next ten minutes she feverishly worked his member, stopping twice to shush him when his moaning got too loud.

"Somebody's coming, somebody's coming," said Bloom using their pre-arranged code to signal he was close to orgasming. He pushed her away, sucked in his abdominal muscles, and started taking deep breaths, while she squeezed the head of his penis. Thirty seconds later, having lost no ejaculatory fluid and still erect, he finished undressing her, put on the condom and got down on his knees. Three minutes later, with his mouth deep in her pubic hair, his phone's ringtone went off during her second orgasm.

"Forget about your phone," she blurted. "I've got one more in me that's begging to come out," she shouted, convulsing it out of her and taking a deep breath. "Forget about your phone and fuck me," she said getting up and getting onto the couch and spreading her legs and pulling him onto and into her yelling, "Empty yourself out in me, sweetheart . . . Your cock feels sooooo good!" she *aahed* a few seconds later.

Bloom was able to quickly take care of the ER call from a prone position while still entwined and inside the blonde's body. They lay together and fell asleep for about twenty minutes. When Bloom awoke, he carefully put his hand into her vagina and squeezed the condom tightly around his penis so as not to let any semen escape when he dismounted.

She cleaned up in the bathroom. When she came out, Bloom was busy signing off on patient reports and dictated office notes. She kissed the back of his neck, told him she loved him and was sorry she had to beat up his penis to keep it from spurting, and left the office via the corridor door. Bloom left two hours later, making a brief call to Missy, who had just finished bringing the groceries into the house.

While driving home, Bloom hummed Starland Vocal Band's 1976 hit "Afternoon Delight."

After dinner Missy prepared a lecture for her medical students dealing with Masters and Johnson's four successive stages of human sexual response while Bloom played Bingo with Peter and Lisa. The children then brushed their teeth, and Bloom put Lisa into her bed and read her *Rumpelstiltskin* for the second time that day. For Peter, he had a riddle about three men who were in an overturned boat. Under what circumstances would not a single man get wet? "Tell me in the morning," he told Peter, not thinking the boy would remember he'd heard this one before. He told Peter to tell him the answer in the morning.

"I'll tell you now," said Peter. "They were married, they were bald, and the boat was not in the water!"

Before going to bed, Bloom and Missy recounted their afternoon activities.

"I can't believe how excited we both got even knowing Aretha was still in the office," began Missy.

"Maybe Wednesdays we should buy her lunch and have her eat in the office and screen my calls," added Bloom.

"I think you should just shut your phone off," she added.

"If I can remember."

"Stopping off at a pharmacy as I did and buying a spermicidal cream and applying it as well as douching had to be helpful," said Missy.

"We'll see. Unrelated to what you did, I went to a bookstore and skimmed through a book of baby names," said Bloom.

"Not funny."

"I agree. How much longer do you think Lisa will be sleeping on the floor in our bedroom?" asked Bloom.

"She's been checked out. There's nothing going on. It took Peter three months."

"So we'll continue in the office."

"Sounds good to me."

"I have some new positions I'd like us to try out," said Bloom raising his eyebrows.

"I'll pencil you in for next Wednesday."

"*Ink* me in," said Bloom after getting a deep kiss goodnight.

CHAPTER 12

HIPAA DAYS ARE HERE AGAIN

"I forgot to tell you I saw Ida Stern today," said Missy in a soft voice, shutting off the light. Lisa was sleeping two feet from them on her mattress on the floor. "This Stine guy got her pretty worked up this afternoon."

"Was he on the TV?" asked Bloom.

"He had been on it a few minutes before I walked into her room. How much do you know about her?"

"Mainly medical stuff. But I got permission today to discuss my history of Ida with you."

"I've done the same for you. What can you tell me about her?"

"She had a kidney removed when she was eight after falling off a horse in Berlin and is still active in the ADL, some Jewish watchdog organization."

"What do you know about her personal life?"

"Not much."

"Do you know anything about her family?"

"She's never mentioned anyone. I know she's had some visitors. I think friends."

"She said she lost her entire family in the war," said Missy.

"I kind of thought she might have."

"She never married."

"Do you think she's ever had sex?"

"You examined her!"

"She refused an internal exam."

Bloom reached for the ringing phone on the nightstand, spoke for a few minutes, then put on the light. "Her bleeding's gotten worse," he said, getting off the bed and hopping to the dresser. "I have to go in."

"Call me when you know what's going on," said Missy putting the TV on low volume. Bloom attached his prosthesis, put on his blue scrubs, and spoke with Ida's nurse, asking her to bring the genito-urinary cart to Ida's bedside along with a three-way size 24 catheter, three liters of sterile water, and an irrigation set. He then put on the house alarm and left, arriving at Ida's bedside twenty-five minutes later.

CHAPTER 13

THE BLEED GOES ON . . . AND ON

"It's me," said Bloom, calling Missy from the nursing station.

"What's happening?" she asked, pushing the mute button on the remote.

"I'm going to be a while. She's bleeding heavily. Hematology's coming in."

"Has she bled before? Other than from her stone and the other night?"

"Not that I know of."

"What are you going to do?"

"Right now, her bladder is distended with clots. I have to irrigate them out and start a continuous bladder irrigation."

"You could have said a CBI."

"Next time I will."

"What is your ETA?"

"Anywhere from a half-hour to an hour-and-a-half. Go to sleep. I'll call you if it's only a half-hour."

They spoke for a few more minutes, then Bloom went back to Foak's bedside, inserted a number 24 three-way catheter and spent the next forty minutes hand-irrigating her bladder.

"Having fun?" asked Foak as Bloom started the CBI and let the irrigant run wide open.

"I was about to ask you the same question," replied Bloom, adjusting the rate to about 180 drops per minute. "You didn't flinch the whole time I was working on you."

"I'm a survivor," said Foak, showing him her left forearm. Bloom noted the tattooed number and nodded.

"Why am I bleeding?"

"Beats me."

"That's what I like about you, your honesty."

Bloom smiled.

"But it doesn't do much to inspire confidence!"

"That's why I've called in a blood specialist."

"They're not called hematologists anymore?"

"No," replied Bloom with a straight face.

Foak smiled.

"Do you think I have a blood dyscrasia?"

"How do you know the word dyscrasia?"

"I do lots of crossword puzzles."

"So do I, and I've never seen the word."

"Do you do the Sunday's *Hematologist's Times* puzzle?"

"Only on Wednesdays. How do you know the word dyscrasia?"

"My father was a blood specialist, maybe even a hematologist."

"Seriously?"

"My father was a doctor."

"Where, in Germany?"

"Uh huh."

"My wife told me about what happened to your family. I'm so sorry."

Ida sighed.

Bloom waited about ten seconds and continued when she nodded okay.

"I've set up this bladder irrigation to help prevent further clots from forming."

"If I'm forming clots, how can I have a blood dyscrasia?"

"Clotting is only one factor. I've already spoken with the hematologist. She'll be seeing you after we get the lab results."

"Sometime tonight?"

"Uh huh."

"I have the CBC results," said Foak's nurse, walking toward Bloom. "Her platelets are fifty thousand."

"Did you call the results into Dr. Winger?" asked Bloom.

"She's on her way in."

"What's the normal platelet count?" asked Foak.

"Over a hundred and fifty thousand," said Bloom.

"I need platelets," said Foak, forcing a smile. "Does this hospital carry them?"

"I'm hoping we'll be able to get them."

"How is Dr. Winger?"

"Dr. Winger's the best! Ask Missy."

"Are you leaving now?"

"I'm waiting until Dr. Winger sees you."

"You should go home," said Foak.

"I need to hang around to see if your bladder needs further irrigating."

Ten minutes later Dr. Winger showed up, spent an hour with Ida, and secured three units of compatible platelets. As Foak's urine cleared, Bloom slowed down the rate of the irrigation but had to irrigate some more before he felt confident that she'd be alright for the rest of the night. At one o'clock in the morning, he said goodnight to Foak and went home.

CHAPTER 14

FROM RAGS TO RICHES

"Your wife is on line 1," said Aretha via the intercom the next morning.

"What time did you get home last night?" asked Missy after Bloom picked up.

"Around 1:30. You put Lisa back in her own bed?"

"You really got me going in the office yesterday and I thought she might stay in her own room and you might come home sooner."

"I had similar thoughts."

"What time did you leave this morning?"

"6:30."

"How's Ida doing?"

"She's still bleeding."

"Shouldn't she have stopped?"

"You'd think so after three units of platelets."

"What does that mean?"

"She may be allo-immune."

"What does that mean?"

"Her body may not be accepting the platelets."

"What does that mean?"

"She may have been sensitized by all her previous transfusions she received after her gunshot wound."

"What does that mean?"

"Hey, broken record. She may need special platelets."

"I repeat."

"She may need HLA platelets."

"Why didn't you say so in the first place?"

"I should have."

"What are HLA platelets?"

"They're platelets from people with the same tissue type."

"So, she needs tissue typing?"

"Correct."

"Who does that? The tissue typist?"

"I guess so."

"Are we still on for lunch?"

"I'm going to have to cancel. From nothing on my schedule, I'll be lucky to get home by three. I had to help Barrow with two of his cases this morning in addition to four new patients I had to see."

At two o'clock the office called Missy and said Bloom was in the OR helping Barrow with another case and said he'd call her when he was finished.

At six he called Missy telling her he was out of the OR and was going to look in on Foak before he left the hospital.

CHAPTER 15

A GLIMPSE OF AUSCHWITZ

"I thought you'd been kidnapped," said Missy, greeting Bloom in the kitchen with a big hug and a kiss.

"What a day!" replied Bloom, giving her an extra one of each.

"How many holes did you play?"

"Ha ha. You can't believe how busy I was. What did you do?"

"I spent some time with Foak."

"You're calling her Foak now?"

"We got into some heavy stuff. Do you know why she calls herself Foak?"

"Foak stands for four of a kind. F-O-A-K."

"You saw the numbers on her forearm."

"6999."

"69999."

"Four nines."

"Right."

"You'd think she'd want to erase that time from her memory."

"You would. But her number was the only constant in her topsy-turvy concentration camp world. It became part of her very being."

"Even so."

"Her four nines made her a VIP, a very important prisoner."

"Still."

"Somehow, she rose to the occasion of her VIP status."

"What do you mean?"

"From what I've learned, she transcended the depths of incalculable adversity. Her entire family was wiped out, some right before her eyes."

"Oh my God! How terrible."

"One day, as she and thirty other prisoners were digging trenches, her mother, who had severe diarrhea and was five feet in front of her, stopped digging for a second to turn her body to the side, so that her loose stool would drain out her pants leg, rather than into her shoe."

"This doesn't sound good already."

"Unhesitatingly, a prison guard who was overseeing them sicced his German shepherd on her mother. The dog severed both of her carotid arteries, and she died within fifteen minutes."

"I can't imagine"

"Her brother was worse."

"Not right now."

"Some of the things she told me were mind-boggling. She said she saw mothers stealing food from their daughters and fathers turning in their sons for extra blankets. There was that and a lot worse. Then there was the goodness."

"What goodness?"

"The goodness was helping others by sharing food with them and helping them with their workload so they wouldn't be killed."

"Unfortunately, some of the good ones were killed if they were caught helping the weaker ones."

"That's true. But rarely would a commandant kill one of his better workers. They'd rather kill the one who was weaker. More likely the next worker appointed to the group might be a better worker."

"Does she believe in God?"

"What do you think?"

"I could give a good case for not."

CHAPTER 16

A GLIMPSE OF A LARGEMOUTH BASS

"Perfect night for fishing," said Bloom looking out from the end of his property line and seeing not a ripple until sixty yards out. There was a slight nip in the air. No wind. "Tonight I'll catch some bass," he said more certain than usual.

He cast out, thought he saw some weeds on the line, and reeled it back in. He cleared the line, checked the plastic worm, and cast again, this time about five feet closer along the shoreline, where there were a dozen or more submerged rocks. He slowly retrieved the line over the rocks, concentrating his tactile acuity when the worm was in free-fall, between the top of the rocks and the lake's bottom. He had learned that it was during this state that a strike was most likely to occur.

"Phone!" yelled Missy, hurrying toward him.

"Who is it?" asked Bloom, completing another cast.

"Susan Winger," replied Missy, waiting for Bloom to reel in so she could hand him the portable phone. "She's calling from her car. You may have trouble hearing her with this phone."

"Hello!" shouted Bloom. "Let me take it inside," he added, getting no response as he handed Missy the rod.

When he returned ten minutes later, Missy was having trouble reeling in.

"What are you stuck on, a rock?" asked Bloom, seeing the line become very taut.

"Probably."

"I knew it," whined Bloom. "I can't let you alone for a minute!"

"Listen, Mr. Big Mouth bass."

"It's Dr., if you will. These worms cost forty cents apiece."

"I'll buy you a worm."

"What about the hook?"

"How much are they?"

"About the same."

"I'll buy you a hook."

"That's not the point."

"Listen, Mr. Fisherman, and I use the term loosely, you couldn't tell the difference between a five-pound bass and a five-pound note."

"You've got a bass on there, don't you?"

"I'd say somewhere between five and six pounds," replied Missy matter-of-factly, starting to strut.

"You saw it?"

"It was too big to see *all* of it."

"Where'd you catch it?"

"Somewhere around here," replied Missy touching Bloom's lips and laughing. "I thought fishing was supposed to be a sport?"

"Let me see this fish," said Bloom, watching Missy giving the line more slack, then reeling in.

"I was doing fine before you came back."

"Don't horse it!" said Bloom as Missy got caught again in the weeds. "You want me to reel it in?"

"I'm doing pretty well by myself."

"I don't want to lose the fish."

"We're putting it back anyway."

"That's true, but I'd like to see it."

"What did Susan want?" asked Missy, now handing Bloom the rod.

"They can't get any more platelets for Foak. You knew she got them through the National Unrelated Donor Registry, right? Well, it seems that the person she got them from was killed when her car was hit by a train."

"Seriously? What does that mean?"

"It means if she starts bleeding again, she's in trouble," replied Bloom, getting his first glimpse of the fish.

"There's no one else in the Registry that matches?"

"No."

"That's bad, isn't it? Keep reeling in," urged Missy again. "I don't want you to lose my fish!"

"Yes. Hopefully she won't need it," replied Bloom, ignoring Missy's comment.

"What's taking you so long to reel it in?"

"I'm thinking."

"Maybe you should spit out your gum."

"You're really hostile tonight."

"I'm sorry. I just have too many patients that are going south right now, and I don't mean to Argentina."

"I have a few of them myself. I'm sorry. Anything I can do?"

"No. I'm going in. Let me know how much it weighed."

When Missy left, Bloom realized the line might break if he continued to reel in, so he opened the bail to take tension off the line and allowed the fish to navigate away from the weeded area. It took fifteen minutes for the bass to get free and head for the deeper part of the lake. Once the fish took off, Bloom gently compressed the line against the spool with his fingers without closing the bail, and when the line stopped releasing, he closed the bail and gently reeled in, not allowing the bass to get entangled in the weeds again. He landed the fish in another ten minutes, then weighed it with his hand-held scale, released it, and went into the house.

CHAPTER 17

FOAK WANTS MORE THAN ONE ANSWER

"Would you have hired me if my name wasn't Aretha?" asked Aretha with a big smile.

"I thought your name was *Urethra*!" replied Bloom with a bigger smile.

"You're too much, Dr. Bloom."

"I must say, your name had something to do with it."

"Ida Stern's on the line," announced Aretha a few seconds later.

Bloom picked up the phone, spoke for a few minutes, then left the office. He walked to the hospital and took the stairs to Foak's room.

"That was quick," said Foak, looking up from her newspaper.

"You sounded very distressed."

"I'd like you to do me a favor, before I become totally paranoid."

"Sure."

"I'd like you to do three things."

"Only three? What are they?"

"I'd like you to find out exactly what happened to me in the ICU, you know, my ventilator."

"If I can. The second?"

"I'd like you to find out about the accident that killed my platelet donor."

"The third?"

"I was out of the country when the initial Sawgrass shootings took place. Can you find out the names of the other two victims?"

"Anything else?"

"I'd really appreciate it."

"No problem. It'll take some time."

"That's okay. See you in ten minutes."

"Make it fifteen," replied Bloom. "I'm very thirsty from all the lox I ate this morning. I'm going to stop off at the doctors' lounge and get something to drink."

"You eat lox?"

"A couple of times a week."

CHAPTER 18

WHY IS HE ASKING ABOUT DR. WINGER

"Mr. Jones is on line 1," said Aretha via the intercom. "Should I tell him ..."

"No, I'll take it now," answered Bloom reluctantly.

Bloom excused himself from his patient, went into one of the empty exam rooms, closed the door, took some deep breaths, and picked up the phone.

"I need the name of a good hematologist," began Jones.

"We have four good ones in this building," Bloom answered, trying a civil tact with Jones.

"How's Susan Winger?"

"She's very good. How'd you choose her?"

"I remember seeing her name somewhere."

"Is that it?"

"Thanks, Doc. You may now hang up."

Bloom placed the phone back on its cradle and stood staring at it for a few seconds. Stine must know Winger is Foak's oncologist, thought Bloom. Could there be a connection between Stine and the death of Foak's platelet donor? He pressed the intercom button and asked Aretha to get Mac and Steven Lambert at the *South Florida Sun-Sentinel*. A second later, thinking through where this could be going, he asked Aretha to cancel the two calls.

CHAPTER 19

WE GET A MAJOR ANSWER

was with Foak today," said Missy, "when CNN announced that William Stine was named head of the Nazi Party."

"What time did you see her?

"Shortly after you."

"How far did she spit?"

"I think she was prepared for it. Supposedly his opponents withdrew their candidacy. She said Stine probably made them an offer they couldn't refuse. What a mamzer!"

Bloom laughed. "She told you what it meant?"

"Everyone knows what a mamzer is."

"Did she tell you about the assignment she gave me?"

"She mentioned it."

"Does she seem paranoid to you?"

"Not really. Oh, one of Steven Spielberg's associates dropped by while I was there. Spielberg wants to interview her for a film he's producing to follow up *Schindler's List*."

"Really?"

"Uh huh."

"That's really nice. Tell me about your session."

"First tell me how big it was."

"The fish?"

"Yeah, the fish."

"It weighed about six and a half pounds."

"You haven't caught anything bigger than that, have you?"

"Nope."

"You can say you caught it."

"I wouldn't do that."

"I saw Bruce Felson this afternoon. It looks like you already have!"

"Uh, did you tell him you caught it?"

"And make you out a liar? Would I do that?"

"Did you?"

"Uh, I don't remember," said Missy in a teasing tone. "Oh, stop whining," she relented. "I didn't tell him."

"I actually told him you caught it," admitted Bloom.

"You did?"

"Yes, I did! I didn't say it to you, especially after my rant about the cost of a lure and a hook, but I was very proud of you."

"Could have fooled me!"

"I really was proud, and it felt good telling Bruce. Now tell me about your session."

"I'll do it while you're massaging my back."

"You're a massage-o-maniac."

"Yeah. And last night you were a necromaniac."

"Not really. I think you moved once. I thought I'd take a chance with both you and Lisa sleeping."

"Just ten minutes worth."

"You're a pain in the ass."

"You're such a pushover."

Missy brushed her teeth and joined Bloom in bed, about five feet away from Lisa, who was asleep next to the bed. After ten seconds of rubbing Missy's back, Bloom stopped.

"Why are you stopping?" whined Missy.

"You haven't mentioned Foak yet."

"Foak."

"Missy!"

"Once upon a time there was a woman named Foak. Start!"

"You mean *resume!*" replied Bloom twiddling his thumbs.

"Something must have happened to her after the war," said Missy, moving her shoulders from side to side, indicating Bloom to continue massaging in that area. "She adjusted to the war with hope and optimism and not only survived the camps but flourished. Yet, shortly after the war ended and she was liberated, she became pessimistic, despondent, and reclusive. Start rubbing."

"Is that so unusual?" asked Bloom placing the tips of his fingers on her shoulders. "The realization that your entire family is gone? That you can't pick up where you left off? Maybe with the war's end she lost her leadership role, her essence for being?"

"But there was still so much more to do."

"Maybe it was just reality settling in."

"I don't think so."

"Then what?" asked Bloom resting his fingers.

"I'm not *happy* with my back massage."

"Which dwarf are you?"

"I'm certainly not Happy. I'm Grumpy. And getting grumpier by the minute. When the hell is the massage going to start, er, I mean, *resume*?"

"Wait!" yelled Bloom starting to make enlarging circles between her scapulas, then stopping.

"Why are you stopping?" whined Missy.

"Now I know what was done when Stine wanted the other two front runners for the leadership of the American Nazi Party to step down and they refused. Remember movie producer Jack Woltz, who refused the Godfather's choice of a lead actress for Woltz's new movie?"

"That was some movie," replied Missy. "Someone was sleeping with the fishes while another was sleeping with Khartoum's head. What did Stine do that that made them unable to refuse his offer?"

"It wasn't Stine! It was me! It was me that did it. I did it!"

"Did what? What did you do?"

"It was the circumcisions! The two that I did!"

CHAPTER 20

WOW!

"The ventilator plug was defective?" said Foak raising her eyebrows.

"That's what I was told," replied Bloom.

"Did you check it out yourself?"

"No."

"Can you do it for me?"

"If I can find the machine. It's probably been already fixed."

"What about the platelet donor?"

"So far, all I know is her name was Constance Withers, and her car was hit by a train. According to one report, she tried to get through the gates as they were closing and got stuck on the tracks."

"What about the other reports?"

"They were sketchy."

"What about the Sawgrass victims? I was out of the country when they were shot."

"I've got their names somewhere," said Bloom rummaging through his pockets. "Here they are," he said holding up a small scrap of paper. "Let's see. Sigmund Hoffmann and Maurice Bern something."

"Bernshtein," said Foak starting to cry.

"You knew him?" said Bloom placing his hands on her shoulders, giving her a gentle hug.

"I . . . knew . . . them," she sobbed.

"Both of them?" exclaimed Bloom hugging her tighter. "From Skokie?"

"The three of us . . . We tried . . . to stop . . . the march!"

"William Stine?" said Bloom softly, slowly nodding his head.

"Yes," answered Foak nodding. "William Stine!"

"Wow! But why now?"

"Payback time and he was making his run!"

"Double wow!"

CHAPTER 21

SITTING DUCK MUST NOW FLY AWAY

"Wow!" said Missy after being brought up to speed. "Have you told anyone else?"

"No," replied Bloom.

"What are you going to do?"

"I don't know."

"Why is he so concerned about an eighty-nine-year-old woman?"

"He's making his run and wants to tie up loose ends."

"I suppose."

"She's a sitting duck in the hospital. I need to get her out ASAP."

"Is she ready to be discharged?"

"I think she can be managed at home, with some medical supervision. That reminds me. Our man Jones wanted to know the name of a good hematologist."

"When was that?"

"A few days ago. Then he wanted to know if Susan Winger was any good. I told him she was."

"I think you quickly changed the subject a few seconds ago," interrupted Missy, "just after you said something about managing Foak at home. You were planning to bring her here, weren't you Jamie? I don't want her here."

"I haven't even thought about it."

"Liar, liar, pants on fire."

"Okay, maybe I thought about it a little."
"She's not coming here, Jamie."
"Okay."
"Did you tell Foak about the circumcisions?"
"No, I've not told her or anyone else."

CHAPTER 22

MAKING HOUSE CALLS
IN YOUR HOUSE

"I hope to get you out of the hospital sometime today," said Bloom reviewing Foak's chart and pulling up a chair at her bedside. "I think you're well enough to leave. But even if you're not, it's immaterial."

"Why is it immaterial?"

"Because you're not safe here."

"Who will take care of me?"

"Me, but only if you promise not to tell anyone I've made a house call."

"I'm sorry for putting you through all this."

"You're worth saving."

"Your wife, also."

"Yes, she's worth saving, too."

"You're a good man, Bloom," said Foak chuckling at Bloom's response.

"What do you know about the two guys running against Stine?"

"It looks like they've dropped out. I don't know why."

Bloom said nothing, thinking about his role in why Stine was now running unopposed.

STARTING THE *WHERE IS SHE GAME?*

"When was the last time you spoke with her?" asked Missy.

"Yesterday afternoon," replied Bloom, attaching the pulsometer to his thumb before he got on the treadmill. "Remember the call I got at 3:30 this morning? That was the hospital telling me she signed out AMA."

"You said there was a pretty good chance she would," said Missy, starting her stationary bike and programming in her daily workout.

"I more or less put the bug in her head."

"Where could she have gone?"

"I have no idea."

"Did you call her home?"

"There was no answer."

"She and you are the only ones who know about Stine?"

"As far as I know."

"Do you think Stine knows you know about him?" The phone rang. "I've got it," said Missy reaching down and picking it up off the side table. "Hello?"

"I'd like to speak with Dr. Bloom," said the voice.

"Which Dr. Bloom?" asked Missy still pedaling.

"It's Mr. Jones."

"Hold on, please."

Missy put Jones on hold and reached forward and handed Bloom the phone.

"It's Jones."

"Surprise, surprise."

"This is Dr. Bloom," said Bloom after a few seconds, maintaining his pace.

"I need your help."

"What is it? I'm on the treadmill."

"Then get the fuck off of it!"

Bloom stepped off the machine. "What can I do for you?"

"That's better. I'm having trouble locating one of your patients."

"Let me guess," replied Bloom mumbling to himself. "Why are you looking for one of my patients?"

"Listen, fuckface, I'll be the one asking the questions."

"Which patient?"

"That's better. Ida Stern."

"She left the hospital this morning, against medical advice. I have no idea where she is."

"I'm sure you'll know by nine tomorrow morning. You may now hang up."

Bloom shut off the phone and handed it back to Missy.

"What an asshole! To answer your question about whether Stine knows I'm onto him, I hope not! Jones wants to know where Foak is by nine o'clock tomorrow morning."

"What if you can't tell him?"

"Or won't tell him?"

"You won't tell him?"

"Not if I can help it."

"That's all well and good, but I don't think you have a choice."

"You're probably right."

"Then what?"

"Then we have a problem."

"That's not good."

"Nope. Let's regroup in 14 minutes," said Bloom, noting the 4:01 reading on the treadmill's timer display.

"Make it 20," said Missy noting the time she had left.

CHAPTER 24

BLOOM'S BED AND BREAKFAST

"Uh, what time is it?" asked Bloom picking up the phone, squinting at the clock on the nightstand.

"3:47," replied the answering service operator. "I just got a call from Mrs. Davis. She wants you to call her. She said it was an emergency."

"Mrs. Davis?" asked Bloom placing his head back down on the pillow. "Did she say what it was about?"

"She said she was having the same problem."

"Can you patch me through to her?"

"Hold on, Dr. Bloom."

"Who the hell is Davis?" mumbled Bloom waiting to be patched through. When he heard Ida's voice on the other line, he spoke with her for a few minutes, then hung up.

"Psst," said Bloom hovering over Missy. "Psst."

"Huh wha... wha... what is it?"

"You have to get dressed."

"I'm already dressed."

"Not for sleep."

"Go away."

"I need your help."

"What time is it?"

"Around 3:55."

"Come back in four hours."

"Missy."

"Four hours. Now leave me alone!"

"I need your help," repeated Bloom nudging her.

"Why me?"

"Missy!"

"Stop calling my name!"

"You have to get dressed. Please! Foak's bleeding."

"I must have missed something," replied Missy turning toward him.

"I may have to bring her here."

"What! We've already had this conversation?"

"This may be the best place for her."

"You've got to be kidding."

"She's frightened to death of Stine."

"Okay."

"So she can't go to the hospital or my office."

"Can't she drive or fly somewhere?"

"Eventually. Maybe it'll be nothing."

"Uh, why do I have to get dressed?"

"I need you to go to the hospital..."

"Me? What for?"

"To drive my car."

"What?"

"I can't go get her in *my* car. I can't take the chance of being followed."

"What are we supposed to do with Peter and Lisa?"

"Nothing."

"I'm not leaving them by themselves!"

"You go to the ER. Stay there for a few minutes, then come home. Call me when you get off I -75. Then I'll leave. Okay?"

"This is crazy."

"She may not have to come here."

"Where else could she go?"

"Nowhere else. Maybe the bleeding is not so bad."

"And if it is?"

"She'll need a CBI and to come here."

"Where do you plan to get the stuff?"

"From one of the other ERs."

"This is crazy."

"I can't abandon her."

"I didn't say abandon her."

"It's really not a big deal."

"It *is* a big deal," replied Missy, sighing as she got off the bed.

Bloom turned on the light, hopped to the oak valet near his dresser, and put on his prosthesis.

"Here, put these on the bed in the guest room," said Missy going into the linen closet and then handing Bloom a sheet, pillowcase, pillow, and blanket.

"Wait a second," said Bloom looking at Missy's hairline, then adjusting her wig. "Do you still need this?"

"Do you still need your leg?"

"That was nasty," replied Bloom, pulling the wig over her eyes.

"I'm sorry, but you asked me the same question this morning!"

"Your hair's grown since then."

"What, a half a millimeter?"

"Maybe two-thirds. I like you with short hair."

"I'll tell you know when it gets short. Let's go."

"You're the one who's going."

"I don't know why I let you talk me into these things." As Bloom started to open his mouth, Missy gave him a look and said, "You'd be smart not to respond." Bloom just smiled.

CHAPTER 25

MISSY THE MAGICIAN

"He just went out the door," said Aretha. She quickly put the caller on hold, opened the door, and shouted Dr. Bloom's name down the corridor.

"What?" asked Bloom turning around and walking back toward the office.

"Mr. Jones is on the phone."

"Shit," he mumbled under his breath.

He went into the office, walked down the hallway, and picked up the phone in the consultation room.

"I gave you an additional six hours," said Jones.

"What?" answered Bloom.

"Where is she?"

"Uh, what?"

"Where the fuck is she?"

"I wasn't able to find out," said Bloom after taking a deep breath and counting to ten. "I must have called a half-dozen cab companies."

"Only four."

"What?"

"I said you called only four companies: All Broward, Atlantic, Yellow, and Checker. She took a Yellow cab to some place on 87th Avenue. What time did you see her?"

"I didn't see her."

"You didn't make a house call?"

"Doctors don't make house calls anymore."

"Didn't you go to 8732, Apt 102? You knew where she was. Didn't you go there?"

"I went there this morning. She had already left."

"Do you know where she is now?"

"I have no idea."

"Haven't you spoken with her today?"

"No."

"Why didn't you tell me you knew where she was?"

"Wait a minute . . ."

"You knew where she was, 8732, Apt 102."

"Right, but now I don't know where she is."

"If you can't tell me where she is by nine o'clock tomorrow morning, well, I'd rather not say right now. You may hang up."

Bloom put down the phone, said good-bye to Aretha for the second time, left the office, and drove home. When he opened the front door, he was greeted by Peter.

"Can the lady stay another day?" asked Peter, chomping on a lemon fruit pop.

"Shh," said Bloom quickly closing the door. "Where's Mommy?"

"I think she's with the lady," replied Peter. "Want a bite?"

"Okay," said Bloom bending down and leveling off Peter's pop. "Thank you, Peter."

"The man was at the bus stop this morning. Mommy saw him."

"Did he talk to you?"

"Not at the bus stop."

"What do you mean?"

"He spoke to me after I got off the bus at school."

"At school! What'd he say?"

"He asked if the lady who came to our house last night was my grandmother?"

"What'd you say?"

"Nothing."

"Nothing at all?"

"I just ignored him."

"Good boy," said Bloom patting him on the head.

"Can the lady stay here?"

"She's not safe here."

"Why not?"

"That man is a bad man. He wants to hurt her."

"Why?"

"It's a long..."

"Forget it."

"Thank you."

The doorbell rang. "I'll get it," said Peter running toward the door.

"Where's Lisa?" asked Bloom.

"She's not feeling well. She's sleeping. Mommy thinks she's getting a cold."

Suddenly, Bloom realized Peter was at the front door. "Don't open the door!" he said quickly. Peter froze.

After twenty seconds, there was knock.

"Who is it?" asked Bloom.

"Dr. Bloom?" came a voice through the door.

"Yes."

"Windmill security."

"What can I do for you?"

"I'm Tom Rogalson, Chief of Security. With me is Lt. Calderone."

"What can I do for you?"

"We need to speak with you."

"What's the problem?"

"We need to talk with you."

"One second," said Bloom walking into the living room and looking through the window, noting a black car in the swale, not the usual white security car with the Windmill Ranches logo.

"I'm sorry," said Bloom now back at the atrium. "What was that?"

"We need to talk with you."

"About what?"

"It'll be much easier if we come in."

"Can you tell me what it's about?'

"We have identification."

"I assume so. What do you want to talk with me about?" asked Bloom ignoring the additional request.

"It's okay, Dr. Bloom. We don't have to come in," said a second voice. "One of your neighbors said she saw a man trying to open your patio door."

"Which neighbor was that?"

"Mrs. What's-her-name, the one catty-corner from you across the lake."

"When was that?"

"About ten minutes ago," said the other voice.

"That was me!" lied Bloom.

"Er, were you wearing a hooded sweatshirt?"

"Sort of."

"Okay," said one of them. "Do you want us to look around before we go?"

"I don't think it's necessary, but you can check the outside."

"Okay, then," the two voices replied in unison.

"Thank you," said Bloom.

Bloom went back into the living room and watched the men get into their car without checking the area around the house. Bloom then walked down the hallway and opened the bedroom door.

"Where's Mommy?" he asked, finding Peter jumping on the king-sized bed, the TV blaring.

"Close the door!" yelled Peter. "Mommy doesn't like this."

"The jumping or the noise?" asked Bloom turning down the volume and then closing the door. "Not so high," said Bloom laughing, catching Peter in midair. "Mommy's right. You can get hurt."

By the time Bloom left the bedroom the two supposed security men were now in the atrium speaking with Missy. He quickly approached the three.

"We've already resolved this thing," said Bloom opening the front door and starting to usher the men out of the house.

"I saw their credentials," said Missy, nodding subtly to Bloom. "Let them do what they have to do."

Bloom took a deep breath and backed away.

"One of your neighbors saw someone trying to open your patio door," began Rogalson.

"We've already..." replied Bloom starting to raise his voice.

"I didn't hear anything," said Missy quieting Bloom with her look. "Maybe you can check things out while you're here."

"We'd love to," said Rogalson, forcing a smile. "A few questions first. How many people live here?"

"Four," answered Missy. "My husband and I and two children."

"Anyone else?"

"Flyer."

"Who's that?"

"Our bird. You can hear him chirping."

Both men smiled.

"Are the children at home?"

"Our daughter is sick. She's in this one here," said Missy opening her door, showing the men no one else was in the room.

"Let's take a look at the rest of the house," said Rogalson starting down the hallway.

"Jamie, I have to be at the clinic in less than an hour," said Missy putting up her hand, momentarily stopping Rogalson. "Can you do me a favor and put gas in my car?"

"Sure," replied Bloom, taking Missy's keys from the pass-through then walking toward the garage.

"I might as well check out the garage first," said Rogalson following Bloom.

Rogalson systematically inspected the garage. He opened each door of Missy's red BMW and took the protective canvas off Bloom's blue MGB and did the same.

"Wait a second," said Rogalson stepping behind the car and trying the trunk. "Can you pop it for me?"

"I think you'd better come here," said Missy running into the garage.

Rogalson quickly looked under both cars, then followed Missy to the back of the house. Meanwhile Bloom got into Missy's BMW, opened the garage door with the remote, and drove away. Missy occupied the two men by having them check out other areas inside the house and the lanai, and when they left, called Bloom to tell him, in case he didn't know, that Foak was in the trunk of Missy's car.

CHAPTER 26

BERLIN CIRCA 1940

loom looked at the next day's schedule, made evening rounds, and drove home.

"Let's walk," said Missy, greeting him at the front door.

"Let me change first," replied Bloom, walking into the house and changing his clothes.

"Where are the kiddies?" he asked joining her at the mailbox.

"They're at my mother's. I thought we'd eat out—just you and me—and then we'd pick them up."

"Want to walk first?"

"Sure."

They left their cul-de-sac and turned right and walked in the direction of the tennis courts.

"I never told you about the phone call I got yesterday," said Missy.

"Yesterday was a giant blur," replied Bloom taking her hand.

"It was from Foak's sister."

"Her sister!" exclaimed Bloom, stopping and turning toward her.

"Her sister."

"Hold it for a second," said Bloom dropping her hand and turning 360 degrees.

"What is it?"

"I don't think we should talk in the house anymore. I'm not even sure we should be talking now. I just read something about electronic surveillance devices. See that guy over there with a headset on, mowing the lawn?"

"Jamie!"

"Maybe not him, but I'm telling you."

"Shall I or shall I not tell you?"

"Tell me, but look away from him when you speak. And speak softly."

"Would you like to read my lips?"

"Let me kiss them first," said Bloom, pressing his lips against hers.

"It's amazing we've never been caught in the office," said Missy, her lips still on his.

"I'm pretty sure Aretha knows what's going on, although she probably thinks it's somebody other than you. By the way, Wednesday is okay."

"Want me to wear a different wig?"

"I like the blonde one, which you really don't need anymore."

"I need another couple of weeks. I think we've already had this discussion."

"When is your next appointment with Dr. Winger?"

"I have some scans sometime this month. My last labs were a month ago. I'd hate to need any more chemo."

"I think you'll be fine."

"I hope so."

Bloom took her hand and started walking.

"Where were we?' asked Bloom, remembering Missy saying something about a phone call from Foak's sister. "I thought her entire family was killed in the war?"

"Ida and her sister Rachel were the only two that survived. Let me speak for a while, okay?"

"The pavement's yours."

"Her sister called to tell me there's a person in Cincinnati who Foak is to go to when she's okay to travel."

"Did she give you the name?"

"You've taken back the pavement so soon!"

"Basically, she's ready to go. I'm sorry. Go on."

"She is?"

"She should be by tomorrow. How long can she stay at your mother's?"

"That's not a problem. My mother's not returning until Sunday."

"I told her sister it probably wouldn't be for another week. I'll have to reach her."

"Do you know how?"

"Uh huh."

"Good."

"When did you last see Ida?"

"This morning."

"How'd you do that?"

"I took a cab from the hospital."

"Good thinking."

"Not as good as you putting her in the trunk of your car."

"You knew she was in there?"

"Not when you told me to fill up your car with gas."

"When? When I popped into the garage and told Rogalson to follow me?"

"Uh huh. He thought she was, I mean, had been there?"

"Obviously."

"Are we finished with Ida for now?" asked Bloom bending down and picking up a stray tennis ball.

"I had quite a session with her before you got home."

"Oh!" replied Bloom moving the ball from hand to hand.

"Her maiden name was Stern."

"I assumed it was."

"She was married to a German named Meyer Berger."

"When was that?"

"She got married in 1934."

"I thought you said before she had never married."

"That's what Foak had told me."

"He died in the war?"

"Foak said she and her sister were the only survivors from both families."

"Foak never remarried?"

"Her sister said Foak had a son."

"A son? He didn't survive?"

"She doesn't think so. Berlin in 1940 was a bad place for Jews. Faced with the possibility of not being able to leave Germany and the prospect that neither she nor her husband would survive and their son would be killed, in April 1940 he was left at an orphanage run by a convent located about two blocks from where she worked as a domestic, the only job she could get after going through two years of dental school."

"Dental school? Really? Did the convent know it was Foak's child?"

"No. The daughter of the person she cleaned for worked at the convent and told her where and when she should bring her son."

"Then the convent didn't know the child was Jewish, right?"

"Right."

"Wasn't he circumcised?"

"No. He purposely wasn't. Foak walked by the convent three times a day, until May of 1940, when she and her husband were sent to Auschwitz."

"What happened when the war was over?"

"She found out the convent had been bombed late in '44. When she went back, there was nothing left."

"Does anyone else know this, other than us and her sister?"

"Her psychiatrist in Brooklyn, Dr. Payne. She died six months ago."

"It would be interesting to see her old records."

"I've already sent for them."

"My, my. Anything else you care to share with me?"

"A pizza and a garlic bread."

"Splendid idea!" answered Bloom, as they turned and headed back to the house.

CHAPTER 27

ENTERS MR. WILLIAM STINE

Forty-five minutes later, Bloom spotted a TCBY store coming up on the right.

"You wanna stop?" he asked.

"Not for me," replied Missy holding her lower abdomen. "Well, maybe for later!"

"You swore you weren't going to eat anything else for the next twenty-four hours."

"I know. I'll be needing something for my heartburn."

"How bad is it?"

"Oh, I don't have it now," said Missy smiling.

"You're unbelievable."

"You've just figured that out?

"University ER," said Bloom hearing his ringtone and seeing University Hospital's ER number on the screen.

"Hi Sherry, whatcha got?" asked Bloom after he got connected.

"Some sixty-something-year-old big shot with a kidney stone."

"What's his name?"

"William Stine. He's got at least five gun-toting bodyguards. Do you know who he is?"

"Yeah. He's head of the Nazi Party. He requested me?"

"Uh huh. Is he a friend of yours?"

"Yeah, he's a member of my synagogue."

"You're not Jewish, are you?"

"That was a joke. Let me speak with the ER doctor."

"I'll put him on. Please hold."

Bloom spoke with the ER physician and told him he'd be there in thirty minutes.

"Crap!" exclaimed Bloom, rubbing his eyes with his thumb and index fingers. "I really don't feel like taking care of this amoral asshole."

"Then don't check his prostate!" said Missy.

"Seriously. This guy's a ruthless murderer."

"He'd like to be Ida-less as well."

"You're on a roll."

"Just take care of him."

"This guy's an abomination."

"You took an oath."

"Missy, this guy murdered more than two dozen people."

"Think of it as guaranteeing your family's life."

"If only that could."

Bloom drove to the yogurt store for a sugar-free raspberry cone for Missy, then drove to the ER, parked, and walked with Missy to the main desk where he spotted the ER doctor.

"Hi Paul," said Bloom. "Why'd this guy request me?" asked Bloom.

"Because your husband is the best," said Paul, smiling at Missy.

"Right," said Bloom sarcastically.

"By law, somebody's got to see him. Anyway, he has a history of stone disease. His last episode was four years ago."

"Calcium oxalate?"

"He doesn't know. This episode started about three hours ago. He's got marked left costovertebral angle and lower quadrant tenderness. His urine shows three plus blood and too numerous to count red blood cells. The CT machine is down. His KUB shows a seven-millimeter right renal stone that does not appear to be in the collecting system and nothing on the left. He has a mild left hydro on ultrasound. I've given him ten of morphine and ten of Compazine. Right now he's fine. Do you want him to have an IVP?"

"Maybe he passed it. Hold off the IVP for now."

"Are you thinking of not examining him?" asked Missy.

"I'm here already. Let me see him."

"Don't you usually see them if you're here?"

"Definitely when the diagnosis is unclear or they're admitted."

"What about when they're neo-Nazis?"

"I don't know. This would have been my first one."

Bloom looked around the ER and noticed dozens of patients in all conditions and attires waiting to be seen. "What are they giving away?" he asked.

"It's been a zoo, Dr. Bloom," replied the triage nurse, wheeling an elderly male in blood-stained shorts into the holding area. "Your patient is in bed 11."

"Please wait for me in the cafeteria," said Bloom to Missy. "I'll be less than thirty minutes."

Bloom dismissed Jones and the rest of Stine's entourage, attended Stine, dictated a note, and discharged him with something for pain, telling him to increase his fluid intake, to call his office in the morning, and under what circumstances he should return to the hospital.

CHAPTER 28

TAT'S NOT ALL, THERE'S MORE

"I counted twelve swastikas," said Bloom standing on the top step of a three-step stepladder, replacing the battery in the smoke detector.

"Where were they located?" asked Missy.

"On his shoulders, hips, the top of his feet, his butt and his back.

"What was he like?"

"Like the guy next door."

"Like Fred?"

"He even looked like him. Same build, five-foot-ten, nice face, and a short brown mustache—like Hitler."

"Sounds like he looks like you, except smaller. Did you examine his amoral asshole?"

"Yes. I'm telling you, he seemed like a good guy."

"You said he murdered all those people."

"He did!"

"Anything else?"

"He's very bright, very personable, and has an excellent sense of humor."

"Is he married?"

"I'm not sure. Why'd you ask?"

"I was thinking of him for your sister."

"Very funny."

"Other than the swastikas, could you tell he was a neo-Nazi?"

"I don't know what neo-Nazis are supposed to be like. Do you?"

"I don't know either. Did he thank you?"

"He was very appreciative."

"Did he make any references to Jews?"

"No."

"Did he say anything about Foak?"

"No."

"Did you?"

"No, but I should have."

"Did he say anything about the circumcisions?"

"No."

"Did you?"

"No, but I should have."

"What's going on with his stone?"

"He may have already passed it."

"Really? Did you send him home?"

"Yep."

"So all in all, it was pretty painless."

"Not for him, thank God. I really shouldn't have said that."

The phone rang. "I've got it," said Missy picking up the portable phone. "It's service."

"Take the message."

"I think you should take it," said Missy after hearing part of it.

Bloom took the phone, spoke for a few seconds, then made two calls.

"Well?" asked Missy.

"His white count was 65,000."

"Whose?"

"Stine's."

"What does that mean?"

"He might have leukemia. I thought something was fishy."

"What do you mean?"

"He refused all blood work."

"So?"

"No one ever refuses."

"Wait a second. Didn't you say his white count was 65,000?"

"I talked him into letting me do an SMA 17."

"That doesn't include a white count."

"One of the lab techs ran a CBC for me, off the record."

"Whose name was on the blood?"

"Nobody's."

"There's no record of it anywhere?"

"Uh uh."

"Can't you get into trouble?"

"I can't see how."

"You think he knows about his white count?"

"I can't see any other explanation."

"What's next?"

"One of the calls I made was to Susan."

"Susan Winger?"

"Uh huh."

"Why'd you do that?"

"Remember a few days ago, I told you Jones was asking about her?"

"Vaguely. She may not be at liberty to discuss his case, and maybe it'd be better if she or Stine doesn't know you know."

"We're too much involved not to have the information."

"What'd she say?"

"She said she couldn't discuss it with me."

"Maybe you shouldn't be discussing anything about Stine with me."

"HIPAA is in a state of flux," replied Bloom shrugging. "I think anything that affects our family's well-being is discussable."

"I think . . . you should answer it," said Missy picking up the ringing phone and handing to him.

"Hello?"

"This is Mr. Jones. I'm just calling to thank you for your urologic expertise."

"I really didn't do anything."

"Nonetheless, I have another envelope for you."

"It's not necessary."

"We'd like to keep you happy."

"I could think of better ways."

"Oh, before I forget. You still haven't told us where to find a certain individual."

"I've told you everything I know."

"June 1 marks the start of the hurricane season."

"So?"

"You were here for Andrew, weren't you?"

"1992. Uh huh."

"What do they issue forty-eight hours before a hurricane is to arrive?"

"A hurricane watch. Why?"

"And what do they issue twenty-four hours before a hurricane is to arrive?"

"A hurricane warning. Why?"

"Did you know that December 1 marked the start of the kidnapping season?"

Bloom did not respond.

"I expect you'll have the information I need tomorrow morning when I call you at eight o'clock," said Jones. "If not, I'll be giving you an advisory on a certain subject. You may now hang up."

Bloom put down the phone and stared at Missy.

CHAPTER 29

THIS THING IS DRIVING US CRAZY

"Do you know where she is?" asked Mac, swiveling to face Bloom, then leaning back in his chair.

"Yes," replied Bloom nervously playing with a chain of paper clips.

"I'd know what I'd do," said Mac now leaning forward.

"You'd tell them?"

"I'm getting paid for this, aren't I?"

"Sorry. Go on."

Mac smiled. "Absolutely," he added.

"They'd kill her."

"You don't know that."

"Right," replied Bloom sarcastically.

"I mean you don't know that for a fact."

"Right."

"Why don't you call her?"

"And?"

"Ask her what she thinks you should do."

"She'll definitely tell me to tell them."

Mac shrugged.

"There's something I haven't told you. I'm pretty sure Stine may have a bad illness."

"How do you know that?"

"I just think," replied Bloom not wanting to go into detail.

"Isn't it strange he's so concerned about killing her?"

"I know. It doesn't make sense. It's probably payback. So you're telling me to call her?"

"Yes."

"Will do."

"Here's what we were able to get on Stine," said Mac, handing Bloom a pile of papers. "Most of it is from the Jewish Defense League."

"Anything interesting?"

"I haven't gone through it yet."

"Mind if I read it here?"

"Be my guest," replied Mac. "I have a meeting down the hall. I'll see you in a half-hour if you're still around."

"Thanks," said Bloom, getting up and shaking his hand.

Bloom sat down and began reading the fifteen-page report:

We were introduced to him on his eighth birthday, when he was questioned in the "accidental" death of a Hasid who fell 252 feet from the Parachute Jump ride at Brooklyn's Coney Island. According to him, the Hasid slipped as he was reaching for his shtreimel, which was starting to blow away. According to the police, when the Hasid hit the ground, the shtreimel was still on his head and the Hasid's safety harness appeared to have been cut. No knife was found, and no charges were filed.

On his ninth birthday he was questioned in the "accidental" death of an elderly Hispanic male who was killed in Corona, Queens. He said someone had pushed him into the male, causing him to fall in front of an oncoming train. No charges were filed.

On his tenth birthday he was questioned in the mauling death of a Black male at the Bronx Zoo. He said the male slipped as he was climbing on the bars of a lion's cage. According to the police he had goaded the much larger and older male onto the bars and pushed him over the railing. No charges were filed.

When he was seventeen he ran away to California and joined his first cult group, an organization advocating mandatory sterilization of Hispanics. It was here he got his first tattoo and officially started his rap sheet.

From 1959 to 1963 he affiliated himself with three other cult groups, got six more tattoos and was credited with at least a dozen felonies and three dozen misdemeanors.

When he was twenty-two he wrote A Guide for the Racist, *a treatise on the psychology of instilling fear. Two years later he wrote* The Holocaust and Other Fairy Tales. *Six months later he was recruited by the White Supremacist Movement.*

For the next nine years, he worked to amass large amounts of money and stockpile an arsenal of weapons for the movement. During this period his name was linked to ten armed robberies, fourteen arsons, and eighteen murders. He also wrote So Many Jews, So Few Ovens.

By age thirty-five he had moved up the ranks and was one of the prime behind-the-scenes men in the Skokie march. When he was forty he wrote Zero Jews by the Year 2000. *At age forty-four, he was among the leading American White supremacists at the Aryan Nations' headquarters in Hayden Lake, Idaho.*

His early life is sketchy. Little is known about him. He lived on the streets between foster homes and attended public schools in multiple states and cities. He was expelled at least four times from public schools and never graduated from high school. His IQ is over 140, and he wrote for his school newspaper. John Denver was his favorite singer. (He suffered from depression after Denver died in 1997).

Bloom's phone rang, and a few seconds later he raced out of Mac's office, leaving Stine's report on the desk.

Driving at least twenty miles per hour over the limit, he arrived home in twelve minutes, his clothes wringing wet, his eyes bloodshot from crying.

"He's okay!" cried Missy meeting him in the driveway. "The school called a minute ago. He's okay!"

Bloom got out of the car and hugged her.

"Peter's okay," she whispered, squeezing him tightly.

"I'll kill them!" shouted Bloom, the tears rolling down his cheeks.

"Shh, Jamie," she whispered.

"I'll kill those Nazi bastards!"

"They had nothing to do with it!"

"What do you mean?" exclaimed Bloom, pushing her away so he could see her face.

"Peter and his friend Larry just wandered off. Stine and whoever had nothing to do with it."

"Are you sure?" asked Bloom wiping his cheeks, getting more composed.

"I'm positive."

"Are you sure Peter's okay?"

"Yes, I'm sure."

"How sure are you?"

"I spoke with him a few seconds ago."

"Tell me again what happened," asked Bloom sighing deeply.

"The school called around 12:30 and told me Peter and another boy were found missing after recess was over. That's when I called you. Just before you got home, the school called back and told me the boys had wandered off and had been watching a man fishing in the canal behind the school."

"Are you sure it was the school that called?"

"I spoke with his teacher, Mrs. Rudolph."

"And you spoke with Peter?"

"I have no problem believing that everything's okay."

"Oh, Missy!" cried Bloom hugging her tightly.

"This is really bending us out of shape."

"I know."

"The phone," said Missy turning toward the house.

"I'll get it," replied Bloom, hurrying inside and picking up the phone on the pass-through.

"Hello?"

"Dr. Bloom?"

"What the fu—what do you want?" said Bloom, recognizing Jones's voice.

"I'm calling to tell you I'm glad your son is okay."

"How'd you—never mind."

"Parents should teach their children not to stray."

"Uh, you're right," answered Bloom biting his lip, trying hard to control himself.

"And also not to get so close to the water's edge."

"Uh, that too," said Bloom biting even harder.

"I didn't know we had such large catfish in Florida."

"Whaa?'"

"On a completely unrelated issue, I need that information now."

"Uh, I hope to have it sometime this afternoon."

"When?"

"By three."

"You may now hang up."

Bloom let go of his lip, hung up, and waited for Missy to come into the house.

CHAPTER 30

U-TURN COMING SOON

"That's what she said," replied Bloom after listening to Mac paraphrase what Bloom had just said. "Well, maybe taking the sleeping pills may be the best way out," said Mac, scratching his chin.

"Come on."

"How old is she?"

"Eighty-nine. What's the difference?"

"Jamie. She's offering you an out. Take it."

"I'm going to the police."

"Don't."

"Why not?"

"You can't win."

"Whose side are you on?"

"Yours."

"I can't let her do it."

"It'll be painless. She'd be much better off."

"That's ridiculous."

"It's her choice!"

"Only because of me!"

"And if you don't tell them, they won't find her?"

"It's a possibility."

"Their hooks are everywhere. Didn't someone call you less than two minutes after the school called? It'd be just a matter of time before they track her down. And who knows what they'll do to her."

"Maybe they're bluffing."

"When is she doing it, tonight?"

"That's what she said. She's already left for Cincinnati."

"When are you supposed to let Jones know?"

"In an hour," said Bloom, sighing and looking up at the clock above his desk. "I'll let you know what happens."

Bloom hung up, left his office, and walked across the parking lot to the hospital. He went into the doctors' lounge, sat down, and went over his options. At two o'clock the call from Jones was put through to him.

"I hope you have the information I need," began Jones.

"She made it easy for you."

"What do you mean?"

"Tonight at eleven o'clock, in a hotel in Cincinnati, she'll be taking a hundred Seconal."

"What's Seconal?"

"A sleeping pill."

"Why are you telling me this?"

"She's checking into a hotel and taking sleeping pills."

"What for?!"

"She thought it would be easier, for everyone."

"What are you talking about?"

"Don't worry, there'll be sufficient proof."

"I don't understand."

"You understand... She cared more about my family that she did about herself."

"I don't understand. What are you saying?"

"I'm saying you can relax. She'll be dead by tomorrow."

"Who wants her dead?"

"Obviously you and your leaders."

"Did I say anything about wanting her dead?"

"Please, Mr. Jones, if that's who you really are? You sniped her on I-75. You sabotaged her respirator. You killed her platelet donor. You've been hounding the hell out of me to deliver her to you . . ."

"You fucking idiot! I need her alive!"

"Well, you're not going to get her alive."

"Well, if she dies, so does your son!"

"Whaaat?"

"You heard me!"

"I don't understand!" exclaimed Bloom, his mouth quivering.

"It's very simple. If she dies, so will your son."

"But... but... why?"

"Why? Because I need her alive!"

"Why?"

"Don't ask anymore questions."

"I don't know if I'll be able to reach her," whimpered Bloom.

"Sure you will."

"Can't we both try?" Bloom pleaded. He had been reluctant to tell Jones where Foak was, but now he had no choice. "She's somewhere in Cincinnati," he said, giving Jones the phone number.

"But like I said, if she dies, so does your son. That's a promise. You may now hang--"

"Please wait!" cried Bloom. "Don't hang up!"

Bloom heard a click, and a dial tone. He immediately dialed Foak's number and got a busy response.

"Thank God," he cried, thinking Foak was still at home.

He kept pressing the redial button until he heard a ringing noise. When no one picked up by the fifth ring, he felt a chill and brushed a bead of sweat from his forehead. After the tenth ring, he hung up and pushed redial, getting the same response. By the eighth ring, he felt the perspiration around his neck. He hung up and hand-dialed the number, this time getting a busy signal. After 15 more minutes of mixed busy signals and no response he stopped calling.

"Were you able to reach her?" asked Jones, calling back a few minutes later.

"No," replied Bloom very distraught.

"You'd better start calling all the hotels in Cincinnati! I hate saying this... but if you don't reach her and she dies, Peter will have to die also."

"But... aren't you going to try?"

"I will, but--"

"Please, I beg you!"

"I won't be doing it for you."

"Please . . ."
"We only go by results. Nothing personal. You may now hang up."
Bloom put down the phone.
"Get me my wife," he said through the intercom.

CHAPTER 31

LET YOUR FINGERS DO THE WALKIN'

"Foak's sister is not home," said Bloom. "Neither is Foak."

"I know," said Missy, sitting down at Aretha's desk. "How do you want to do this?"

"I'll take A to M," said Bloom, sitting at the new thirty-eight-year-old employee Cathy's desk and looking over Cincinnati's hotel list. Bloom looked at Missy's watch, dialed the first hotel on the list, and asked to be put through to Ida Stern.

"You know what room she's in?" asked the hotel operator.

"No."

"Please hold."

"Count the number of hotels," said Bloom, turning to Missy as he looked at her watch again and noted twenty seconds had already elapsed.

After twenty additional seconds, the operator got back on.

"I'm sorry. How you spell that?"

"S-T-E-R-N."

"What's the first name again?"

"Ida. I-D-A."

"Please hold."

"How many do you estimate?" asked Bloom, turning back to Missy, noting the forty-five-second mark.

"I'm sorry," said the operator coming back on. "But we don't have an Ida Stern registered here."

"What Stern's do you have?"

"I'm sorry. I can't tell you that."

"Do you have any Sterns here?"

"I can't tell you that either."

"Can I speak with the manager, please?"

"Surely. Please hold."

"Over a hundred," said Missy, doing some quick calculations.

After ten irritating minutes waiting for and speaking with the manager, Bloom did not know if there were any Sterns staying at the hotel.

"This is bad," he said to Missy after hanging up. "It took over 11 minutes and we can't say whether or not Ida's at that hotel."

A similar thing happened when Bloom called the next one and when Missy called the third.

"If each call takes ten minutes and each of us calls fifty hotels, it'll take us roughly eight hours each to call all the hotels," said Bloom. "And we can't even consider the information we've received to be accurate. There's got to be a better way." Bloom thought for a few minutes. "I've got an idea," he said. "I remember I spoke with a Walmart pharmacist last year when I called in a prescription for Ida. I think his first name had a 'Z' in it. The Walmart was on Colerain Ave." He looked up the number of Walmart's Pharmacy on Colerain, dialed the number, said he was Dr. Jamie Bloom, the doctor of Ida Stern, and asked to speak with the pharmacist. When someone named Zev Blumberg announced himself, Bloom smiled and told him he had spoken to him last year when Ida Stern was visiting Cincinnati. He reminded him she then was eighty-seven and a Holocaust survivor and told him he needed his help.

"You're in Florida, I remember," he said. "What can I do for you?"

"Actually it's for Ida and for me. It's very convoluted and I'll try to be succinct."

"We're very busy here."

"I appreciate you taking the time," began Bloom. "Ida, along with two other people, tried to stop the neoNazis from marching in Skokie," began Bloom.

"I remember. I came to the U.S. in 1977 just before the march."

"Two of the three were murdered by William Stine this year."

"I know who he is."

"A few months ago Ida was shot by him and almost died on the OR table from a hole in her ventricle. Since that time Stine's been looking to finish the job he started. She came back to Cincinnati this week to take her own life with Seconal because she wanted to die her own way and not by Stine's doing. For some reason they have changed their mind and now want her alive, and they have threatened me with kidnapping and killing my seven-year-old son if I don't tell them where she is. My wife and I are trying to call every hotel in Cincinnati in order to find her. So far, it's taking us ten minutes per hotel to find out that they can't tell us whether or not she's there. One of the problems is whether she's registered as Ida Stern, Ida Berger, Mrs. Meyer Berger, or Foak."

"Foak?"

"In Auschwitz she was Foak—her arm tattoo had four nines in it. I call her Ida. She sometimes calls herself Foak—four of a kind."

"Have you gone to the police?"

"I think my son would have been dead already," replied Bloom choking on the words.

"I agree. Okay, this is too crazy to be made up. I can help. I know the people at Ho-Jo's, Ramada, Hyatt, and Holiday Inn. Concentrate on the other ones, and if it seems they're holding back information let me know whom they are."

"Oh God, thank you. Thank you so much."

"How many hotels have you called?"

"We just started, so only three. None that you've mentioned. The first one said there was no Ida Stern there and wouldn't answer any other questions. The second said the same. The third said there was a Stern there but not an Ida and wouldn't tell me the Stern's first name."

For the next seven hours they called the hotels not assigned to Blumberg. "How are you doing?" asked Bloom after finishing his last call. "I'm going into my consultation room and lay down on the couch. "My back and tush are killing me."

"I have four more to go," said Missy. "Any word from Blumberg?"

"So far he hasn't had any luck. He hasn't heard yet from Ramada."

"Why don't you take a look at the large manila envelope I got from Dr. Payne. I brought it in with me and put it on Aretha's desk."

Bloom picked up the envelope, walked into his office, and literally plopped down on the couch after putting the envelope on the nearby chair. Missy joined him fifteen minutes later and snuggled under his armpit. In three minutes they were both asleep. Twenty minutes later Bloom was awakened by his phone. He got up and raced to it. It was Jones.

"Yes," he said, hoping it was good news. "Were you able to reach her?" he asked anxiously.

"I found her. Your son is safe."

"God bless you!" said Bloom heaving a sigh of relief. "Is Ida okay?"

"All you should care about is your son. Your services are no longer needed."

"But--"

Bloom heard a click and a dial tone. Because of Jones's abrupt and incomplete answer, he called Ida. He dialed her number and was quite nervous about what he might find out. All that ended when Ida answered on the first ring.

"I might have been better off in the long run to have taken the Seconal," she said. "Stine and his mob has made me a burden to you and your family. I've lived long enough. And now he wants me alive. Why? Does he want to kill me himself? Is that it?"

"Ida, we love you. You're not a burden. I want you to live. Please don't take the pills."

"I won't, because if I do, he'll probably come after you."

"Good. So you won't take them?"

"Correct."

With that he hung up and hurried to Missy to tell her the news.

Missy was soundly asleep so he let her be. He opened the manila envelope, took out its contents, grabbed a throw pillow from the couch to put behind his back, and sat down on the chair to start reading.

I turned the corner and had a most uncanny feeling and immediately thought of Dorothy when she arrived in Munchkinland after her house landed on the wicked witch. The dull, dark, dismal Berlin street with its dull, dark, dismal church and orphanage from Foak's description appeared before me in vivid color. I felt warm in my topcoat, even though it was only twenty degrees, and squinted from the brilliant sun. I counted forty-six to Foak's forty-nine paces from the corner to the iron gate, which led to the courtyard in front of the orphanage. I recited from memory the inscription over the orphanage entrance, partially obscured by the leafless branches of a bending oak. I now see why Foak was so anxious when I told her I was traveling to Germany.

The orphanage was still intact, although I had learned it had not been functioning as such for the past forty-six years. For a second, I thought I heard the screaming of Foak's son as his butt was branded with a lit cigarette when she and her husband realized his days as a Jew in Berlin were numbered and wanted some way to be able to reclaim him when they returned. I continued to walk along the six-foot fence and, at thirty paces, stopped in front of the clerestory that housed seven concrete slabs, formerly seven scenes from the New Testament, and counted the hundred and fifty bricks beneath it.

"She never went back for her son," muttered Bloom to himself.

At that point Missy started to get up. When she saw the open envelope and Bloom holding its contents, she asked him what he found out. He paraphrased what he read and reiterated she never went back for her son.

"What do you think?" he asked Missy.

"I have no idea. Did you read the rest of it?"

"Uh huh."

"And?"

"Foak refused to talk about it."

"What did Payne say?"

"She didn't say anything . . . What do *you* think?"

"Maybe as a result of a posttraumatic stress disorder, she repressed his memory."

"How would that explain the fact that she said the orphanage had been destroyed?"

"Maybe it wasn't until many years later, either though therapy or on her own, that she became aware of her son."

"And by that time it was too late to do anything about it?"

"Maybe she tried, but she wasn't able to find him."

"You think she made up the story about the bombing to make it easier to accept?"

"Or maybe she learned something in Auschwitz or after the war that discouraged her from looking."

"You think her sister may know something?"

"Very possibly."

"You think Ida still believes the bombing took place?"

"Possibly. I think right now she's getting ready to be dead."

"Not me. Right now, I think she may want to be alive . . . for now!"

"How can you say that?"

"Because I spoke with her while you were sleeping."

PLEASE SAY IT ISN'T SEW, AGAIN

"Dr. Bloom's office, Cathy Eder speaking, may I ... oh it's you, Dr. Bloom," began Cathy. She was a relatively new member of Bloom's staff, having recently moved to Florida with her husband and eight-year-old son from Albuquerque four months ago. "Your first patient is filling out his forms."

"I'm just pulling into the hospital," said Bloom.

"Take your time, Dr. Bloom."

Bloom hung up and pulled into the canopied doctors' parking lot.

As he finished securing the roof on his MGB, orthopedist Bob Stevens was getting into his own vehicle. "Jamie, the ER is looking for you," he said.

"Any idea what it's about?"

"I think a Bobbittectomy."

"Are you kidding? Not another one!"

"You're the maven. Good luck."

Bloom locked the car and sprinted to the ER, his abnormal gait hardly noticeable.

"Whatcha got?" he asked arriving at the main desk, not happy about what he was about to find out.

"You're the man," said ER physician John Ringer. "He's brown bagged it," he added, "but it's not his lunch."

"Self-inflicted?"

"Like the last one."

"How long ago?"

"About two hours ago. He just got here."

"Did you look inside the bag?"

"It's not a sausage link," said Ringer, directing Bloom into room 4.

Bloom's eyes were drawn to the patient's blood-soaked gown. Then he noticed the patient's blood-stained hands, the right one holding a brown bag.

"I'm Dr. Bloom," he said, double-gloving and shaking the patient's hand after relieving him of the bag and looking at its contents.

"I'm Shorty," replied the patient.

"Shorter?" asked Bloom.

"No, Shorty!"

"Shorter," mumbled Bloom to himself. "What happened?"

"I cut my thing off."

"Why'd you do that?"

"It wouldn't behave itself."

"Has psych seen him?" asked Bloom turning to Ringer.

"I don't need a psychiatrist," said the patient.

"Not yet," said Ringer

"Do you have a psychiatrist?" asked Bloom looking at the patient.

"What for?'

"Can I take a look at you?" Bloom asked moving toward the patient. "I'll be very gentle."

Bloom approached the patient's midsection and gently lifted his gown, taking care not to dislodge the huge blood clot now occupying the space of the once-attached organ.

"When did you eat last?" asked Bloom.

"Eleven last night," replied his accompanying nurse.

"Was there anyone with him when he came in?" asked Bloom.

"No," replied the nurse.

"Put the penis in a sterile basin filled with normal saline," said Bloom, stepping out of the room and dialing the OR, alerting them of the emergency. He went back into the room, spoke with the patient for a few minutes, then rushed out, wrote the necessary orders, and sprinted to his office.

"Good morning and let me see today's schedule," said Bloom as he bolted past Aretha and Cathy into his consultation room and called the OR and the on-call plastic, vascular, and neurosurgeons, learning that the OR would be ready to go in thirty minutes, and that none of the specialists would be available for at least two hours.

Bloom went back into reception area, told his staff of the emergency, giving them only the most rudimentary details, and asked Aretha to change all of the day's appointments after the first eight patients and to make sure all the emergencies came in before 10:30.

Bloom arrived home eleven hours later.

CHAPTER 33

I THOUGHT I HAD SAID NOOKY

"I referred a patient to you today," announced Bloom walking into the family room and sitting down on the leather couch.

"Come again," replied Missy entering the family room from the other side of the house.

"First give me a kiss," said Bloom, puckering up.

"I heard you had a fun day," replied Missy, bending down and planting a kiss on his open mouth.

"Where are the kiddies?"

"It's ten o'clock!"

"Everyone's okay?"

"Have you eaten yet?"

"Two crackers and a glass of apple juice. That was it for the day."

"Want a hot dog?" she asked facetiously.

"Ug," cried Bloom making an ugly face. "Never again! The circumcisions were nothing compared to this. I said I referred a patient to you."

"Not this guy."

"Afraid so."

"When he asked if he'd be able to get erections, did you say it wouldn't be long now?"

"Ha ha. I gave him a copy of Lorena Bobbitt's new book on weight loss titled 'How to Lose Inches While You Sleep.'"

"Very good. Should I defrost some pizza?"

"Sounds good."

"Was this another pro bono radical circumcision like the last one?"

"Nope. Guess the name of his insurance company."

"I give up."

"You give up too easily."

"State Farm."

"Why State Farm?"

"The good hands people."

"That's close. John Han(d)cock."

"Is it really?"

"Uh huh."

"That's funny."

"How about a hand on this cock . . . and some nooky?"

"Okay," replied Missy, hitting him gently on the top of his head with the knuckle of the middle finger.

"Hey!" shouted Bloom flinching. "I didn't say noogie!"

CHAPTER 34

"HE'S BACK!"

As Bloom picked up the portable phone on the night table he glanced at the clock. It was 3:17 a.m. He was greeted by Denise, the midnight secretary at University's ER. He hopped with the phone to the kitchen, put on the light, and sat down on one of the chairs.

"It's 3:17. What's so good about it?" replied Bloom responding to Denise's "Good morning."

"Time to rise and shine, Dr. B."

"Spare me, Denise."

"Yes sir, Dr. Bloom."

Bloom laughed.

"Your guy is back."

"He cut it off again!"

"I heard about him," replied Denise laughing. "No, not him."

"Which guy?"

"Your buddy, the neo-Nazi."

"Is he holding a brown bag?"

"You're funny for three in the morning."

"I'm even funnier at four. What's he got, another stone?"

"Bingo. Mid-ureteral on the left with moderate hydro."

"How big?"

"The report says six millimeters. He also has a nonobstructing seven-millimeter stone in the right kidney, which was present on his last admission. This six millimeter one is probably the one we didn't see on his last visit when the CT scanner was down. His pain subsided and he said he had strained his urine for two weeks, although he admitted he had missed a few urinations when he didn't have his strainer with him."

"How much pain is he having?"

"He's already had ten ccs of morphine and five of Dilaudid."

"Let me speak with a nurse. Are any of his henchmen around?"

"Only three. Jones is one of them."

Bloom spoke with the nurse, gave some orders, spoke with Jones, then spoke with the nursing supervisor and scheduled the emergency cystoscopy and lithotripsy for the early morning.

Bloom hopped back to bed and tossed and turned for the next three and a half hours. Thoughts of how to kill Stine on the OR table pervaded his thoughts. He couldn't think of any possible urologic way to do it. Of course, he could perforate a ureter or bladder or cause bleeding, but these complications could easily be treated by him or any other urologist. Then there were the repercussions—lawsuits and the danger to him and his family. An anesthetic death would be easier, but that would have to involve another person, unless he used the potassium chloride he had on hand to diagnose interstitial cystitis. No, killing Stine was not an option for now. And wasn't Bloom told that he and his family now were safe? On the other hand, could he rely on the word of a sociopath and murderer?

After the morning surgery, Bloom went to see Stine in recovery. "Here's a chunk of the culprit," he said, holding up a closed container.

"Did you get all of it?" asked Stine.

"The rest was pulverized and will come out when you urinate. We'll need to analyze it to see what kind of stone it is. It'll probably be made of calcium oxalate or uric acid, the latter of which is radiolucent and would not have shown up on a plain film. Hopefully there'll be something I can prescribe to try to help them from forming."

"I feel like I have to pee."

"That's because of the catheter. It'll come out in about an hour. There's another tube in you that will need to stay in for about a week. I'll take that one out in the office."

"Where's that one?"

"Between your kidney and your bladder."

"When can I go home?"

"Probably this afternoon. I have to make sure whatever pain you have is controlled with oral meds, that you're eating okay, and that you're able to urinate okay. Before I forget, do you remember you still have that seven-millimeter stone in your right kidney? It's not causing a problem so it's not worth going after it at this time. It's possible this stone may never be a problem, or it can become one tomorrow. Again, there's no medical indication to do anything now, but the medicine I'm going to put you on to help prevent stones will not help the stones that have already formed. Getting back to your urination, because of the anesthetic you received today, plus the big instruments I used to laser, grab, and pull the stone out, it may be a little more difficult to urinate. I will see you before you're discharged. And I also need to speak with you regarding other matters."

Stine nodded. Bloom went to his office, saw today's and some of yesterday's rescheduled patients, checked his post-ops, and had that long-awaited conversation with Stine.

Meanwhile, in the University of Cincinnati Medical Center Hospital, Foak was bleeding out with a hemoglobin of seven and a platelet donor search revealing only a single match, which was nonsuitable.

CHAPTER 35

LEAVING ON A JET PLANE

"Somebody's home!" shouted Bloom, putting his key and fanny pack on the pass-through.

"Mommy's on the phone with that lady's sister," yelled Peter as he galloped down the hallway on his hobby horse with Lisa right behind on hers.

"This is a toll road," said Bloom, crouching down to Peter's level, anticipating a kiss or a hug.

"The tolls have been waived," replied Peter, not slowing down.

"What'd you say?" asked Bloom, catching him before he could pass.

"The tolls have been waived," repeated Peter.

"Where'd you hear that word?"

"Tolls?" answered Peter.

"Waived. You know what I mean."

Peter laughed. "I heard it on TV last year. They said that the tolls would be waived because of the hurricane that was coming."

"What does that mean?"

"It means they can get through without having to pay the toll—like now!" yelled Peter trying to get away from Bloom's grasp.

"Dehr," said Lisa, trying to squeeze through under Bloom's arms.

Bloom grabbed both of them and carried them, horses and all, onto the family room couch where he smothered them with hugs and kisses.

"Anything left for me?" asked Missy, walking into the family room and sitting on Bloom's lap.

"Of course," said Bloom giving her the same treatment.

"I need to talk with Daddy," said Missy a few minutes later. "Peter, please take Lisa into your room, just for a little while. Okay?"

"Wead Dindawella, Petah."

"Oh, no!" replied Peter.

"Wead Dindawella."

"I'm sick of Cinderella!"

"Can Peter read something else?" asked Missy starting to laugh.

"No White," said Lisa.

"Snow White?" said Peter.

"Dehr. No White."

"Just once,"

"Dindawella."

"No Dindawella. No White just once. Okay?"

"Oday."

"Good, I'm glad we got that settled," said Missy, gently nudging Peter and Lisa off the couch. "I just got off the phone with Foak's sister. What do you want first, the bad news or the very bad news?"

"Is Foak alive?" blurted out Bloom.

"Yes, she's alive."

"What's the very bad news."

"She's dying."

"From blood loss?"

"Uh huh."

"And the bad news."

"We're going to Cincinnati."

"Why?"

"She wants us there."

"What for?"

"She's dying. She wants to see us . . . and she wants us to find her son!"

"Is he in Cincinnati?"

"You're an idiot."

"Is his name Waldo?"

"You're still an idiot."

"But I'm a funny idiot. How can we possibly find him? Let me call her attending and find out what kind of time frame we have."

"According to her sister, there isn't any."

Bloom's phone then rang.

CHAPTER 36

WHO'S IN CHARGE HERE?

Bloom stored their carry-ons, took out whatever he needed for the trip, and got ready for their departure from Ft. Lauderdale to Cincinnati via Atlanta.

"Tell me about your discussion with Stine," asked Missy, putting her laptop under the seat in front of her and fastening her seat belt.

"It wasn't much of a discussion. He basically denied everything."

"What about the circumcisions?"

"That, too."

"And the twenty thousand dollars?"

"He intimated that Jones was acting on his own."

"And you believe him?"

"He's very good."

"You mean as a liar and a conniver?"

"Things don't add up about him."

"Like what?"

"I don't know. He doesn't seem like that bad of a person. I guess he may treat different groups of people differently—you know, the Eddie Haskell syndrome based on the *Leave It to Beaver* character."

"Okay, so why does he now want Foak alive? He certainly doesn't like Jewish people."

"Beats me. He might have leukemia, but I don't know where that fits in. Ida's probably a loose end he needs to tie up. You know what?

I'll ask him when he comes to the office next week . . . or when we play golf!"

"Ha ha."

CHAPTER 37

IN ROOM 623

Even though Bloom had recently learned that Foak was doing better, he was still very apprehensive when he walked into room 623, expecting to see the urinary drainage tubing with its rapidly flowing irrigant pushing massive clots from the bladder into the drainage bag, a bright reddish-black-colored urine, and a minimally responsive eighty-nine-year-old woman. Instead, he saw no irrigation, a slowly dripping rose-colored urine, and an alert warrior. He was ecstatic. Teary-eyed, he rushed over to her and gave her a big hug. He held her for two minutes and then wiped the tears from his eyes.

"So is your catheter in someone else? I was told yesterday you were bleeding out, your blood count was not compatible with life, and there was no blood available to give you! What's responsible for this miracle?" he asked. "Tell me what happened here." He reached for her wrist and felt that her pulse was about 90 and strong.

"The blood bank called yesterday afternoon and said they located four units of compatible platelets," said Foak.

"Out of nowhere?"

"I didn't question it."

"It would be nice to know from where in case you need more. I'll try to find--" He was interrupted by the hospital sound system, another code blue. "That's three they've called in the last ten minutes!"

"Relax doc, they're off limits to you," replied Foak. "You're only visiting."

"A doctor's work is never done. The only problem is that I don't have an Ohio license."

"I won't tell anyone," said Foak smiling. "How was your flight?" she asked, turning toward Missy.

"They were both uneventful, just the way we like them. You look all scrunched up in the bed. Are you comfortable?"

"She makes a living," replied Bloom smiling.

"Hey, that's my line," said Foak. "That's only said by Jewish people." Missy laughed.

"I really appreciate you coming here," said Foak. "I've never imposed myself on anyone before or put anyone in harm's way . . . like I've done to your family," she added, looking emotional.

Bloom put up his hands signifying that what he and Missy were doing was no big deal. Trying to switch topics, he said, "I'm so glad they found a donor for you. I had assumed the doctors here were unable to find another platelet donor after the last one . . . died."

"That mamzer!" hissed Foak, recalling Stine's alleged role in pushing the platelet donor's car onto the railroad tracks.

"You're not going to start spitting, are you?" asked Bloom backing away. "By the way, you're not going to believe this, but your mamzer asked us to come here."

"What?"

"And paid for our flights."

"Why?"

"And I really shouldn't be telling you this, but I was more or less forced to take care of him a few days ago when he came to the ER. I actually operated on him yesterday."

"You had a chance to kill him?"

"It entered my mind."

"You told him about me?"

"He knew about you before your sister called us."

"Did he want you to come here to finish the job he started?"

"I wasn't supposed to tell you that," replied Bloom with a deadpan expression, then smiled broadly.

"My husband—your doctor—is an idiot," interjected Missy.

"Nolo contendere," said Bloom. "I spoke with Stine yesterday. He basically denied killing your two friends from the ADL, denied killing your platelet donor, denied trying to kill you, and denied wanting you dead."

"And you believed him?"

"Of course. He denied it!" Bloom said sarcastically.

"Why does he want me alive?" asked Foak. "Guilt? That can't be! The man has killed at least two dozen people and maimed countless others. The man has not one shred of guilt in his entire body."

"Stine has leukemia and will probably need treatment."

"That mamzer!"

"That mamzer wants me and Missy to make sure nothing happens to you."

"I don't want to talk about him anymore. Let's concentrate on finding my son. Can you bring me the blue suitcase from the closet?" asked Foak, lifting the head lever on the bed frame so she could sit more erectly.

Bloom located the suitcase and placed it on the tray table as Foak reached into her hospital gown and removed the chain and key that was around her neck. She opened the suitcase and removed a frayed gray notebook.

"Either of you speak German?" she asked.

"Nein," replied Bloom.

Foak raised her eyebrows.

"That's the extent of my German."

"Do you know Yiddish?"

"Ida, how many gentiles do you know that know Yiddish?"

"I keep forgetting."

"What is this book?"

"My mother's diary up until 1942. Pull up some chairs and make yourself comfortable."

"Danke schoen."

Foak smiled.

"Let me give you some background. My father, Mendel Stern, was born in 1884, my mother, Sophie Berg, was born in 1888, both in Germany. They married in 1913 and had three children—me in 1914, my brother Simon in 1916, and Rachel in 1917. I was married to Meyer Berger in 1934. Neither of my siblings married. In 1938, after four years and no pregnancies, I went to a Berlin clinic and got artificially inseminated using my husband Meyer's semen. Our son Sigmund was born in 1939, and in 1940 we left him at a convent in Berlin. I assume you know why."

Missy and Bloom nodded.

"In December 1940 we were herded into boxcars and transported to our first death camp. After that, I never saw Meyer or my father again. My mother and brother died in the camp we were in, my mother killed by a German shepherd, my brother had his eyes poked out with a hot iron for reading a prayer book he had hidden in his mattress."

Missy and Bloom sighed.

"After my mother died, Rachel and I found her diary in her mattress, the most popular hiding place in the camps, when we were going through her sleeping area. Most of the prisoners slept on wooden floors that had some straw strewn on it. Some lucky ones, like Simon and my mother, had paper mattresses filled with wood wool, which gave potential hiding areas. After Rachel and I were transferred to our second camp, Rachel was taken to a medical facility where she was inseminated and kept for three months, after which time her uterus was removed with the fetus intact. Three weeks later she was returned to our camp. I was inseminated, but I luckily miscarried, probably because I repeatedly fell onto heavy, pointed objects wherever I could find them."

"Mengele?" asked Missy.

"Rachel thought so. He was referred to as Dr. Joe and her description of him matched the textbooks. Her hysterectomy was done without anesthesia."

Ida waited a few minutes for Missy and Bloom to regain their composure.

"You commented on my blue eyes when you first examined me. Remember?"

"Uh huh," replied Bloom.

"I'm the only one in my family with blue eyes, and the only one with fair skin. Anything I've said ring a bell?"

"Not really," replied Bloom after a few seconds.

"What about you, Missy?"

"No, not particularly."

"You're either really good friends," said Foak, acknowledging their reluctance to respond, "or you're not that familiar with the Holocaust."

"We're really good friends," said Missy.

"The Boys from Brazil?" said Bloom.

"Bingo!" said Ida.

Foak opened the notebook and skimmed the pages, her index finger coming to rest on the entry dated February 21, 1939.

"Wir...." she began. "Sorry, I'll translate and speak English. This is in my mother's handwriting."

We just returned from the hospital in Berlin where Ida was artificially inseminated by Dr. Josef Mengele. He said that although this was a new technique, he had performed more than fifty of these procedures and was optimistic in its success.

"That doesn't mean he didn't use Meyer's semen," interjected Bloom.

"He's not a great listener," said Missy frowning.

Bloom smiled.

Foak skimmed the next four pages, then continued with the entry dated March 21, 1939. "Mendel, du bist ein .... Sorry, again," said Ida.

Mendel, through one of his colleagues—

"I told you my father was a physician."

"A hematologist you said," interrupted Bloom.

Mendel, through one of his colleagues, learned that our Dr. Mengele had been conducting experiments using fair-skinned, blue-eyed mothers and that Meyer's semen might not have been used for the insemination. Mendel told me not to say anything to Ida or Meyer.

Bloom nodded. Missy showed no expression. Foak flipped through another few pages.

As expected, Mendel's office was closed down today. He can no longer practice medicine. Cousin Fritz offered him a job in his shoe store.

The next entry was August 17, 1939.

Ida is seven months pregnant. Through a nurse, Mendel found out that none of the fifty inseminations—now seventy-five—performed at that clinic used the husband's semen. The nurse thinks Mengele used his own and Hitler's semen. I won't tell Ida and Meyer. We need to leave Germany.

"Vital signs check," announced an LPN pushing a small rolling cart to within a foot of Foak's bed. "How are you doing? Your urine finally looks like urine."

Bloom glanced at the almost clear fluid in the drainage bag tubing.

"We'll step out?" said Bloom starting to get up.

"Give us a few minutes, okay?" replied the nurse.

"We'll get a quick bite," said Bloom. "Want anything from the coffee shop?"

"A latte would be nice," said Foak.

"One latte coming up. See you in a bit."

Bloom and Missy exited the room and walked in the direction of the elevator.

"Now we know why she didn't go back for him," said Bloom, pushing the down button.

"Assuming she got this information before the war was over," replied Missy.

"It looks like she did."

They took the elevator to the ground floor and went into the coffee shop and sat down.

"Would you look for him if it was your son?" asked Bloom looking over the menu, spotting chocolate mousse cake in the dessert section.

"He's at least half hers, unless they implanted a fertilized egg in her. They couldn't have done that, could they?"

"I think it had to be the mother's egg. Want to share an egg salad sandwich?"

"Ha ha."

"But knowing that Mengele might be the father?"

"We don't know that for a fact."

"You're right. Maybe Hitler was!"

"Wasn't he busy doing other things?"

"I didn't say Hitler actually may have had sex with her."

"There's no wrong or right answer."

"Are you surprised she never told her psychiatrist?"

"She was never dying before now."

"You think that's it?"

"I'm sure we'll find out in due time, that is, if you don't keep interrupting!"

HOLDING DOWN THE FORT

"Dr Bloom's office, Aretha speak . . ."

"I need you to get him right now!" interrupted Jones.

"Excuse me. This is Dr. -- "

"I know who the fuck I called! I need you to get him right now!"

"Who is this?"

"Listen, asshole! Just get him for me!"

"And you are?"

"You know the fuck who I am!"

"I'm sorry," said Aretha hanging up.

A few seconds later the caller was back on the line, having the same conversation and ending with the same result.

The third time, Aretha took a deep breath and counted to ten before hanging up.

"Don't fuck with me lady, and don't hang up," began Jones on his fourth try.

Despite Aretha's attempts to be patient and counting to ten, she hung up again.

Aretha put all three phones on hold. She went into the third examining room, picked up the portable phone, and tried unsuccessfully to get Bloom on his phone. She left a message, shut off the lights, put the phones back on, closed the office, and drove home as fast as she could. She didn't want to be anywhere near the office in case the caller decided to stop by.

CHAPTER 39

SEND IN THE CALVARY

Missy picked up this month's *Cosmo* and a latte and handed them to Bloom, who was in line paying the cashier.

"Anything else?" asked Bloom taking them from her. He spotted a piece of chocolate on the corner of her mouth and wiped it off, licking the tip of his finger. "You're welcome," added Bloom, noting her frown.

"You're in rare form today, Dr. B."

"Thank you."

Bloom paid in cash—the coffee shop's only acceptable form of payment—handed the latte and magazine back to Missy, visited the men's room, and accompanied Missy back to the sixth floor.

"Code blue, sixth north!" heard Bloom as the elevator door opened. He quickly looked in the direction of 623 and saw a flurry of activity. He raced to the room. Two nurses were attending Foak, who appeared unresponsive.

"Did anyone see her arrest?" shouted Bloom nearing Foak's bedside.

"You'll have to leave," said one of the nurses.

"I'm a physician," said Bloom. "Ida!" he screamed, feeling no pulse and seeing no respiratory motion. "What happened?" he asked again.

"We don't know who you are," replied the nurse. "You have to leave."

"Where's the code team?" asked Bloom, flattening the bed, thumping Ida's chest, sweeping her mouth and removing her dentures, and starting sternal compressions.

"They're on the way. Please leave."

"Where's the crash cart?" shouted Bloom seeing none.

"You'll have to leave right now. Get the supervisor!"

"Yes, get the supervisor," shouted Bloom, noting no respirations. "Just get me the crash cart," yelled Bloom continuing with the chest compressions. "We're losing her. Someone get me an amp of epi … I don't care where you get it from! I also need an EKG machine."

"Crash cart and EKG machine are here."

"Someone hook up the leads and give her an amp of epi," said Bloom continuing the compressions while eyeing the IV and making sure it was running.

"Leads are on. I'll be giving the epi in a few seconds."

"Flat line on EKG."

"Epi given."

"Get another amp of epi ready, but don't give it until I tell you." After thirty seconds, Bloom asked what the EKG showed.

"Still flatlining."

"Give the second epi." said Bloom still compressing.

"V fib," said the nurse monitoring the EKG.

Bloom looked at the EKG and yelled, "Paddles!" The defibrillation paddles were taken out of their cases and placed on the bed.

"Everyone, stand clear!" shouted Bloom greasing the paddle and putting it on Foak's chest. "Give me 250 joules. Clear!" yelled Bloom, giving a warning he was about to press the button on the paddles.

A few seconds later, Foak's body convulsed on the bed.

"One more time!" shouted Bloom, still seeing V fib on the EKG. "Clear," he yelled once again. Ten seconds after the next shock, the EKG reverted to sinus rhythm. Bloom continued the compressions until he felt a good radial pulse.

"The code team has arrived," announced one of the team members.

"Thank God and thank everyone," said Bloom.

"You saved her, whoever you are," said one of the nurses.

"We all saved her," corrected Bloom.

CHAPTER 40

TOO MUCH THINKING GOING ON

"Dr. Winger's on line 2," Cathy said through the intercom, eyeing Bloom coming out of exam room 2.

"I assume this is about William Stine?" said Bloom picking up the phone, answering Dr. Winger's questions as quickly as she asked them. "He was almost parked outside my door . . . Cincinnati . . . to see Ida Stern . . . It's a long story . . . Where are you now, in the office? . . . Let me call you in ten minutes, okay?"

Bloom hung up, finished talking to the patient seated in front of him, then asked Cathy to call Winger back. He had learned—unofficially through Jones, then officially through his weekend coverage Dr. Katz, and now from Dr. Winger—that Stine needed treatment, intense chemotherapy with or without a bone marrow transplant.

"Your friend Mr. Jones is on line 2," announced Aretha interrupting Bloom again. "What shall I tell him?

"Tell him to go fuck himself," replied Bloom under his breath. "Tell him I'll be with him in a minute," he said louder to Aretha.

"He's already called twice."

"Put him through," said Bloom.

"I need an update on Stern's condition," began Jones in a menacing tone.

"Why are you so concerned about her well-being?"

"I'll ask the questions," he answered gruffly. "Do you have the information I requested?"

"Her doctor's not in yet. I thought you guys were going to leave me alone?"

"You have thirty minutes. You may now hang up."

Bloom put the phone back on the cradle but kept his hand on the phone.

Why would Stine, with all his problems, thought Bloom, be so concerned about Foak's health? Unless, he continued musing to himself, *unless his health depended on hers.* Bloom knew from Dr. Winger that there was some degree of match between the two, but he didn't know the extent of it. Stine hadn't had any chemo and he was a long way off for even being considered for a marrow transplant. But would he even consider receiving marrow from a Jew? If he did, his career would be over. The neo-Nazi party would have nothing to do with him. Unless . . . unless he got her marrow without the rest of the world finding out. But how could he do that? And again, even if he could, would he? It would go against every shred of his moral—more like amoral—fiber. Bloom continued to try to think the situation through. Foak would never agree to it, although it could be done illegally. But maybe she would, if it was somehow related to the well-being of her sister, or to Bloom and his family. Maybe that's why she didn't follow through with the Seconal.

Bloom spent the next five minutes ruminating, then blurted out. "Maybe this has nothing to do with Stine! Aretha, get me Dr. Winger again," he said into the intercom.

CHAPTER 41

WELL, WELL, WHAT DO YOU KNOW?

da Stern's on line 1," said Cathy, spotting Bloom walking down the hallway. "She has a question."

"I'll take it in the lab," replied Bloom, sitting down at the microscope to look at the slide of the next patient's urine. He then picked up the phone.

"Hi, Ida. When'd you get in?"

"Rachel and I got in last night. I scheduled my cysto with the office for next week. I never got my CAT scan, but I'm not bleeding. Is it absolutely necessary? My urine looks like tap water."

"I'm afraid so. Cathy said you had a question."

"Yes, do you know what city or state Stine was from?"

"I told you what I had found out about his earlier life and checkered past."

"I'm an expert on his checkered past," interrupted Stern. "I thought you might know what city or state he was *from*."

"For some reason I'm thinking Kentucky or West Virginia."

"Where'd you get that?"

"I don't know. I'm going to see him in a few days. Other than killing him, is there anything else?"

"Killing him would be sufficient."

"Ida, I spoke with Dr. Winger yesterday."

"Oh?"

"I know there's a tissue match between you and Stine."

"That man will never get marrow from me! She shouldn't have told you."

"You signed a statement with her office giving Dr. Winger permission to discuss your medical condition with me and Missy as well. It's called HIPAA."

"What else did she tell you?"

"She told me the finding of the match came about quite by accident."

"How was that?"

"She said that you and Stine and were hospitalized around the same time and you needed HLA matching for platelets, while Stine, when the leukemia was found, underwent typing for a possible bone marrow transplantation, and somehow they got compared. You asked me about his birth date. April 20 was the date he gave to the hospital when he came to the ER. It's also Hitler's birth date. He also said his middle name was Adolph. Stine changed the spelling of his last name when he was eighteen to Stine. I don't know what it was before. He claims his earliest memories are from Kentucky and West Virginia. I know this is a lot. You know we can talk any time you like."

"It's not your problem."

"Ida, please talk to me . . ." Bloom heard a click and the line went dead. Bloom hung up and kept his hand on the phone for a minute.

Bloom had an early lunch and spent the rest of the day reversing vasectomies on two patients who had recently remarried. Afterward, he apprised Missy of his conversation with Ida, returned his calls, made evening rounds, and went home. As he got onto the Sawgrass area, he thought about how his conversation with Ida had ended. He could not remember having seen this side of her.

"Have you spoken with Ida Stern since I spoke with you this afternoon?" asked Bloom, leaving Lisa's room after having read *Cinderella* to her for the second time that day. He walked into the family room and found Missy relaxing on the recliner.

"No."

"I'm calling her," said Bloom walking into the den and sitting at the desk.

Missy changed the recliner to the sitting mode, got up, and followed Bloom into the den. Bloom dialed Ida's and her sister's numbers, but got no answer. He called University Hospital's medical record department and was told they had no additional phone numbers for the Sterns. He thought for a few minutes then redialed medical records and got both the sisters' addresses.

"Going for a ride," said Bloom getting up.

It took twenty-four minutes to get to Ida's house. Rachel's house was around the corner from her sister's. No lights were on at either house. No one answered the bell, and both front and back doors were locked. Both cars were gone. Bloom called both houses and listened to make sure the phones were working. He rang the bells of the four next-door neighbors and after explaining who he was and what he wanted, he didn't learn anything new. As far as they knew, no ambulances had been to either house during the day, and they had no knowledge where either of the women might have gone. Bloom gave them his card and asked them to call if either one should return home. Bloom wasn't sure whether or not they would, except for Rachel's right-side neighbor, who was one of Bloom's patients. He taped his card with a message on each sister's front door, spoke with Missy, then sat in his car for fifteen minutes before heading home after passing by each sister's house one more time. Four minutes into his ride, he received a phone call from Jones telling him it wasn't safe and against the law to drive without a seatbelt.

"Mr. Jones," said Bloom recognizing his voice. "Are you going to call the police?"

"Much worse if you don't do what you're supposed to do."

"And what is that?"

"Deliver her."

"I thought we were working together."

"New game, same rules."

"I don't know where she is."

"But I have every confidence that'll change. You may now hang up."

CHAPTER 42

HOUSE CHECKS

"Mr. Jones is on line 2," said Cathy, seeing Bloom open the office door, holding a medium-size brown bag and placing it on the shelf next to the water cooler.

"I'll take it inside," replied Bloom, taking two containers out of the bag and putting them into the refrigerator. "The bagels are hot," he added, putting on his lab coat and going down the hallway.

"Let me make myself clear," began Jones. "Your job is *not* to buy vegetable cream cheese, whitefish salad, and bagels for your office staff, but *to locate Ida Stern.* Your job is *not* to see Louis Masters at 9:15 and Susan Del Campo at 9:45 and do an office cystoscopy on Sam Rothman at 10:15, but *to locate Ida Stern.* Your job is *not* to have lunch with Dr. Jeff Grant at 12:30, but *to locate Ida Stern.* Am I making myself clear, or do I have to mention your family's names? I hope you're shaking and you feel your neck getting tight and you've already loosened your pretty tie-dyed blue pastel tie. I am giving you five minutes to think about what I've said and will call you back at 9:05. You may now hang up."

"To do my job better," began Bloom, "I need to know the following from you, because the doctors won't talk to me. I need to know what's going on medically with William Stine. The doctors won't tell me squat!"

But Jones had already hung up and did not hear any of Bloom's words. Three minutes later Bloom was back on the phone with Jones and paraphrased his missed request for more information.

"Mr. Jones, I need some help to do my *new* job."

"Go ahead, Dr. Bloom. Tell, er, I mean, ask me what you want me to do for you?

"What a complete asshole," said Bloom to himself. "I called Ida and her sister and left them both messages this morning. I haven't heard back yet. I plan to try their homes again this afternoon. Stern was feeling okay yesterday morning when I spoke with her. She's supposed to see me in the office sometime next week. I know Stine has leukemia, but I don't know where he is, how badly he's doing, and what treatment he's on or what's been recommended to him. I realize that my family is at risk here and helping you is in my best interest. The more information I have though, the better I'll be able to get her to you."

"I'll get back to you this afternoon or evening. You may now hang up."

Bloom completed his morning schedule, saw two added-on emergencies, one requiring removal of a mascara brush from the bladder of a woman who was bleeding, the other requiring dilation of a urethral stricture and placement of a catheter in a man with a distended bladder. His lunch with Dr. Grant was interrupted by a twelve-year-old boy who came to the ER with testicular torsion, requiring emergency surgery to save the testicle by surgically untwisting it and securing it and the other testicle in the scrotum so that neither testicle would have a similar problem in the future. He then saw two consults, checked his post-op patient, and spoke with his office, finding that Jones had not called. He then drove to the Stern sisters' homes, after calling them and getting no answer. He started with Ida's house. There was no car in the driveway or on the street. He heard the doorbell when he tried it. The card that he had placed was still there. The door was still locked. He bent down, opened and looked in the mail slot, inhaled through his nose to test for the presence of gas, and yelled her name three times. He then checked the back door. Inspection of Rachel's house was likewise negative. He drove back to the hospital, discharged his pediatric patient, and drove home.

CHAPTER 43

PROBLEM SOLVED

"I feel like a yo-yo," said Bloom after recounting what was going on with Jones and the Stern sisters. "Stine and company know where I'm going, what I'm wearing and buying, whom I'm seeing, and when I'm seeing them."

"'And why are they bothering me?'" added Missy smiling, as if she were speaking for Bloom and completing the fifth W used for good reporting.

"Exactly. And why are they bothering me?" repeated Bloom.

"What's your next step?"

"I can't do anything until I speak with the Sterns and Stine tells me what he wants with her."

"I think he wants her bone marrow or at least wants to know where she is so he can coerce her or, if need be, physically take it from her."

"I told her I wanted to help her, and she said it was not my problem."

"It may be that she's already made up her mind—to take her life."

"All Jones has asked me is to give him her location."

"Maybe Stine hasn't told Jones what to tell you yet."

"That's a possibility."

"That's your ringtone," said Missy, pointing toward the kitchen.

Bloom turned around, hurried into the kitchen, and picked up his phone. It was his answering service asking him to call Rachel Stern. He took the number, walked back into the room he left, sat down, and dialed her number. She told him that Foak had had a massive stroke while in Miami yesterday and was now in the ICU at Cedars of Lebanon Hospital. He found out which ICU she was in, her bed number, and the name of her attending physician. He told Rachel to go the hospital and sleep there if necessary. He asked her to make sure she gave the ICU nurse her number and that if the ICU called her, she should call him immediately. He told her he would see Ida tomorrow.

Bloom took a few minutes to bring Missy up to speed.

"That explains why they weren't home," said Bloom.

"Do you think Stine and company know about Stern?"

"It's hard to say. At any rate she should be safe while she's at Cedars."

"You'd think so."

"Any thoughts on whether or not I should alert Jones?"

"I'd wait until he calls."

"I could curry favor by giving Jones a heads up."

"By now, you should realize you can't curry favor with those guys."

"Jones, anyway. You're right, as usual."

"As usual."

CHAPTER 44

ADIOS GOON JONES (WE HOPE)

"Dr. Bloom, it's service calling," waking him up. "Please call Mr. Jones at--."

"Can you please patch me through," interrupted Bloom, eyeing the clock and noting it was 4:03 a.m.

"Can do. Please hold on."

Boom quickly got up and went into the guest room with the phone.

"Why didn't you call me?" shouted Jones.

"You should have called me yesterday," said Bloom. "I was waiting for your call."

"You knew where she was!"

"Yes, I learned late last night."

"And you didn't call me," he growled.

"Mr. Jones," said Bloom taking a deep breath. "Obviously, you know where she is."

"No thanks to you."

"Mr. Jones, please tell William Stine if he wants to contact me, he should please do it himself. Tell him I no longer want to deal with you. You may now hang up," added Bloom speaking very softly, then hanging up. Bloom then called his service and told them to write Jones's name and number in large black letters on Dr. Bloom's account number, instructing them not to call him or transfer any more calls to him from Jones.

CHAPTER 45

STINE CONFIRMS ADIOS

"William Stine is on the line," shouted Aretha, catching Bloom out of the corner of her eye as he passed her on the way to his office. "He called at 9:00 and then again at 9:35."

"I'll take it now," replied Bloom, going into his office and picking up the phone.

"Mr. Stine," said Bloom cordially.

"Dr. Bloom," replied Stine also cordially. "I hear you're not getting along well with Mr. Jones."

"Your hearing is excellent."

Stine chuckled. "He can be a little difficult."

"I wouldn't mind a *little* difficult."

Stine laughed. "What would you like to know?"

"Tell me about your nonurinary health."

"I have leukemia. I'm being treated by Dr. Winger. I'm very happy with her."

"I'm glad about that. She's an excellent oncologist."

"She said I'm going to need a bone marrow transplant."

"Going to need or might need?"

"Going to."

"What's the timetable?"

"Soon. Very soon."

"Where does Ida Stern come in?"

"We match. I think you know that."

"I do. But I don't know how good the match is. Have you spoken to Dr. Winger about this?"

"No."

"You should speak to Ida also."

"Ida won't take my calls."

"Are you surprised?"

"No."

"You must have heard from Jones that she had a stroke yesterday while she was in Miami. Her sister said it was massive. I plan to see her later today. I can let you know how she's doing."

"Yes, that'll be good. I'll give you my number."

"One more thing. In the future, I would like to deal with you. I don't want Jones calling me anymore. He woke me up at four o'clock in the morning today to reprimand me for not telling him something he already knew."

"I'll tell him."

"Tell him twice."

The two men laughed, exchanged phone numbers, and cordially hung up.

STINE NOW ON NOTICE

"Hi, Cathy," said Bloom, opening the office door and looking down at the patient schedule. "Please call Peter Mulett, the pediatric patient that I operated on yesterday, and see how he's doing. I'd like to speak with one of his parents. I also need to speak with William Stine and Dr. Winger."

"Which one you want first? Peter?"

"Uh huh. I'll be in the lab looking at the urine cultures." Bloom put on his lab coat and took the culture plates out of the incubator. He recorded the results, notified the patients, and called their pharmacies after verifying they were not allergic to the antibiotic he was going to prescribe.

"Mrs. Mulett is on line 1," announced Cathy. Bloom picked up the phone and learned that Peter was doing well. He had no fever and minimal pain. She was told to continue with the ice packs and make an appointment for him to come in on Thursday.

"You have two semen samples to look at, Dr. Bloom," said Aretha walking into the lab. "One's post vasectomy, the other's post vas-reversal."

"When do you want the other two calls?" asked Cathy via the intercom.

"What time's the first patient?" asked Bloom.

"You've got fifteen minutes."

"You can call Stine in five minutes." Bloom gloved, put a drop of the post-vasectomy specimen on a microscope slide, covered it with a cover slip, and looked under high power. He saw an occasional non-motile sperm. He wrote a note in the patient's chart, told the patient he needed to continue to use birth control until the last few sperm were eliminated, and to bring in another specimen in four weeks' time. He discarded the slide and replaced it with another one using the post vas-reversal specimen and went through the same procedure, seeing a fair number of active sperm. He wrote a note in the chart, told the patient what he found, and told him to start using something for birth control if he was not planning to have a child at this time.

"William Stine is on line 2," said Aretha via the intercom.

"I'll take it in my office," answered Bloom going into his consultation room and picking up the phone.

"Good morning," began Bloom, surprised by Stine's quick callback, considering he had spoken with him at length last evening, after he had seen Ida. "You have already signed a form giving permission for Dr. Winger to discuss your case with me. This includes things like marrow and data bank registries. Right now, I have some questions I'd like to ask you."

"Sure."

"Do you have any living relatives? Parents? Siblings? Children?"

"I was adopted. I know nothing of my family history. I never married, and I have no children."

"Where were you born?"

"What state?"

"First, what country?"

"Why'd you ask that?"

"You said you were adopted."

"I was. The United States."

"What state?"

"Not sure."

"A Southern state?"

"Not sure."

"Do you have a birth certificate?"

"Why do you need my birth certificate?"

"If Ida Stern dies or is physically unable or refuses to give you her marrow and you can't get a reasonable match, we'd have to try to expand the donor pools."

"Isn't that's what the registries and banks are for?"

"Only a small percentage of matches are known. There's nothing wrong with being proactive."

"I don't have a birth certificate."

"Have you gone outside our medical community to get help for the leukemia?

"No, but I probably will."

"Have you made any appointments yet?"

"No."

"I'll do whatever I can to help you," said Bloom. He waited a few seconds to see if there was a response. Hearing none, he cleared his throat and continued. "You know Ida Stern is a patient as well as a friend of mine?" Again Bloom paused, and Stine did not reply.

"I learned she went to Cincinnati to die by her hands, not yours. And you threatened killing my son if we didn't help you find her and then again when we could not help you find her after you changed you mind and wanted her alive. Did you change your mind and decide to kill her yourself after she decided to kill herself? What happened to make you change your mind, and why was my son's survival based on your whims?" Bloom again paused.

"When Jones told us you were not interested in harming her, my wife and I called every hotel in Cincinnati trying to reach her. We subsequently learned that Jones had contacted her. Do you have anything to say about all this?" Again, Stine had no response.

"I am very worried about my family's safety. My son's existence has been threatened countless times, and our family has been living in fear of Jones's reprisals. You've kidnapped my surgical skills to operate on people who did not want to be circumcised. I had to hire a lawyer. The money you've given me will be used to pay for the lawyer and hospitalization of one of the persons I operated on. And I will have to deal with the consequences of operating on people without their will. You've basically caused me a lot of stress and distress." Still, there was no response from Stine.

"I took an oath many years ago, and you are now my patient. I have given you the same care I would have given my brother, despite what you've done to me and my family. Guarantee Stern's and my family's safety, and I will work to get you through your potentially lethal illness."

"I will need her bone marrow to survive," said Stine when Bloom stopped talking, neither refuting nor apologizing for what Bloom said he had done.

"I have no idea how good a match she would be. When they say 'match' it could be an excellent or a very poor one or somewhere in between. It's too soon to discuss matches. First you have to get through the chemotherapy. Meanwhile we can start with the data banks. The reason I'm asking you all these questions is to see if we can find a sibling or a relative if there is one that might be a better match than Ida Stern. Right now Stern's unable to give her marrow to you even if she was willing. She suffered a heart attack on top of the stroke." Stine did not reply. Finally, Bloom hung up the phone.

Bloom sat back in his chair and closed his eyes. "A few loose ends here," he mumbled to himself thinking about Stine's nonresponses to any of his charges, to the guarantee of safety proposal, and to Stern's worsening condition and her probable unavailability as a donor. He knew Stine should have agreed to the proposal in any event since he could always not honor it and gotten her bone marrow illegally using whatever methods were available to him. Rubbing his eyes in frustration, Bloom decided he would need to revisit these subjects later.

CHAPTER 47

QUICK REVIEW OF WHERE WE STAND

"Thanks for seeing me on such short notice," said Bloom, getting up from his seat in Mac's office to shake his lawyer's hand before sitting back down.

"I missed all the excitement," replied Mac, likewise sitting down at his desk.

"Huh?"

"I'm Peter Mulett's grandfather. We just got back from Italy this morning. I heard you saved both of his testicles."

"We usually fix the untwisted testicle at the same time, so we don't have to untwist that one at a later date. Peter's a good kid. His mother and father are very nice. His mother is your daughter?"

"She's one of five daughters."

"Any sons?"

"Just sons-in-law. My secretary said you sounded distressed. What's up?"

"It could have waited until you got settled."

"You're here now. What happened with your Ida Stern? I thought a lot about her while I was away."

"That's not what vacations are for."

"Is she alive?"

"Yes. That's water under the bridge. Quick review: Remember she went to Cincinnati to hide and commit suicide, in the meantime getting away from Stine and taking the pressure off my family?"

Mac shrugged. "I wasn't sure it was going to take the pressure off your family."

"You're so right!"

"Go on."

"When Jones called me and asked me again where she was and I told him she'd no longer be a problem and explained why, he became furious with me and said that if she dies, so will my son. He didn't tell me why, but after speaking with Stine recently I learned he might be needing a bone marrow transplant and Ida Stern might be a good match. At that time, I gave Jones the only number I had for Stern and somehow he was able to stop her, whether he used threats against Stern's sister Rachel or my family, I don't know. While in Cincinnati, Stern had to be hospitalized for bleeding and Stine 'summoned' Missy and me to fly there to make sure she was receiving the best care she could. I'll skip the part where she had a cardiac arrest. She came back to Florida a few days ago and refused to give Stine her bone marrow. Naturally, I was called (and threatened) by Jones to deliver her to him. I told Jones I was no longer going to deal with him and I set up a meeting with Stine, which I then had. By the time I learned about Stine's possible need for a bone marrow transplant down the road, Stern was in Cedars of Lebanon Hospital in Miami after suffering a heart attack complicated by a stroke. I saw her in Miami two days ago. The heart attack was minor, but the stroke was not. I told Stine Stern's present condition precluded her from having a marrow biopsy even if she agreed to it and that we needed to look for alternative donors. I also told Stine I no longer wanted to deal with Jones and I'd continue to help him if he would 'guarantee' no further threats to Stern, her sister, or my family. I didn't mention to him any of the 'goods' I had on him, but I did mention how he kidnapped my surgical skills and ethics when he had me perform the circumcisions. He did not comment on anything I said and did not guarantee anyone's safety. This is where we stand. Stern's sister wouldn't give as much as a drop of blood to see if she was even a match. Both Stern sisters absolutely detest Stine. And right now, I wouldn't put it past Stine to do whatever he had to do to get Stern's bone marrow, like hijacking someone else's skills to get the biopsy and/or to do the transplant. You are now up to date."

"Phew! Jamie, you need to find out how imminent Stine's bone marrow transplant is. You have to worry about the safety of your family. You can't rely on any guarantees from Stine. Right now, it looks like you're on the hook to help Stine get what he needs."

"How could I possibly provide a donor?"

"Okay, maybe not provide a donor, but you could be coerced into having Stern's sister tested and/or having either of them 'donate' their marrow."

"To repeat, Stine has not guaranteed me anything or admitted to anything he's done to me or my family. He suggested that Jones may have been acting on his own. I asked him how Jones could be allowed to do things on his own, but he didn't answer me. I've got the feeling Jones does the dirty work and Stine refuses to take responsibility for what happens and condones whatever Jones does. This leaves me and my family in a dangerous situation."

"I don't disagree."

"When do I involve the police?"

"Call Stine and tell him he's in an untenable situation, and you can't go on living with the continued threats from his organization."

"And what if he doesn't answer me?"

"He will answer you if he's the person you seem to think he is."

"Then I shouldn't just go to the police."

"Absolutely not. At least not now."

"Even if he agrees to what I want, he can still do whatever he wants to do."

"Yes, he can always do that."

"So I shouldn't threaten him just yet?"

"No. Not yet."

"It would be silly and even stupid of him not to agree with me at this time. He hasn't gotten any treatment yet. I think he's thinking about getting other opinions. If he decides to be treated by Dr. Winger, it will take a number of months of chemotherapy before he could receive a bone marrow transplant, if he's to receive one at all. He knows this. He's an intelligent man, so why not say yes and receive the status quo.

He could succumb to the chemo and/or we could find another donor or two for him."

"So we're finished for now?" asked Mac, getting up and shaking Bloom's hand.

"To be continued," sighed Bloom.

CHAPTER 48

PLUTO OR ANYWHERE ELSE

"Dr. Winger's on line 2 and William Stine's on line 1," said Cathy, seeing Bloom come out of the exam room.

"Tell Dr. Winger I'll be with her in a minute. Tell the patient in the exam room to wait for me in there. I'll take William Stine's call in my office." Bloom sat down at his desk and picked up the first line. "Good morning, Mr. Stine. This is Dr. Bloom. I have Dr. Winger on the other line."

"Change of plans, Dr. Bloom."

"How so?"

"I'm seeing another oncologist at the Cleveland Clinic in Weston."

"Let me know what's happening," said Bloom reflexively, really wishing he would be treated by a different community or planet, hoping he would never have to deal with him again.

"Will keep you in the loop."

"Bye," replied Bloom hanging up and picking up line 2.

"Susan, are you on the line?"

"Yes, Jamie. I just got off the phone with William Stine. He's getting another opinion at the Cleveland Clinic, Weston, Florida."

"Did he say anything else?"

"No."

"Did you know that Ida Stern is in the Cedars of Lebanon ICU in Miami with a CVA and an MI?"

"No. How bad was the CVA?"

"Pretty bad. I saw her yesterday."

"Down there?"

"Uh huh. Off the top of my head, Susan, for as little as I know about oncology, shouldn't a person be in remission before they get a bone marrow transplant?"

"Then you know something, Jamie!"

"That's why someone might get a second opinion if the first opinion recommended an initial course of chemotherapy?"

"No comment," said Winger remembering her conversation with Bloom that only nonreputable institutions would do a bone marrow transplant before getting a remission with chemotherapy.

"Assuming someone had a noncomplicated course of chemo—if there is such a thing—when would they get the bone marrow transplant?"

"A decision is made at that time to have a bone marrow transplant or not after the successful chemo, or wait to relapse and then again respond to chemo and receive the bone marrow transplant."

"Suppose they don't get a remission with the chemo?"

"They try a different chemo."

"Suppose they still don't get a remission?"

"That's a bad situation. Maybe a different type of bone marrow transplant."

"How successful are those transplants?"

"Not very. That's why in the elderly, say over sixty, we try to encourage a bone marrow transplant whenever possible."

"Like with Stine?"

"Some patients would prefer not to have additional chemo, which the transplant would entail."

"Okay, thanks, Susan. Still trying to piece all this together," said Bloom, thinking about the safety of his family, and of Ida Stern.

CHAPTER 49

GETTING OUT OF DODGE

"Time to plan a vacation," announced Bloom, putting his keys in the bowl on the pass-through and continuing into the family room, finding Missy sitting between Peter and Lisa reading *Rumpelstiltskin.*

"What's the occasion?"

"Stine and company are going to leave us alone for a while."

"Is that what they said?"

"No, that's what I said! Stine needs chemo, and Ida is not well enough to give her marrow to anyone."

"Can we go to Disneyworld?" asked Peter.

"Yeah," said Lisa smiling.

"YEAH!" exclaimed Missy, surprised by Lisa's new word.

"Peter, that reminds me of your talking farm pull-toy," said Bloom chuckling. "Do you remember that?"

Missy and Peter laughed.

"Peter, do you remember what happened?" asked Bloom.

"You told me I was three when you gave it to me. I remember that when I pulled the string it said, 'The dog says 'bow wow' or 'the horse says 'neigh' or 'the cow says 'moo' or the 'the pig says 'oink oink' or the cat says 'meow' or the donkey says 'hee haw.'" That's all it kept saying. I played with that toy every day. I stopped playing with it two years ago. Last week I found it at the bottom of the toy chest and pulled the string."

"And what happened?" asked Missy laughing.

"It said, 'The rooster says "cock-a-doodle-do."'"

"It never said 'cock-a-doodle-do' before that time, did it?" asked Missy.

"No. Never. That's why it was funny!" said Peter.

CHAPTER 50

PLUTO IS PROBABLY OUT

"Dr. Bloom, good morning," said Cathy through the intercom, seeing the lights on in his office and hearing his voice. "Dr. Winger's on line 1. Should I tell her you'll call her back?"

"I'll take it now," replied Bloom, terminating his call and hitting the flashing light.

"Deb, er, Susan. Sorry. Debby Winger was one of my all-time favorite actresses."

"I liked her in *Black Widow*."

"I saw it three times. How are you doing with your patient and his buddy Jones?"

"Not great, but probably much better than you."

"It's been a nightmare!"

"I can imagine."

"Any threats?"

"I'll tell you when I see you."

"What did you tell him?"

"That he needed chemo."

"What'd he say?"

"He wanted a bone marrow transplant instead."

"Is that why he's going to Cleveland Clinic?"

"That and to get another opinion."

"Do you think he'll get one?"

"An opinion? Yes. Not a bone marrow transplant from a reputable oncologist."

"Is it possible to get one from a black-market oncologist?"

"Seriously?"

"If he offered someone ten million dollars?"

"Where would they do it?"

"I don't know. If I could think of the possibility, so could he. Let me ask you something. If you've tried every type of chemo available and are still unable to get a remission, what's left?"

"Basically, nothing. Doing a transplant without a remission is expensive and a waste of time. Following a remission, we usually give two to three more months of chemo to consolidate the remission. Sometimes, in isolated cases, we don't wait for a relapse. We go straight to transplant."

"If I understand correctly, chemo can induce a complete remission on its own and be used to produce a remission in disease that has recurred. Following that, a bone marrow transplant can then be used."

"You understand correctly."

"Just trying to keep track of all the possibilities. Thanks, Susan."

CHAPTER 51

FOREIGN BODIES: PART OF CHART

"Your first patient is ready for you, Dr. Bloom," announced Cathy through the intercom. "Her urine's on a slide."

"I'll come get her," answered Bloom. Walking into the waiting area, he said good morning to Rebecca Johnson, the only patient there. He walked her into his office and went into the lab to check her urine. "Your urine looks fine," he said when he came back into the room. "Any urinary complaints?"

"No. Is there still blood in it?"

"The blood is gone."

"I'm not missing any more small objects from my vanity."

"I wasn't going to bring it up" replied Bloom smiling.

"I thought you might be interested in how it got there."

"Nope."

"Can I have it back?"

"The hospital keeps it."

"Why is that?"

"It's part of your medical record. It's been put in toxic solutions. You wouldn't want to use it."

"You're probably right. Have you told anyone about it?"

"No."

"Not even your wife?"

"I've told nobody."

"Have you ever removed a mascara brush from anyone else's bladder?"

"Not a mascara brush."

"Wha else have you removed?"

"Pens, lollypop sticks, chains, matches, drinking straws, stirrers."

"Pens? Chains? Were these people crazy?"

"Some of them. Is that why you asked me if I told my wife? She's a psychologist.'"

"No. I didn't know that."

"You were the first with a mascara brush. If it fits in the urethra, it's probably been fished out of someone's bladder. Although sometimes the object gets stuck in the urethra and represents an emergency. When I first saw you a few weeks ago, I had no idea what was causing the bleeding. Your urine wasn't infected, and you had no urinary symptoms, so I needed to check out your entire urinary tract to find where the bleeding was coming from."

"I'm glad you did."

"I would have found it when I had looked inside the bladder."

"Couldn't you have fished it out in the office?"

"I considered it. But I needed larger instruments, and it might have been too difficult and uncomfortable for you."

"I'm glad you chose to do it in the hospital. My boyfriend told me what happened."

"Please don't tell me what he said."

"I can tell you in a minute," said the patient appearing disappointed.

"That's between you and your boyfriend," said Bloom writing a note in her chart and getting up. He said goodbye to Johnson and handed her chart to Cathy.

"Your next patient canceled," said Cathy, taking the chart from Bloom. "The third patient is on her way in. She's a new patient. I'll call you when she's ready."

Before Bloom could sit down at his desk, Cathy buzzed him on the intercom.

"That was fast!" said Bloom. "What is it?"

"Dr. Merrill's on line 1."

"The gynecologist or the rheumatologist?"

"He didn't say. Should I ask him?"

"No. I should recognize his voice, although they sound like each other."

"He wants you to see his wife."

"Sure. Get her in as soon as you can."

"She's in the hospital."

"University?"

"Uh huh."

"I got it," said Bloom picking up line 1.

"Hi," said Bloom.

"Jamie, it's Rudy. I've got a headache for you."

"I don't get headaches. I give them. What's doing with Mary Jo? She's pregnant with twins, isn't she?"

"Seven months and in the University ER with twin kidney stones."

"That's not good."

"One in each kidney,"

"Both causing problems?"

"Very much so. She's diabetic and her creatinine is 3.5."

"I know she's diabetic. Is the creatinine due to the stones?"

"Uh huh."

"Has she had any films?"

"They're on the screen in X-ray."

"I'll see you in ten minutes."

"I'll meet you in X-ray."

Bloom told Cathy to hold down the fort and that he was going to the ER and would call her in fifteen minutes.

"Should I give the patients on the schedule a heads up?"

"Not yet. Let me see where I'm going with Dr. Merrill's wife. I'm going to need to do something, but I can't tell you right now what or when."

"10-4."

When Bloom got to X-ray, the radiologist got up and pointed to the renal ultrasound on the X-ray screen.

"Looks like bilateral five-millimeter proximal ureteral stones with moderate hydro," Bloom told the radiologist. He then turned to Merrill, who had just entered and was looking at the offending stones and blockages on the films.

"How tall is Mary Jo?" asked Bloom.

Merrill gave Bloom a quizzical look.

"She may be needing ureteral stents. The size of the stents depends on her height."

"She's five-foot-six."

"Does she have a diabetes doctor or a nephrologist?"

"Steve Myers is her primary. He takes care of her diabetes. Bill Caruso is her obstetrician. Do you think she needs a nephrologist?"

"I'd leave that up to Steve. Let me see her. Then I'll speak with you, Steve, Bill, and the anesthesiologist and we'll talk to Mary Jo."

"What are your thoughts?"

"We need to make her comfortable, improve her kidney function, and not interfere with the pregnancy."

"What about the stones?"

"I'll decide after I examine her, look at her chart, and we all talk."

"What about the stones?" Merrill asked again.

"That's not for now. That's for after she delivers healthy babies."

Both doctors left X-ray and headed toward the ER.

"I'll need to see her chart," said Bloom before ducking behind Mary Jo's curtain.

"It's at the nursing station," replied Merrill.

"I'll get it. I'd like to speak with her nurses anyway."

Bloom found one of Mary Jo's nurses hanging a patient's IV bottle. "Hi Phyllis, are you taking care of Mrs. Merrill? When you get a chance, I'd like to speak with you for a few minutes."

"Sure, Dr. Bloom. I can speak with you now. Let's go to the nursing station."

"Thank you."

They both left the room and went to the chart rack to pick up Merrill's chart.

"I haven't seen her yet," said Bloom. "How is she doing?"

"She was sleeping a few minutes ago."

"Has she received a lot of pain meds?"

"Nothing in the last two hours. She came in three hours ago. She initially got some Demerol/Vistaril, which was supplemented with 5 ccs of Dilaudid."

"Any nausea or vomiting?"

"She hasn't asked for anything to treat that. Her vital signs are stable, and she has fetal monitors, which have been normal."

"Very good. She's been kept NPO?"

"Of course, Dr. Bloom. Except for a few ice chips."

"You have a urine on her?"

"It should be on the chart. Here it is."

"Was it a catheterized specimen?"

"Dr. Bloom! Of course. We thought you might be seeing her."

"Good job," replied Bloom smiling. "Where was her pain when she came in?"

"Mainly in her back."

"Right or left?"

"Both."

"Traveling anywhere?"

"Into both groins. The urine shows mainly RBCs, some whites, no bacteria, esterase and nitrites neg. What are the last two for?"

"Breakdown products of WBCs, signifying infection. She's diabetic. What was her blood sugar? Let's see. 135. Not too bad. And creatinine? I heard it was elevated. 3.5. That's not good. Who's seen her so far?"

"Nobody else. She has two stones I hear."

"Yep."

"Dr. Bloom, what's your plan?"

"I need to examine her first. Then we need to put our heads together with the Merrills, Dr. Caruso, Dr. Myers, and the anesthesiologist, and possibly a nephrologist. We need to unblock her kidneys, reduce her pain, and keep her pregnancy intact. As of now, I'm planning to leave the stones alone and take care of them after she delivers two healthy babies."

"Are you going to put up stents?"

"If and when you want to leave this place, I'll have a job for you in my office."

"You probably say that to every nurse."

"Just to anyone who could figure out that the proper thing to do here is to put up stents! Let me call my office for a sec, and then we'll see Mrs. Merrill."

Bloom dialed his office and was told that the new patient had car trouble and had rescheduled, and the next patient had just walked in. He told Cathy to rearrange the schedule and tell the patients he has an emergency and would be a little late, maybe forty-five minutes before he was in the office. He went behind the curtain with Nurse Phyllis, examined Mary Jo, and met with the three other doctors plus the anesthesiologist. He then discussed at length with the Merrills what he recommended for Mary Jo, wrote a note in her chart, dictated his consult, and hurried to his office.

CHAPTER 52

A GRANITE STATER APPEARS

"Dr. Winger's on line 2," said Aretha through the intercom, hearing Dr. Bloom coming out of the second exam room.

"I'll pick it up in room 1," replied Bloom, realizing he had already asked the patient he had just seen to meet him in his office. "I may be on the phone awhile with Dr. Winger, so ask Cathy to look in on me say in ten minutes."

"Will do."

"Hi, Susan," said Bloom picking up. "What's doing?"

"Two things."

"Is one of them Ida Stern or William Stine?"

"Three things."

"You're on."

"What's doing with Ida Stern?"

"She's not bleeding, thank God. That was as of this morning. She's leaving Cedars tomorrow and going to rehab in Sunrise."

"Is she on blood thinners?"

"No, because of her platelets."

"Right. How's she doing neurologically?"

"Surprisingly, she's made lots of progress. I spoke with her this morning. She comprehends and answers questions. Some of her words seem a little garbled, but it's good that she's aware of it."

"That is good! Which brings me to William Stine."

"Number two?"

"Number two. William Stine is back in the fold."

"That's extremely bad news."

"I agree."

"Cleveland Clinic doesn't want him?"

"They do. But he wants us."

"Don't say us, Kemo Sabe."

Susan chuckled.

"Did he have a fight with them?"

"Probably."

"What has he agreed to?"

"To doing it with me."

"Me is a much better word than us. Doing what?"

"The chemo."

"What about the bone marrow?" asked Bloom nervously.

"No bone marrow for now. He's also agreed to additional chemo if necessary."

"Then, Cleveland Clinic said no to the bone marrow?"

"As the initial treatment. I knew they would."

"What's the timetable?"

"Two to three months for the chemo, assuming everything goes okay and he goes into remission. Then one or two more cycles to consolidate the remission. Then we leave him alone and see what happens."

"No bone marrow transplant?"

"Not sure. In younger individuals we usually wait for a relapse and go ahead with the bone marrow after they go back into remission. In someone like Stine, who because of his age may be more likely to relapse and more difficult to get a second remission, we may elect to go straight ahead with the transplant."

"Do we need to think about a bone marrow donor?"

"It wouldn't hurt."

"Ida's our only candidate so far?"

"I'll take care of that."

"Can I have that in writing?"

Susan laughed.

"Does Ida's sister Rachel need to be tested? From what I know about her, I don't think she'd be a match, and she'd certainly never agree to do anything to help Stine."

"First let's see what I can do."

"What's behind door number three?"

"A New Hampshirite who thinks he may have prostate cancer."

"How old is he?"

"Forty-three. He's CEO of some mega electronics company."

"What's his name?"

"Russell Clark III. You're seeing him tomorrow."

"Thank you, Susan. Do you want to see Ida when she's in rehab?"

"Only if she has a problem."

"Can I tell her Stine's not going to need a bone marrow transplant at this time, and never if he remains in remission?"

"I wouldn't say anything about never needing a bone marrow transplant. And I would certainly never use the word *never*. We'll see how he does with the chemo."

"Will do. Thanks again. I'll call you after I see Russell Clark III."

CHAPTER 53

RUMINATIONS

"Dr. Parsons is on line 2," said Aretha through the intercom, after watering the basil plant and placing it back on the sill.

"Got it," replied Bloom picking up in his office. "Hi, Ed, how've you been? Any more holes in one?"

"No, but I got an eagle on Saturday."

"Where was that?"

"Eagle trace."

"Never played it. Whatcha got?"

"It's about Mary Jo Merrill."

"Uh huh."

"Rudy asked me to see her."

"I'm not surprised."

"Why's that?"

"He wanted me to remove her stones. I told both of them and the doctors in the room with us that under different circumstances I would have opted to do that. But not now. Have you seen her yet?"

"I just finished."

"And?"

"And what?"

"And what do you think?"

"I think the stones should be removed."

Not at University Hospital, thought Bloom. *Not even at Coral Springs Hospital where they have obstetrics,* he continued in thought. *And not pregnant with twins and two months away from being delivered. And not with maternal diabetes and impaired renal function and uncertain anesthesia time and X-ray exposure associated with the procedure. Just unblock the kidneys with stents and take care of the stones after she delivers. Too many possibilities for things to go wrong if you go after the stones now.* But he said nothing.

"I guess that's why they called me," added Parsons after the short pause.

"You read my note?" asked Bloom not wishing to state what he had just been thinking, knowing that it was all in the patient's chart for Parsons to look at.

"Uh huh."

"Anything you want to ask me?"

"No. I'm doing it at University tomorrow at 10:30 a.m."

"If you decide to just put up stents, I'll be happy to help you."

"I don't need your help for that," replied Parsons, hanging up.

"You're welcome," mumbled Bloom after hanging up. Then through the intercom, "Aretha, can you find out Clark III's PSA for me please?"

"Will do. He was kind of strange, wasn't he?"

"I'd say. He also looked strange."

"He looked like a football linebacker."

"Did you read his chart?"

"No, I never look at the charts."

"Good. You shouldn't. Also find out his free PSA and let me know when the first patient is ready."

"He's not here yet. You have at least thirty minutes. Remember, you have Peter's softball game at four."

Bloom sat back in his chair and closed his eyes. *That was kind of strange for Merrill not to let me know he was calling Parsons to see his wife,* thought Bloom. *And again, not to tell me Parsons was doing the surgery. I hope Parsons thought it through before consenting to do it. It would have been kind of bad for Parsons to have agreed just because Merrill wanted it done. I wonder if he would have recommended removing the stones if he had been the first urologist to see Mary Jo. Sometimes the second opinion doctor tells the patient or referring doctor something different in order to gain their confidence so they decide to use him instead. For example, in cases involving a man with prostate problems—symptoms of frequent voidings day and or night, hesitancy or slowing of the stream, and urinary incontinence related to an enlarge prostate—there are many ways we can help patients with this condition, such as cutting back fluids, making sure their bladder is emptied before leaving the house, avoidance of certain foods and liquids, and using many medications that have the ability to open up or shrink the prostate. All urologists are familiar with these methods of treatment and use them to try to make the condition manageable. When they've exhausted these options and the patient is still unhappy, they may recommend minimally invasive procedures. If these are not successful, there are the more invasive procedures that have been time-tested that can be offered. Sometimes if the symptoms are not too bad, we suggest the patient live with the condition, especially if the more invasive procedures would carry a high degree of risk. Whenever I recommend one of the more invasive procedures, it is always after I've exhausted all the other options. Usually by the time we get to that point, the patient has been with me for some time and sees I've been trying hard to help him. What I'm getting at is that when I tell the patient he needs to have the more invasive procedure I tell him he can get another opinion. The next urologist, if he knows me, will usually know that everything that can be done has been done and concurs the patient should have the surgery. If the other opinion doesn't know me, some urologists may untruthfully mention there are things he can offer that makes my surgery unnecessary at this time, such as suggesting a generic of the medicine the patient is already receiving, thus misdirecting him, hoping down the road he can perform the surgery himself. This is not uncommon. In general, the patient or patient's family should have almost no say what surgery should be done. The outcome in Mary Jo Merrill's case would probably have been the same if I had recommended Merrill get another urologic opinion, especially if Merrill's choice would have been Parsons. And this has nothing to do with me not doing the surgery and getting further referrals from Merrill. I'm used to telling my patients to get other opinions if I feel they don't feel good about my recommendations. In this case, all the urologists I know and work with would not have removed the stones, or at least would have not made the decision until they had a full picture of the number, size, and locations of the stones, Moreover, if removing the stones was a possibility, they would have transferred the patient to a hospital that had obstetrics, which University Hospital does not have. Getting into trouble*

Two minutes later Aretha startled Bloom via the intercom. "I have Clark III's results."

"I must have dosed off," replied Bloom, stretching his arms over his head. "Whatcha got?"

"PSA and Free were both normal. PSA was 0.6 and Free 30 percent."

"Do you have a hard copy?"

"Yes."

"Send it to Dr. Winger with my dictated note. And get her on the phone for me, please. What time is my last patient?"

"Three o'clock. Just a urine check."

"Anyone who calls in who's having a problem, make sure they come in sooner."

"Yes, sir!" replied Aretha, well aware of Bloom's routine. "Do you want to speak with Clark III about his results?"

"Yes, please. I think we both should call him Mr. Clark."

"Mr. Clark, it is. Hold it. Cathy is waving to me. I think Dr. Winger is on line 2. Yes, she's on 2."

"I've got it," said Bloom picking up the line. "Hi, Susan. Your patient Clark? His exam, PSA, and free PSA were normal. Did you see him in the office?"

"No. It didn't make any sense to, especially when he said there weren't any records."

"How did he get your number?"

"He said one of my patients told him about me?"

"From New Hampshire?"

"That's what he said."

"The reason why I'm asking you is that he's never seen a urologist, has no evidence of prostate cancer, and his exam and PSA and free PSA were negative. He also gave no family history, has no children, and has never married. You and I both take care of a confirmed neo-Nazi who is president of the American Nazi Party and shortly is to begin a fair amount of chemotherapy, and who may be out of commission for a number of months. When I examined Clark, I noted he was uncircumcised and had four fair-sized swastikas on his back. I haven't looked yet into his past, but I've got the feeling he's not in Florida solely to run an electronics company or go to an electronics convention. I think he's here to insinuate himself with you, me, William Stine, and if necessary, Ida Stern. I must add that I am an amateur writer, so my mind travels in these directions."

"Considering what you and your family have gone through with Stine and his cohorts, there's reason to come to such a conclusion."

"When does Stine begin his chemo?"

"Next Tuesday."

"Cure him and I'll be your best friend."

When Bloom hung up, Aretha called Clark.

"Hi, Mr. Clark," said Bloom a few minutes later. "Good news. The two prostate tests we did were negative. I've sent a report and a copy of your tests to Dr. Winger. Normally, I wouldn't need to see you for a year, but with no previous tests to compare with and no family history to go by, I think I should see you in six months. If the next visit is negative, I can then see you on a yearly basis. You can set up an appointment now or call in four months. Good luck in Florida." After he hung up, he told Cathy he was not doing Mary Jo's surgery tomorrow morning, but she was to keep the two-hour time slot allotted for the surgery free in case he was needed in the OR. A minute later, Cathy let Bloom know that William Stine was on line 2 and wanted to speak with him.

CHAPTER 54

REHABBING IN HEALTH SOUTH

"I'm Dr. Bloom and I'm here to see Ida Stern," said Bloom, stopping at the information desk at Health South in Lauderhill.

"Dr. Jamie Bloom?" asked the receptionist, looking up and giving him a big smile.

"Marilyn Moskowitz!" he exclaimed, now looking for a way to get inside her office and properly greet her.

"It's Jacob now," she replied, getting up and signaling him to walk around to the left.

"You're no longer Marilyn?" replied Bloom as he started moving to the right. "When did you come back to Florida?"

"Six months ago," she replied laughing. "I got married two years ago. My husband was recently transferred here. I called your office when we got here. Aretha said you had just hired someone."

Bloom made his way to her desk and hugged her. "How's your pancake kidney doing?"

"I think okay. I've not seen anyone since I left here."

"When was your surgery?"

"September will be six years."

"When was your last follow-up?"

"Three years ago with you. Just before I left for Atlanta."

"And your mom? I haven't seen her in a few years."

"She's fine. You must have cured her."

"What does your husband do?"

"He's CFO of PetSmart. Just promoted."

"Very nice. Have any pets or children?"

"Two pets. One non-pet on the way. I'll be leaving Health South soon. I'm actually giving them notice tomorrow."

"Before you leave do you think you could give me Ida Stern's room number?"

Marilyn laughed. "You always make me laugh." She looked at the patient sheets then added, "She's in room 113."

"Does your OB know you have a pelvic kidney?"

"He sure does."

"Whom are you using?"

"Dr. Merrill."

"Does he know what you went through?"

"He sure does."

"When did you see him last?"

"Three weeks ago. Should I see you?"

"Because you're pregnant, yes. Call his office and give him permission to send me your lab work. Make an appointment to see me in two weeks. And you need to get back to work before you get fired before you quit. I have to see that lady in 113." They hugged one more time and Bloom headed for Ida's room, the last room at the end of the eastern corridor next to the emergency exit. The door was ajar and Ida was on the phone. Bloom smiled, thinking that Ida having a conversation probably meant she was making further improvement from her stroke. He gently knocked on the door, and when Ida turned her head in his direction and smiled, he took a few steps into the room.

"C-Come in D-Dr. B-Bloom."

"Whom are you speaking with?" he asked

"Y-You," she replied with a big smile.

Bloom laughed. "Are you on the phone with Rachel?"

Ida nodded.

"Can I speak with her?" asked Bloom approaching her.

Ida nodded and handed him the phone. After they spoke for a few minutes, Bloom asked Ida if she could tell Rachel to call back in twenty minutes? Ida nodded, complied, and hung up. He then reached down, and they hugged each other. "Ouch," he exclaimed feeling his body being compressed by her hug. "You're still pretty strong, Ida," remembering her unusual upper body strength.

"W-Want to go for a w-walk?"

"By myself?"

Ida laughed.

"Let me ask your nurse if it's okay," said Bloom, putting her back into a reclining position. He left the room and came back two minutes later.

"You're on," said Bloom getting her robe from the closet.

She shook her head, waving off putting on the robe. Bloom helped her out of bed and stood holding her for a few seconds until he felt she was steady, then turned her around and took a few steps still holding on to her.

"Where to?" he asked.

"O-Out of this r-rehab p-place."

"They'd throw me in the clink for kidnapping you."

"I-I'm not a k-kid."

"Let's walk to the nursing station."

"I-Ice c-cream?"

"You *are* a kid!"

"Y-you m-make me f-feel like a kid," said Ida giving him a big smile.

"What flavor do you want?"

"C-Choc-c-co-l-late. I o-only eat c-cho-c-co-l-late."

"Me too! When you lived in New York, did you ever go to Jahn's?"

"Of course. Many t-times."

"Did you hear what you just said?"

"Course and many."

"Yes, course and many."

"C-Can I get out of here n-now?"

Bloom laughed. "You need to leave it up to your therapists to say when. Just know that you don't have to be 100 percent to get out of here. I'll tell you about my visit to Jahn's when I was fourteen after I get you your ice cream. Let's sit over here," said Bloom taking her to a table across from the pantry and helping her get seated. He took two cups of chocolate ice cream from the freezer and put them on the table along with some spoons and napkins. He took the lids off the cups and put them into the nearest basket and handed her a spoon.

"When I was twelve," began Bloom, "my friend's father invited ten kids to Jahn's Ice Cream Parlor to celebrate his son's birthday. We were told we could order anything on the menu. Items on the menu included Super Duper for Two, The Bombshell, Suicide a la Mode, Joe Sent Me, and a mini Kitchen Sink. I had a Tall in the Saddle—twelve scoops of chocolate ice cream with hot fudge, whipped cream, jimmies, and a cherry. I had no problem finishing it, and I managed to eat dinner that night. I have some form of chocolate almost every day, most of which is dark chocolate. I see you've finished yours, and I've already had some today for lunch. Have mine," he said pushing the cup in front of her. "Ess."

"H-How'd you k-know t-that w-word!"

"My best friend was Jewish. When his mother put something on the table for me to eat she would say 'ess,' eat."

"W-Where was t-that?"

"In Brooklyn. Somewhere in Bed/Sty. I don't remember the street."

"H-How o-old were y-you?"

"We left there when I was six."

"I-I'm full," said Ida after the third spoonful, pushing the cup away. "T-Time to get m-me b-back to my r-room."

Bloom got up, cleared off the table, wiped Ida's hand and face with a wet napkin, got her up, walked her back to her room, and put her in her in bed.

"I'd like to talk to you about our buddy," said Bloom thinking of Stine.

"B-bud-dies," replied Ida thinking of Stine and Jones.

"When was the last time you heard from either of them?"

Ida shrugged her shoulders.

"I don't think you will, at least not for a while."

"G-Good."

"He's got leukemia."

"V-Very g-good. The w-worst type?"

"I think so. Your worst enemy is becoming your best friend."

"T-That's n-not g-gonna h-happen. H-He s-still w-wants m-my m-m-marrow?"

"He's getting chemotherapy now and does not need it right now."

"B-But h-he m-m-may s-some t-t-time in the f-fut-ture? Th-Th-thin k-king a-a-bou-bou-bout h-h-him is d-e-ef-f-fin-i-t-e-ly n-not h-h-help-ing m-m-my s-s-speech!"

"That's for sure. Do you want me to get you some more ice cream?"

Ida shook her head and laughed. "B-But t-there's a p-pos-si-b-bili-i-ty the c-chem-mo w-won't w-work or h-he r-re-lapses and w-will n-need one?"

"Yes, that's a possibility."

"N-Not f-from m-me."

"Let me tell you a couple of things. He's not stupid. His IQ is—or at least was—over 140. He wrote for his school newspaper. He knows what he's doing. Yes, he tried to do you in."

"M-more than t-twice."

"Yes, three or four times. He was your enemy then."

"S-S-Still is!"

"But now he's looking out for you."

"He o-only l-looks out f-for h-hims-self."

"He was the one who got you platelets when you were bleeding out in Cincinnati. And he was the one that gave Missy and me plane tickets to make sure they were taking good care of you there. And he was the one that got you the only private room in this rehab facility."

"D-Dr. Bl-loom, w-why are y-you t-telling m-me th-this?"

"Just to keep the record straight."

"D-Did h-he r-re-n-o-n-o-unce h-his le-leadersh-hip in th-he Na-Nazi P-Party a-and d-did he l-let you c-circ-c-cumc-c-cise him?"

"Not yet," replied Bloom, laughing.

"He a-aint g-gonna g-get m-my m-m-mar-row!"

Bloom smiled and nodded. He hugged Ida goodbye and left her room, passing and waving to Marilyn on his way out of the facility. He got into his car, closed his eyes, and sat back in the seat. "For Ida and my family's preservation, I've got to portray her as a possible marrow donor for Stine," said Bloom to himself, rationalizing why he spoke about Stine to Ida before leaving her room.

CHAPTER 55

AN ALTERNATIVE TO IDA'S MARROW

"We need to finalize our Disney World trip," said Bloom clearing off the kitchen table and washing the ketchup and mustard containers and placing them upside down in the door shelf of the refrigerator. "Too bad what happened at River Country last year."

"That was terrible," replied Missy, putting the soda and tea beverages away.

"Two children drowned and two died from amoebic infections."

"Something like that."

"I think Magic Kingdom would be the best thing."

"It's probably best to go on a Tuesday and come back the same or next day, avoiding the weekends."

"Book it Dano."

"10-4," said Missy, humming the "Hawaii 5-0" theme song.

"I ran into Marilyn Moskowitz today at Health South when I visited Ida."

"Isn't she supposed to be in Atlanta?"

"Now she's married. Marilyn Jacob."

"How's her waffle kidney?"

"It's called a pancake kidney."

"Whatever."

"She's pregnant. Her husband was just made CFO of PetSmart."

"That's very nice! What was she doing at Health South?"

"Finishing her last week of work. She had called my office six months ago looking for a job while her husband was in Georgia. Surprised Aretha didn't tell me."

"What's doing with Ida?"

"She's coming along. Her brain seems okay. She's still stuttering, though less. When I mentioned Stine she started regressing."

"Why'd you do that?"

"I probably shouldn't have, but there's a reasonable possibility he might need a bone marrow transplant after he goes into remission, and we could be back to square one. So I thought I should tell her that Stine was responsible for getting her platelets when she was bleeding out in Cincinnati and that he also gave us the plane tickets to visit her there and that he was also the one who got her the only private room in Health South."

"What did she say about that?"

"Whatever she said it came with a barrage of nonstop stuttering. She said he was doing it for himself. I didn't disagree with her, but I thought I should mention it anyway. By the way, Stine started his inpatient Ara-C and Daunorubicin chemo today."

"Isn't Ida no longer a donor candidate? And isn't Susan Winger in charge of procuring a donor?"

"Both are theoretically correct. But Ida not being medically able and Susan's supposedly being responsible will put Ida and our family in Stine's crosshairs again. We need to be proactive."

"What about Rachel?"

"She hates him also. Do you really think she'd agree?"

"To help her sister?"

"Ida wouldn't allow it. She'd try to kill herself again first! This brings us back to being proactive."

"Obviously you have something in mind."

"I do."

"Want to share?"

"It'll require work and/or travel."

"For whom?"

"One or both of us."

"Tell me about the work?"

"Finding out where Stine was born. Finding his parents or siblings, if they're still alive."

"Where do we start?"

"Talk to Stine. Get more history. He said he thinks he lived in Kentucky or West Virginia before moving to New York."

"You said he was adopted."

"He didn't have a birth certificate or driver's license."

"Are Kentucky and West Virginia those travel places?

Bloom nodded, then added, "And ..."

After a ten second pause Missy opened her supinated her palms. "And what?"

"And what about the possible donor Ida left behind?"

"In Berlin?"

"Ja."

"Is that German for *yes*?"

"Ja."

"Is that also another travel place? No more 'Ja'!"

"Peut-etre."

"But we'll probably have a problem finding birth records. According to his hospital chart, his birth date is April 20. I googled that date."

"And?"

"A famous person was born on April 20. Care to guess?"

"Give me a clue."

"He had a mustache and created a furor!"

CHAPTER 56

PATIENT DISMISSAL

"Please bring Mrs. Green into my office," said Bloom, exiting the cysto room after fulgurating multiple small recurrent tumors in Mr. Green's bladder.

"Yes, Dr. Bloom," replied Aretha, getting up and going into the waiting area.

"How's my husband?" asked Mrs. Green, stepping into Bloom's office.

"I found a few more small tumors, which I took care of."

"That's not good."

"Today was supposed to be an important day regarding his care."

"I know that."

"He smelled from cigarette smoke," said Bloom reluctantly. "Breath mints fell out of his pants pockets when he undressed. You'd think after his last cysto, when I burned out five tumors and told him I would no longer be treating him if he didn't stop smoking, he'd at least not come in smelling of cigarette smoke. I've told him at least five times to stop smoking. I'm very saddened by what I have to do."

"He was good for six weeks and then started taking long walks by himself, and I began to find breath mints everywhere."

"I never smoked so I don't know how difficult it is to stop. I've already put all the different available agents into his bladder to try to stop these cancers from coming back. He'll soon be at the point where his bladder will have to be removed. That's a multihour operation with lots of risks and potential complications, as well as a long recuperation and a possibly altered lifestyle."

"Can't he continue this way?"

"You mean with him smoking?"

Mrs. Green nodded.

"Greta, I can't practice medicine this way."

"You've kept him alive this way for five years!" said Mrs. Green pleadingly.

"I'd rather be a good doctor than a good guy."

"You're both, Dr. Bloom. Bernie loves you."

"It's mutual," replied Bloom likewise nodding. "Again, I'm saddened what I have to do." Bloom paused for a few seconds. "He needs to make an appointment with another--."

"Suppose he stops smoking?" interrupted Mrs. Green.

"Hopefully he'll stop smoking with his next urologist. My secretary will give you the names of three urologists he can see, or you can choose a different one. Ask your friends who they use."

"They all use you!"

Bloom smiled. "I'll give him a month to see the new urologist. I'll also see him if he has a problem before his appointment with him or her. My secretary will make a copy of his chart and will call you when it's ready."

"Are you going to tell Bernie now?'

"I told him a little while ago."

"What'd he say?"

"He nodded."

Bloom got up and hugged Mrs. Green. He walked her back to Aretha's office and asked Aretha to make a copy of her husband's chart and call them when it was ready to be picked up. He went back into the cysto room, told Green about the discussion he had had with his wife, and the two men hugged. Bloom went back to his office, wrote a note in Green's chart, sat back in his chair, and closed his eyes. I was so upset when I walked into the cysto room and smelled the cigarette smoke and saw the breath mints, thought Bloom. I was hoping his bladder was free of cancer. But now what? Bloom thought about some of his lung cancer patients when he was at the VA, who two weeks after having their lung cancer removed, were found with a lit cigarette inhaling through their tracheostomy tube. *And if his bladder was free of cancer, would I have told him the same thing? Honestly, yes.* Bloom sat for another ten minutes, then got up and brought Green's chart to Aretha's office. But when he saw Aretha and the Greens embraced in a hug, he turned around and went back to his office. He sat for a few more minutes, and when he heard the Greens leave, he buzzed Aretha.

"This was very sad," said Bloom. "If he can stop smoking for the next urologist, I would be ecstatic."

"But even if he stops, down the road he may still need to have his bladder taken out," said Aretha.

"Yes. You're so right. And smart."

"Do I smell a raise?"

"What you smell is cigarette smoke!"

"Dr. Bloom!"

"Can you please get Dr. Winger for me?"

"Good job changing the subject, Dr. Bloom."

"Changing the subject is my subspecialty."

"You want her now?"

"Please."

"Is it about Stine?"

"Yes."

Bloom did some paperwork while Cathy cleaned up the cysto room, soaked the instruments, and labeled Green's bladder biopsy specimen.

"Dr. Winger's on line 2," said Aretha via the intercom.

"Got it," replied Bloom, picking up.

Within five minutes Bloom was brought up to speed on Stine. He had been on in-patient IV Ara-C and Daunorubicin for his one-week induction phase with virtually no significant complications. Minor side effects included dry eyes, mouth sores, and a few lower extremity petechiae. His consolidation phase was to begin shortly using the same drugs in cycles of treatment and rest. A decision would then be made to either start maintenance postconsolidation with reduced dosages for months or years, or to proceed with bone marrow transplant. Steps to procure a bone marrow donor had been taken. Ida was still a very good match, a lot better than the ones they'd found so far.

Bloom was only concerned about this last part: the possibility of a bone marrow transplant for Stine and that as of right now Ida Stern would be his best donor marrow match. Somehow John Denver's "Take Me Home, Country Roads" and Stephen Foster's "My Old Kentucky Home" popped into his head. He also remembered that in 1986 the word "people" was substituted for "darky" and "darkies."

Aretha brought Stine's chart into Bloom's office. He read Dr. Winger's last note and added what he had just learned. He looked at the face sheet of Stine's first hospital admission and noticed that he had a middle initial of "A." He looked further and learned it stood for Adolph. With the combination of an April 20 birth date and Adolph as a middle name, Bloom concluded that both were probably added after he was born, but nonetheless he would begin with William Adolph Stine born on April 20 after 1940 but would concentrate on any William Stine or male Stine born around that time in Kentucky, West Virginia, and their surrounding states. He would have to speak with Stine before he could go any further.

Doing so, he learned Stine's father's name was William and his mother's name was Barbara. He didn't have any cousins, aunts, or uncles. He couldn't remember the names of any childhood friends. At age eight or nine, his father left home, and his mother took Stine and moved to New York. He left his mother at age sixteen before he was to graduate from high school. At age eighteen, he added a middle name Adolph and adopted his birthdate as April 20. He's had no further education. Then he remembered reading something that Stine's original name may have been Stein, and he had changed it to Stine when he was eighteen, because Stein was too much of a Jewish name.

For the next three days Bloom spent his office free time searching the internet for all the abovementioned people in fifteen states between 1940 and 1958 and came up with seventeen names. It took him another two days to eliminate these people and another three days to search the rest of the US states plus Alaska and Hawaii (not part of the US when Stine was born) and Canada, and another three days to clear the thirty-four names that cropped up.

"Did you look up the American Nazi Party and neo-Nazis?" asked Missy after Bloom had told what he had found so far. "And other members of the Party?"

"Did all that. I don't know what else to do. I must say I have no idea where he was born."

"It's probably not that important."

CHAPTER 57

SEARCHING FOR SIGMUND

"Welcome back, Dr. Bloom," said Cathy, seeing him coming into the office. "How was your vacation?"

"I'm happy we took the extra three days. The weather was great, and the crowds were small."

"The kids loved it?"

"Yes. Lisa hadn't yet been to the Magic Kingdom. And we were surprised how much Peter enjoyed Epcot. Anything I have to know right now?"

"You've gotten a request from Mary Jo Merrill's lawyers for her office chart."

"Already? That was fast! Dr. Reilly told me about it when I checked in with him last night."

"Is she still in the hospital?"

"I don't know. I don't have all of the facts."

"I heard she lost one of her babies."

"That's what he said. How terrible! I'm glad I wasn't involved in her surgery."

"I thought I heard you say you'd be available to help."

"I did. But Dr. Parsons never took me up on it."

"Do you think the outcome would have been different had you been there?"

"Who knows? Can you get me her chart?"

"Will do."

"Let me ask you something. If I hadn't come back yet, would you have sent the lawyers a copy the necessary papers?"

"I don't know."

"Wrong answer."

"What should I have done?"

"*Never ever* send anything to a lawyer that I haven't reviewed! *Never ever. No exceptions.*"

"Why's that?"

"There could be typos or inaccuracies. It's much harder to correct them once the lawyers have them. Whatever you send must always be authorized by me. Even after you've picked out exactly what I've asked you to send, I must see what you've picked out before you have me send it. Also please bring me Ida Stern's chart."

Bloom went through Merrill's chart and took out and clipped what pages he wished to send along with a note for Cathy. He jotted down all of Rachel's phone numbers in Stern's chart and put the charts on Cathy's desk. He reached Rachel on her phone and tried bringing her up to date on Stine's progress, mentioning the possibility he might require a bone marrow transplant. When she interrupted Bloom the third time telling him there would be no way Ida would consent to being a donor, Bloom said, "Rachel, Rachel, I will never ask Ida to donate her marrow. I'll say it again. I will never ask Ida to donate her marrow. Please listen to what I have to say."

"Go ahead, Dr. Bloom."

"When did I not become Jamie?"

"Go ahead, Jamie."

"Dr. Winger is obtaining a donor for him. My staff and I are also looking for a donor for him. We think Stine was adopted. He has no birth certificate or driver's license. He's never married and has no children. We've spent days calling hospitals, county clerks, and foster homes without success. I am looking at other possibilities. Other than Ida's son, you are the only living family member, correct?"

"There's no way in hell I'd be a donor!" interrupted Rachel. "I wouldn't even give up a drop of blood to see if I was a match for that Nazi bastard!"

"Wow!" exclaimed Bloom. "Can I please continue!"

"I don't like where you're going!"

"Like I've said before, I have no intention of asking you to be a donor. I will never ask you to be a donor. I know this is difficult for you, but I need to continue."

"Go on."

"I would like to check out the church and orphanage where Ida's son was brought. His name was Sigmund, wasn't it?"

"Yes, Sigmund."

"I need to know the name and address of the church as well as the family Ida cleaned for, and their family member that 'found' Sigmund when Ida left him at the church. I would also like to know Sigmund's date of birth in 1939, his handedness, eye color—although that may have taken a couple of years to become permanent—and if he had any identifying marks, like Mongolian blue spots, which usually disappear by early childhood. Ida's psychiatrist mentioned that Ida's husband burnt Sigmund's butt with a cigarette in order to be able to identify him at a later date. I would also like to know the date he was brought to the church and the last time she saw him. The convent would know the date he entered and left or was adopted. I know it was thought that your sister may have been inseminated with Hitler's or Mengele's semen when she went to the infertility clinic. Sigmund may lead us to his siblings and maybe other donors. Do you think I should have this conversation with Ida? I understand that she may not want to be reminded of this period in her life. But she did ask me to help find her son not so long ago."

"When was that?"

"When Missy and I visited her in Cincinnati."

"Let me ask you something. Why are you going through such lengths if Stine doesn't need a transplant and if Dr. Winger is getting a donor for him?"

"Great question! Now we're getting down to the nitty-gritty. I'm not certain of anything I'm about to say about Stine. He's got a terrible past from what I've read and what Ida has told me. I have no proof of what he's been accused of recently—the shooting of the three Skokie march protesters, sabotaging her ventilator, killing Ida's platelet donor, even getting me to do the circumcisions. He may have been complacent about these things, but he may not have actually physically organized or carried out what was done. I can say he will stop at nothing to get what he wants. If for some reason he needs the bone marrow transplant and Dr. Winger can't find a match as good as Ida, regardless of her condition and her absolute refusal to give permission, he might try to get it. If it means kidnapping her and securing her marrow with or without anesthesia, he might do it. Once he learns he needs the transplant, the kidnapping may still take place, based on her previously leaving the state to take sleeping pills to kill herself so she wouldn't be killed by him, even if Dr. Winger says she's found a match as good as Ida's. Ida wants to know why she's still alive. Do you know the reason?"

"Yeah. He found out she was a match for him."

"I think there's more to it than that."

"I don't."

"Did Ida tell you he helped get her platelets when she was hospitalized in Cincinnati?"

"And paid for your flights to Cincinnati and got her a private room at Health South--yada, yada, yada," said Rachel. "He wants her marrow. And after he gets it, he'll want her dead."

"Nah," said Bloom. "He'd probably want her alive in case he needs another transplant."

"And what will happen if she doesn't give it to him and for some reason he can't get her marrow some other way? He'll threaten to kill me or someone in your family."

"You say that so matter of factly, so cold-bloodedly."

"I don't mind if he kills me."

"What about me or my family?"

"I rather he doesn't do that!"

"That's all, Rachel?"

"That's all."

"Wow!"

"That's two 'wows' in ten minutes!"

"Yes, Rachel. Do you think you can do the things I've asked you to do?"

"Okay, Jamie. I'll try."

CHAPTER 58

STRANGE CASE IN THE ER

"Dr. Bloom, University ER's on line 1," said Cathy via the intercom. "Can you pick up?"

"Tell them I'll call them back in three minutes," replied Bloom speaking with Mrs. Green on line 2.

"Buzz me when you're ready," answered Cathy.

Bloom finished his conversation with Mrs. Green, telling her to bring Bernie into the office right now.

"Bernie Green is bleeding," Bloom told Cathy. "He's coming in now. You can get the ER on the line now."

A few seconds later, Cathy shouted, "ER's on 1."

"This is Dr. Bloom."

"We've got a strange case here, Dr. B," said the charge nurse.

"Hi, Lois. Is it a male carrying something non-food in a lunch bag?"

"It's stranger than that."

"Is it something that's no longer attached to his body?"

"We think so. You have eighteen questions left."

"Is part of his body missing?"

"We think so. Seventeen."

"Does he have a wound?"

"Yes, we think so. Sixteen."

"Is it in his scrotum?"

"No. Fifteen."

"Near his penis?"

"No. Fourteen."

"Flank?"

"Yes. Thirteen."

"Someone removed his kidney?"

"Bingo. We think so."

"Is the patient drugged or drunk?"

"He's alert and talking."

"Does he speak English?"

"Yes. He speaks English and says he knows you. He's from Brooklyn. Moved here two years ago."

"What's his name?"

"Robert Gold."

"Does he know what happened to him?"

"Yes. He said someone removed his kidney."

"Is he having a lot of pain?"

"Not a whole lot. I didn't want to give him anything until you saw his CT scan."

"How are his vital signs?"

"He's afebrile, pulse is 100, BP is 96/60. He has RBCs in the urine. His labs are okay except for a Hb of 8 and a Hct of 24. Right now he's in X-ray."

"He'll be needing blood if and when I take him to the OR. Type and crossmatch him for four units. Tell me about his wound."

"He has a towel wedged in his left flank. He came in this way."

"Where's he from and how'd he get to the hospital?"

"He lives in Colony West in Tamarac. Someone found him in a sand trap on the third hole. EMT brought him in. I said it was a strange case."

"Today's not still April 1, is it?"

"No, it's the second."

"Is someone with him?"

"Just his caddy."

"That was very good!" replied Bloom laughing out loud. "Very good. Do me a favor."

"Sure."

"Call me when he gets back from X-ray. Also see if you can get the CT result. I'll need to look at his films before I see him. Keep him NPO."

"He's been NPO since he was brought here."

Bloom hung up and went into the cysto room and made sure the cystoscopes he used that morning were now sterile and ready for use.

"Mr. Green is here," said Cathy. "His urine is on the microscope."

Bloom went into the receiving area, greeted the Greens, and brought them into his office.

"When did you start bleeding?" Bloom asked Mr. Green.

"An hour ago," Mrs. Green replied.

"Are you back on the blood thinners?"

"He restarted them this morning."

"Was your urine clear when you started it?"

"Yes," replied the patient.

"Have you made your appointment with Dr. Levy yet?"

"No, not yet," replied both of them, shaking their heads.

"Thanks for seeing him," said Mrs. Green. "He stopped smoking," she added.

"I can smell that, or rather not smell that!" replied Bloom smiling. "I'm proud of you. I hope it will continue. Are you passing any clots?"

"No," answered the patient.

"Any fever, pain, or burning with urination?"

"No fever, but I have urinary urgency and slight burning when I urinate."

"Let me check your urine," said Bloom, getting up and walking into the lab. He smelled Green's urine. It smelled infected. He looked at the slide under the microscope, checked the dipstick, and then rejoined the Greens. "It looks like you have a urinary tract infection. I'm going to give you some antibiotic samples. Take them every twelve hours. Call me tomorrow morning after nine and let me know how you're doing. It may take a few days to determine what type of infection you have. Hold off on tomorrow's Coumadin. Don't have any alcohol or spicy food and try to drink more water than usual."

"Are you going to do a cystoscopy?" asked the patient.

"Not today. It may be necessary if the bleeding worsens. The infection may be what's causing the bleeding,"

"When do you want to see me again?"

"Good try. See if you can call Dr. Levy's office and set up an appointment with him."

"Bernie stopped smoking!"

"I'm really very happy to hear that. I've got to go to the ER now," said Bloom, getting up, shaking their hands, and leaving the consultation room. "I'm going to the ER," he announced to Cathy leaving his office. He stopped off at X-ray to see if the CT scan had been completed. It had, and he was told the patient was back in the ER. He looked at the X-ray's revolving view box and located the films on Robert Gold. Normal right kidney, ureter, and bladder. Foreign body—presumably the towel—in left flank, absent left kidney, left ureter not visualized. He saw things that looked like clots next to towel. Bloom found the radiologist and asked him to look at the films. After the radiologist confirmed Bloom's findings, Bloom went into the ER and reintroduced himself to the patient.

CHAPTER 59

WHO CALLED?

"I had an unusual day today," said Bloom, opening the door from the garage to the laundry room and seeing Missy on the couch sitting between Peter and Lisa watching an old DVD.

"Daddy, you were on TV!" screamed Peter getting off the couch and running around to him.

"Yeah!" yelled Lisa following suit.

"Yeah!" echoed Missy stretching her head and neck back and allowing Bloom to plant a kiss on her lips.

"Strange case," said Bloom, hugging Peter and Lisa. "There will be an investigation."

"I should hope so," replied Missy. "Daddy will watch the rest of the DVD with you," she added getting up, kissing Peter and Lisa goodnight and leaving the room. After the movie, Bloom got them both ready for bed, reading Lisa *Rapunzel* and asking Peter a riddle before kissing them goodnight. He found Missy in the study preparing for her upcoming lecture to her medical students on empathy.

"Give me ten more minutes," said Missy, holding up both hands.

"I'll be watching the Marlins game in the bedroom," replied Bloom, leaving the study. Fifteen minutes later Missy came running into the bedroom.

"Why are you screaming?" she shouted. "The kids are trying to go to sleep."

"How do you try to go to sleep? Did you ever try to go to sleep?"

"Whenever you try to tell me about your surgical cases."

"Whoa! Did you take a double dose of your mean pills today?"

"That's what Paul Revere said at the end of his famous ride warning that the British were coming."

"Opening day," added Bloom with a make-believe tip of his cap and complementing Missy on her reference to the silversmith and his horse. "First inning, Chicago's up. The Marlins pitcher walked the first three batters, then went 0 and 2 on the next batter and the pitcher served up a 50-miles-per-hour change-up that flew out of the stadium! A 50-miles-per-hour meatball over the plate with an 0 and 2 count. It's four to zip. I'm sick."

"Shut it off and tell me about the kidney donor."

"I remembered today's patient from the Brooklyn Hospital where he worked in the radiology department. He moved out of Brooklyn two years ago and now lives in Colony West."

"I'll be sad when Lisa starts saying 'yeah' regularly."

"Me, too. Okay. Let me tell you about Robert Gold. According to him, he signed up with the National Kidney Donor Registry five years ago when his 40-year-old niece needed a kidney transplant. He wasn't a match. Sadly, she died before she could get a transplant. Three years ago, he was contacted by the Registry who told him he was a match for a 47-year-old male with end stage renal disease who needed a transplant. He said he had told the Registry when he learned he was not a match for his niece, he no longer wished to be a donor. He never heard back from them. He said a month ago he received a non-Registry call asking him to donate his kidney. He declined. He said he was offered $100,000 if he'd accept. Again, he declined. Last night he drove to an ice yogurt creamery near his home at 10:00 p.m. and went inside the store with his car running. When he got back to his car after his purchase he was chloroformed or something like it and didn't remember anything until waking up in a sand trap in Colony West at 2:30 a.m. He called 911, and the paramedics brought him to University Hospital. I saw him later in the morning and took him to the OR to explore his wound, control the bleeding, clean out the clots, see the extent of what was done, copiously irrigate the wound, place some drains, and close him up."

"What'd you find?"

"His kidney was gone, along with a large portion of his ureter. The 'surgeon' did an excellent job."

"What do you think's going on?"

"Somebody's getting or has just gotten a kidney transplant."

"You think so?"

"Something along those lines. The patient has already told the police about his dealings with the Registry and the $100,000 offer."

"That's good. I wouldn't say anything to the police or to Mac or to Ida."

"Of course not. But just as I was leaving the office, Cathy said Ida Stern had been looking for me. I called her a few times but wasn't able to reach her."

"What time do you have?" asked Bloom, looking down at his wrist and realizing his watch was in his car. "Is it too late to call Ida?"

"Yes, it's too late to call Ida."

"You haven't even looked at your watch!"

"How long have we been married?"

"I don't know, I left my watch in the car."

"Ha ha. I don't own a watch. And I don't want one. And I don't want you renting one for me."

"How do you know what time it is?"

"Have you ever heard me tell you, 'Yes, it is okay to call someone at this time?'"

"No. But now you don't know what time it is."

"That's true. I don't need to know the time. I just know *when it's too late to call!*"

"Do you think our kids will have that talent?"

"Only Lisa. It's a woman thing. I'll remind you to call her in the morning."

"I'm going to watch a few more innings of the game," said Bloom, going into the TV room.

"I'll be here trying to finish the book I started a few days ago."

"Still four to nothing," mumbled Bloom, seeing the score on the TV screen. "I guess that's good." In the fifth inning with the score tied 4-4, his phone rang. Not recognizing the number and the call not having come from his answering service, he deleted it. After the third call from that number, he let it go to voice mail and listened to the message: "I am calling about your patient Mr. Gold. Please call me." Bloom played the message four times but could not recognize the voice. It sounds a little like Jones, but it's muffled, thought Bloom.

Bloom lowered the TV volume and went into the bedroom. Missy was asleep, the book still in her hands. He removed the book and her glasses, covered her, kissed her goodnight, shut off the light, and closed the door. He checked the kids and went back into the TV room. "What to do about this call?" he muttered.

Bloom returned to the bedroom. He tossed and turned for most of the night and then left the bed and finished watching the ball game. Thinking that he'd been doing a lot of tossing and turning recently, Bloom started to sing the old Bobby Lewis hit song. Whether or not to call Jones was the first decision he had to make. Initially, Bloom decided he didn't want to have anymore information. Gold was not getting his kidney reattached. Bloom would have to go to the police. What would he tell them? That the neo-Nazis may be involved in removing the kidney, based on the say-so of one of their henchmen. That could stir up a hornet's nest and incur Stine's wrath and possibly aggravate Stern. He decided to get some sleep and call Jones when he got up in the morning. Obviously getting more sleep was not going to happen. He went into the garage, got his watch, and noted it was 5:00 a.m. *Slept more than I realized*, thought Bloom. *Actually I need to get going and make rounds. I'll call Jones and Mac later this morning. And also Ida.*

CHAPTER 60

REACHING THE BERLIN ORPHANAGE

"Good morning, Bob," Bloom said, entering Gold's room and seeing him sitting up in bed eating breakfast. "Need some help opening the syrup?"

"I'm not a syrup guy, Doc," replied Gold, taking another forkful of the pancake. "How's my kidney function today?"

"Your good kidney got a message that it's mate is gone and has started bulking up."

"Says who?"

"Says me and all the physiology textbooks."

"Already? Who sent the message?"

"Your departed kidney."

"How'd it do that?"

"It came as a work order. It was told to ramp up production by dint of an increase in the amount of waste product it inherited."

"Seriously?"

"Would I lie to a brother Brooklynite?"

"And a Brooklyn Hospital Brooklynite!"

"Your remaining kidney started to hypertrophy while you were in the sand trap. Your own kidney will enlarge up to 30 to 50 percent in size in three to six months."

"What if the person who got my kidney rejects the one he got from me?"

"Call your insurance company and see if you're covered for a full-time kidney, er, I mean, bodyguard."

"Don't make me laugh!" warned Gold holding his left flank.

"Your Colony West urologist or general surgeon did an excellent job. See if you can get his name. I may be looking for someone to join me in a few years."

"Stop with the jokes," cried Gold, laughing and regrabbing his flank.

"Sorry. Your kidney function will improve steadily. Now it's about the same as yesterday's. Your blood count is a little lower than yesterday's. I expected that. The body makes up for the blood volume you lost by shunting body fluids around, which results in the dilution of your blood count. I'll look at your wound to see how much bleeding you're having and decide if the dressing needs to be changed. I left a drain in there, which I will gradually advance and remove as the drainage subsides. You'll need to stay here at least two to three more days to check your blood count and temperature. You're on an antibiotic, which will be discontinued before you're discharged, depending whether or not you have an elevated temperature or an infection. You have no idea where the surgery was done?"

"All I remember was walking to my car and waking up on a golf course. And whoever did the surgery or drove the vehicle must have eaten my ice cream."

"Or they may have shared it! I have a question for you. You said yesterday that you were called by the Registry three months ago today to donate a kidney, which you declined to do, and then a month ago someone who had nothing to do with the Registry called you and was willing to pay you $100,000 for your kidney. Correct?"

"Correct."

"Do you remember what day or date the Registry person called? The name of the Registry person? Or the name of the non-Registry person, or day or date they called? Or their phone number? Did that person ask you what you'd be willing to take for it? Just as an aside, would you have taken $1 million? How about $2 million?"

"I remember the date the non-Registry person called. It was on my birthday."

"What about the Registry person? If you have any numbers at home that you could give me, I would appreciate it."

"Why are you so interested?"

"This is a global problem. In New York City, Central Park is a major victim dropoff site."

"Have you seen it in Florida, other than in me?"

"We have our share," said Bloom, thinking of Ida Stern.

"When are you going to look at my wound?"

"Finish breakfast. I have other patients to see. I'll be back in thirty minutes or so."

Bloom left the room and took the stairs to the ICU, bed 6.

"Mr. Bloom, no relation, how are you doing today?" asked Bloom speaking extra loud to the 102-year-old World War I veteran, two days post-laser treatment of a five-millimeter mid-ureteral stone in a solitary kidney, having lost the other kidney in the war.

"When am I getting the hell out of here, Doc?"

"Today. But you're just leaving the ICU. You're not going home. Today is Tuesday. I'm not sending you home before Thursday. Repeat what I just said."

"I heard what you said. I'm not a parrot!"

Bloom chuckled. "Your wife will drive your car home. You are not to drive."

"My wife's a terrible driver. And she can hardly see."

"Do you have a relative that can drive you home?"

"All my relatives are dead."

"What about a neighbor?"

"Ditto."

He checked Bloom's catheter and drainage bag. The urine was a slight rose color, consistent with the surgery. "I'm calling your wife to tell her we're moving you out of the ICU, so she doesn't have a heart attack when she doesn't see you in your bed. See you tomorrow on the third floor, that's of course assuming your primary doctor doesn't want to keep you in the ICU."

Bloom waved goodbye to the patient and took the stairs to the ER to see a patient he had just been called about. He saw the patient and took the stairs back to Gold's room.

"I see the nurse brought in the supplies," said Bloom, looking over the tray table. He put on surgical gloves, asked the patient if he was allergic to iodine, opened some surgical dressings, and gently peeled off the surgical tape. "Doesn't look like much drainage." He gently yanked on the drain and pulled it out a few centimeters, removed some of the superficial bandages, swabbed the wound with Betadine and replaced the top dressing and surgical tape. His phone went off, and he found out Ida Stern was looking for him. He went into an empty room and dialed her number. After the normal pleasantries, Ida told him she had some answers for him.

"Ida, great! Hold for a second while I get a piece of paper. Bloom went to the nearest nursing station to get a piece of scrap paper and sat down at an unoccupied desk.

"I'm ready," said Bloom."

"Meyer and I lived in Wilmersdorf, Berlin," began Stern sounding fully recovered from her stroke. "As you know, at the beginning of 1939, after four years of a childless marriage, I was artificially inseminated, and Sigmund was born later that year. Shortly after that Meyer's office was confiscated, and I got a house-cleaning job a few blocks from us in nearby Charlottenberg, Glesebrecht Str 3. I worked for Ludwig and Margaretha Albrecht. Their nineteen-year-old daughter Lena worked at the Catholic Church/orphanage on Kurfürstendamm, which was midway between our house and where the Albrechts lived. Sigmund was born at home, so there would be no record of his birth. Our sister-in-law performed the delivery. Sigmond was not circumcised in case we were forced to leave him somewhere. His checkups and care were given by friends that came to the house. Outside of our family, only the Albrechts knew about Sigmund. Lena came to our house almost every day, wearing more bulkier clothing in preparation, if need be, for transferring him with the intention of placing him in the orphanage, and if that was not possible, raising him as her own. Within five months, she and Sigmund had bonded. By the time he was four months old, it was no longer possible for the three of us to leave Berlin. We started calling him Sigmund Conrad Schultz, and decided once we got the okay from the Albrechts, we would make the transfer. One month before the intended transfer, while I was at work, Meyer applied local anesthetic to Sigmund's butt and held a lit cigarette against the anesthetized area in order to produce a scar to help us in reclaiming him down the road. When he was fully healed, I brought him to the Albrechts so Lena could get him into the orphanage.

"He had brownish-gray eyes and congenital Mongolian blue spots on his lower back in addition to the scar on his left buttock. He had not demonstrated any dominant handedness. I had asked Meyer why he had scarred him when he had already had the large blue spots on his back, and Meyer said that those blue spots would have faded in two to four years. We were ecstatic to learn that the Albrechts might consider adopting him once he was placed in the orphanage. One month after he was in the orphanage, Meyer and I and our extended families were sent to Auschwitz. Prior to leaving, we had given all our money and whatever possessions we had to the Albrechts."

"I know Meyer and the rest of your family other than Rachel did not survive Auschwitz."

"That's correct."

"You did not look for Sigmund after the war, correct?"

"Yes, that's correct," replied Ida hesitatingly."

Bloom took a deep breath. "I know you're uncomfortable about this, but I'd like to know why?"

"I'd rather not talk about it."

"Does it have something to do with the possibility of Hitler or Mengele being Sigmund's father?"

"Yes."

"I'm looking to find Sigmund for other reasons."

"I know that from Rachel."

"So I'm going to try to find Lena and the Albrechts if I can."

"Promise me you won't tell me what you've found."

Bloom agreed. He thanked her for her information, commented on her remarkable speech improvement, and made small talk with her for ten minutes. After he hung up, he looked at another patient's recent KUB, noticed the stone was no longer present, told them the good news, and discharged them. He walked over to his office, handed Cathy the face sheet on today's new patient, and told her about who he saw on rounds. He was then able to get the phone numbers for the church and orphanage on Kurfürstendamm.

"Your first patient will be here in fifteen minutes. I'll let you know when he's ready. Dr. Railly called a little while ago. He'd like you to attend the M & M surgical conference on Mary Jo Merrill next Tuesday at noon."

"Tell him I'll be there. Please remind me on Monday before I leave the office. Make sure I'm free from 11:45 to 1:30."

"What's M & M?"

"Morbidity and Mortality, we discuss adverse things have that have happened in the operating room. It's a learning session we have every month."

"Are you going to speak?"

"Maybe. But I'd rather not."

Bloom checked the time. Noting the six-hour time differential between Miami and Berlin, he dialed the orphanage. The message in German suggested he push numeral one for English. After waiting twenty minutes with no interspersed recordings and Cathy notifying him the patient was ready, Bloom hung up. By the time he finished with the patient, Bloom thought it was too late to call again.

The following day Bloom made early rounds and got to the office when it was 2:00 p.m. in Berlin. He had asked Cathy to get there early so she could help with his call. He dialed the orphanage, transferred to the English-speaking person, and was put on hold. After thirty minutes the line was picked up.

"Hello, this is Dr. Jamie Bloom from the United States. I need help in locating a male orphan that was brought to the orphanage on April 9, 1940, his name could be Sigmund Schultz or Sigmund Albrecht. He may have been abandoned and found by one of the workers at the orphanage, Lena Albrecht."

"And this is who?"

"This is Dr. Jamie Bloom. I'm calling from Tamarac, Florida, in the US," he continued spelling out the city, state, and his name.

"You said April 9, 1940?"

"That's correct."

"You need to speak with archives. I'll transfer you. Please hold."

"Thank you." After fifteen minutes of phone silence, Bloom yelled for Cathy to get on the line.

"Yes, Dr. Bloom," said Cathy.

"I'm on hold, supposedly being transferred to the orphanage's archives. I'm expecting a dial tone soon. I need to do some things in the lab."

"I'll hold on. Aretha is here if we need her."

"I'll pick up the lab phone if someone comes on."

Bloom read yesterday's urine cultures, recorded the results in the lab book, wrote notes in the patients' charts, and left messages for the patients.

"Archives is on the line," said Cathy covering the mouthpiece with her hand.

"This is Dr. Jamie Bloom," began Bloom after picking up the lab phone. "I'm calling from Tamarac, Florida, in the US."

"This is Maria Knoop in archives. You're looking for Sigmund Schultz?"

"Yes. He was abandoned and left at the orphanage on April 9, 1940, and was found by one of the workers."

"Hold, please, Dr. Bloom."

"Maria, please take my phone numbers in case we're disconnected," said Bloom quickly, giving her two numbers. After another fifteen minutes of silence Bloom asked Cathy again to wait on hold for him. Ten minutes later Cathy told him there was a dial tone. Ten minutes later Maria was back on the line with the office.

"Maria, thanks for calling back," said Bloom taking over the call.

Within ten seconds he found out that the Albrechts had adopted Sigmund Schultz on June 6, 1940. They could not give Bloom the Albrechts' address or phone number. I doubt Ida still has or knows their phone number, thought Bloom, and whether a different phone system is now in use. Ludwig and Margaretha are probably dead, he thought. Lena may be alive and may be living in Charlottenberg at Glesebrecht Str 3 or some other place with Sigmund Schultz, or with some other name. She may no longer be an Albrecht.

Using all the information he now had, Bloom made a list of names, addresses, and places that needed to be called and what questions to be asked. He made two additional copies so he could keep one under his desk blotter, one in his wallet, and one in his top pocket to be left at home. He called Ida, but she did not remember or have access to the Albrechts' number. She did not ask any questions about Sigmund, nor did he mention Sigmund's adoption by the Albrechts in 1940.

CHAPTER 61

A CAN OF WORMS

"And when you Googled those four names, nothing came up?" asked Missy having been brought up to speed by Bloom, who was now putting the last dinner plate into the dishwasher.

"Google's been around only a short time," replied Bloom, putting detergent into the well, closing shut the dishwasher door, and pushing start.

"What's next?"

"I'll call the orphanage and speak again with Maria Knoop."

"And ask her what? She's already told you she can't give you any more info."

"Either I'll tell her what actually happened in 1940 and/or ask to speak with her supervisor. I don't know why there's so much fuss about what happened almost sixty years ago. Nobody now is looking for a child they gave up that many years ago, certainly not Ida, who wants no part of this."

"You're right about that. But suppose Lena doesn't want to talk to you. Suppose when 1945 came around and Ida or Meyer never showed up, for whatever reasons, she didn't tell Sigmund about Ida or even that he was adopted. Then what?"

"What if she did tell him? Suppose he knows about what happened and the reason why Lena and her family adopted him. Wouldn't he wonder why they never came back for him?"

"I would think so, if especially if he knew one of them were still alive. Okay, so assuming he knows about his birth mother, and he's interested in meeting Ida, and Lena agrees, then what?"

"I guess I'd then speak to Ida and see what she says."

"They'd want to know why you were calling. What would you tell them? Suppose they wanted to speak to Ida."

"Then, Houston, we have a problem!"

"Okay, assuming Ida decides to speak with them. What should she tell them?"

"That's her problem."

"Seriously."

"She would figure out what to say before she spoke with them. Eventually she would mention her medical problem."

"You're not thinking about mentioning the neo-Nazis, are you?"

"Are you serious? No. Of course not. I'm talking about her medical problem with her platelets. Sigmund might even have a bleeding disorder himself. But if not, it's possible he might even be a match for Ida with his platelets."

"That's possible."

"I'll try to call Maria Knoop sometime tomorrow."

"I hope you're not opening a can of worms!"

CHAPTER 62

HOLDUP IN GERMANY

"Good morning, Dr. Bloom," said Cathy, hearing Bloom unlocking the door and seeing him come into the office. `

"I'm glad you're still locking the door when you're in the office by yourself before nine."

"That's what you taught us. But you don't start today until ten. What brings you in so early?"

"I thought I'd speak with the Berlin orphanage again."

"Maria Knoop called earlier this morning and left a message with the answering service for you to call her. The number is on your desk."

"Did the service say what it was about?"

"No. You want me to get her for you?"

"Yes. Thank you. I'll be in my office."

Bloom leafed through this month's *Journal of Urology* table of contents and began reading the article "The Efficacy of a Reduced Dosing Schedule in the Treatment of Minimally Invasive Superficial Bladder Cancer."

"Maria Knoop had to leave her office today," said Cathy, finding Bloom. "Her office said she would try to call you later in the day or tomorrow."

"And her office had no idea what it was about?"

"No. But they said she said it was important."

"Great," replied Bloom sarcastically, wishing he could be making more progress regarding Sigmund.

Bloom made rounds, saw his office patients, had lunch in the doctors' lounge, saw his afternoon patients, and left the office, all the while thinking about what important bit of information Maria Knoop had for him. "I hope it's something good," said Bloom feeling they could use a break.

Maria was not in the office the following day nor the next, and when Bloom was able to get through to the orphanage, he learned that there was a serious problem in her family, and she wouldn't be returning for at least two weeks. Fortunately, he was able to reach one of the higher-ups, who reassured Bloom that after he had been given all the facts of the case he would have some information for him in a day or so. Three days later Bloom learned the M & M conference was canceled because of the imminent lawsuit. Stine was now septic and had been moved to the ICU, and there was still no news from the orphanage. *Things may take care of themselves,* Bloom thought to himself. *Stine might actually succumb to his sepsis. It would be fitting, but life, or death, doesn't work that way. That would be too easy. Hippocrates must be turning over in his grave right about now,* he mused.

CHAPTER 63

NOTE LEFT ON DOOR

"Dr. Winger's on line 2," Aretha announced via the intercom.

"Got it," said Bloom picking up the phone.

"Hi, Susan. Thanks for getting back to me. What's doing with William Stine? I know he's septic."

"He had some crackles at his left base this morning. His chest CT showed a small patch of pneumonia. Infectious disease saw him this morning and started him on antibiotics. He's still on his same leukemia meds. I have no plan to stop them."

"Is Ida Stern still number one on the donor list?"

"You're still worried about her?"

"As long as they're both alive I'll worry."

"Jamie, she's still numero uno … You'll be the first to know when she's not. Again, I'm not planning on any bone marrow transplant."

"It's the unplanned one that worries me. You heard about my patient that had his kidney removed and was left in a sand trap in Tamarac?"

"Colony West. I heard. Do you know who received the kidney?"

"I may have been a day trader at one time, but kidneys weren't one of my commodities," replied Bloom chuckling. "The answer is no. The CIA, FBI, local police, and National Kidney Registry are working on it. And as far as I know, Ida is not aware of it. Regarding Stine, he has a recent history of kidney stones. Is his urine okay? And does he have any urinary complaints? Does he have a catheter?"

"He has no complaints and doesn't have a catheter. Do you want to see him?"

"Not really. I would stop in to say hello, but without any urinary findings, my presence would not help his sepsis."

"Okay. I'll call you if I need you."

"I'll second that," replied Bloom, saying goodbye and hanging up.

"Dr. Bloom, you've got a call on line 1," said Cathy via the intercom. "It's Mr. Jones," she added, unhappy about giving Bloom the message. "It's *that* Mr. Jones! What should I tell him?"

"What does he want?"

"To talk to you."

"Hang up on him."

"This is the third time he's called."

"Hang up on him."

"I've tried that."

"I said hang up on him!"

Five seconds later the phone rang.

"Let it ring," said Bloom.

The next day when Cathy came to the office, she found this taped to the door.

I'm glad Ida Stern has recovered from her stroke. How are Missy, Peter, and Lisa doing? It's a shame about Bob Gold.

Does Ida know about what happened to him?

Upset by Jones's menacing note, Bloom decided to speak with Missy.

"Hi, Jamie, what's doing?"

"Yesterday afternoon Jones called the office, and I refused to take his call. This morning we found this three sentence note on the office door.

Bloom read it to Missy.

"Didn't Stine say Jones would no longer be a go-between for you and him?"

"Yes, that was a while ago."

"Are you going to tell Stine?"

"Don't you think I should?"

"Yes. You said yesterday he was septic? How is he today?"

"Infectious Disease saw him. He's got pneumonia. He's now on antibiotics."

"I'd wait a few days. Did you say anything to Jones?"

"No."

"Good. Are you okay now?"

"More or less, after speaking with you. But it took me a full hour to recover from reading that note, even after hurling a boatload of derogatory epithets at him in absentia and being assured twice by Dr. Winger that Stine would not be needing a bone marrow transplant at this moment and that he still might succumb to his sepsis."

CHAPTER 64

ORPHANAGE PART 1

"Good morning, Dr. Bloom's office. This is Cathy speaking. I hope you are having a good day. How may I help you?"

"Hi, Cathy," said Bloom. "And a good morning to you. I am having a fine day myself. And thank you for asking how can you help me."

"Dr. Bloom!" squeaked Cathy. "You could have interrupted me."

"I like listening to your spiel."

"What can I do for you?" Cathy asked, laughing.

"I'm coming in early to try to speak with the orphanage."

"We don't start till 10:30.'"

"That's okay. It's 3:00 p.m. now in Berlin, and I think they leave work at 4:00."

"Do you want me to see if Aretha can come in?"

"No, that won't be necessary. Anyway, she said she's getting her hair cut this morning."

"I forgot. Okay, see you in a while."

Twenty minutes later Bloom came into the office.

"I forgot to lock the door when I came in," said Cathy. I just locked it a few minutes ago."

"You should try to keep your door locked, especially if you're here by yourself."

"I'll put a sign on the computer that I'll see when I get into the office."

"Good idea. Can you please call Maria Knoop at the orphanage archives? The number's in your desk drawer."

"I'll get you when she's on."

"I don't think she'll be there. You may have to ask for the archives director."

"Okay."

Bloom went into the lab, looked at the urine cultures, and recorded the results.

"Maria Knoop is on line 1," announced Cathy.

"Maria Knoop?" asked Bloom getting on the phone.

"Sorry I didn't get back to you," said Knoop. "Everything's okay. My son who was missing at sea was picked up by another boat. Just a major scare."

"I'll bet. That must have been awful. I'm happy he's safe."

"I called you a few days ago because the information I gave you was just partially correct. Sigmund was adopted by the Albrechts on the day I said, June 6, 1940. I read a little further and found out that he came back to the orphanage three months later after there was a gas explosion in the Albrechts' house. All three Albrechts were killed. Sigmund survived unhurt.

"Oh, my God. That's terrible! What happened to Sigmund?"

"I've looked through thirty years of records and didn't find his name again. Nothing. Not a mention of another adoption, sickness, or death. Sigmund was your Jewish patient's child who was brought to the orphanage to escape the Nazis, correct?"

"Yes."

"Your patient survived the camps?"

"Survived Auschwitz with her sister. Her husband and eleven members of her family died there."

"That's terrible. Sigmund was her only child?"

"Yes. She never remarried."

"Maybe Sigmund ran away. Children run away from orphanages."

"What do you suggest I do?"

"Let me do some more digging for you."

"That would be great! She'd appreciate anything you could do for her."

"I don't want to raise her expectations."

"According to the archives, his name was still Sigmund Albrecht? I thought he came into the orphanage on April 9, 1940, as Sigmund Schultz, and his name was changed to Sigmund Albrecht when he was adopted."

"I'll check and get back to you."

"Great. I'm very happy about your son."

"I hope I can help you. What's your patient's name?"

"Ida Stern. Her husband was Dr. Meyer Berger. They lived in Wilmersdorf, walking distance from the orphanage on Kurfürstendamm."

"I live in Wilmersdorf! What street?"

"I'm not sure. I think somewhere near Dusseldorfer and Leibniz."

"That's where I live! On that corner!"

"How long have you lived there?"

"Thirty years. My parents bought the house in 1972."

"Small world."

"It would be nice to find her son."

"Yes, it would."

"It's never too late, Dr. Bloom."

"Call me Jamie."

"I'm Marie."

"Danke Schoen, Marie."

"You're welcome, Jamie."

"Marie, what I can do at my end?"

"Being in Germany, I have a lot more resources than you. Let me have a go at it."

"You're too nice, Marie."

"I'm not Jewish, but I have some Jewish friends who'll help me."

"Bless all of you."

CHAPTER 65

SHORT VISIT WITH STINE

"Dr. Winger is on line 1," said Cathy via the intercom.

"Hi, Susan," said Bloom picking up the phone in the lab.

"William Stine's been afebrile for the past two days," began Winger. "His chest sounds much better. You can see him today if you wish. Just the usual mask, gown, and gloves are needed."

"Should I wait a few more days?"

"You're just talking to him?"

"Yes."

"Today is fine. You want me to write a consult order?"

"That's not necessary. I looked at his CAT scan. It shows a seven-millimeter kidney stone that hasn't increased in size since his first admission. Other than a few red cells, the urine is negative. His upper tracts and bladder have already been evaluated. I don't have to examine him. I'll just write a note in his chart. Thanks for letting me know. Bye."

Bloom hung up, called Stine's floor, and told the nurse he'd be there in ten minutes."

"Someone was with him," said the nurse. "Do you want me to call you when the person leaves?"

"Yes please. What does he look like?"

"He's very muscular."

"Do you know his name?"

"You want me to find out?"

"Please. Did you see him when he was in Stine's room?"

"I saw him both in and out."

"Was he fully gowned, masked, and gloved when he was in the room?"

"Yes."

Twenty minutes later the nurse called Bloom's office and said the visitor had left and that his name was John Michaels. Bloom made a copy of Russell Clark's office ID photo and took the stairs to the third floor, found the nurse, and showed her Clark's photo.

"That's him," she said.

Bloom went to room 307 and knocked on Stine's door. He announced himself, and hearing Stine's "come in," he entered the room, donned the required attire, and proceeded to Stine's bedside.

"Long time no see," said Stine smiling.

"Lucky you," replied Bloom also smiling. "Looks like your temperature is down and your pneumonia is improving."

"I'm very happy about that."

"I'm not here to examine you. I'm here to write a note in your chart and tell you about two incidental findings that don't require further evaluation at this time."

"Why couldn't Dr. Winger tell me?"

"They're urologic and need to be documented by a urologist. Your CAT scan showed the seven-millimeter stone you had when I first saw you. It hasn't gotten any larger and it's in the same location, so nothing needs to be done about it."

"I think you told me about that. What's the other thing?"

"Blood cells in the urine."

"What causes them, stones?"

"Stones and other things. The other things have been ruled out when I looked inside your bladder during your first kidney stone procedure and also by your recent CAT scan. While I'm here I'd like to discuss something with you. My office got a call a few days go from Mr. Jones. He asked to speak with me, and I refused to talk to him. The following morning, we found a note on our office door that started out pleasant enough, expressing good wishes for my wife and children, but also asked if Ida Stern was aware about what happened to my patient Bob Gold, the one who was left for dead in a sand trap after being abducted and having his kidney removed."

"I'm sorry about that. I was aware of that patient, but I certainly didn't tell him to call you."

"Can you remind him not to call me?"

"Will do, Dr. Bloom."

"Thanks."

"One more thing. That call from Jones reminded me that although a bone marrow transplant is not in your cards, we still need to find you a suitable donor if you should ever need one, assuming Ida is not available by illness, death, or refusal to accommodate you. As of right now, she is still your best option. With that in mind, what's the earliest memory you have and where were you living at that time?"

"I'd say age six in West Virginia or Kentucky."

"We could not find any William Stines around your age registered in the US, England, or Canada. Was S-T-I-N-E the only way it was spelled?

"I didn't have any other spellings or names as far as I know."

"What were the names of the people who adopted you?"

"Frank and Barbara Stine. I was told Frank left my mother and me a few months after I was adopted, and my mother and I moved to New York City."

"Wait a minute. Didn't you change your name when you were eighteen?"

"You're right! My parents were not Stine. I think they were Stein!"

"I'm going to need to recheck my search using the other spelling. And you had no brothers or sisters?"

"Nor did I have any aunts, uncles, or cousins, at least not that I knew about."

"What about school?"

"I dropped out of high school just before graduation."

"Where did you live?"

"On the streets."

"How did you survive?"

"I just did. I did a lot of bad things, which I regret and wish not to discuss."

"What about college?"

"I didn't go to college."

"Have you ever had an interest in finding your birth parents?"

"I did for a while when I was on my own."

"Not now?"

"No, not now."

"I'll check out Frank and Barbara Stein."

Bloom thought about calling Stine out on Clark's unauthorized visit but decided he'd speak with Dr. Winger and see how she wanted to handle it. Obviously security was breeched because Clark didn't have permission to see a patient that was in isolation. *But at least he wore protective gear,* thought Bloom to himself, *and it did confirm the relationship Bloom suspected between Stine and Clark.* Bloom said goodbye to Stine, walked into the inner room, and started taking off his protective gear.

"Thanks, Dr. Bloom," shouted Stine through the closed door. "And also, thanks for not bringing up John Michaels."

Bloom immediately stopped taking off his protective gear, turned around, refastened his ware, and went back unto Stine's room.

"Only because you mentioned his name did I decide to come back in and speak with you. I was going to let Dr. Winger handle it. By bypassing hospital security, Clark did a potentially dangerous thing. We have a strict protocol about visitors going into the room of a patient in isolation. They have to be screened by the infectious disease nurse. I'll speak with Dr. Winger, and she'll speak with the infectious disease nurse and see if anything else needs to be done and if Clark needs to return to the hospital."

Leaving the room, Bloom felt satisfied the Clark situation had been addressed.

CHAPTER 66

ORPHANAGE PART 2

"Dr. Bloom, Marie Knoop's on line 2," said Cathy, catching Bloom coming out of the exam room.

"Guten Mittwoch, Marie," said Bloom picking up. "How are you?"

"Fine, and good Wednesday to you," replied Marie. "And how are you?"

"Also, fine," said Bloom. "What have you got?"

"I began reading the daily notes concerning the orphans," continued Knoop, "starting when Sigmund Albrecht came back to the orphanage after the explosion in 1940. On any one day they had from five to nineteen orphans in the orphanage. If there was a different number from the day before, it was usually because some new orphan had come in, or an orphan had been adopted, or one had gone to the hospital. During that year, the person responsible for signing off each day was Adele Becker. On February 2, 1941, there were eighteen on the census. On February 3, 1941, there were sixteen. Adele's comment on the third was that Sigmund and another child were transferred out. No mention was made as to the sex or age of the other child or where they went. Sigmund was younger than eighteen months old."

"They went out together?"

"I'm not sure. Oddly enough, that was the last day Adele worked at the orphanage. I could find no further mention of her after that date.

Looking ahead over the next twenty years, I could not find any other occasion of an undocumented incoming or outgoing orphan or anything about the two children."

"Were you able to find anything else on Becker?"

"No, but we're continuing to work on it."

"That could turn out to be very important."

"It could be."

"Thanks a lot, Marie."

"You're welcome, Jamie."

They said goodbye and hung up.

Dr. Winger called ten minutes later and left a message for Bloom saying she had taken care of the Clark thing and that he didn't have to go back to the hospital.

"Dr. Bloom, it's noon and I've signed out to you," said Cathy. You start tomorrow at 8:30. Need anything before I leave?"

"I've got some stuff to do. I don't need any help. See you in morning."

"Bye," said Cathy, leaving the office.

Bloom did some paperwork, then he made rounds at two hospitals and went home. When he arrived home, he found a note on the fridge:

The kids have play and dinner dates.

Call me when you get home.

Bloom scribbled something the at the bottom of the note and called Missy.

"I'm home. Did you see Dr. Winger yet?" he asked.

"Yes. My next visit is in six months."

"Great! Any more chemo?"

"No more chemo!"

"YIPPEE!"

"Yes, YIPPEE!"

"We need to celebrate."

"The butter churner?"

"I'm ready already."

"I'll be home in fifteen minutes," said Missy. "Wait for me."

"Hurry up. I'm going into the shower. We'll need to stretch for at least thirty minutes. Remember the last time?"

"Wait for me. We'll shower together. Like last time, I'll drop the soap times two, and we'll both get two turns."

"I'm already out of my underwear."

"And mine is starting to feel damp."

CHAPTER 67

I'D LOVE TO KILL JONES

The next day while on the way to the Festival Flea Market Mall in Pompano Beach with his family, Bloom received a call from his answering service telling him his patient Ida Stern was crying inconsolably from a call she just received from a Mr. Jones.

"Can you patch me through to her?" Bloom asked his service, clenching his teeth. He took a deep breath, pulling off to the side of the road and parking at a Dairy Queen. "Take the kids with you and get some good stuff," Bloom told Missy, ushering them out of the car trying to recover from the news.

Bloom listened quietly to Ida for a few minutes. "It was a mistake," he said, "I also got a call from Jones a week or so ago about the same thing."

"Didn't Stine promise Jones would no longer be calling us?"

"Uh huh."

"Some promise!"

"You know that Stine is responding to his chemotherapy and there's no plan for him to have a transplant."

"But that doesn't mean he may not need one," interrupted Ida tearfully.

"That is right. But nothing has changed medically. He is doing well. What has changed is that because of Stine's uncertain condition, with death being more of a possibility than a bone marrow transplant, a new person has been brought into the picture, someone who is monitoring Stine's treatment and who at any time may take over leadership of the Nazi Party. I think he may have been the one to have gotten Jones to call both of us. When I spoke to Stine a few days ago, he assured me he was not responsible for Jones calling me."

"And you believed him?" interrupted Ida still tearful.

"I think Stine's illness may be making him a tad more humane. I've already spoken with him about Jones calling my office and putting a sign on my door about what happened to Bob Gold, the one whose kidney was removed. I'll call Stine and tell him to tell both the new guy and Jones not to call either of us. You have my number. Please call me any time you want to speak with me. And by the way, your speech is perfect."

Bloom said goodbye to Ida, exited his car, and joined his family. Looking around and seeing the three of them scarfing down their sundaes, he ordered a large Extreme Chocolate Brownie Blizzard, knowing they would soon be surrounding him like vultures and swooping down on him with their red spoons. After their treat, they continued on to the Flea Market, where they bought some sour and half-sour pickles, a baseball glove for Lisa, a basketball for Peter, a Mahjong set for Missy, and some fishing lures for himself. Bloom made his call to Stine, who was accommodating. He then ran through the Dairy Queen chocolate choices with Ida and told her he'd be at her house in twenty minutes with the Blizzard of her choice.

CHAPTER 68

BUSY DAY, LONG DAY

"I just finished," said Bloom, calling from University Hospital recovery room. "Everything went well. I'm writing the post-op orders. I need to dictate a note and speak with Miller's family. I should be in the office in thirty minutes. Anything doing?"

"Where should I start?" asked Cathy.

"Anything bad? That reminds me of a joke. Four women were in a restaurant--."

"Not now, Dr. Bloom," interrupted Cathy. "William Stine arrested. He's in the ICU bed 5."

"Oh God. When was that?" asked Bloom, surprised that he cared whether Stine lived or died.

"Two hours ago. Dr. Winger just called and said he was doing okay. Bernie Green started bleeding this morning. He's been here in the office for over two hours."

"Isn't he seeing Dr. Levy?"

"We called Levy's office. He's in Israel and won't be back for ten days."

"Who's covering for him?"

"Dr. Walton. He's away. There's illness in his family."

"Who's covering for him?"

"I have no idea."

"Please find out who and get me the number. What does Bernie's urine look like?"

"It's loaded with clots. Should I set up a cysto?"

"I'll need to examine him first. What else?"

"Your mother ran out of her dulcolax and Bystolic."

"I'll take care of that. What else? I sound just like the people who work in a bakery. I go in there telling them I only want this one item, and they keep asking me what else? I'm sure the owner makes them ask."

"They do the same thing in the deli," Cathy laughed.

"That's true. What else?"

"You got a request for records on Mary Jo Merrill from another lawyer."

"Get ready to send the same thing you sent to the first lawyer. Make sure I see it before it goes out."

"Of course, Dr. Bloom! Of course! What are you going to do with Bernie Green?"

"Nothing right now. Give him some water to drink. Do a urinalysis and call me with the results, unless you've already done it."

"It's not been done yet. I need help looking under the microscope."

"We'll try to spend some time doing that with you later today."

"Good."

"Remind me later to go through the CPT codes for today's surgery."

"Okay. There are some messages, but you can see them when you get in."

"Anyone else need to be seen?"

"No. Oh, Marie Knoop called earlier the morning."

"What'd she say?"

"Something on Adele Becker. I told her you were in surgery. She left her phone number."

"Let me have her number."

Cathy gave Bloom the number and hung up.

Bloom dictated his operative note, spoke with Miller's family, saw Stine who was sitting up in bed and was conversant, looked at Miller again, and walked to the office.

"What time did you start today?" asked Cathy, seeing Bloom entering the office.

"Getting Miller on the table, prepping and draping him, scrubbing, gloving and gowning, I'd say ten before seven."

"The surgery took about seven hours?" said Cathy looking at her watch.

"The patient and I have both been NPO since midnight."

"Doesn't that bother you?"

"You get used to it. I almost never eat breakfast and frequently miss lunch, unless I'm at home, on vacation, or if someone is treating me."

"That's not good for you."

"Probably. I try not eating anything too spicy or salty the evening before my long cases. In a pinch someone in the OR slips a straw under my mask and gives me some liquids."

"I was just about to call you. Aretha came in and looked at the urine and dipstick,"

"And?"

"She thinks Green has an infection. She cultured his urine. She also told me what to look for on the dipstick and how to use the microscope."

"That's why she gets the big bucks. Plus, she's been working here since I opened the office. Let's look at his urine."

Bloom took Cathy into the lab and picked up the container holding Green's urine. "The red color and clumps representing clots suggests bleeding. Can you have red urine and not have bleeding? The answer is yes," said Bloom answering his own question. "Some medicines cause the urine to look reddish. Eating beets can produce a red urine. This condition is called beeturia. Some over-the-counter medicines can also discolor the urine. Specifically Azo, prescribed for burning with urination, causes an orangey-red urine. Infected urine looks cloudy, not clear like water. Infected urine usually smells," continued Bloom, putting the cup up to the tip of his nose. "I smell all the questionable urines," said Bloom, pointing to Aretha as she burst out laughing.

"We'll tell you later," said Aretha trying to control herself. "Looking at the dipstick, we see he has white blood cells and nitrites in his urine, signifying infection. Red blood cells on the dipstick signifies blood in the urine." Bloom put the slide under the microscope and focused it. "There's RBCs, that means red blood cells, and I also see some bacteria. All the tests—looking at and smelling the urine, the dipstick, and the microscopic findings—tells us he has an infection. The question is,

should we do the cysto if the patient has an infection? The answer is . . .
Aretha, what's the answer?" Immediately Aretha answered, "No! First
treat the infection."

"Why is that, Cathy?" asked Bloom.

"Infection may be the reason he's bleeding."

"And why else?" asked Bloom.

"Doing a cysto on a patient who's infected can push the bacteria
into the blood stream and make them septic."

"Excellent, Cathy! See if he's on blood thinners. If he is, get permission from his doctors to stop them. Push fluids and reevaluate him. If
the urine culture is negative, which is unlikely, he'll need a cysto. If it's
positive, treat him appropriately and see what happens with the bleeding. If it persists, we'll need to do more tests to see where the bleeding's
coming from, like an IVP or CAT scan. Mr. Green is no longer our
patient. But that doesn't matter. We're going to take care of him like he
is, which means doing what we discussed. I'm going to examine him
and make sure his bladder is not distended. If it is, that may change our
plan. I'll bring him and his wife into my office, and you guys can sit in
our discussion. Basically, it'll be what we discussed. I will get permission
from him if you'd like to sit in." Aretha and Cathy nodded. "Meanwhile
put together what's necessary for Mary Jo's attorney."

Bloom went into the waiting area, said hello to the Greens, brought
Mr. into the exam room and put Mrs. in his office. After examining Mr.
and finding only 50 ccs on his bladder, he brought him into his office
and obtained consent for his staff to sit in for his consultation with the
Greens. Finding that Mr. was on Coumadin and it was okay to come
off of it, Bloom told the Greens to temporarily stop the Coumadin.
Based upon accepting Bloom's plan, Green was given two Cipro 250
mg tablets to take today, told to drink plenty of fluids, and come to the
office at 8:45 tomorrow morning. After the Greens left, Bloom told
Cathy why Aretha was laughing. "About five years ago, when I entered
the office one morning, I told Aretha I had been at the hospital from
1:30 a.m. until 5 a.m. that morning taking care of a patient who was
bleeding. I told her that I was drowsy and almost got into an accident
coming to the office for my 9 o'clock patient and that I was glad I didn't
have to do any surgery that morning. In the lab I saw she had the first
four patients' urines in a clear plastic cup with their names on it with a

microscope slide of the patient's centrifuged urine sitting on the top of it along with a printout of the dipstick. When Aretha had to leave the lab to go to the front desk I quickly got up, looked at the fourth patient's urine, slide, and dipstick. Then I wrote a note in the chart and threw the cup in the garbage. I got a new cup, took a hospital apple juice container from the refrigerator, and poured some into the cup. Then I rewrote the fourth patient's name on it, made a fake slide and dipstick, and put it on top of the container. When Aretha came back into the room, I told her I was drowsy and that I might have to leave early but not to cancel any of the patients. For the first three patients I looked at the urine, dipstick, and slide. I smelled each one of the urines and threw them all into the garbage after writing a note in the patient's chart. I yawned as I picked up the last cup, looked at the dipstick and slide, and after I had thrown them into the garbage, I lifted the cup to my nose and instead of smelling what was in the cup, I began drinking it. Aretha screamed, 'Doctor Bloom!' and knocked the cup out of my hand, its contents splashing me, her, and the walls. When I opened the refrigerator and showed her the half-filled container of apple juice and laughed, she grabbed the container and poured what was left on my head!"

"True story," said Aretha, shaking her fist at Bloom.

"Okay," said Bloom. "Time for the CPT codes for today's surgery. Cathy, tell us what I did today to Mr. Miller."

"You removed his bladder cancer and made him a new bladder that empties his urine through a hole in his abdomen into a plastic bag which is attached via adhesive to his skin."

"Very good, Cathy," said Bloom. "Aretha, how did I do it?"

"The first thing you did was to make a lower abdominal incision and removed his pelvic lymph nodes to determine whether the cancer had gotten into them. You sent those nodes to the pathologist to get frozen sections. When no cancer was found in them, you extended the incision to check the liver and spleen and the nodes along the aorta and vena cava—the large vessels that supply the lower half of the body. When these were found to show no tumor present by touch, you proceeded to fashion his artificial bladder using a piece of his small bowel. This required isolating a piece of bowel and rehooking the bowel back together. Then you detached his ureters from his bladder and tunneled them into the piece of bowel. Then you removed his bladder and made an opening in a predetermined area in his lower right abdomen and brought the end of the new bladder outside the body cavity and attached a plastic bag around the new opening and closed the incision."

"Excellent, Aretha."

"The three numbers Aretha just checked off are in summary the complete operation you performed?" asked Cathy.

"Yes. A year ago, I had Aretha come into the OR to watch one of these, but there were so many people in the OR, she couldn't see anything and thought it was a waste of time, so I didn't bring you in for this one. The next time I have a less complicated case, I'll try to get you into the OR. You're not squeamish are you and you don't eat Raisinets, do you?"

"Like Kramer?" said Cathy smiling.

"Like Kramer," repeated Bloom laughing.

"Did you call Marie Knoop?"

"Thanks for reminding me," said Bloom, taking her number out of his lab coat pocket. "It's too late to call her," he mumbled. "It's 11:00 p.m. in Berlin right now. Please remind me to call her tomorrow morning."

"Why were there so many people in the room when Aretha was in the OR?"

"In addition to my surgical assistant, whom I must have in the room with me for every major case, similar to having a co-pilot, and the anesthesiologist, there were two nurses, one handing me the instruments and one circulating in case I needed something that wasn't already on the sterile field. There were also observing medical and nursing students and a cell-saver person who collected the suctioned blood that was lost during the case and given back to the patient via a separate IV line. We only use a cell-saver if we're expecting significant bleeding."

"The patient also had blood from the blood bank on hand if needed, right?"

"Yes. We don't operate without blood on hand if blood loss is a significant possibility. Obviously you need blood for open heart surgery and aortic aneurysms. Sometimes the patients themselves donate their own blood prior to their surgery, which is stored for their use."

"What do you do about Jehovah Witnesses?"

"That's a good question. Some doctors won't operate on them."

"Would you?"

"I've operated on a few of them. And one was a fairly difficult case."

"Did any change their mind just before going under?"

"One did, but he had already been given a pre-operative medicine and his subsequent consent was ruled invalid."

"What'd you do?"

"We waited twenty-four hours to obtain consent for obtaining and receiving blood."

"Did you ever run into bleeding on such a patient?"

"Luckily, no."

"Can I go home now? It's way after five o'clock."

"You're the one keeping us here with all your questions!"

ANXIETY/SLEEP DEPRIVATION

"This is Nancy Severin from University Hospital ICU, Dr. Bloom," heard Bloom after picking up the portable bedroom phone, seeing it was 2:34 in the morning. He got up and left the bedroom for the computer room so as not to wake Missy.

"I'm calling about your patient Harris Miller in bed 7," continued the nurse.

"This is Dr. Bloom, go ahead."

"His hourly urinary output has been 8 ccs for the last two hours. Do you want me to increase his IV rate by 10 ccs per hour?"

"What are his vital signs?"

"92/60, 96, 16, and temp of 99.4."

"His lungs are clear?"

"Yes, Dr. Bloom."

"What was his last H and H and blood sugar, and when was it?"

"9.2 and 33 and 147 at 11:00 p.m.."

"He's hypovolemic. I wouldn't give him any blood. Yes, keep raising his IV rate by 10 ccs per hour until his output increases."

"Will do."

"He has blood work ordered for the morning?"

"Yes. CBC, SMA 12, and electrolytes."

"How much pain is he having?"

"He's not complaining."

"Call me in two hours if his output hasn't picked up."

"Will do. Thanks, Dr. Bloom."

"No. Thank you!"

Bloom hung up and continued sitting in the computer room. He knew he wouldn't be able to get back to sleep. It never was worth trying. Never. Although low urinary output was to be expected following a seven-hour surgery for of the removal of his cancerous bladder, a patient such as Miller with preexisting conditions added to Bloom's usual anxiety following such procedures. He had taken care of Miller since Miller got off the plane, the day he moved from Roslyn, New York, and urinated blood in the Ft. Lauderdale airport. That was six years ago. Since that time, he had close to twenty cystoscopies for superficial, precancerous, and now invasive bladder cancer. He had two courses of BCG therapy before the most recent biopsy. Bloom was aware that most of his colleagues in his area would have referred Miller, who had diabetes and two prior heart attacks, to Miami or Cleveland Clinic once a recurrence needing a second course of BCG was found and especially after the finding of invasive bladder cancer. Bloom thought that probably more patients could have died on the table or immediately post-op after any operation and not because of surgical, anesthetic, medical, or nursing error but because of patient age and poor protoplasm. Bloom did not feel his surgical skills were better than the other urologists in his area. As a matter fact, he thought that some of them had better skills than he in some aspects of urology, and he told them so. He just felt a responsibility to care for those patients that trusted him, and together with his level of competence he could keep his patients' care close to home, where there was familiarity with the hospital and its surroundings. He never put down the other urologists for referring their patients to another institution or distant communities. He did not want any of them to refer their patients to him—nor would they; he thought it might make them lose face as well as their patient. Might they be unhappy with him for doing these difficult cases in their own backyard? Maybe. But he could not help that. Bloom looked at the clock next to the computer and saw it was now 4:17 a.m. "Must have dozed off," he said, not aware he had closed his eyes since coming into the room. He dialed the ICU and asked to speak with Nurse Severin about Harris Miller.

"Dr. Bloom, his output has more than doubled to almost 20 ccs per hour," said Severin. "Do you want me to slow down his IV?"

"Check his lungs. If they're clear, leave him at that level. If you hear any crackles, cut it back down by 5 ccs per hour. I'll be in to see him at 6:30."

"Make it closer to 7:00. The labs won't now be back until then."

"Thanks for the heads up. See you at 7:00."

Bloom hung up and set the computer room clock alarm to 6:15.

CHAPTER 70

MORNING ROUNDS AND MARIE KNOOP

loom took the stairs to the ICU and slipped behind the bed 5 curtain.

"Good morning, Nancy," Bloom greeted Nurse Severin, who was checking Miller's urinary drainage bag.

"His output has continued to improve." said Severin. It's still over 20-25 ccs per hour even after a reduction in the fluid rate. I heard a few basilar rales, as did Dr. Morris."

"When was he here?"

"A half hour ago. He would like the patient to get some blood."

"Were you here with him?"

"Yes."

"Did he see today's labs?"

"He said cardiac-wise he was doing okay, but he expects his blood count to drop even more as he equilibrates, and with his history he thinks it's a good idea to give him a unit of packed cells."

"I definitely agree," said Bloom.

"Brilliant minds think alike, which is why I've already called for it."

"Which brilliant minds?"

"Dr. Morris and mine, of course!" Severin replied, laughing.

"I thought you'd say that."

"I didn't hear any bowel sounds. I assume you're going to keep him NPO."

"Let me examine him first."

"I'll give you a few minutes," replied Severin, stepping outside the curtain.

Bloom examined Miller's heart, lungs, and abdomen. The ileal bladder's stoma looked nice and pink. The urine was slightly blood-tinged. There was no leakage around the drainage bag. Bloom examined Miller's legs. There was no edema or calf tenderness, and his compression stockings were fine.

"Yes, we'll keep him NPO," said Bloom catching up with Severin. "Can you swab his mouth with glycerin-impregnated Q-tips prn?"

"Write the order. Also Dr. Morris would like you to tell him when he can restart his Coumadin."

"Let me check his labs," said Bloom, walking over to the nursing station and returning a few minutes later.

"They're okay, except for the low H and H," said Bloom "His renal function and blood sugar are okay. I'll see tomorrow if we can resume the blood thinners. I'd like him to get out of bed Q shift."

"Write the order."

"Yes, Nurse Ratchet, er, I mean, Severin," comparing her with the strict nurse in the Jack Nicholson film *One Flew Over the Cuckoo's Nest*.

"I'll remember that," replied Severin, making a mock fist.

Bloom put a note in Miller's chart and wrote a full page of orders, including the afternoon labs and requests for dietary and physical therapy consultations. He called Miller's son in Paris and was able to converse with him almost totally in French. He told him his father tolerated the seven-plus hours of surgery and was alert and would be in the ICU for a number of days and that he would need a fair amount of convalescence that might require him to go to rehab for a while. Bloom said he would try to call him on a regular basis and gave him his office, home, and cell phone numbers.

Bloom visited Stine in the ICU, reminding him again about Jones and adding the Granite Stater to the mix, saw two more post-op patients and a consult, and hurried over to his office to make his long-awaited call to Berlin.

"Guten Morgen, Marie," said Bloom when Marie Knoop answered the phone.

"And good morning to you, Jamie" Marie replied, recognizing Bloom's voice.

"That's most of the German I know," answered Bloom starting to laugh.

"That's fine," said Marie also laughing. "How are you?"

"I'm okay. How are you . . . and your son?"

"We're good. The seas are still rough. He hasn't been in the water since."

"What does he do?"

"His job is with the equivalent of your Coast Guard."

"I must say your English is quite good."

"Most Americans only speak English."

"Je parle un peu de Francais."

"Je parle cinq langes."

"Tres bien."

"Let me tell you about Adele Becker. I couldn't find her anywhere. There's been no mention of her after August 19, 1944. I did find, however, an Adele Bekker. She got a government position right after the boys were taken out of the orphanage. And there's no mention of her anywhere before August 19, 1944.

"If that's true, it doesn't make a whole lot of sense."

"To me either."

"What kind of government position?"

"I don't know. Right now I'm looking for both Becker and Bekker in assisted-living and nursing facilities. Also homeless shelters and prisons."

"If she's alive she has to be at least in her eighties.

"Or nineties! I have another call I have to take. I'll be in touch. Goodbye, Jamie."

"Tschuss, Marie. Danke."

CHAPTER 71

YOU PICK 'EM, EAT 'EM, THEN PAY 'EM

"Dr. Winger's on line 2," Aretha called out, trying to catch Bloom before he went into the exam room.

"I'll take it in my office," Bloom replied, going into his office and picking up the blinking phone line. "Hi, Susan, what's doing this fine Saturday morning?"

"You have office hours today?"

"Are you having a problem?"

"No, I'm fine," she answered, starting to laugh.

"Good. No office hours today. I'm doing a vasectomy on someone who can't do it during the week. Whatcha got?"

"William Stine."

"I saw him yesterday. He looked good. What happened to him?"

"I don't know. I don't think he actually arrested. Possibly he had a seizure. Cardiology and neurology saw him. All his tests were negative. I called to tell you Stine has completed his induction phase."

"Great!"

"Great?" asked Susan quizzically.

"Susan. Can you call me back on my cell? My number is 954-723-8424."

Bloom hung up and answered his phone when it rang.

"Hi, Susan. My 'great!' was the usual necessary response. Obviously, between you and me, it would be better for me, Ida Stern, and the rest of the world if he died. But I must say, when I learned he survived his cardiac arrest, I inexplicably felt happy. Don't ask me why. I spoke with Ida a few days ago when we spoke about Stine, I told her he sounded a little humane. 'Well, he still won't be getting my marrow!' was her reply. But, I must say, he's told me a number of times how he appreciates what you and I have done for him," said Bloom. "He's really been a good patient. What's next for him?"

"A bone marrow biopsy in one week."

"What is that going to show?"

"Hopefully a hypocellular marrow with 5 percent or less blast cells. That would mean he was in remission."

"And what if it's more than 5 percent?"

"Either repeat the bone marrow biopsy in another week or go another round of chemo, with the same or different drugs, plus or minus a bone morrow transplant."

"And if he's in remission?"

"Then he gets consolidation therapy."

"Which is what?"

"Several cycles of chemotherapy and/or a bone marrow transplant."

"Bone marrow is still a possibility?"

"It's always been a possibility."

"Do you have a donor?"

"No one's as good as Ida so far."

"Do you have any at all?"

"Not really."

"Is that a no?"

"Yes, that's a no. What about her sister?"

"Rachel wouldn't do it, and Ida wouldn't let her do it. And from what I know about Ida, I don't think Rachel would be a match. What about an autologous bone marrow transplant?"

"That's an option. Right now, let's think about getting a remission."

"Do you remember what happened when she thought Stine and his henchmen were going to kill her after she survived their murder attempts on the Sawgrass and again in the hospital?"

"You told me about it."

"Did I tell you they threatened to kidnap my son if I didn't tell them where she was after she left the hospital? And this was after I surgically removed Stine's kidney stone! If she doesn't agree to give him her bone marrow, Stine or Clark and his goons will take it from her, just like someone took my patient's kidney a few weeks ago and left him to die in a Tamarac golf course sand trap."

"Wow!"

"Yes, wow! Susan, there's a lot more to this story than I've told you. It's hard for me to think just about remission, but I'll try."

Bloom finished his conversation with Dr. Winger, saw one more emergency in the office, and called it a day after signing out to one of his covering physicians. He had promised to take his family to the not-so-nearby U Pick'em fields for tomatoes, corn, strawberries, and peppers and had already put the hand wipes, water, and saltshaker in the big car this morning. In addition, he left a note on the steering wheel to remind him to bring two more items from the house for the trip—canisters of plain and chocolate whipped cream.

After two hours of vegetable and fruit picking with the help of the saltshaker for the tomatoes and the canisters for the strawberries, they needed to pay for what they picked. Bloom popped the trunk and an attendant removed the bags and baskets, separated and weighed each type of produce, closed the trunk, and told Bloom the amount he owed. Bloom paid and they left the farm with their bellies full and their canisters on empty.

CHAPTER 72

THE PLOT THICKENS

"Dr. Bloom, Marie Knoop's on line 1," announced Aretha through the intercom.

"I'll take it in exam room 2," replied Bloom noting there was a patient in exam room 1 and another in his office.

"Guten tag, Marie," began Bloom.

"Hello, Jamie. I think I have something for you. I've found Adele Bekker in an assisted-living facility fifty miles southeast of Berlin. She's ninety-one and has had full-time care for the last four years, after having a stroke. She's able to speak, though haltingly, and with some help is communicative. I learned from her aide she was Hitler's personal secretary."

"Was she working the day the boys were taken from the orphanage?"

"She was reluctant to speak about it." Marie paused. "Then I said to her 'one of those boys was sent to the orphanage by its Jewish mother before she was sent to Auschwitz so he wouldn't be killed.' Adele Bekker remained silent for a full minute, then I heard her sobbing."

Bloom remained silent for about thirty seconds then spoke. "Did Adele say anything after that?"

"I asked her if she took the children? She answered yes through her sobs. I was going to tell her that I was sorry I upset her and tell her that I'd call her back in a few days, but I thought she'd probably not take the call, so I continued."

"Did she say why or to where she took them?"

"She said she was told by Hitler's office to bring them to the embassy."

"Which embassy?"

"I would imagine the German embassy."

"Did she say for what reason?"

"She said those were Hitler's orders."

"Do you know where the children went from there?"

"She wouldn't say."

"You think she knows?"

"I think yes."

"Do you have any idea?'"

"No. I hope to call her in a few days."

"Marie, this is very interesting. Danke."

"It is. You're welcome, Jamie. Bye."

"Bye." Jamie hung up, still keeping his hand on the phone, and thinking for a few minutes. "Very interesting, indeed."

CHAPTER 73

READING ASSIGNMENT

"Dr. Bloom, Marie Knoop's on line 2," said Aretha spotting Bloom coming out of exam room 1.

"I'll take it in my office," replied Bloom going back into the exam room and telling Mr. Janowitz to wait for him there. He then went into his office and spoke with Marie for ten minutes, jotting names and dates on a piece of scratch paper.

"Dr. Winger's on line 1," announced Aretha, seeing Bloom coming out of his office heading back for the exam room.

"I'll take it in my office," answered Bloom, turning around and picking up the phone in his office. "Whatcha got, Susan?"

"Stine's bone marrow biopsy showed 8 percent blast cells."

"Repeat the biopsy or restart the chemo?"

"I'm repeating the biopsy in a week, giving the chemo more time to do its job."

"Sounds like a plan. Have you told him?"

"I'm going there now."

"I'll stop by later."

Bloom hung up and asked Janowitz to bring his wife into his office.

"I took a biopsy of Mr. J's bladder," Bloom told Mrs. J.

"I know. I heard him screaming."

"That was when I told him I was going to do the biopsy. He didn't make a peep when I actually did it."

Mrs. J. laughed.

"This is the first biopsy I've had to do on you in ten years," Bloom told Mr. J. "Remember how long it took to rid you of your bladder cancer?"

"Is that unusual after so many years?" asked Mrs. J.

"I see it every so often. That's why I see him at least once a year. You never know if or when this bladder thing will raise its ugly head. You stopped smoking ten years ago." Bloom frowned as he watched as the couple looked sheepishly at each other.

"He's smoking?" Bloom asked, looking at Mrs. J.

Mrs. J. sighed.

"Since when?" asked Bloom.

"Tell him, Reuben," Mrs. J. said.

"I stopped smoking a week ago."

"Because you were coming to see me?"

Mrs. J. nodded.

"When did you start?" asked Bloom.

"Six months ago. Will you have to put all those terrible chemicals in me again?"

"Let's see what the biopsy shows. I will need to check out the rest of your urinary tract if the biopsy is positive. Hopefully it was caught early and there'll be nothing else. Obviously, you're not going to smoke anymore. Right?"

"I stopped."

"And will stay stopped."

"And will stay stopped," echoed the patient.

"He'd better," added Mrs. J., shaking both fists at him.

"Aretha will give you two antibiotic samples. You'll take one now and one before you go to bed. Call me tomorrow morning and let me know how you're doing. Have Aretha make you an appointment for next Tuesday to check your urine and discuss the biopsy result."

"Your last patient rescheduled for tomorrow," said Aretha. "I see you've already made all your calls. You just need to see Stine before you go home."

Bloom nodded. "First I have to search the internet to see what was happening in Germany and the US in the 1930s."

"Is that's what Marie Knoop suggested you do?"

"Basically."

"And that may have had something to do with why the boys left the orphanage?"

"Presumably."

"I'll be leaving in thirty minutes." said Aretha. "You start tomorrow at 8:30 a.m. Cathy will be here by 8:15."

Bloom nodded again, said goodbye, and then spent almost an hour on the computer.

CHAPTER 74

SPANKY AND HIS GANG

"Did you know that in May 1933 Nazi Deputy Fuhrer Rudolf Hess gave German immigrant Nazi Party member Heinz Spanknobel permission to establish the American Nazi Organization in Detroit and then the pro-Nazi Friends of New Germany in New York as its Bundesleiter?" asked Bloom, opening the door from the garage to the laundry room, spotting Missy folding one of Peter's T-shirts and putting it on top of the shirt pile.

"And you're having baked beans for dinner," replied Missy, starting to fold Lisa's red shorts. "I bet you didn't know that."

"How could I've known that?" asked Bloom. "You just told me when I came into the house!"

"You're losing it, Jamie," answered Missy. "You just can't think fast enough or you would have quipped one of Heinz's other fifty-six varieties and mustered up something better than that."

"First of all, there are fifty-seven varieties, and I don't relish what you're saying."

"Has your brain been frozen by the chili sauce?"

"Don't be a crab-apple."

"I'm so far ahead of you. You'll never ketchup."

"I purposely left that one for you."

"I know. That's why I love you."

"Where are the kiddies?"

"Doing Peter's puzzle."

"The 500-piece one?"

"Don't go in there and sneakily steal a piece so you can put in the last one!"

"Would I do that to my kids?"

"Especially your kids!"

"You really think you know me, don't you? I happened to take two pieces so they could each finish the puzzle together."

"Really?"

"Really," answered Bloom showing her the two pieces. "I took them this morning."

"My apologies. Are you finished talking about the Bundesleiter who enjoyed spanking his baroness lover?"

"You're a good listener."

"That's what I do for a living. I'm a psychologist. You can continue."

"The spanker also developed a presence in Chicago and in 1936 established the German American Bund in Buffalo for citizens of German Descent, with training camps in New Jersey and Yaphank, New York, and organized a rally of 20,000 Nazi supporters in Madison Square Garden. Its purpose was to promote a favorable view of Nazi Germany to the US. That's all she wrote."

"And your purpose in telling me?"

"That's a great question! According to my Berlin connection, it may have had something to do with the disappearance of Sigmund and company from the orphanage."

"On who's say so?"

"Another great question! The person who took them from the orphanage."

"Really? Does this person have a name?"

"Adele Bekker."

"She's got to be at least in her eighties, maybe more."

"She's ninety-one and is in an assisted-living facility about twenty miles out of Berlin. She had a stroke a month ago and is in rehab."

"How'd you manage to find her?"

"Marie Knoop found her."

"Who's Marie Knoop?"

"I told you about her some time ago. She works in archives at the orphanage. Her son's in the Berlin Coast Guard and had been lost at sea a few weeks ago. He was eventually rescued."

"That's good. And Adele told Marie all this?"

"With reluctance. The fact that my patient is a Holocaust survivor and put her son in the orphanage to be saved from Hitler, the two women were somewhat compelled to help me. All right, maybe not compelled. But not opposed."

"You've always been more optimistic than I, Jamie."

"Marie said Adele has never told anyone else about what she did."

"Do you know why she did it?"

"Marie's on it."

"Is Marie your NBF?"

"Newest Berlin Friend?"

"That was very good!"

"Give me a hint."

"Basically, you've got it. New Best Friend."

"Is NBF a common abbreviation?"

"I guess not as common as I thought."

"To the ENT doctor it would stand for epistaxis or nose bleed—Nasal Blood Flow."

"You're hopeless," said Missy, rolling her eyes and laughing.

CHAPTER 75

THANK YOU FOR CALLING

"D r. Bloom, Ida Stern's on line 2," said Cathy. "She'd like to speak with you."

"Sure," replied Bloom, hanging up with Cathy and picking up the second line.

"Hi, Ida. Que pasa?"

"I'm only calling you because I love you."

"Go on."

"I wasn't going to call you."

"Go on."

"I'm bleeding with some clots."

"Who were you going to call, a plumber?"

Ida chuckled. "It took a lot to call you."

"I'm happy you called. And you know I love you too."

"I know."

"When did the bleeding start?" asked Bloom, trying to segue from the implied seriousness of her situation to the nitty-gritty of her medical problem.

"Two days ago."

"Are you able to urinate?"

"Yes, but I'm passing clots."

"Any other symptoms?"

"Pain when I'm having trouble passing the clots. I don't feel like it's an infection."

"Are you taking any blood thinners?"

"I stopped them two days ago. Dr. Bloom, isn't it time for me to die?"

"Not yet. I'll tell you when it's time."

"Promise?"

"I promise."

"Am I near?"

"We're all nearer than we were yesterday."

"You wouldn't lie to a ninety-year-old, would you?"

"You're only eighty-nine. Did I miss your birthday?"

"You'd never miss my birthday. Where are you going to get the platelets?"

"Platelets R Us if you need them. We need to first see where you're bleeding from. Remember you never got the CAT scan and cysto I wanted you to have before you got your stroke."

"I remember."

"Come to the office. After I see you, I'll speak with Dr. Winger, and we'll decide what needs to be done. We'll see. You may need to be hospitalized. Do you want me to speak with Rachel?"

"That's not necessary."

"Does she know what's going on?"

"No . . . I was planning to die!"

"I know. Can I tell Missy? It's important she sees you."

"I guess so."

"I'll want to call Rachel and ask her to bring you here. Is that okay?"

"Okay," replied Ida sighing.

"I'm calling her now. Hold on."

Bloom put her on hold, called Rachel, and explained the situation. He hung up when she said she'd bring Ida to the office. When he tried to get back on the phone with Ida he got a dial tone. When he could not reach her by phone, he called Rachel and told her to immediately get to her sister's and call him.

CHAPTER 76

ONE MORE LEASE ON LIFE

loom followed Ida into recovery, dictated the operative note, wrote the post-op orders, spoke with Dr. Winger, and joined Rachel in the waiting area.

"She did very well," said Bloom. "I didn't find any additional tumors. There was minimal blood loss. For precaution's sake she's going to the ICU. She doesn't need a private duty nurse tonight."

"I'm surprised she called you," began Rachel. "We had discussed a short time ago what would happen if she started bleeding. At that time it was only about not being able to get platelets, not because her marrow was about to be hijacked and she would lie dying in a sand trap, or about pressure being put on you and your family to comply with Stine's requests. Not calling me or you and dying at home was a reasonable action."

"The only problem was that she had a treatable condition and did not require platelets. This is not to say that things can't or won't change."

"Will she need any additional treatment?"

"I'm not planning any."

"What about Dr. Winger?"

"She agreed."

"What kind of follow-ups?"

"Urine tests, office cystoscopies, occasional X-rays. What kind of work did Ida do?"

"JDL work—Jewish Defense League—office work, meetings, some involving travel."

"Did she smoke?"

"Not that I know of."

"Did she ever work in a beauty shop or handle chemicals or dyes?"

"No. Will she be having much pain?"

"Very minimal. It'll be from the catheter and that should be removed tomorrow."

"When can I see her?"

"I will take you to see her in recovery in twenty minutes. Go back to the waiting area. I'll get you. "

"Okay."

Bloom went back to recovery and waited for the nurses to do their work before approaching Stern.

"Ida, you're in recovery," said Bloom gently nudging her. "Your surgery is over. Everything went well. Do you have your hearing aids in? Nod with your head."

"I hear you."

"You were bleeding from a small superficial bladder tumor, which has been removed. You have a catheter in you, which may be removed tomorrow. You shouldn't have much pain."

"I don't have any pain. Where's Rachel?"

"I saw and spoke with her. Your nurses need some time to settle you in. You will see Rachel in a few minutes. I'd like you to stay overnight."

"Thank you, Jamie."

Bloom gave her a hug, brought Rachel into recovery, stayed with the both of them for a few minutes and went to his office.

Seeing him, Cathy said, "Marie Knoop's on line 2."

"I've got it," he replied, looking past Cathy and seeing two patients in the waiting area. He hurried into his office and picked up the line.

"Hello, Marie, I've got a lot of stuff going on here. Can I call you back in an hour?"

"It's about Adele Bekker. She doesn't want to speak with you any more. She wants to speak directly with Ida Stern. I'll hang up now. Call me back when you can."

"Thanks. I'll call you soon."

Bloom hung up but kept his hand on the phone. He took a deep breath and sighed. "I thought this might happen," he said sighing again. He saw the two patients, then called recovery to see if Ida had gone upstairs to her room. When the nurse said yes and that Rachel went up with her, Bloom asked Cathy to get Marie Knoop back on the phone.

"Hi, Marie," said Bloom. "Sorry I couldn't speak with you before. Ida Stern just had surgery this morning and will speak with Adele in a few days. Why did Adele say what she said?"

"How'd her surgery go?"

"It went well."

"Good. From what I've gotten from Adele, probably two reasons. One, she may have information that could lead Ida to finding her son. And two, she has stuff regarding Hitler plus things about herself that she's never told anyone that she feels needs to come out. Her age and recent stroke have made her think she won't be able to, and I quote, "relieve herself of this information" before she dies. I think Ida has given her this opportunity."

"She should definitely speak with Ida," said Bloom. "But I think either Rachel or I should be on the phone with Ida because Ida's hearing is not so good."

"I'll run it by her and get back to you."

"That would be great."

Bloom got Bekker's contact info from Knoop as well as the best days and times to reach her, then thanked her and hung up. Looking at his watch and noting it was 11:52 a.m., he called Missy and told her what Knoop had said, hoping as Ida's psychologist, she would talk to her. But Missy said it would be a hard sell to get Ida to call Bekker and said she rather not do it. Bloom decided he would speak to Ida but would first run things by Rachel.

Bloom saw four more patients and went back to the hospital to see Ida, who was now sleeping. Rachel was sitting by her side. The urine in the drainage bag was slightly rose in color. He whispered to Rachel to stand up and motioned her to follow him away from the bed.

"I'd like to speak with you," he said leading her out of the room and into an unoccupied room on the same floor. "I couldn't be happier with what I found. The tumor appeared superficial and was easy to remove.

As I said before, no additional treatment is required. An office cyctos-copy will be needed in three months and every three months for the next year. But what I want to talk to you about is her son Sigmund and what he may represent for her future health and well-being."

"What? Why? I don't understand."

"Let me explain. Right now she's not bleeding. But we still don't have access to a supply of platelets if she does."

"That bastard Stine killed her platelet donor."

"That may be the case. But he was the one who got her the platelets when she was in Cincinnati."

"How'd he do that?"

"I don't know."

Rachel raised her eyebrows and gave a quizzical look.

"Right now," continued Bloom, "Stine does not need a bone marrow transplant, and he may never need one, but doctors don't like to using the word 'never,' and if he ever does, I know Ida would never give him hers. I'll never ask her to change her mind."

Seeing Rachel starting to raise her hand to speak, Bloom raised his hand silencing her. "I also don't want her going to Cincinnati or staying at home alone to kill herself because of the bone marrow situation. And I don't want her kidnapped and her marrow taken from her and dying in a sand trap."

"Ida told me one of Stine's henchmen called her and told her about the sand trap incident."

"I spoke with Stine about that, and he said he had nothing to do with that call."

"And you believe him?"

"That's not the issue here. Let me continue."

Rachel gave a small nod.

"Here's what I'm getting at. When Ida gave me the go ahead to locate Sigmund for the purpose of obtaining a possible platelet donor for her, she also may have given Stine a different option for a bone marrow."

"Is that it?"

"No, there's lots more I have to speak to you about."

"I'd like to get back to my sister now."

"Sure," replied Bloom getting up.

"When should I see you?"

"I start seeing patients at 9:00 am tomorrow. Come to my office at 8:30."

"Tomorrow? 8:30?"

"You can come later ... What we don't finish tomorrow, we can finish the next day."

"Seriously?"

"Rachel, I have some important things to discuss with you, and I need to do it before I talk to Ida."

"I can do it now, then."

"No, now go see your sister," said Bloom motioning her to get up. "I'll see you in the morning."

"See you at 8:30, Jamie."

Bloom said goodbye to Rachel and left the hospital.

He had just gotten into his car when he got a call from Dr. Winger telling him that Stine's repeat biopsy showed 6 percent blast cells and that she was going to repeat the same regimen he had just completed. She added that this would have been the same regimen even if the blast cells had come down to 5 percent, and at this time, there was no plan for a bone marrow transplant but that one may be needed after this therapy is completed.

He stopped to get food for Flyer and ice cream surprises for Lisa, Peter, Missy, and something for himself and went home. He paid the sitter and played hide and seek with the kids and started a load of wash while they each did a puzzle.

"I saw Ida a little while ago," said Missy, coming in from the garage, seeing Bloom putting the end of the wash load into the dryer before turning it on.

"Was Rachel with her?" asked Bloom

"Yes."

"Was Ida up?"

"She was alert and looked pretty good. She said to thank you again. So, thanks!"

"How'd her urine look?"

"Her drainage bag was on the other side of the bed."

"They must have switched it after I left her. Sometimes they do that when the patient has a visitor, but they shouldn't be doing that on a post-op urologic patient. Did you say anything to them about it?"

"Am I a urologist's wife? Of course I did! How else can they know how bloody or clear the urine is and how well the catheter is draining the bladder and what's the urinary output?"

"You did me proud. What did the nurse say?"

"She gave me two thumbs up."

"Did she move the drainage bag and tubing to the front side of her bed?"

"Yes. Did you get a chance to speak with Rachel?"

"We spoke for a little while. I told her I'd speak with her tomorrow in the office before my first patient."

"Did she seem receptive?"

"I don't know yet. Rachel's always been a little difficult."

"I'd give her a pass. You've never had your uterus removed without an anesthetic."

"That's true."

"Are you interested in what information Bekker has for Ida?"

"Yes. But she wants to talk to Ida, and I need to get Ida to agree. Marie Knoop said it would probably be okay for Rachel or me to be on the line also."

"Do you think Ida will agree to speak with her?"

"That's what I have to talk with Rachel about."

"You think Ida may have changed?"

"As she's nearing her end of life and even thinking about ending it herself, there may have been changes, just as there were for Bekker."

"I hope you're right."

CHAPTER 77

DILEMMA RESOLVED

"Miss Stern, Dr. Bloom was just called to the OR," said Cathy, as Rachel walked into the office. "One of the doctors had an emergency that required his help."

"Did he say how long he'd be?"

"At least two hours. Maybe more."

"I'll visit Ida. Can you have him call me when he gets in?"

"Will do. He may have patients to see. Right now I'm rescheduling at least two hours' worth."

"What about tomorrow at 8:30?"

"I'll ask him when he comes in."

"Fine," replied Rachel, leaving the office.

Bloom returned to the office three hours later and called Rachel to confirm the next morning's 8:30 time slot, saw patients till 5:30 p.m., saw Ida and the man he had just operated on, and drove home.

"I heard you saved a kidney today," said Missy, greeting Bloom with a kiss as he opened the laundry room door. "What happened?"

"Roberts removed a pelvic colon mass that contained a six-centimeter piece of ureter."

"What'd you do?"

"My first choice would have been to get a transplant surgeon to relocate the kidney and reimplant the ureter. I could do the nephrectomy, bowel replacement surgery, or hitching it to the other ureter. I decided to speak to our vascular surgeons and those in Miami and then speak with the patient's wife. I told her if the surgeon was not available or transfer was impossible, I'd hitch the left ureter to the right or use the bowel and hope for the best."

"I assume finding a transplant surgeon and relocating the kidney and transferring the patient to Miami was not available."

"Correct."

"So you wound up doing something."

"Correct. The easiest, safest, and most expedient thing to do would have been to remove the kidney."

"Which you did not do."

"Correct."

"So you either hooked up the left ureter to the right one or got GI to help you use some bowel to bridge the gap, both of which you've never done or seen before."

"Correct."

"Did you tell that to his wife?"

"Yes, of course! I added that I didn't think any of these procedures had ever been performed at this hospital and told her it would be a good idea to get another urologic opinion."

"What'd she say?"

"She agreed. She suggested Parsons!"

"*The* Dr. Parsons?"

"The very same!"

"What'd you do?"

"I called the patient's primary physician and explained the situation. I told him what I had planned to do and that because of all the options and complexity of the situation I wanted to get another urologic opinion. I told him that I had spoken to the patient's wife and she suggested Dr. Parsons. I asked her to call you and ask you if you could call him."

"What did the primary doctor say?"

"He told me to call Parsons."

"What'd you do?"

"I called Parsons."

"You did?"

"I was not happy about it."

"I'm sure that was not a fun thing to do. How'd it go?"

"I was succinct and polite. When I told him the patient was missing seven centimeters of his left ureter he said to remove the kidney. I asked him if he could see the patient and put a note in his chart. He said he couldn't. I told him that he needed to call the attending and tell him that."

"What'd he say?"

"He hung up."

"That's it?"

"I called him back, and he wouldn't come to the phone."

"Yikes."

"Exactly."

"What'd you do then?"

"I called the attending and told him that Dr. Parsons couldn't see the patient and without seeing him he said he'd remove the kidney. I then told the attending I would be calling another urologist myself. He said okay."

"Who'd you call?"

"Barnes, who was doing a cysto next door."

"Did he see the patient?"

"Uh huh."

"What'd he say?"

"He wanted to know if the edges of the resected mass and remaining ureter were free of tumor. And he said that if I was going to connect the two ureters he would love to assist me."

"Did you discuss the other options?"

"He brought all of them up and we discussed each one."

"And?"

"We did the hookup."

"How'd it go?"

"Very well. It was a pleasure working with him."

"Had you ever worked with him before?"

"Not really. As we were starting the surgery he said he had actually done two of these operations in his residency program."

"Wow, that's great, Jamie. Is he your NBF?"

"My very best NBF!"

"So you were able to save his kidney after Parsons said he'd remove it. And you documented your conversation with Parsons with a phone conversation with the attending."

"Time will tell if the kidney has been saved and I haven't injured the good kidney. And if everything turns out right, Parsons will deny he ever spoke with me. But remember, removing the kidney was on my option list."

"Did you get a chance to speak with Rachel?"

"Tomorrow."

"I saw Ida a little while ago. She was out of bed and sitting in a chair."

"How was her urine."

"Slightly rose."

"I love that shade."

"I thought you loved clear or yellow."

"I was referring to post-op shades."

"Well, excuse me!"

CHAPTER 78

FINALLY, THE TÊTE-À-TÊTE

"can't believe we're finally having our conversation," said Bloom. "How's Ida doing?"

"I think she's doing well," replied Rachel. "She's still weak, I guess from the blood loss. She's taking her iron and stool softener. Her urine is almost clear. She's not taking any pain medicine. Does she still need the stool softener?"

"The stool softener is for the iron. Iron is very constipating."

"How long will she need to be on it?"

"We'll see after next week's labs. I think she'll probably still need to take it. Would you like some water or a soft drink before we start?"

"No thanks. I'm fine. I think I'm ready."

"When Ida started bleeding," began Bloom "she knew there would be no platelets available for her and since she had no new urinary symptoms to suggest a treatable condition, she resigned herself to die alone at home. She didn't tell you or me and did not ask for help. I don't know why she decided to call me, but luckily, she did. You and I spoke a short while ago about finding alternative platelet sources. She can't take your platelets and Stine's platelet source is no longer available."

"He killed her donor."

"That may be. But he did get platelets for her when she was in Cincinnati."

"I still don't believe that."

"Some time ago,"Bloom continued, not wishing to dwell on Rachel's reply, "Ida allowed me to look for another platelet donor. She gave me permission to search for her son Sigmund and any children he might have under the condition I wouldn't give her any unwanted information. I should have, but I never questioned her what that meant. On two prior occasions when her life was at stake and she was about to resign herself to die, she asked me to find him. I'm wondering this time, when she was bleeding and was accepting death, did she say anything to you about finding him."

"I never knew she was bleeding or was resigned to dying."

"Has she said anything to you about him since her surgery?"

Rachel shook her head.

"I don't know if you are aware, but Sigmund was adopted by the family that Ida cleaned for and he came back to the orphanage less than a year later after an explosion in his house killed everyone but him. And shortly after that he was 'taken' from the orphanage. I have been in contact with the orphanage and indirectly with the person who 'took' him. Her name is Adele Bekker and she has decided wants to speak with Ida. She says she has a lot to tell her that she's not told anyone else and would like to talk with her before she herself dies."

"This has nothing to do with me."

"This woman is in her nineties and just had a stroke and may not get this opportunity again."

"She can tell somebody else."

"She feels that what she has to say would have meaning for Ida and no one else."

"You want me to tell Ida to speak to her? I'll tell you right now I won't."

"Adele had been working directly under Hitler for six years and somewhat strangely began working at the orphanage one week before Sigmund was taken. It is probable she personally transported Sigmund to the United States and set him up with his new family."

"Why would Hitler have done that?"

"My feeling is he's Hitler's son. And it's probably yours and Ida's feeling as well. I think that's why Ida never went back to the orphanage after the war. Anyway, by that time, Sigmund was probably already in the United States and Ida never would have found him."

"All of this you know as fact?"

"To be confirmed if and when Ida speaks with Adele Bekker. I didn't expect you'd get involved, but I wanted you to understand where this could go."

"What does that mean?"

"You and Ida thought Hitler's or Mengele's semen might have been used for Ida's insemination in 1939 based on what was in your mother's diary from Auschwitz. Adele Bekker may know for sure. If Hitler's semen was not used, her son is from her and her husband. If that's the case, she might want to reconnect with Sigmund. And Sigmund might also be a match for her platelets. If Hitler's semen was used, then she might be able to justify her decision about giving up on him, but then there'll still be a strong likelihood Sigmund would be a match. Let me add this. Even if she was inseminated with Hitler's semen, Meyer still could have been the one who got her pregnant. My primary responsibility is to Ida—to get her platelets and keep her out of the hands of Stine and his henchmen."

"And my responsibility is also to Ida—not to cause her any emotional distress."

"I recognize your responsibility."

CHAPTER 79

A GOOD BAD REASON
TO SEE A DOCTOR?

"Guess what happened this weekend?" asked the almost completely white-haired Abe Buxbaum as Dr. Bloom applied a tourniquet to his right arm.

"You got a hole in one?" asked Bloom.

"Guess again."

"You caught a five-pound bass?"

"Last guess."

"You got the best erection of your life?"

"All great guesses. I turned eighty yesterday."

"Mazel tov," shouted Bloom and removed the tourniquet.

"Why'd you do that!?"

Bloom looked Buxbaum in his eyes and recited a variation of his patented soliloquy. "The practice of urology is evolving. For men over the age of eighty who have comorbidities and stable urologic examinations and no change in urinary symptoms and a stable PSA, the likelihood of finding a cancer that needs to be treated is unlikely and probably more harm would come from the diagnosis and treatment of the cancer than from the cancer itself. Cancer of the prostate is unlike other cancers. Ovarian and breast cancer needs to be totally removed to affect a cure, whereas for prostate cancer, where we can diagnose it in close to 80 percent of all men eighty years of age, only a small number of them need to be treated."

"You don't love me anymore, Dr. Bloom?"

"Of course I love you, Abe," replied Bloom, putting his arm around him. Then he replaced the tourniquet. "This'll be your last PSA. Okay?"

"I love you too, Dr. Bloom," replied Buxbaum. "And I trust you," he added removing the tourniquet himself.

Bloom smiled, then examined him, checked his urine, and told Aretha to make an appointment for one year.

"Why one year?" asked Buxbaum. "You see me every six months!"

"Abe, I think once a year is enough."

"You're telling me to find another urologist?"

"No! Of course not, Abe!" said Bloom chuckling.

"I love coming here!"

"I know that. And I love seeing you."

"Dr. Bloom, I go to many doctors. Almost every visit results in either making another visit to the same doctor who has found something else wrong with me or to an another physician or to a trip to a facility that does more tests. When I go to Dr. Bloom's office, he finds nothing wrong with me and he tells me everything is fine and to come back in six months. Now you're saying twelve months. I love coming here. You never find anything wrong with me!"

"Maybe Dr. Bloom is not a very good doctor," replied Bloom laughing. "Maybe you should see a urologist who can find something wrong with you. Aretha, I've changed my mind. Give Mr. Buxbaum an appointment for six months!"

"Dr. Bloom, Ida Stern is on line 2. She's been holding for ten minutes."

Bloom shook Buxbaum's hand, gave him a hug, and went into his office to pick up the lit line.

"I'm doing well, thanks to you, Jamie," said Ida. "Life is short."

"Sadly, yes, it is for many of us."

"Rachel and I talked yesterday, and I decided I want to hear what Adele Bekker has to say."

Bloom smiled, shook his head, and fist bumped himself. "Good. You're seeing me next Tuesday, right?"

"Uh huh. At 9:30 a.m."

"Let me see if the day and time are okay for her. I'll let you know."

"Okay. Should I bring Rachel with me?"

"Yes. That would be good. Speak with you soon. Goodbye."

Bloom hung up. He was able to get Marie Knoop to confirm Ida's call with Adele for that time and day and also get Adele's phone number. He called Ida and told her things were set. "This is exciting," he said out loud. "But I pray, as Missy said before, we haven't opened a can of worms."

CHAPTER 80

THE CALL

"Either of you want some coffee or something to drink before you make the call?" asked Bloom, getting ready to leave the consultation room.

"I'm fine," replied Ida. "I don't want to have to pee," she added, sitting in Bloom's black swivel chair, reaching for a phone, and glancing down at the white index card containing Adele Bekker's number.

"Same here," answered Rachel, seated on the pink couch next to the desk.

"I'll wait for you to make the call and then I'll be in the lab if you need me. Remember, speak slowly and loud enough for her to hear you. She speaks fluid German and English. There's writing pads and pens for both of you. Rachel, there's a clipboard on the desk for you. You may find it easier holding it while you're sitting on the couch. Even though you haven't asked for any, I've put two bottles of water on the desk for you. Try to write down as much as you can. Rachel, if you need to hear better, go into one of the exam rooms and pick up the lit line."

Bloom went into the lab and checked yesterday's urine cultures. He recorded the results in the patients' charts, spoke with them and called their pharmacies if necessary. He walked back to the consultation room door, which was ajar, peeked inside, and left after receiving a thumbs up sign from Rachel. He dictated some patient notes and spent a half hour on his phone. When he peeked in again, this time he got a thumbs up from Ida. He found Rachel, now in one of the exam rooms, and she like-wise gave a thumbs up. He left Rachel's room and relayed his pleasure to Cathy when she asked how things were going. After another twenty minutes when Bloom approached his consultation room, it appeared the conversation was winding down. Ida was crying as she thanked Adele and made plans for a second conversation. Rachel then joined Ida in the consultation room. Bloom waited in the other exam room and allowed the sisters to interact without him being in the way. Rachel was the first one to exit the consultation room. She appeared moved by what had transpired. Bloom allowed her to pass and approach Cathy. It was another ten minutes before Ida exited. Bloom now decided to exit the room and found the three women sobbing and hugging each other and made it a quartet without asking any questions or learning a single fact of the two women's conversation with Bekker. The office phone rang, and Cathy let it ring.

CHAPTER 81

THE HAPPIEST TIME OF HER LIFE

got stopped for speeding this afternoon," announced Missy, spotting Bloom walking into the family room from the garage via the laundry room.

"You got a ticket?" asked Bloom, opening his mouth and raising his eyebrows, giving her his best bewildered look. "You never speed. How fast were you going?"

"He said sixty. One of my long-term patients, whom I saw yesterday, tried to commit suicide this afternoon."

"Is the person okay?"

"Yes, she's doing better. No, I did not get a ticket."

"I'm glad. Where are our kids?"

"Playdates."

"When do we have to get them?"

"In an hour. Tell me about Ida Stern and Adele Bekker."

"And Rachel."

"She was there? I never would have let her be there."

"Ida wanted her there."

"How did that turn out?"

"Between the two of them, their entire conversation with Adele was chronicled. They started out in my consultation room, but after ten minutes Rachel went into one of the exam rooms and was able to hear

Adele and Ida better on the other phone. They both took notes. It's all here," added Bloom, showing Missy Aretha's and Cathy's typed pages.

"Should I read it?" asked Missy.

"You can, but I can tell you everything from memory, reading, and paraphrasing."

"Do you have time now?"

"It'll take less than ten minutes," replied Bloom putting the pages on the kitchen table.

"As we knew," began Bloom, "Adele was eager to tell her story. She said she had been a single woman working alongside Hitler from 1934 to 1943 and knew that he was concerned with his legacy and wanted a child. But she said Hitler was born with a severe penile deformity called hypospadias that required him to squat to urinate and made it impossible for him to use his penis to procreate. She also said that the incestuous relationship with his sister's niece Geli Raubal and the one with Eva Braun did not result in pregnancies and that she was pretty certain he hadn't had relations with either of them. She said there would be more about this at another time.

"When Mengele was experimenting with insemination, Hitler saw a pretty, fair-skinned, blue-eyed woman in the clinic who had two years of dental school training. So in 1939, when Ida went to the Berlin infertility clinic, he convinced Mengele to use Hitler's own semen instead of Meyer's for the insemination. Either he didn't know or care the woman was Jewish. Adele said that at the time of the insemination, Ida was told to refrain from having relations for a month following the insemination and to return in six weeks for a second insemination, again using Hitler's semen in place of Meyer's. Hitler had her pregnancy followed and knew where she delivered and who gave Sigmund his post-natal care. He also knew Ida worked for the Albrechts and had planned to get Sigmund into the orphanage and subsequently get him adopted by them. Adele said Hitler was upset with Meyer for burning Sigmund with a cigarette for his later identification, but was happy he had given him an anesthetic. He said under the circumstances Meyer probably did the best he could do, but in any event he knew Meyer would be dead shortly.

"Hitler regretted the Albrecht adoption. He was upset how Sigmund was taking to them. He wanted more control of how and what he was taught. He believed the easiest way to do this would be to get rid of the Albrechts. While Sigmund was out at the park with the Albrecht's maid, Hitler had someone come into their house and detonate a bomb, killing all three family members. As there were no other living relatives, Sigmund was brought back to the orphanage, and Adele Bekker was put in charge of orphanage activities. Hitler told her he wanted Sigmund to have an older brother. Three days later Edsel, who was older by two years, was brought over to the orphanage. Three months later, when Adele told Hitler the boys were bonding well, Hitler instructed Adele to take them out of the orphanage at 5:30 a.m. one morning and bring them to a home in his Berlin compound. They lived there for about two years. Adele primarily took care of Sigmund, and Gertrude Strauss took care of Edsel. Every day Adele spoke to Sigmund about Adolph Hitler and read to him for five hours, three in German and two in English. She also spent an hour each day showing him pictures and saying the names of German fighter planes and battleships, eventually teaching Sigmund to say *Der Vater* and *ich liebe dich Vater*. Gertrude Strauss treated Edsel similarly, but not with the same intense enthusiasm as Adele. She was older than Adele, had been married before, and likewise had no children. Edsel was already talking when she met him. She became attached to him but not to the extent Adele was to Sigmund. All four of them lived in the same house and a love developed between the boys, who spent almost all of their 'free' time playing with each other.

"Once a week Adele brought Sigmund to Hitler who hugged him and lifted him in the air. On a different day of the week, Gertrude brought Edsel to Hitler, who likewise lifted and hugged him. Hitler actually loved Sigmund, initially for his genetic makeup but later on due to Adele's teachings and showing reverence for him. But the love that Hitler felt for Sigmund was nothing compared to the love Adele felt for Sigmund. She said it was the happiest time of her life, seeing him waking up each morning, his smile, his giggle, his hugs and kisses, his first steps, his first words, the way he pronounced the names of the aircraft and ships. She said she cried when he spontaneously said to her *ich liebe dich mutter*. She thought Sigmund was the cutest, smartest, and sweetest child she had ever seen and didn't want to give him up. The best chance, she thought, for her and Sigmund to remain together would be for Germany to lose the war. But, she thought, wasn't that already happening? Didn't Great Britain and France declare war on Germany after the Germans invaded Poland in 1939? Weren't the Allied troops safely evacuated in the spring of 1940 in the Battle of Dunkirk, and didn't England defend itself against the German Luftwaffe in the summer of 1940 in the Battle of Britain? Didn't the Germans lose the Battle of Moscow in 1941? Didn't the U.S. enter the war in 1941 after Pearl Harbor? What about the Battle of Midway that Japan lost in 1942? And the Battles of Stalingrad and El Alamein? She had all these thoughts as the war went on. 'I'm glad no one was able to read my mind,' she said when these things were happening. 'And then it hit me, like a bolt out of the blue. Sigmund was not the Albrechts' son. He wasn't Hitler's son. He was not my son. He was Ida Stern's son. And I must hold onto him and pray Ida survives the war and she finds me or I find her! This is too much for me,' Adele added. 'I can't talk any more.' Then she hung up."

"Wow," said Missy teary-eyed, reaching for a tissue.

CHAPTER 82

WORRIED ABOUT ADELE

"Dr. Bloom, Ida Stern's on the second line," said Aretha, seeing Bloom entering the office. "Do you want to take it here or in your office?"

"I'd prefer my office," replied Bloom, nodding hello and walking past her and down the corridor into the consultation room. "Hi, Ida," said Bloom after picking up the phone.

"She's not answering her phone," began Ida.

"Who?"

"Adele Bekker."

"How long have you been trying?"

"Three days now! You remember she hung up abruptly?"

"I remember."

"I'm worried about her."

"I'll see what I can do."

"You'll let me know?"

"Of course."

"I like that lady."

"We all like her."

"I hope nothing happened to her."

"I'll call you as soon as I know."

"I hope she's okay."

"So do I. I'm hanging up now," said Bloom doing so. "Is the first patient here yet?"

"Mr. Gleason called and said he'd be a few minutes late," replied Aretha.

"Can you please get Marie Knoop for me?"

"Now?"

"Uh huh."

"Will do, Dr. Bloom."

"Thanks."

Five minutes later, Aretha said, "Dr. Bloom, Marie Knoop's on line 2."

"Hi, Marie," said Bloom. "Ida Stern called me today and said she's been unable to reach Adele Bekker. Is Adele okay?"

"As far as I know," said Marie. "You told me the day they spoke that they had a wonderful conversation with her. You also said Adele was so emotionally overwhelmed that she couldn't speak anymore and had to hang up. I haven't heard anything, and I don't have any other number for her other than the one Ida called her on. But I may have the name of the rehab facility where she's staying, hold on a second." After two minutes, she got back on the line. "She's at the Charite University Hospital in Berlin. I'll send you the number. Any questions, please call me. If you contact her, let me know how she's doing."

"Danke," replied Bloom. "Will do," he added then hung up.

Twenty minutes later Marie sent Aretha the hospital's number and Adele's room number. Bloom saw his first two patients and then had Aretha call Adele's hospital.

"The hospital is on line 1," said Aretha via the intercom.

What Bloom was able to learn, considering he was not related to the patient and was not the patient's physician and was calling from outside Germany, was that Adele had a TIA while speaking on the phone three days ago, and although she is now doing well, according to her physicians, she is no longer allowed to take calls from the United States, specifically from Ida Stern or her sister or anyone asking questions about her life in Germany during World War II. Bloom then called Marie Knoop and told her what he learned.

Marie said she would call Adele herself.

Bloom saw three more patients and called Ida to tell her what he had learned. An hour later Bloom got a call from Marie Knoop, telling him that she just spoke with Adele. Adele had said that she was told by her neurologist that her recent TIA superimposed on her CVA, which bodes an ominous prognosis, and so she must curtail all possible excitement. However, she felt that telling Ida the rest of her story needed to override whatever harm may come to her as a result.

The next patient was a quick wound check and the patient after that was still filling out his new patient forms. So Bloom took the opportunity to call Stern himself and tell her about the recent phone conversation Marie had with Adele.

"What do you think we should do?" asked Ida. "I certainly don't want to put Adele's health in jeopardy."

"Of course not," said Bloom. "But I wonder what's so important that she'd take such a chance with her life?"

"Maybe the name of the people to whom they entrusted Sigmund."

"I'll speak with Marie and see what we can do. I'll let you know what we come up with. How are you doing?"

"In what way?"

"Let's start with the information you've gotten so far from Adele. Sigmund had loving formative years with the Albrechts, Adele Bekker, and even Hitler to some degree. Hitler was gone from his immediate life before he was five. With what you know now, how do you feel about wanting to see him?"

"Yes, I would want to see him."

"Good. And how does Rachel feel about it?"

"The same."

"Good. Now tell me about your urine."

"It's fine. No more bleeding."

"Call my office to schedule a cystoscopy in about ten weeks."

"To follow up on the tumor you took out of my bladder?"

"Yes. Meanwhile I'll see what I can do about getting together with Adele."

"You spend a great deal of your free time worrying and taking care of me."

"You and Rachel are my family. It started when you saw my butt."

"I never forget a tuchus," replied Ida laughing.

"Touché," said Bloom meaning "tushie," trying to use another Yiddish butt variation.

"Marie Knoop's on line 2," came Aretha's voice over the intercom.

"Gotta go," Bloom said to Ida. "Gotta take another call."

"Okay, Jamie, I'm hanging up."

"Everything okay?" asked Bloom, surprised to hear from Marie so soon.

"I've been thinking," began Marie. "Adele's hospital is twenty minutes from me. I can pay her a visit and she can use my phone to call Ida, or you can call me when I'm with her and I'll hand her my phone. I can watch her face for any signs of upsettedness without hearing any of the conversation. I can run it by her if you and Ida want me to. What do you say?"

"I don't see why not. But I'll run it by Ida first. I'll let you know. Thanks."

"I'm off Sundays and Wednesdays. Either day is fine."

"I'll get back to you shortly. Thanks, Marie. You're a good person."

"Jamie, you're the best. Goodbye."

"Auf wiedersehen."

Bloom called Ida and immediately got the go-ahead for either day.

"The OR needs you, Dr. Bloom," said Cathy, now in the office using the intercom. "They can't get a catheter into a guy who's on the table."

"Okay, tell them I'm on my way," replied Bloom, telling her to ask the OR to get a 10 cc syringe, a tube of KY Jelly, a number 16 coude catheter, and the filiforms and followers. He then went into his waiting area and told the two patients in there that he had an emergency in the OR and should be back in about fifteen minutes.

He returned twenty minutes later, after injecting the patient's urethra with 10 ccs of KY Jelly and easily slipping the coude catheter in to drain his bladder.

CHAPTER 83

ADELE IS BACK IN THE LOOP

"This is Cathy from Dr. Bloom's office calling," said Cathy when Marie Knoop picked up the phone.

"Hi, Cathy. How are you?"

"I'm fine. So are all of us here. How are you?"

"As you say in the U.S., 'we're hanging in there.' You're calling about Ida?"

"Yes, this Saturday works for her. Is that okay with you?"

"Yes. I should be there with Adele by 9:00 a.m. your time. I'll call Dr. Bloom's office."

"Would you rather we call you?"

"Calling you is fine."

"You sure?"

"I'm sure."

"You have our office number?"

"I've dialed it a number of times."

"So we're on for this Saturday at 9:00 a.m. our time."

"Speak with you then. Goodbye."

"Wait, before you hang up, Dr. Bloom said you need to find out if Adele will let you stay there while they're talking. There may be some sensitive things she may not want to say in front of you. You may have to leave the room. Will that be okay? Or would she rather make the call herself with no one else in her room? We don't want her stifled. She's been waiting for over fifty years to tell her story."

"I'll ask her and get back to you."

"Danke."

One second after Cathy hung up, Dr. Winger called.

"Dr. Winger, hello," said Cathy. "Dr. Bloom is out of the office today. Can I take a message?"

"Please give him the message that William Stine is halfway through his chemo and is doing well. Hopefully he'll have a good second half. Dr. Bloom does not have to call me."

"Thank you. I'll tell him that when he calls in."

CHAPTER 84

THE UNMADE DECISION

"Hallo, Adele. Das ist Ida. Wie geht's. Ich bin hier mit Rachel."

"Hello, Ida and Rachel," replied Adele in English. "English is fine."

"Bist du sicher?" asked Ida.

"Yes, I'm sure. I will speak English."

"Okay," said Ida.

"I felt the war was lost when we invaded Russia in June 1941," began Adele. "By October 2, with little progress made and winter coming soon, we made a last-ditch effort to reach Moscow, but with the rain and ice our infantrymen were unable to advance. When we got to within seventeen miles of the Russian capital in November, the temperature was thirty degrees below zero. Our tanks froze, and we were still in our summer uniforms. On December 7, Japan bombed Pearl Harbor and the U.S. joined the war. We retreated from Moscow, and from then on we took a more defensive stance.

"In 1940 Hitler began to remove Jews from Berlin and put them into death camps—*Judenrein*, the clearing of the Jews from Germany. It was completed on June 16, 1943. Ida, when were you taken to Auschwitz?"

"Our entire family was taken to Auschwitz by boxcar in May 1940."

"Ida, Sigmund was born in October 1939?"

"October 13," added Ida.

"And brought to the orphanage in April 1940," continued Adele. "He was adopted by the Albrechts in June 1940, brought back to the orphanage in September 1940 after the explosion, and brought to Hitler's Berlin compound with Edsel in February 1941, where he stayed with me. At that time, I was thirty years old, unmarried, without children, and had worked closely with Hitler for eight years.

By 1942 Hitler thought Germany would lose the war. He became obsessed with two things. He wanted to be able to kill all the Jews his armies had gathered by building more death camps and making those already in use more efficient, and he wanted his son Sigmund to be embedded with a German family where he could be educated and finish the work Hitler had started.

I had other plans for Sigmund. But as the war progressed, the writing was on the wall, and the higher ups in the German high command became more concerned with their families' safety and began to plan exit strategies from Germany. This included shipping paintings and precious metal objects and all sorts of lootings from abandoned German homes and museums. Hitler became concerned with Sigmund's safety and talked about placing him in a German family outside of Germany. We'd butt heads regarding where Sigmund should be placed. I said I would stay and raise him here in Germany. Hitler disagreed. I thought of leaving Germany myself with Sigmund but realized we wouldn't get very far, and I would be executed. I didn't care about that except Sigmund would be left without someone who truly loved him. So, listening to Hitler, me taking Sigmund out of the country to be embedded with a German family, hopefully with me as his nanny, became an acceptable alternative. And of course, once Hitler was out of the picture, preferably dead, I'd look for Ida or whatever family members I could find and reunite them with Sigmund. I knew the German American Bund that had been established in 1936 had its headquarters in New York and was a possible place for Sigmund to be embedded, but I had no idea how he'd get there."

"I have a question," asked Ida.

"Sure," said Adele.

"How did Hitler accept the fact that Sigmund and Sigmund's mother Ida were Jewish?"

"He never mentioned it. I guess carrying on his dream and legacy were more important."

"Wasn't there a question also about Eva Braun's Jewishness?"

"Yes, there was."

"Was she ever impregnated by Hitler?"

"I wasn't going to get into it, but since you mentioned it, I don't think she could have gotten pregnant. She was diagnosed with Mayer-Rokitansky-Kuster-Hauser Syndrome, which is a congenital reproductive anomaly that results in an underdeveloped vagina and an absent uterus. As far as I know, she never became pregnant. And it's possible they never had relations. By the way, she and I were born on the same day February 6, 1912."

"Really? Did you know her?" asked Rachel.

"The public never saw her. I saw her on a few occasions. She was Hitler's private photographer. I was not with them when she and Hitler were married on April 29, 1945, nor the next day when they committed suicide and their bodies were burned. Enough of her."

"How are you doing?" asked Ida, remembering their last conversation. "Do you want to take a break?"

"No. I'm fine. Let's go on. Basically everything heightened over the next year. Hitler focused on the killings, insisting on daily death reports from all labor and death camps as well as the ones on the streets caused by dogs, drownings, falling off rooftops, and being runover by steamrollers. Hitler's obsession with numbers also resulted in the killing of hundreds of non-Jewish Germans by Germans. He started seeing Sigmund twice a week and had a small Ferris wheel constructed in his compound along with a petting zoo.

"In December 1942, when I was bringing Sigmund to Hitler, I overheard Hitler on the phone with Pope Pius Il. Two days later Hitler told me I was going to New York with Sigmund and Edsel within the week, traveling first by train to Rome and then by ship to New York. Two weeks later we left Berlin at 5:00 a.m. and arrived in New York at 9:00 a.m. two weeks and a day later. Both boys loved the train and ship. They had window seats whenever they could. The ship's captain let them hold the wheel. It was a pleasure to have them with me. When we passed Customs, we were met by four German-speaking men and women (two couples) who transported us to a very nice home in Brooklyn. They all spoke German and English fluently. Both couples were childless and both wives suffered three miscarriages. One woman was twenty-eight, the other thirty-two.

I told them the boys were born in Germany, had no living relatives, and were raised together in the same household in Berlin by two caregivers for the past two-plus years. I told them the younger one, Sigmund, was recently three and the son of a high-ranking German official and the older boy, Edsel, was five and that the boys could not be separated. I took the liberty—I never discussed it with Hitler—of telling them I would be their nanny for at least six months or more depending on their needs and that I would be paid by Germany. I showed them the boys' birth certificates and passports, which they inspected and took. One couple said they only wanted the younger child; the other wanted both. That made things easy. I asked the latter couple to be taken to their home along with the kinder and our luggage. On the way to their home, we passed many stores that had German signs in their windows. Their house was a two-story home across the street from an elementary school with an attached playground.

"The next morning I made a collect call to Berlin and brought Hitler's personal secretary up to speed. I told her I thought I should stay with the new family for a while during the boys' transitioning, especially before I gave them any money. His secretary said Hitler'd get back to me. The next day his secretary replied that the Fuhrer was pleased and said I should stay and use some of the money I was to give to the family for my personal use as necessary and that I should give the Fuhrer weekly updates."

"Great!" said Ida and Rachel together.

"After staying with the parents Oskar and Karen Fuchs and the kinder for six weeks," continued Adele, "Karen asked me how long was I planning to stay with them. I told them I had planned for six months and then we'd see if it'd be okay for me to go back to Germany. Karen thought she and her husband and the kinder were doing well together and asked me how I thought things were progressing. I told her I thought they were progressing nicely and that the difficult period would be when I left. I said I would remain in the U.S. during the next transition period.

"One day they decided to take the boys to the Prospect Park Zoo. I asked them if they'd like to go without me and they said I could take the day off and return that night or the next day. I asked them again if the next day would be okay and they said yes. The next day Oskar and Karen couldn't wait to see me.

Karen asked me, 'Did you know they knew the name of every animal in German and English?'

I nodded.

'And did you know that Edsel could read English and German? I guess you did. Did you teach him?'

'Someone named Gertrude Strauss taught him. I taught Sigmund.'

'Why are you smiling?' asked Karen.

'You'll see that Sigmund can also read, though not as well.'

Karen frowned.

'Do you have a book nearby?' I asked.

'German or English?'

'Either.'

'Let him sit on your lap, give him the book, turn to a page, and ask him to read.'

After she did, Sigmund said, 'Then Jaaack climmed the been stork.'

'Amazing!' said Karen.

'Not only are the boys amazingly smart, but they're also amazingly good. As for Sigmund, he also has a very good memory. Maybe he's just remembering what you've read to him. Next time try him on something he's never heard or seen. Regarding the animals, we lived within walking distance of a petting zoo. I also taught him the names of the German fighter planes and Battleships.'

'You said he was recently three?'

'Yes, three months ago. I showed you his birth certificate.'"

After a brief pause, Adele said, "Let me continue telling my story. One day Edsel came to me crying, and I remember what was said like it happened this morning.

'What's wrong Edsel?' I asked, hugging him. 'Don't you feel okay?'

'When is die mutter coming to take care of me?' he sobbed.

"I knew this was coming. I was surprised it hadn't come weeks before. I hugged him again and then too started to cry. 'I am leaving soon, too. Your new mutter will be taking care of you. You and Sigmund will be brothers and Karen and Oskar will be your new Mutter and new Vater.'

'I don't want a new Mutter,' cried Edsel. 'Does Sigmund want a new Mutter?'

'No. But Gert and I live in Germany. We were taking care of you until we could find you and Sigmund your own Mutter and Vater. Karen and Oskar will be your new Mutter and Vater.'

'I want Gert to be my Mutter.'

'What about your Vater?'

'Oskar can be my Vater but I want Gert to be my Mutter.'

'Karen and Oskar will be a good Mutter and Vater for you and Sigmund and you will be Sigmund's brother. Isn't that nice?'

'Why can't you be our Mutter?'

'I have to go back to Germany.'

'Why can't I go back with you to Gert?'

'Because Germany is not safe. There is a war going on there. That's why I've brought you both here, to get a new Mutter and Vater and become a family. Don't you love Sigmund?'

'Yes, very much.'

'And he loves you very much.'

'I know,' said Edsel. 'I don't want you to go,' he sobbed. 'Sigmund and I love you. Don't you love us?'

"I started to cry, and Edsel hugged me. 'Of course I love you both. And Gert loves you. You will understand when you're older,' I said, now sobbing.

'When will that be? Why can't I understand now?'

'You will someday.'

'I'm telling you now that I won't,' said Edsel sobbing more than before.

"At that moment I wanted to pick him up, grab Sigmund and take them out of that house and hide somewhere with them forever. Looking ahead, I'm so sorry I didn't. So sorry," said Adele sobbing. "I need to stop now," she said. "We'll continue some other time. I'm hanging up."

"That sounded ominous," Ida commented to Rachel.

"Maybe because later she and Gert lost contact with the boys."

"We'll call her back in a few minutes and make sure she's okay."

CHAPTER 85

A VERY RARE CONGENITAL ABNORMALITY

"When they called her back, her line was busy," said Bloom, speaking from home, after telling Marie Knoop the circumstances of the abrupt hang-up from Adele.

"Did you call Charite Hospital?" asked Marie.

"I had Ida call. I thought she'd have a better chance of getting through."

"Did she?"

"It was busy."

"I'll try in a little while and let you know if I learn anything."

"Or not. Thanks, Marie."

"Or not," dittoed Marie.

While he was waiting for the call back, a ninety-year-old woman with urinary bleeding called Bloom's office and said she was born with untreated bladder exstrophy, but had been doing okay until that morning when she started to bleed. She said she had called five other urology offices who told her they didn't treat that condition and was told to go to the University of Miami ER. When the woman called and spoke with Aretha, Aretha spoke with Dr. Bloom, who told her to make an appointment for the woman today. "You want me to call Miami?" she had asked. Bloom laughed.

"No!" he replied, "not Miami. Make her an appointment with our office! For today!"

Bloom came to the office without hearing from Marie. The new patient had arrived there twenty minutes before. Bloom read Aretha's intake note on Alma Dixon prior to seeing her. She was born in 1910 in Macon, Georgia. According to her mother, the attending physicians had said her daughter had exstrophy of the bladder, meaning the bladder was missing its front wall, and nothing could be done to fix it, that she should be brought home and she would probably die in a week or two, and if she happened to survive, her mother was told she'd be incontinent of urine her entire life. She survived and has been in diapers for ninety years. She married at age forty and has been married for fifty-two years. She had normal menstruations and had gotten pregnant and miscarried five times. Bloom was concerned about the possibility of bladder cancer because cancer was very common with bladder exstophy due to the long-term irritation to the bladder wall from the urine and diapers.

"Alma could not give me a urine sample," said Aretha as she brought Mrs. Dixon into the consultation room. Bloom smiled at the patient, and she nodded and smiled back. Both knew that bladder exstrophy patients cannot store their urine and thus cannot give a urine sample. The patient looked younger than her stated age. She was attractive, well dressed, and well made up.

"You are Congresswoman Alameda Dixon, aren't you?" asked Bloom.

"How could you possibly know that?" she replied surprised, her jaw dropping.

"The Georgian Peach," added Bloom smiling.

"How do you know about me?"

"I read the newspapers."

"I haven't been in the papers for over fifty years, and that's way before you were born."

"My grandfather's always talking about his brother and about you."

"Who's your grandfather's brother?"

"Was. He died in 1944."

The patient froze and stared into space. It took thirty seconds before she was able to speak. "Was you grandfather's brother James Bloomington?"

"Yes, ma'am."

She gasped, swallowed hard, and began to breathe rapidly. She spoke after composing herself. "We were supposed to be married in June 1945," she said sighing. "He died in 1944."

"I know," said Bloom, nodding. They both took deep breaths.

"I'm Jamie Bloom. I'm his namesake!"

They both stood up, walked toward each other, and embraced. When they separated, they each reached for the tissue box on the corner of the desk.

A few seconds later, Bloom said, "That happens about two to three times a week here."

Alma blinked, then said, "You have James's sense of humor. Let me bring in my husband."

"We'll bring him in after I see you."

Bloom took her history, brought her to the exam room, and told her to wait for Cathy, who would get her ready for the examination. Before he took Cathy to the exam room, he took her into his office and showed her on a piece of paper what she would be seeing.

"The patient is missing the front of her bladder. You're going to see a raw area that has two little mounds quirting urine from her kidneys onto the sheet covering her. Don't gasp, turn away, or say anything. You will never see anything like this again. This is the way she was born. There is surgery to fix this, but it was not readily available where and when she was born. In time she came to accept this as herself. Have her undress from the waist down and cover her with a sheet. I will be very upset with you if you don't look at her abdomen when I remove the sheet."

Bloom brought Cathy to the patient and put them in the exam room. Five minutes later Cathy yelled "ready," and Bloom came into the room. He had the patient sit up, and he tapped both costovertebral angle regions. He then put her back down, put on gloves, and palpated her kidneys, epigastrium, and upper abdomen. He gently pulled down the sheet to expose her lower abdomen. The front of her abdominal wall was missing. The posterior bladder wall contained two small mounds with nipples representing the ureteral orifices, which were separated by the trigone. Clear urine was seen intermittently spurting from each ureteral orifice. On the trigone there was a friable raised erythematous irregular area about 1.5 centimeters squared that was bleeding, most likely an adenocarcinoma, the most common type of cancer with this condition. Both the urethra and vagina were shortened, and the vagina was stenotic. Bloom was unable to penetrate her vagina with his pinky. Her clitoris was bifid. On examination, the uterus was normal as was the rectum. Bloom thought about the ordeal they probably had to go through to have intercourse, if that was even possible, and for her to become pregnant. He thought that had she been seen at a major institution after she was born or any time thereafter, she could have been made continent and, with gynecologic surgery, could have been able to have had normal intercourse and possibly carried a pregnancy to term. He told the patient to get dressed after he left the room and to ask to get whatever supplies she needed from Cathy and meet him in his consultation room where he would bring in her husband. Bloom found him in the waiting area, introduced himself, and brought him to his office where he was to wait for his wife. Bloom waited a few minutes for Alma to join her husband and waited a few more minutes for them to speak with each other before he entered.

"Another ordinary day at Dr. Bloom's office," said Bloom, sitting down.

"You were the last name on the list," said Alma.

"All the others should have seen you."

"Why did you see her?" asked her husband, Charlton.

"I've seen bleeding with this congenital anomaly before, and it turned out to be a skin irritation, which responded to a cream. You never know what you're going to find, an irritation, an infection, a stone, a tumor."

"What did you find?"

"She has a lesion on the tigone between the ureteral orifices. It needs a biopsy."

"What do you think?" asked Charlton.

"Tumors are very common with exstrophy. The lining gets irritated by the urine and whatever is used to cover the open bladder. With newborns we construct a new bladder so the urine no longer stays on the surface. And we do plastic surgery on the vagina to permit normal intercourse and pregnancies. These options were not yet fully developed ninety years ago but are now widely available. You managed to go through life unscathed except for the incontinence. Having relations had to have been an ordeal, if even possible. The same for the pregnancies.

I'll need you to tell me when your last doctor's visit was, what blood tests you have had, whether you have seen a gynecologist recently, and what recent X-rays you have had. You'll need a CT of your abdomen and pelvis to see the status of your kidneys and see what's doing behind the back of your bladder."

"What if it's cancerous? Am I better off at a major center?" asked Alma.

"It's always better to be at a major center. There's always the possibility that a cancer might be able to be treated with instruments that don't involve making a cut. Most bladder cancers are handled by scrapping and burning away the cancerous tissue, not excising it with a scalpel. The most important issue in treating cancer is the extent of the cancer and whether it is curable by surgery or some other form of treatment. In your case, your age will probably not include extensive bladder surgery, and radiation might be the option that's recommended."

"Is your grandmother alive?"

"Yes. She's four years younger than you."

"Where would you take her if she had what I had?"

"I'd take her to see a urologist at a major medical center that treats bladder cancer. And I would say no matter how much or little cancer they found, she would probably not have a major operation. Where do you live?"

"We live in Raleigh, North Carolina. Right now, we're on vacation."

"Let me ask you a question. If you find you don't have cancer and nothing needs to be done, are you content with your life as is or would you go through surgical reconstruction to make you continent and make sexual relations more enjoyable. Let me say first, because of your age, you may not be able to find surgeons who would be willing to put you through the necessary surgeries to accomplish this."

Nearly in unison, they both said they didn't think they would do it.

"Tell us what you would recommend," said Charlton.

"Some lab tests, a CAT scan, medical clearance, an anesthetic, and a bladder biopsy."

"Can you do a biopsy in the office?"

"No, you need to get a good biopsy. That means not only determining whether there's malignancy present but also the extent or degree of invasiveness if there is. And tumors bleed. There's always a possibility of severe bleeding during and after a biopsy. It needs to be done in a hospital setting, maybe as an outpatient. I would go to Raleigh for starters."

"And do what?"

"Find a urologist with a background in oncologic surgery to do the biopsy. If you can't find one, I'll find one for you. Depending on the extent of the cancer and your general health, a team will decide what's the best option for you. It may be radiation is recommended, but we're getting way ahead of ourselves. I'm not terribly familiar with those areas of the county, but anything that needs to be done can be done there. Again, all things being equal, the biopsy should be done close to home."

"Does she definitely need a biopsy?"

"The short answer is yes. The problem is if the bleeding gets worse, you don't want to be on the road. And that could happen after a biopsy. The more I think about it, the more I feel the safest thing to do is go back to Raleigh, sooner rather than later. Can the bleeding stop by itself and nothing needs to be done? I'll vote for that!"

"Me too," said Alma and Charlton together.

"If that should happen, please see someone anyway in Raleigh."

The couple nodded.

"Here's my phone number," said Bloom, writing it on his business card and handing it to them. "Also, if you're having a problem when going north, the Mayo Clinic Jacksonville would be a good stopping point. Now that I've thoroughly confused you, what do you think you're going to do?"

"Dr. Bloom, Marie Knoop is on line 1," Aretha said through the intercom. "Do you want to come and take it up front?"

"I need to take this call," Bloom told the Dixons.

"Sure," replied Alma.

Bloom left and returned two minutes later. He was smiling.

"Everything okay?" asked Charlton.

"Very much so," answered Bloom. "Thank you."

"We're leaving today and hope we don't have to stop before getting to Raleigh."

"Remember, for now you need to see a urologist if you're en route and the bleeding gets worse, and once you get to Raleigh see a urologist who treats bladder cancer. Exstrophy does not seem an issue at this moment. You have my number. Let me add my home number," said

Bloom, taking his card back and adding the number. "Come with me to the front desk and take your supplies with you. If there's severe bleeding, apply a pad or two, scrunch up a towel, put it over the area that's bleeding and apply pressure, like this," added Bloom, taking one of the towels and making a ball out of it and pressing it against his abdomen.

"I forgot to tell you something."

"I'm listening."

"I'm on blood thinners. I don't know how I forgot."

"For what?"

"A fib."

"What are you taking?"

"Coumadin."

"Are you bleeding anywhere else?"

"No."

"Have you ever had any blood clots?"

"Both legs."

"When was that?"

"The last time was ten years ago."

"When were you put on blood thinners?"

"Six years ago."

"For A fib?"

"Yes."

"Do you have a cardiologist?"

"Yes. You want his number?"

"Please. I need to speak with him. Is he in Raleigh?"

"Yes."

"I'm probably going to take you off your Coumadin because you'll need to be off it anyway for your biopsy if it needs to be done. There should be no problem if you're off it for a few days. We'll need his address to send him a copy of our office notes."

Bloom accompanied the Dixons to Aretha's station and had her call the cardiologist.

"Call me when you get him on the phone."

Bloom went back to his office, wrote some additional notes in Alma's chart, and started to dictate a summary of today's office visit.

"Dr. Woodmont's on line 1," came across the intercom.

Bloom spoke with the cardiologist and got permission to stop her Coumadin. He then said goodbye to the Dixons, finished dictating Alma's office visit, and called Ida to tell her that Adele is fine and was just having trouble with her phone but said she would be back in touch soon.

CHAPTER 86

WHAT TO DO ABOUT GOLD

"Robert Gold is on line 2," said Cathy via the intercom. "He said he needs to speak with you."

"Do you know what it's about?"

"It sounded serious."

"Tell him I'm finishing up with a patient. Ask him if I can call him back in ten minutes."

"Will do."

"You don't have to buzz me again if it's alright."

"How many times have you ejaculated since your vasectomy?" Bloom asked the new patient.

"About six times."

"How long ago was the vasectomy?"

"Six weeks."

"Your exam was normal. You're too soon after the procedure to expect complete clearing of the semen of sperm. Continue with birth control and bring in another sample in four more weeks. I don't physically have to see you."

"Is this normal?"

"It can take a couple months for the sperm to clear. Did your urologist show you the pieces of vas he removed?"

"I don't remember him showing them to me."

"Some urologists do and some don't."

"So I shouldn't worry?"

"Just continue using birth control for now. Ask the nurse for a container as you're leaving. Just remember, you must continue using something for birth control until a urologist tells you no longer need to do so. My secretary will give you a sheet you must sign before you leave to this effect."

When the patient left the office, Bloom asked Cathy to call Mr. Gold.

Two minutes later, Cathy said, "He's on line 2."

"TTRVM," shouted Robert Gold, following up with, "TCAM!"

"What?" said Bloom.

"TCAM! TCAM!"

"I don't understand!" shouted Bloom.

"Through the rearview mirror, they're coming after me! Through the rearview mirror, they're coming after me!"

"Who's coming after you, Bob? Who's coming after you?"

"They are! The people who took my kidney!"

"Why are they coming after you, Bob?"

"They're coming after me, Dr. Bloom!"

"Tell me, why are they coming after you, Bob?"

"They want my other kidney! I got a call a week ago from someone who knew I was once on the National Tissue Registry, like last time. They said they were a match for my kidney, and they wanted me to be a donor. I told them I only have one kidney now. They said they knew that. They offered me $500,000. I told then I wasn't interested and hung up. They called back the next day and said they'd pay me a million dollars. I said I still wasn't interested and hung up again."

"Do you have a name or phone number?"

"I have nothing."

"Have you called anyone?"

"I didn't know who to call."

"Did the voice sound familiar?"

"No."

"Last week was April 1st. Do you have any friends who might be playing a trick on you?"

"No. I'm very scared, Dr. Bloom. Very scared."

"Do you have the National Kidney Registry's number and any other numbers regarding kidney recipients and donors? Do you have a registry number or the name of a person you can speak with?"

"Shouldn't I go to the police?"

"Probably. Let me think about it. I need to see some patients. I'll try to call you later."

Bloom hung up and sat back in his chair. *Maybe scratching my head will help me think how to get him out of this dilemma. I'm sure when I speak to Missy, she'll ask me why is this dilemma my dilemma? It's my dilemma because he's my patient and he's asked for help. Although it's a kidney problem, it's not a urologic problem, but my acquaintance with Stine may allow me to play some sort of role in getting him to act on Gold's behalf. Missy will probably say Stine will then expect a quid pro quo, like persuading Ida to give up her marrow. You never want to put yourself in a position like that, she'll say. And I'll say, like old times, I'll . . . we'll always be in that position. So, I'm probably spinning my wheels talking to Missy. Maybe she'll surprise me. Nah.*

He called Gold back. "Are you still going to that ice cream store? If you are, don't go there anymore. Speak to the police. Get a gun, learn how to use it, and carry it with you. Hire a bodyguard. Ask to be put in witness protection." *Or take the million dollars,* thought Bloom to himself.

CHAPTER 87

ADELE: FINAL CHAPTER

"Adele Bekker's on line 1," said Aretha via the intercom.

"Got it," replied Bloom, jumping up from his seat in the lab and rushing into his office and picking up. "Hi Adele," said Bloom, surprised by the call. "How are you?"

"I'm fine. You have time to talk now?"

"Of course!"

"Are you with a patient?"

"There'll be none for the next thirty minutes."

"I won't be that long."

"We appreciate very much what you're doing for all of us, and that certainly includes me."

"It's nice what you're doing for her, and me."

"We love you, Adele."

"And I love you all, too. I know I dropped a bomb right before I hung up with you a few days ago. Sorry, poor analogy," she said chuckling.

"I appreciate the humor."

"I'm glad. Basically I'm sorry I said what I said about grabbing the boys and whisking them away from that family."

"Yes, we thought something ominous was coming and it wasn't just that you wouldn't be seeing them much again."

"That's why I called to speak with you. I have nothing more to say that's good. I only have a lot to say that's bad. But I don't want to tell them."

"Ida and Rachel? You're calling to tell me instead?"

"I'm not sure you'll be okay after you hear this."

"Were they alive and in one piece when you last heard about them?"

"That they were."

"That's good. So why don't you tell me."

"You're easy to talk to, Dr. Bloom."

"Please don't call me that. My name is Jamie."

"Okay, Jamie. Here goes. From what I've already told you, you can see that I was in no hurry to leave the Fuchs house. After four more months in Flatbush, Karen suggested it was time for me to leave, which was sooner than the six months I had anticipated, but Sigmund and Edsel appeared to be satisfactorily adapted to Karen and Oskar, their home, and surroundings. Edsel had started Kindergarten and Karen taught third grade at the school across the street, while Sigmund remained with Oskar, who was a writer and worked at home. I had developed a relationship with the nanny from next door, also named Adele, who cared for two girls who were about the same ages as our boys.

"In June 1943, when Karen told me it was time for me to say goodbye to Sigmund and Edsel, that was the most difficult day of my life. I'm sure it was as well for the boys. When Karen saw us crying inconsolably, she asked me to leave on the spot. I told her I'd remain in New York for three weeks and she could call me any time. She said she wasn't going to call me and that I could go back to Germany that day. She also said she needed more money for their children's care, as was promised her. I gave her five hundred dollars. When she asked when she could be expecting the next payment, I told her it was dependent on how the boys were doing and how well she kept us informed of their progress. Karen wasn't particularly thrilled for me to call her regularly, even though I said I was calling for a high-ranking German official. I kept tabs on the boys via the other Adele. I never asked to speak with either Sigmund or Edsel, although I heard on several occasions when they knew I was on the phone and asked to speak with me. I heard Karen say to them, "She can't talk now." When I told Hitler about her reluctance to speak with me, he asked me if they were still getting their money, and when I told him yes, he said to continue giving it to them. When she refused to take any calls, and I found out the money was now in my name, I decided to withhold a tidy sum of one million dollars from them. In December 1943, 1 heard from Adele that Edsel was caught exposing himself and kissing the genitals of boys in his class. When Karen found naked pictures of Sigmund, Edsel, and Oskar in Oskar's closet she confronted Oskar, and when he denied it, she called the police and eventually Oskar was removed from the house. Karen, Oskar, and the boys underwent whatever counseling was available at that time and continued to stay as a family without Oskar. In April 1944, Karen was diagnosed with breast cancer and as she had no family members that could stay with or care for the children, she hired a nanny while she was receiving treatment. Karen died a year later, on the same day Hitler and Eva Braun committed suicide, and the New York courts refused to allow Oskar custody of the boys. They became wards of the state. Japan surrendered in August after bombs were dropped on Hiroshima and Nagasaki. The war was nearly over. I remembered thinking, if only there was a way to get the boys back to Germany. I remembered the passports Hitler gave me in case the boys were ever to come back, but I had given them to the Fuchs. Since the boys now had no family in the U.S., I thought maybe they could be sent back to Germany. But who would accept them? I certainly would have and so would Gert. But being a single parent in the world's climate those days meant it would not have been permitted.

"Hitler was gone, so was his clout. I think if Ida had come back to the orphanage after the war, both boys still would have been gone, but because of what happened to them in the U.S. they might have been sent back to Germany. I certainly would have paid for the transportation. I asked Adele if she could find out the name, address, and phone number of the place where the boys were taken and she did. God bless her! I called Flatbush Ave Foster Care and learned they were there. I told foster care who I was and asked to speak with the head nurse. They told me her name was Nancy Washington. When she got on the phone, I told her my relationship with the boys and that I was the one who took care of them in Germany where they were born. She asked me If I was familiar with their history and told her I was the one that brought them here from Germany and stayed with them and their adoptive parents as their nanny for around four months. When I said I wanted to speak with Edsel, I was told his name was now Eddie and that he didn't want to speak with me. I asked about Eddie's brother and was told that neither Eddie nor Ziggy wanted to speak with me. I mentioned that when

I brought them to the U.S. to be adopted I gave their passports to their adoptive parents Karen and Oskar Fuchs and that Oskar still might have them. I told her I'd like the boys to be brought back to Germany. Nancy asked me if the birth mother was alive, and I said she was sent to Auschwitz during the war, and I was waiting for her to return to the orphanage where she dropped Sigmund off before she was taken to the concentration camp.

'Is there a family in the U.S. that can take them?'

'I don't know if there are any alive relatives anywhere. I honestly was raising Ziggy with the hope of finding his mother Ida Stern and handing him over at that time. Ziggy met Eddie in the orphanage and they were raised as brothers. That's why I took them both to New York to be adopted by a German family. I raised Ziggy, and my friend Gertrude Strauss raised Eddie. We raised them together in the same house. I don't know who Eddie's parents were. Ziggy and Eddie have been together almost since birth and had lived as brothers. The last time I saw them was two years ago when they were three and five. They were wonderful boys.'

'They may have been wonderful two years ago,' said Nancy 'but they're anything but wonderful now.'

'This has been a rough year for them. They need all the love they can get, and I want to give it to them. Did you know that both boys were reading by age three? They were also fluent in English and German also by age three.'

'Are you married?' asked Nancy.

'If I were, I would have been down there already.'

'Start looking for a husband.'

'Can I come down there and fly back with them to Germany and wait for Ziggy's mother?'

'There's no question that you may be the absolute best person to have these kids and it's a crime against mankind that you can't obtain custody of them. Maybe in a more civilized world and in a different period of time, this might be commonplace.'

'Aren't there cases where exceptions to the rule result from what's in the best interest of the children? After listening to me and hearing their story, might the powers that be allow me to transport the children to Germany where I will deliver them to Ziggy's mother or raise them as my own, assuming their adopting father agrees? The judge knows Oskar can never see them or live with them.'

'What attempt have you made to contact Ziggy's mother?'

'Hitler's dead, but the war is not officially over. Japan has been bombed twice. I think they just surrendered yesterday. Thousands are still in concentration camps. There's no list yet of the dead or survivors.'

'First, no matter what, you have to find out if Oskar is willing to give up or by law can be forced to give up his children. I don't think by law he can be forced, but I may be wrong. And second, there's the question of whether an unmarried woman or two unmarried women or men can adopt.'

'Could you possibly run this by someone who had some experience with these situations?'

'I think you'd have to speak with Oskar Fuchs yourself. I'll try to find someone who might be helpful. I can't promise anything. My advice is for you to speak with Oskar Fuchs first. He may want some money to do this and not just a one-time payment. And he might be happy to shed the burden of being a father with no rights. I would also look for a husband. Basically, you need a husband and a lawyer.'

"I was happy and surprised, mainly happy that Nancy didn't ask me why I was bringing two German boys out of the country to be adopted, especially since one of the boys and his mother was Jewish and he was adopted by a non-Jewish German family. Hitler would probably have been brought into the conversation."

"I thought the same thing. So what did you do?" asked Bloom.

"I called Oskar Fuchs."

"How was he?"

"He was mourning his wife. He missed the boys. He said he'd been going to therapy three times a week. He'd wanted to get the kids back, but he didn't think that was going to happen."

"Did you ask about giving up the boys?"

"He said only if he could never see them. He said he'd wanted to see them with supervision. But, again, didn't think that was going to happen."

"So then what?"

"He said he might have to think about giving them up. But not now or in the near future."

"Did you ask him if he was thinking about himself and not his kids?"

"He mentioned that to me."

"Did you tell him you wanted to take care of his kids?"

"He knew that."

"Did you tell him you might be able to give him supervised visits?"

"No. But he asked me."

"What'd you say?"

"I said I would if it was okay with his psychiatrist."

"And what if it wasn't?"

"Then, no," I said. "I told him that when I said that Sigmund and Edsel are wonderful boys, Nurse Washington said the boys may have been wonderful when I knew them, but they're not so wonderful now. I also told him their names were now Ziggy and Eddie."

"'I know their behavior took a turn after you left,' said Oskar. 'When Karen got cancer,' he said, 'we should have called you to come back to Brooklyn to be their nanny. Not calling you was a mistake. With her being sick and me not having a presence in the house, the boys were neglected. I hope they haven't gone too far astray.'

'I've given a lot of thought of getting married and coming to the US to live,' I said, 'but if you're not ready to have me take care of them, there's nothing I can do. Right now, they don't want to talk to me. They probably feel that I've abandoned them, which I have. Honestly, that was Karen's and your doing. Karen was upset with the boys' attachment to Gert and me. She literally thew me out of the house when she saw them sobbing when I had to leave. She wasn't mature or secure enough to understand their attachment to Gert and me. We each spent five hours each day speaking German and English to them, along with teaching them German history and giving them a huge amount of history and science and hugs. Sigmund spontaneously called me *mother* one day. I truly loved him.'

'I know that,' he said.

'So, I'll start working on getting a husband.'

'I'll think about what you told me. I hope we don't lose them,' he said. I remember thinking to myself, I think we may already have.

"So that was my conversation with Oskar," said Adele to Bloom. Do you want to talk some more or continue some other time?"

"Adele, you're truly amazing. Are you sure you're not Mother Teresa?"

"Mother Teresa died five years ago. The only thing she and I have in common is that we were both born in 1910."

"On the same day as you and Eva Braun?"

"Almost. Should I go on?"

"Please."

"Obviously time was of the essence."

"I'll say."

"And we needed to get Gert involved in order get to Eddie."

"Of course. Eddie wouldn't even speak with you."

"Eddie should have had a better memory of Gert than Ziggy of me."

"So you didn't think you had to worry about Oskar at that point?"

"I thought his best chance to legally see his kids was if they were with us. Of course, he could always have tried to see them illegally when they were outside their facility."

"You think he was already doing that?"

"Very possibly."

"Did you and Gert go Brooklyn?"

"That we did. We flew into La Guardia airport, which opened six years before. Nurse Washington greeted us and took us into her office.

'Do you want to see them together or separately?' Washington asked.

'Let's see them both together,' I said.

'Is there a different room where we can see them?' Gert asked. 'Where we can have some privacy?'

'Yes, come with me,' Washington said, walking them down the hallway and putting them in an empty room. 'Do you want me to bring them in now?'

'Please,' Gert answered.

Washington left the women and returned two minutes later with the boys. She waited a few seconds to make sure there were no outbursts and closed the door behind her. The boys walked to the back of the room and faced the back wall. Gert spoke first.

'Eddie, do you know who I am?' she asked.

Eddie did not reply.

'Do you know my name?' she asked.

Still no answer.

'Would you like to say something to me?' Still no response.

'You can say anything you want. Anything. I just want to hear your voice.'

'Fuck you, Gert,' said Eddie.

'Fuck you, Gert. Anything else you'd like to say? Soon we'll be gone, Eddie. Don't lose this opportunity to say what you really want to say!'

'I said what I wanted to say.'

'I taught you to express yourself better than that.'

After a few seconds Eddie spoke. 'You abandoned us and left us with a faggot father and an unfit mother.'

'Eddie, that wasn't our plan. You didn't belong to us. You were on loan to us. We had no control of your future. We thought we were leaving you with a good mommy and daddy. We know now the people who adopted you were no good. We came back because now we have a say in your future.'

'What's done is done. We are now what we'll always be.'

'And what is that, Eddie?'

'We're bad. We lie, we hurt, we steal, and we cheat. They say we have no regard for human life. And we can't change. You deserve better than us.'

As Gert started to move toward Eddie, he cried out, 'Don't try to hold me. I will resist you with all my might. I'm taking Ziggy and we're leaving you now. You'd better not stop me. I have a knife in my pocket, and if you were anybody else I would have used it already.'

'Okay, Eddie,' said Gert stopping in her tracks, 'please allow Adele some time with Ziggy. Let them have their day.'

'He doesn't even know who she is. He's never mentioned her name.'

I wondered whether that was true and whether the answer would be of any value. But I said, 'Please take Ziggy to Adele.'

Eddie lifted Ziggy and carried him within five feet of me, Ziggy still facing the wall.

'Sigmund, have you ever seen me before?' I asked. When he didn't respond, I asked him what his favorite cookie was. When he didn't answer I opened my purse and took out a Mallomar and held it up. 'Do you know what this is?' I asked putting it out to him. 'Is this still your favorite cookie?' Quickly, he turned around and lunged forward, grabbing the Mallomar and stuffing it into his mouth. 'And Sigmund, do you remember what you called your pet llama?'

'Yama,' he said.

'Yes, Yama,' I echoed standing up and starting to move toward him to give him a hug, but seeing Eddie standing five feet from me with his hand in his front right pocket, possibly holding his knife, I stopped and sat back down.

'Can I ask him if I can hug him goodbye?'

'You can ask him,' said Eddie.

'Ziggy, can I give you a hug and say goodbye?'

Ziggy looked at Eddie, then turned and shook his head and said, 'No.'

"Gert and I then got up, went to the door and summoned Nurse Washington. We spoke with her for the last time and never saw or heard from or about her again. The same for the boys."

CHAPTER 88

A MAN'S WIFE SHOULD ALWAYS GO WITH HIM TO THE DOCTOR

"Who's next?" asked Dr. Bloom, walking into the lab and sitting at the microscope.

"Mr. Montgomery," replied Aretha, placing the patient's spun urine under the microscope. Bloom looked at the urine, put a note in the patient's chart, and took him into room 2. He examined him, performed renal ultrasounds, and brought him back into his office, where Cathy had his wife waiting.

"Both kidneys are normal," said Bloom, showing and explaining the films to the couple.

"He's feeling a lot better since you removed that tube," said the patient's wife.

"Do I need to see you again?" asked the patient.

"You're going to see me a lot before I'm through with you. I need to repeat the ultrasound in a month. When's your next appointment with Dr. Roberts?"

"I don't need to see him anymore. I'm going to follow up with a GI guy in three months."

"What about Dr. Winger?"

"I saw her last week. I don't need any additional therapy."

"That's great! Let me ask you a question. What sports do you play? I know you've played football in the past."

"I think just two-hand touch for now. I thought I'd start this weekend."

"Your football days are on hold for now, and possibly forever."

"You're kidding me, Doc."

"One good hit to your abdomen and you'll sever the newly made connection from your left to your right ureter. You need to wait at least a year, and if I were you, I'd not play football again. One good bullet pass to your gut would completely disrupt the surgery. I shudder thinking about it."

"Come on, Doc."

"Don't make me put you in a total body cast."

"Doc, you're killing me."

"That's one of the reasons I put your wife in the room—to hear this conversation."

"My life is over, Doc."

"It will be if you disrupt that suture line."

"Doc, I thought you were my friend."

"Who said anything about me being your friend? Did you ever hear me saying anything about me being his friend?" Bloom asked, looking at the wife.

"I never heard that," she answered.

"I'm not happy, Doc."

"You want to be happy? Go to Dairy Queen and get a large Extreme Chocolate Brownie Blizzard. Have one on me," added Bloom, taking a ten dollar bill out of his wallet and handing to Montgomery. "You can give me the change when you see me in a month."

"We'll see about the change, Doc," said Montgomery, putting the bill in his wallet.

"Call me if you're having any problems."

"Like what?"

"Shh. I don't want to give your body any ideas!"

"You're too much, Doc," replied the patient, shaking Bloom's hand and giving him a hug.

"And by the way, I am your friend," said Bloom.

"I know that, Doc. I know that. Maybe you'll get your change." Bloom sent the Montgomerys on their way, saw three more patients, and got the call he'd been waiting for.

"I'll take it in my office," said Bloom through the intercom.

He went into his office and picked up the phone.

"Hi, Ida," he said.

"Have you spoken with Adele?" she asked.

"Yes, she's fine. When is your cystoscopy?" asked Bloom, not yet prepared to discuss the situation with the boys with her.

"On Wednesday."

"I assume Rachel will be coming with you?"

"Definitely. Did Adele tell you anything more about Sigmund or Edsel?"

"I'll tell you and Rachel together on Wednesday."

"Are they alright?"

"They were fine the last time she spoke with them."

"When was that?"

"It was some time ago."

"But they were fine?"

"Yes."

Bloom hung up with Ida and asked Aretha if it was too late to get Adele on the phone for him.

"It's okay to call her now," she answered. "Do you want me to get her?"

"Please. "

Bloom dictated a note for the last patient's chart and got on the line with Adele.

"Hi Adele," said Bloom. "Is this a good time to speak with you?"

"Yes. Is everything okay?"

"Yes. I haven't spoken in detail to either Ida or Rachel about our last conversation. It sounded so final."

"It was."

"You said something about letters and phone calls. Do you remember the places you called other than the one where you briefly saw them? Did Gert have any success? Did she have other numbers? Did any of the letters come back to either of you? Did you speak again with Nurse Washington? Do you have any suggestions about who or what organizations to call? If they were adopted, where would that record be? Do you have Oskar Fuchs's number or the name of anything he got published or the name of his publisher, or what he wrote about? As far as you know is Gert still alive? If she is, do you have a way to contact her?"

"I'm over ninety and have had a stroke and TIAs. One at a time, please!"

"Sorry, Adele," replied Bloom, starting to laugh. "Regarding your letters, did any come back to you?" asked Bloom, regaining his composure.

"The first five or so letters did not come back. The rest of them came back."

"They all went to Flatbush Ave Foster Home?"

"All the letters and calls went there. None of the calls or letters were answered. I assume the letters were received. After six months, I was told they no longer were at that foster care facility."

"Did they say where the boys went?"

"They went to Ohel Milton Schulman Foster Care in Brooklyn."

"Why did they go there?"

"All I learned was there were disciplinary problems with Eddie."

"Did you to speak with them there?"

"They wouldn't come to the phone."

"What about the letters?"

"They didn't come back."

"So you think they were received?"

"I know they were received. Ohel Schulman told me so."

"How were they doing there?"

"Same old, same old. They then went to Sheltering Arms in Manhattan. We lost track of them after that."

"Were they ever adopted?"

"I can't say."

"Did Sheltering Arms say where they went?"

"They ran away, and the shelter didn't know where they wound up."

"What about Oskar Fuchs? Did you know anything about his writings?"

"No."

"When was the last time you contacted him?"

"In 1946, about a year after we got back from New York."

"Had he had any contact with them?"

"He said no, not because he hadn't tried."

"Do you know where he was living?"

"Somewhere in Brooklyn."

"Do you still have his number?"

"A land line from over fifty-five years ago?"

"Yes."

"Let me see if I can find his number. Hold on." Two minutes later she gave Bloom Fuchs's number. "I'll call you back if I get another one."

Adele hung up and called Bloom back a few minutes later.

"Would you believe it's the same number as 1946?"

"I believe it." Bloom paused for a few seconds then added, "What am I thinking? The likelihood he's still alive and can speak on the phone is probably less than zero. He has no idea whom I could possibly be. Even if I spoke fluent German, he wouldn't have any idea what I was talking about. Adele, could you please call the number?"

"You want me to find out if it's him and what happened to the boys, are they alive, were they adopted by anyone else, where are they now, and whatever else I can think of?"

"Yes. And tell him that Ida Stern is Sigmund's mother and survived Auschwitz and wants to speak with him. Find out all you can about him and Eddie, and tell him that Ida Stern and her doctor may be calling him."

"You now speak fluent German?" asked Adele.

"Nein," replied Bloom. "And that's the extent of it. But he may no longer speak German. If he did, it would be with a Brooklyn accent!"

"I'll try to call you in a little while," replied Adele, chuckling as she hung up.

CHAPTER 89

A FEW MORE THINGS TO CHECK

"Good morning," Bloom greeted Ida and Rachel on the phone. "I just got off the phone with Adele. She's fine and says hello. Can you hear me okay?"

"Yes," they both answered

Bloom summarized all the information he had gotten from Adele.

"Adele and Gert then went back to Germany. Eventually, despite writing letters and trying to speak with them by phone, they lost track of the boys. We know that some of the letters they sent early on were received and not answered. They unsuccessfully tried to have the boys brought back to Germany and even considered finding men, getting married, and traveling to New York to adopt them. But since they could not locate the boys, that plan was scuttled. Do you remember what Adele said at the end of your last session with her?"

"She wanted to pick them up, take them out of that house, and hide with them forever," said Ida.

"Exactly," responded Bloom. After a pause and some sighs, he added, "We have the names, phone numbers, and addresses of three facilities where they stayed, along with other facilities that were open around that time. We're also waiting for a call back from Oskar Fuchs and Gert. In the past, they've said they've not seen or heard from either of the boys."

We don't know if they're even alive, Bloom thought to himself.

"Dr. Bloom, Oskar Fuchs is on the other line," said Aretha walking into Bloom's offce. "Should I tell him you'll call him back?

"No, I'll speak with him now," replied Bloom, quickly answering Aretha, not wanting to lose Fuchs, and telling Ida and Rachel he had Oskar on the line and will get back to them shortly.

"Oskar Fuchs?" announced Bloom, picking up the blinking line. "It's so nice hearing from you. I appreciate you're getting back to me. I am the doctor and close friend of Ida Stern, the woman who gave up her son to the convent and whom you and Karen had adopted in 1943."

Bloom spoke with Fuchs for about fifteen minutes, asking him about himself and all the questions he had asked Adele to ask him. He thanked him, wished him well, checked to make sure he had his number, and got back on the line with Ida and Rachel.

"I just got off the phone with Oskar Fuchs," began Bloom. "He said in retrospect he should have given up his children to Adele in 1945, even if they were taken back to Germany and he never saw them again. He said he would have felt good about the kind of life they probably would have had. He said that the decision still bothers him today. But he did have some information on them."

CHAPTER 90

ONE MORE THING TO CHECK

"I'm going to medical records to dictate some charts," said Bloom, having walked into the office and learned the first patient hadn't yet arrived. "Call me when the patient is ready to be seen."

"10-4," replied Cathy looking at the day's short schedule. "Are you and the Mrs., er, I mean, doctor playing golf this this afternoon?"

"We're going to play nine holes."

"Is Dr. Barrow covering?"

"Yep," replied Bloom, leaving the office.

Bloom used the north entrance to enter the hospital and walked to medical records, passing outpatient surgery, X-ray, the OR, and the main and doctors' entrances. In front of the entrance to medical records, Bloom saw one of the female pharmacists showing a photograph to three medical record secretaries, so he stopped and looked at the picture.

"He has his father's eyes," said one of the secretaries.

"He has your smile," said another.

"He has his mother's mouth," said the third.

"Very nice," said Bloom, nodding and smiling. He stood around with them for another minute, then went into medical records, dictated his charts, and left. As soon as he got back to his office, he called medical records and asked to speak with Sylvia, one of the women who was looking at the photo.

"Are you alone?"

"Yes," she replied.

"What were you all looking at?"

"Why?" she answered, starting to laugh.

"Why are you laughing?" he asked.

"No reason," she volunteered, not wanting to get into a discussion.

"Really, what were you looking at?"

"Why are you asking?" she said, starting to laugh again.

"Why are you still laughing?"

"You laughed first."

"No, you laughed first."

"I'm not laughing now."

"Were we looking at a human? Or was it a jackal or a hyena? And did it have a head?"

By this time Sylvia was laughing out loud uncontrollably.

"Seriously, what was it?" asked Bloom.

"It was her grandson."

"Can you please tell me what *you* saw?"

"I'm not sure."

"You were the one that said, 'He has his mother's mouth.'"

"I didn't know what else to say. I had to say something. You said, 'Very nice,' and smiled. We all had to say something. You get a pass because you're a man and you're not a good friend. Women need to say something."

"What did you honestly think?

"It was fine."

"What was fine?'

"That was her grandson."

"I saw a lot of fur and a tail."

"Don't get me started."

"I thought you were real idiots."

Sylvia started laughing out loud. She paused a few seconds and composed herself.

"We were all trying to say something nice to one of our friends."

"I understand that."

"We're all good friends."

"Will you speak to any of the others?"

"Certainly not today."

"So, I'm not crazy?"

"And you're also not a good friend. But you did well under the circumstances."

"When I tell my wife about this she'll be happy and surprised I didn't say anything stupid."

Sylvia laughed.

"Mainly surprised," said Bloom. "Gotta run," said Bloom. "TBC," he added hanging up.

Bloom looked at his watch and called Missy. "Are we still on for golf?"

"Are we still on for golf?" she answered.

"I asked you first."

"You asking me first usually means you're not going to be able to make it."

"Usually, but not today."

"I have a few minutes, and I forgot to ask you how the girls responded to your follow-up info from Adele, Gert, and Oskar."

"They more or less knew what was coming from Adele's previous doom and gloom conversation ender. What I and the girls got from her were the names of the foster care facilities where the boys had once stayed, some of which are no longer open, and a dozen other facilities where they might have stayed in the mid-1940s, also some of which are no longer open. Adele has had no contact with Gert after the marriages and adoptions plans were scratched. Ida and Rachel sobbed uncontrollably after learning Edsel died in a car accident. A year later Sigmund was adopted for the second time, but the name or address of the adopting couple was never found out."

"Who told you that?"

"Oskar Fuchs."

"He was the one that told you both things?"

"Uh huh."

"How'd he know?"

"After Karen died, the boys were legally taken from him. He pushed for obtaining supervised visits, but that was denied. He said he once spotted Sigmund on a train presumably with his parents, but did not contact him, respecting the court's decision. However, twenty minutes later, he got off when they got off and followed them to a movie theater. When they went inside, he bought a newspaper, walked across the street, and waited on a bench. After two hours the theater let out and the manager locked the door. Sigmund and his family had apparently exited from a different door. Oskar walked to the train station and waited for half an hour. When they did not show up, he went home. He said he used his contacts with newspapers and law enforcement people from his writings but was unsuccessful in obtaining the names of the adoptive parents or where they lived. I need to speak with Oskar again," said Bloom telling Missy he was going to hang up. "I want to get him before he leaves. I'll be home in an hour. I'll try to get a tee time for 1:30."

"Better make it 2:00," said Missy, hanging up.

Bloom called Oskar and was excited to learn he had a copy of Sigmund's fingerprints in addition to his passport and asked him if he could make copies and/or fax them to the office. Hitler's method of being able to recognize Sigmund seemed a lot less painful than the method used by Dr. Meyer Berger, and Hitler's method definitely may be the way to go to locate Sigmund, continued Bloom, even though he knew fingerprints could change over one's lifetime. But, in order to be effective, Sigmund's fingerprints must have to have been registered somewhere, for example, if he committed a crime or required fingerprinting for lawful reasons. *One more call to make,* he thought, *then I'll call the golf course.* He dialed Adele's number and told her he spoke with Oskar and learned that he had Sigmund's passport and fingerprints. She said she remembered giving them his passport but didn't remember the fingerprints.

CHAPTER 91

AN UNENVIABLE SITUATION

"Dr. Bloom, Mrs. Gold is on line 2," said Cathy. "And she's screaming."

"What does she want?"

"Her husband is missing. She thinks you know where he is."

"Me? How long has he been missing?"

"Since ten o'clock last night."

"Has she called the police?"

"She called them last night."

"I'll speak with her."

As soon as Bloom announced himself, Mrs. Gold started to scream.

"Annette, take a deep breath and count to nine," said Bloom calmly.

"Why nine?"

"Take another deep breath and count to seven."

"They've got him, Dr. Bloom. They've got him."

"Who's got him?"

"They've taken out his other kidney," she screamed.

"Annette, take another deep breath and count to five. Then tell me what the police said. I assume you told them everything. Take another deep breath and count to three."

"I'll try."

"Did you call all the local hospitals?"

"The police said they did. Wait a minute, there's someone at the door."

"Thank God, officer," Bloom heard her cry and then heard her hang up.

"I wonder what just happened?" said Bloom, hanging up and scratching his head.

"Your old buddy Mr. Jones is on line 1," said Cathy.

"Take a message, er, never mind, I'll take the call," replied Bloom, changing his mind in case Jones said something he might not want Cathy to hear.

"Yes, Mr. Jones," said Bloom.

"Friends help out friends," he said, then hung up.

Bloom hung up, put his elbows on his desk, rested his head in his palms, and sighed. He thought about the conversation he should have had with Missy about Gold and sighed again. He thought about the uncomfortable conversation he did have with Stine after Gold decompensated on the phone regarding the imminency of him losing his only kidney and the annoying follow-up call Bloom had gotten from Jones hinting at the consequences from bucking demands. *The difficulty with the Stine conversation,* thought Bloom, *was that it kind of implied Stine might have a connection with someone of that ilk who was involved in removing organs from people against their will. It also hinted Stine might have already played a part in Gold's first nephrectomy.* Bloom did not specifically tell him to leave Gold alone, but he wanted him to know that Gold was a good man and a patient of his, and that if the other kidney was removed Gold would probably die after years of dialysis.

After he saw his twelfth patient of the morning, he was put through to Gold himself, who was on line 2.

"Hello, Bob. What's going on?"

"I went to my favorite ice cream place last night."

"That's not a good nighttime activity."

"They have the best ice cream."

"Did you get to eat it?"

"No, my captors ate it."

"The same ones from before?"

"I didn't see them either time."

"Did they chloroform you, or used what they used before?"

"Probably. I had the same dry mouth and heartburn."

"Where'd they take you?"

"Nowhere."

"Nowhere? What did they do?"

"Nothing."

"I fell asleep right away. They must have given me a larger dose than before. As I was waking up, they dropped me off near the police station."

"Are you bleeding?"

"No."

"Do you have any pain?"

"No."

"Did they speak?"

"No, but I heard one of them say some words as I was being dropped off."

"What words?"

"Something like 'high places.' I have no idea what that meant."

I do, Bloom thought to himself. *It means you have friends in very high places, friends like me. I sure hope he doesn't figure that out. Gold was supposed to get me the info from his time with the Organ Registry, but he didn't. He's lucky I called Stine, which I now regret, certainly not for Gold, but for Ida and my family.*

"Did you speak to someone about me?"

"You were supposed to get me your info from the Organ Registry. You never did."

"Do you think this was a warning?"

"I have no idea. Have you been praying?"

"I'm a secular Jew."

"You can still pray. Have you asked anyone to pray for you?"

"No. Have you prayed for me?"

"Yes, I pray for all my patients. I'm not Jewish, but that shouldn't matter."

"You're not Jewish?"

"No. A lot of people think I am."

"Didn't I see you eating in Ben's Restaurant a few months ago?"

"Yes. I even have a Ben's Friends rewards card."

"What do I do now?"

"Keep off the ice cream at night."

"Really, Dr. Bloom."

"Wait for another offer."

"Then what?"

"What do you mean then what?"

"What do I do after that?"

"You do nothing if you don't get an offer. They will probably either leave you alone or make another offer. Hopefully they'll leave you alone."

"What do I do if I get another offer?"

"You hire a bodyguard. Witness protection will probably not be available, but it may be worth a try. Do you have any information to give up? Right now, I would buy a gun, learn how to use it, and start carrying it."

"They sneak up on me at night."

"I think you should be fine until you get an offer. Then start carrying your gun and don't go out at night. You'll have to change your lifestyle. Speak to the police and bodyguard agencies. I'm not an expert in any of this. Or you can take the offer!"

"Take the offer?!"

"At least you'll get some money, and the anxiety will be much less, and you won't have to carry a gun. And you'll be able to eat ice cream from the good ice cream store every night."

"If they remain in business. I guess I can eat ice cream with no kidneys."

"There you go!"

CHAPTER 92

THE BEST DARN ULTRASOUND EVER

"I'm still waiting in X-ray for my ultrasound," whispered Ida, seeing one other patient seated and three burly/surly men at the entrance of the room.

"How's your back doing?" asked Rachel.

"It's been fine since last night. Maybe I don't need this study."

"You're there already. You might as well have it. I have one more errand to do. Call me when you're ready to be picked up. Good luck."

"Thanks," answered Ida, hanging up.

"William Stine," announced the technician walking into the waiting area.

Stern as well as Stine stood up. Stern had her oversize hat covering her face.

"I think he called me," said Stine.

"Remember me?" asked Stern, now almost face-to-face with Stine.

"I don't think so," Stine replied turning away, walking toward the technician.

"Let me refresh your memory," said Stern following him. As Stern caught up to him, Stine's bodyguards moved toward her. Stine stopped walking, turned around, and motioned his men to back off. "You first met me on January 19, 1977, at Dunkin' Donuts in Ft. Lauderdale, the day it snowed in Florida," continued Stern. "You came to Florida to organize a march in Skokie for the following year. You and I had hot chocolates with whipped cream and sat next to each other. We saw a boy and his bike get hit by a bus and we rushed to save him, and when you saw the Star of David hanging from his neck you bolted and left him to die. Do you remember that? Do you remember killing my friends who tried to stop the Skokie march? Do you also remember having me shot and my platelet donor killed in her car on the train tracks? And do you remember wanting me killed after I survived all your other attempts? I'm sorry I didn't bring my gun with me to the exam today. Maybe one of your goons can lend me theirs." She looked at them as a group, then one at a time. "I'd have no problem killing you right now. Nothing would give me greater pleasure."

Waiting for some response and getting none, she continued. "So I guess this will have to do," she said, clearing her throat and spitting in Stine's face.

"Have a great day, Miss Stern," said Stine, motioning his men to still keep away as he wiped off the spit and started to walk away.

"Oh, this has already been a great day, Mr. Nazi bastard."

"And Ida, you're still as pretty and charming as you were twenty-five years ago," he said with a smile. "And good luck with your exam," he added, walking into the exam room, his men following closely behind.

After Stern's study was completed, Bloom was called by the radiologist and was told the study was normal. Bloom then called Stern and told her the good news and told her he'd check her films himself and meet her at his office.

"That was the best ultrasound I ever had," said Stern, when she saw Bloom.

"Was it the exam or the prelude?" asked Bloom smiling.

"Who told you about the prelude?"

"The tech."

"After my diatribe I was waiting for him to say something, but he didn't."

"I guess you thought you had to do something, but that wasn't very smart."

"No, it wasn't, but it sure felt good!"

"What'd you think of his response?"

"He didn't seem upset. His self-control and politeness infuriated me even more. I tried but I couldn't gather enough saliva to fire another salvo. It's funny, not really so funny, but he seemed like the guy I met before he pulled the disappearance act at Dunkin' Donuts."

"What does that mean?"

"I don't know." After a few seconds, she added, "I'd still kill him if I got the chance."

"Changing the subject, how's your pain?"

"The pain is gone. What do you think it was?"

"Your tumor was very close to the ureteral opening. A scab may have temporarily blocked off the opening."

"I did pass a smallish clot last night about the size of the tip of lead that comes off the tip of a lead pencil."

"You know that there's no lead in a lead pencil."

"And Panama hats are made in Ecuador!"

"Exactly. That certainly could have caused your pain. Do you want to stay a day to make sure?"

"No. Especially with the goon squad so close by."

"Let me ask you something."

"If it's about Stine, think before you ask me."

Bloom remained silent.

"I don't want to get into a discussion about him. He's an evil man who does evil things."

"Dr. Bloom, Dr. Winger is on line 2. It's about William Stine," Cathy announced over the intercom.

Bloom said goodbye to Stern and picked up line 2.

"Hi, Susan. Whatcha got?"

"Your buddy successfully finished his consolidation phase and is being discharged. His bone marrow biopsy is scheduled for next Wednesday."

"What's after that?"

"Nothing or a bone marrow transplant."

CHAPTER 93

IS ZERO HOUR NEAR?

"Or a bone marrow transplant!" exclaimed Bloom to Missy, repeating the astonishing and admonishing, sentence-ending bomb Dr. Winger had dropped over the phone the day before. "Where did that come from?"

"What'd she say when you asked her?"

"She said that it had always been on the table."

Bloom recounted the conversation. "Whose table? It certainly wasn't on mine or your table."

"I know it's a very sore subject for you and your family, and I don't want to get into an argument," she said, "but it's really been on the table since it was diagnosed. It's just now closer than before to actually being done than it had been before. If the repeat biopsy shows no blast cells, he can be watched, although almost every oncologist I spoke with at my international meeting last week said anyone over the age of sixty should have a bone marrow transplant even if the biopsy is negative for leukemic cells."

"Has she found a donor for Stine?" asked Missy, breaking in.

"Yes, two. Putting it in simplistic terms, she said she would rate her two a 15 and a 16 out of 20."

"And Ida's?"

"A 19 out of 20. I don't know if they can be numerically compared, but clearly she thinks Ida would be a better match. How much better, she didn't know."

"Stine will get to learn about all the potential matches, right?"

"I would think so."

"Ida has already told him she won't donate her marrow, right?"

"She told us she had. Many, many, many times over."

"Have you asked her under what conditions she would do it?"

"Ida and I have never had that or any other conversations about a transplant ever being a possibility."

"Would she have one with Stine?"

"I would say definitely not."

"Do you think it would be good if they had one? You never know what might happen."

"Yes, but there's no way she would do it. And Rachel wouldn't allow her do it."

"If just Stern and Stine and no one else was present? And they checked their pistols at the door."

"Maybe it would be better if they each brought two pistols with them."

"Shouldn't they wait until he's had his biopsy?" asked Missy, ignoring Bloom.

"I think she should have them ready and know how to use them."

"Are you serious?"

"Or maybe Ida should take an expectorant and drown him in her spit!"

"You're an idiot," replied Missy laughing.

"And funny."

"No, just an idiot."

"You laughed," said Bloom, eyeballing her. "You could admit it's a little bit funny."

"Okay, maybe a little bit, but no more than that," said Missy, eyeballing him back.

"I'll kiss to that," added Bloom, embracing and then kissing her.

"They're smooching again," yelled Peter, running into the room, Lisa right behind him.

"Yeah, mooching again," said Lisa.

"I have some things I must do," said Missy, separating herself from Bloom. "Why don't you fish for a while. Then we'll have dinner."

CHAPTER 94

SOLICITATIONS

"Good morning, Dr. Winger," said Bloom, picking up. "Whatcha got?"

"Our friend's marrow biopsy showed no leukemic cells, and I've recommended a bone marrow transplant."

"What'd Stine say?"

"He wanted to know the time frame. I told him now would be the time to do it."

"What'd he say?"

"He asked if he should get another opinion. I told him yes. Then he asked me about his possible bone marrow donors, and I told him about his two. He asked me if those were the only two donors that would be available to any oncologist who had him as a patient."

"And I said if I was the world's best oncologist and he was the president of the United States or Russia there would be only two donors available for you. 'Isn't Ida Stern available?' he asked. But he wouldn't know about Ida's match. She's never put herself out as a donor and she's not on any donor list. I gave Stine my handout for what's involved in a transplant. It's my variation of the national/international protocol. I have to be in your building sometime this afternoon. I can drop a copy off at your office."

"Great! I'd appreciate that. Thanks. Susan, I'd like you to let me know what he's decided."

"I'll do the best I can. If he goes somewhere else and I'm out of the loop I won't be able to help you much."

"I realize that. Is it possible after he gets his second and third opinions and understands the protocol and sees what's involved going forward he elects to do nothing at this time?"

"I would say that considering what he's already gone through he could go either way, but more likely he'll proceed if all the opinions agree he should go ahead with it."

"Is there any way another comparison with Sterns's blood might not show a better match?"

"Do you think if it did he'd believe it?"

"If a doctor other than you told him. Could recently receiving a load of platelets alter the result?"

"Do you have any more straws you want me to grasp?"

"If I had I would have put them out there."

"Ida Stern's on line 2, Dr. Bloom," said Aretha. "She called earlier his morning and again when you were with Dr. Winger. Should I tell her you'll call her shortly?"

"Tell her to stay on. I'll be with her in less than two minutes."

Bloom finished his call with Dr. Winger and picked up the second line.

"Ida, good morning," began Bloom. "We've been very busy. What's doing?"

"Stine called me this morning."

Surprise, surprise, thought Bloom to himself.

"He announced himself," continued Ida, "and he said he understood why I spat in his face. I hung up on him."

"Good," said Bloom.

"He called back and I didn't answer."

"Good."

"What should I do?"

"Nothing."

"He's probably going to keep calling me."

"I guess so."

"I don't want to speak with him."

"Don't answer the phone."

"He's called Rachel, too. I know what he wants, and he's never gonna get it!"

Don't say any more, said Bloom to himself.

"Should I call the police?" asked Ida.

Bloom chuckled. "And tell them that you spat in his face and he called to tell you he understood why you spat in his face?"

Ida laughed. "Nah, I don't think that would be a good idea."

"The next time he calls, don't hang up. Listen to what he has to say."

"And then what?"

"And then we'll know what he said, that is, if he has anything else he wanted to say."

"Okay. That sounds easy enough. I'll hang up after he says or doesn't say something."

"Sounds like a plan, Ida."

CHAPTER 95

GIVE IT UP FOR STEPH KWOLEK

"Hi Jamie, this is Rachel. Have you spoken with my sister today?"

"No. The last time I spoke with her was two days ago."

"I went to her house. She's not home, her car is gone, and she left her phone at home."

"She's done that before, hasn't she?"

"Not very often."

"Did she take her handbag?"

"Yes, she took it."

"Did you check her appointment book?"

"I'm back home now. No, I'll do that."

"When did you speak with her last?"

"Last night."

"What did you talk about? Did she say what she had to do today?"

"Nope."

"Did she say don't worry?"

"If she had, I wouldn't be worried."

"That makes sense. When's the earliest she ever leaves the house?"

"We live separately so it's hard to say. It depends on if she has any appointments and what time and where the appointment is."

"Check to see if her appointment book is still there and see what time her clock is set for. Call me in 10 minutes."

Ten minutes later Bloom heard from Rachel.

"Her clock alarm had been set for 4:00 a.m. The radio was still on and was beeping. Maybe she took a flight, but that doesn't make any sense. She wouldn't do that without me. There are no dishes in the sink. The house is in order."

"Is there an appointment book or any note pads on her desk?"

"I didn't see an appointment book, but there is a pad with today's date on it with big black capital letters D DAY and in red capitals NN. What do you think that means?"

"I think it means today is the day she goes after the neo-Nazi. Does she own a gun?"

"Not that I know of."

"Any guns or empty cartridge cases lying around?"

"No."

"Take the note off the pad and put it in your pocket. Do it now! Do you think I'm going overboard with all this?"

"I think you've already gone!"

"I can't say I have a good feeling about what's going on. D Day means the day of the launching of an offensive, in this case against William Stine. She's mentioned a number of times that she had the opportunity to kill him but did not have a gun. She actually asked one of his henchmen if she could borrow his gun when all of them were in ultrasound. As of two days ago Stine was out of the hospital. Could Ida have arranged a meeting with him? I have Stine's cell and home number as well as one of his henchmen's numbers. I have some things to do. If I'm not at home, I'll have my phone. Let's stay in touch."

Bloom hung up, sat back in his black swivel chair and rocked. "What to do, Jamie?" he said out loud. "What to do?" He rocked some more, using the tips of his toes to push off the floor. Then he sat back to think. *Nothing may be going on here. So let's not get bent out of shape,* he thought to himself. *If that's the case, Ida'll return home shortly, completely intact with a reasonable explanation, and we'll yell at her for not taking her phone and not telling us where she was going. This includes meeting with Stine and returning home without killing him and not getting killed. On the other hand, something bad may be happening/have happened to her. First things first. I'll check the radio and TV and see if Stine has anything going on locally.*

After twenty minutes of phone calls and checking the TV, Bloom learned that Stine was holding a hastily scheduled rally at the large pond at the old site of the former Crandon Park Zoo in Key Biscayne. According to the station, he had been out of the public eye for the last four months and was anxious to resume his leadership role. The rally was to start at 11:30 a.m. It was already 11:00 and it would be more than an hour before they'd be able to get down there. He called Rachel and told her what he had learned and said he was going down to Miami if she hadn't heard from Ida. Rachel said Ida hadn't called and said she'd go with him to Miami. He said he'd pick her up in ten minutes and asked her to get directions to the pond in Crandon Park in Key Biscayne.

Ida had set her alarm clock for 4:00 a.m. with the alarm and music set at a very low volume and went to bed in the second bedroom with this alarm set for 7:00 with the alarm and music set at a normal volume. When she awoke she shut off the alarm in the second bedroom and raised the volume in her bedroom and left the alarm and music playing. She made the bed she slept in and left the house at 8:15, purposely leaving her phone in the kitchen and putting a burner phone in her handbag.

At 9:30 she found a location two hundred yards not facing the sun and not visible from the staging area in Biscayne Bay and by 9:45 sat blanketed in a chair, wearing sunglasses, holding binoculars, with her AK-47 under her blanket.

At 10:00 a.m., using her burner phone, Ida directed Sophie, widow of murder victim Maurice Bernshtein, to her location. Sophie had metastatic pancreatic cancer and only a few weeks to live and wanted to witness Stine being shot. At 10:15 they watched from an unobstructed view of the podium a dais being set up with eight chairs placed in a semicircle, separated by flag holders containing large flags with swastikas. When Ida spotted four Stine henchmen setting up rows of chairs in front of the podium, she smiled and nudged Sophie with a thumbs up.

At 10:45 a.m. guests started to arrive and occupy the podium seats. Using the high-powered binoculars, all podium guests were visible. By 11:00, neither Clark III nor Stine had been spotted. By 11:15 they still had not arrived.

"Can we reach Stine from here?" asked Sophie.

"Only if he shows up," replied Ida smiling, patting her Avtomat Kalishnikova under the blanket. "It's my baby from the years I fought in the Israeli army," she added, patting the rifle again. She had already used the ballistic trajectory calculator for a distance of 200 yards to know she needed to aim seven inches above her target.

At 11:20 Rachel and Bloom were on 1-95 heading south.

At 11:30 a.m. Ida spotted Clark getting onto the dais. "The football player is here," she announced.

"Who's that?" asked Sophie.

"A guy named Clark. He looks like a bull. I think he's the number two man. "Here," said Ida, handing Sophie the binoculars.

"A short bull," said Sophie, spotting Clark and scanning the rest of the dais. "I think numero uno has arrived," she added, handing the binoculars back to Ida.

"That's him!" agreed Ida, watching him sit down next to Clark. "Clark will probably introduce him. We have a while to go. There's a number of seats on the dais that need to be filled as well as some empty seats in front of the podium."

"It's 11:55," said Ida. "All the seats are filled. Clark is standing and motioning to someone on the dais. And that someone is now heading toward the microphone. I don't know who he is." Ida took his picture. The individual welcomed everyone, spoke for a few minutes and introduced Clark. After the applause, Clark came to the microphone, lowered it, spoke for ten minutes, and introduced Stine. After the applause died down, Stine raised the microphone and began to speak.

It was 12:20 p.m. and Bloom had just passed Jackson Memorial Hospital on 1-95.

"Nervous?" he asked.

"Uh huh," replied Rachel. "You?"

"A little bit."

"That was a huge ovation," said Sophie, two minutes later.

"He's pretty charismatic," answered Ida. "And quite the charmer. I'll tell you some other time." She continued uncovering the AK-47, aimed the rifle seven inches above the middle of Stine's chest, and placed her index finger on the trigger.

"Break a leg, er, break his leg."

"I'm not aiming at his leg. Unless he breaks it when he falls after I've hit him."

It was now 12:30 p.m. and Bloom was commenting on the number of emergency vehicles going onto the Rickenbacker Causeway from 1-95. As their car continued southeast toward Biscayne Bay, two helicopters flew overhead appearing headed toward Jackson Memorial Hospital.

"What do you think?" asked Bloom.

"About the choppers and the emergency vehicles?"

"Uh huh. See if you can find out anything on your phone."

"Do you think we should turn around?"

"No. We should be there in 15 to 20 minutes. Here, take my phone. Look up Cathy's number, call her, and give me the phone. You don't have to speak with her."

Rachel took the phone and found and dialed Cathy's number and handed the phone back to Bloom. When Cathy answered, Bloom told her he needed her to find any news channel—radio or TV—and see if there's been a shooting in Crandon Park or Biscayne Bay.

"I'm watching something right now," she said. "Three people have been shot and are on the way to Jackson Memorial Hospital."

"Any names given?"

"Just one. William Stine."

"What about the other two?"

"Those names were not given."

"Male or female?"

"Not given."

"Anyone dead?"

"It just happened."

"Are they going to Jackson Memorial Hospital?"

"They're being helicoptered now. Where are you?"

"They just flew over us. I can't talk. I'll call you as soon as I can."

"Okay. Bye."

"We're going to Jackson?" asked Rachel.

"Yes," replied Bloom, looking for a place to make a left or U-turn. He asked Rachel to look up directions on his phone.

"Get us to the Ryder Trauma Center," said Bloom. "That's where the helipad is."

In two miles Bloom made a creative U-turn and headed north on 1-95 to get to Jackson Memorial hospital. As a physician accompanying the sister of one of the possible three gunshot victims, he was able to learn where the Key Biscayne gunshot patients were taken. Rachel found out Ida indeed was one of the victims but couldn't find out whether she was alive or dead. She was told to wait where she was and someone would come out and speak with her.

"I teach here," Bloom told Rachel as they walked toward the doors to the outside. "Reception is poor inside the hospital and I need to make some calls. I'll just be outside."

Rachel nodded.

"Hey, Professor Bloom," said Chief Urology Resident Stu Goldberg coming into the room from the outside. "Whatcha doing here?"

"Remember my eighty-nine-year-old Holocaust survivor patient I presented a few weeks ago?" asked Bloom.

"The one with a solitary kidney and a tumor in the bladder/ureteral orifice?" replied Goldberg.

"She got into a gunfight with the president of the American Nazi Party, also my patient."

"The one that just happened at Key Biscayne?"

"Yes. Are you seeing a patient in the ER?"

"I'm seeing a guy with a knife in his kidney."

"See your patient. If you have some hang time, see if you can check on my patient Ida Stern. Her sister, Rachel, is that pretty woman sitting over there," said Bloom pointing her out.

Bloom went outside and called Missy, his answering service, Cathy, and three patients and came back into the waiting area to sit down next to Rachel.

"Professor?" she asked

"My official title is Assistant Volunteer Professor of Urology. Dr. Goldberg likes calling me professor. He hasn't come back to speak with you, has he?"

"He just left. Ida is alive. She has some bruising from the bullets and is getting a CAT scan of her heart, lungs and abdomen. She will be staying in the hospital."

"She must have been wearing some kind of vest," said Bloom. "She also must have shot Stine."

"Stine is also alive but has a lung laceration and is bleeding into his chest. In addition, he has a fractured hip. Goldberg also said there was a third person, a woman, and she too is alive but doesn't know anything else about her. You're a good man, Dr. Bloom," said Rachel giving him a hug.

"A mensch?" asked Bloom.

"Yes, a mensch," she replied, hugging him again.

"I've finally made it to mench-dom."

"You're a mensch, Professor Jamie," she added, hugging him a third time.

It was 9:00 p.m. when Dr. Jim Colburn came to see them. Bloom told him he was on the teaching staff of the hospital, was Ida's physician, and was waiting with Ida's sister Rachel. Colburn nodded and said Ida was in the ICU and that she had sustained non-life-threatening sternal abrasions and fractures and also a contusion of her esophagus. He further said her pulmonary, cardiac, and remaining abdominal studies were negative. Because of the bleeding from her esophagus, he said he had to reverse the action of her blood thinners, that she would need to remain in the ICU for 24 to 48 hours, and that she would be kept NPO except for ice chips, which may be used if the esophageal bleeding continued. He said also that Ida kept saying Stephanie Kwolek saved her life.

"And also the life of the guy she shot," added Bloom, shaking his head laughing.

"Do you know who this woman is?" asked Colburn

"My father's a chemical engineer. In 1966 he worked at Dupont with chemist Stephanie Kwolek, who had been working with canvas, denim, and leather to make a lightweight plastic that would prevent itself from shredding and thus dissipate the force of a bullet."

"Kevlar," said Colburn. "Both Ida and William Stine were wearing Kevlar. And I think so did the other person who was shot."

"Do you know anything about this other woman?"

"Not a whole lot. I know she's stable."

"We'd like to see Ida for a few seconds," said Bloom, deciding not to persist learning about the other woman. "Is that possible?"

"She's been sedated for her sternal pain. Don't rouse her. She also has full-time security watching her, so you'll have to square things with them."

Bloom gave Colburn a quizzical look.

"She did shoot somebody," said Colburn.

"We're happy about the security," replied Bloom. "The guy she shot is also my patient."

Colburn chuckled and gave Bloom a quizzical look.

"Yes, the neo-Nazi."

Rachel and Bloom went with Colburn to the ICU, passing two of Stine's men en route, and met the police officer stationed in front of the ICU's entrance, who asked to see their driver's licenses and took photos of them and their licenses. They were told to wait for Ida's nurse, who would take them to see her.

Ida was sleeping. Her IV was running slowly, and her monitor showed a slight tachycardia with a normal BP and respiratory rate. The urine in her drainage bag was clear. Bloom asked Rachel what she was planning to do, and she replied she was staying at the hospital. He asked her if she wanted him to go to Ida's house and gather some clothing for her and bring it tomorrow. She said it wasn't necessary. He said good night, that he'd call her in the morning, and left the hospital. Before he got in his car, he called Rachel and told her to make sure she charged her phone.

CHAPTER 96

A QUICK FEED AND BACK TO JACKSON MEMORIAL

"What time did you get in?" asked Missy, still in bed, stretching out her arms and yawning. "What time is it?" she asked, rubbing her eyes, trying to focus on the night table clock. "Did you change the time on the clock?" she asked, reading the time as 11:30 a.m.

"Which question do you want answered first?" asked Bloom, sitting down alongside her. "The kiddies are asking for lunch."

"Is it really lunch time?"

"It is for most of us."

"What time did you get in last night?"

"After one. There was an accident on 1-95. It happened right in front of me. Five cars. All the lanes were blocked. I had no choice, being a first responder."

"Did you have to do anything?"

"I've already seen myself on the news. You can read about it in the papers."

"Anything new about Ida?"

"She's doing okay. She'll probably stay another day in the ICU."

"How's the bleeding?"

"It doesn't seem to be a problem. Her H&H is good."

"Is she eating?"

"Not yet."

"Still off her blood thinners?"

"Yes. PT is seeing her. She's wearing compression stockings and will probably ambulate this afternoon."

"Find out anything on the other woman?"

"Sophie Bernshtein? She was the wife—now widow—of one of the two Sawgrass Expressway victims, Maurice Bernshtein. You remember, Ida was supposed to be the third."

"Sophie could have gotten killed!"

"She wanted to witness Stine getting shot."

"And possibly get killed herself?"

"Sophie has stage four pancreatic cancer with less than a month to live. She didn't even want to wear a Kevlar jacket. I think she wanted to die thinking Stine was dead."

"Sorry about that. She knows Stine hasn't died?"

"Hasn't died, yet."

"Why 'yet'?"

"In addition to his gunshot wound, he's bleeding into his chest from a lung laceration and also has a fractured hip that will need surgery. I forgot to tell you Ida has a policeman guarding her."

"I would imagine."

"Why do you think?"

"So that Stine's henchmen don't kill her?"

"Guess again."

"So that Ida won't try to kill Stine?"

"You have one more guess left."

"I give up. I'm not like you. It's too early to think."

"It's almost noon! She's been arrested for shooting Stine."

"When did shooting neo-Nazis become a crime?"

"Everyone has equal rights under the law."

"That's the problem with our legal system. I'm ready for breakfast."

"That ship has sailed."

"You say it's been 1-a-unched?"

"I couldn't say it any better."

"Or any wittier."

"We have a cousin in Whittier, California."

"And she's probably eating breakfast right now."

"What would you like for breakfast?"

"French toast with bananas and chocolate and coffee."

"What's your second choice?"

"What are the kids having for lunch?"

"They're making pizzas."

"With caramelized onions?"

"I have to go down to Miami. I don't have time to caramelize the onions."

"I'll also have an iced decaf coffee with skim milk and five sugars."

After serving the one breakfast and the two lunches, Bloom cleared his messages with his service, touched base with Rachel, and left for Miami.

CHAPTER 97

SOMEONE IS UNDER ARREST?

"How was last night?" asked Bloom, finding Rachel in the sitting area just outside the ICU.

"It wasn't terrible."

"After I spend some time with Ida, I can take you to her car and you can go home for a while if you want."

"That sounds like a plan."

"Or I can drive you home if you wish. Did you take her keys from her handbag?"

"Yes," replied Rachel, waving them.

"Do you want to go in with me?"

"I was just there."

"How was she doing?"

"She said she was uncomfortable."

"That's breastplate pain caused by trauma to the sternum when the bullet was stopped by the Kevlar vest. Stine has bleeding from the lung in addition to the injury to his sternum, also from the vest. Has the doctor seen Ida yet?"

"That was a while ago."

"Did you speak with him?"

"He said she was stable. He didn't think the bleeding was a problem. Her chest is clear and her labs were okay."

"Did PT see her?"

"I don't think so."

"Okay, I'll be back in a few minutes," said Bloom, walking into the ICU. He was greeted by a different policeman from the one he saw last evening, who took a picture of his driver's license and directed him to Ida Stern's nurse.

"I'm Dr. Bloom," he said, approaching the nurse and introducing himself. She led him into Ida's room. When he didn't notice a urinary drainage bag on the side he was on, he moved around to the other side of the bed.

"What are you looking for?" asked the nurse.

"She had a foley in her last night. I wanted to see if it was removed."

"Are you a physician?" she asked.

"I'm her urologist as well as the urologist of Mr. Stine."

"Are you on staff here?"

"I teach the urology residents here. I see her catheter is in. Her urine looks okay. Can I rouse her a little?"

"She goes in and out."

"Is she having much pain?"

"It's not too bad."

"Has she been out of bed?"

"Not yet. We're waiting for PT."

"Is she still NPO other than the ice chips?"

"Yes. She hasn't asked for any ice chips yet."

"I'm going to gently touch her shoulders," said Bloom, leaning over her and softly making a *psst* sound.

"Jamie," she said, opening her eyes. "Where am I?"

"You're in Jackson Memorial Hospital."

"How'd I get here?"

"By helicopter."

"How is Sophie?"

"She's okay. A little shaken up. She's a few curtains to the left."

"What about my buddy?"

"Stine?"

"Okay, he's not my buddy. Is he dead?"

"Not yet."

"Almost?"

"He's got more problems than you."

"What problems do I have?"

"A bruised sternum."

"Stephanie Kwolek saved my life."

"Yes."

"That's the third time she's done that. She's also saved Sophie's."

"And probably your buddy's."

"That bum was wearing a vest?"

"It looks that way."

"Where's my other buddy?"

"Who's that? Rachel?"

"My buddy from Israel," replied Ida, patting her right thigh.

"Your AK-47?"

"You've got that right!"

"They have a policy here. You have to check your buddies at the door."

"Can you find out where it is?"

"I assume the police have it."

"Have I been arrested?"

"I don't know your particular status. There's an officer sitting outside the entrance to the ICU."

"How bad is the neo-Nazi?"

"You shot him in the chest and, like you, he was wearing a Kevlar vest, so his sternal injury is probably comparable to yours. Your esophagus was mildly traumatized, and they're watching it. They may keep you NPO for a day or two or not at all. Stine's lung was injured and he's having significant bleeding from it. He also sustained a hip fracture that needs to be treated."

"That's funny," said Ida giving a short chortle. "Just before I pulled the trigger, Sophie told me to break a leg. She then corrected herself quickly by saying 'his leg, not your leg!' I said that since Stine was standing at the podium I would not be surprised if he broke his hip when he fell down after the shot to his chest. In war we are taught to aim at the chest and not the head. In war the enemy is more likely to be moving. Since the bullet loses gravity as it moves toward its target, I had to aim about seven inches above his chest to hit his chest. If I had aimed to hit his head and I was off, I might have missed him completely or hit him in the neck. "

"Did you know you hit him?"

"I never told you I spent all those years in the Israeli army with my AK-47 buddy. I used a 7.62x39 123 grains bullet, which hit him after losing half its energy and falling six inches in 0.3 seconds. The rifle has a telescope. It was like I was standing next to him. I saw exactly where I hit him. I watched him fall backward and saw him hit the ground. I would say he broke his left hip."

"Then what? What'd you do?"

"I looked for Clark."

"Why was that?"

"I thought I might as well take him out, too."

"What about the rest of the people on the dais?"

"Yeah. Why not?"

"Seriously?"

"Not really. But it probably would have been a worthwhile thing to do while I was in the neighborhood."

"Wouldn't it have been a mitzvah?"

"Now you're talking!"

"You want me to stop in on Sophie if I can?"

"Absolutely!"

"Did her family know what you and she were doing?

"Of course not!"

"When did you learn about the rally?"

"The day before it took place."

"What about the rifle, Kevlar jackets, target distances, and gravity drop-offs?"

"Rifle and vests were in the back of my linen closet."

"What about the gravity drop-offs?"

"That chart has been imprinted in my brain since 1971. If my car hasn't been impounded, look for it across the pond just to the left of the trees. Send Rachel back in and I can tell her what I'll need her to bring back to the hospital."

"Will do. Ida, can you tell me what happened to you and Sophie?"

"You mean while I was admiring my handiwork and looking for Clark et al. instead of hightailing it out of there?"

"Something like that."

"The people on the dais scattered. Someone returned fire and that was it. I felt a sharp pain in my chest, did a posterior trunk tilt, and fell backward. I have no recollection of any helicopter ride or being in the ER. Send my sister in and then go fetch my car."

"What kind of car do you have?"

"My sister knows."

Bloom found Sophie's nurse, learned whatever he could, and relayed it to Ida. When Rachel returned to Ida's room, she and Bloom left the hospital and took I-95 to the Rickenbacker Causeway and arrived at what was left of Ida's car 15 minutes later.

"Do you remember what Sonny's car looked like after going through the toll plaza?" asked Bloom.

"Sonny did not look too well either."

"That could be Sophie's car," said Rachel pointing to another car 50 yards away that got similar treatment.

Rachel opened the car's trunk and driver's door, took out anything of importance and closed the car. She took a number of pictures of the bullet-laden auto and drove off with Bloom to Ida's house.

"Don't open the door," said Bloom, grabbing the key from Rachel's hand. "Just wait a second." He opened the outer screen door, bent down, lifted the mail slot cover, put his nose in the slot, and took a deep breath. He coughed and closed the slot. "There's gas in the house."

"Ida doesn't have gas stovetops. She has electric ones."

"Does she have a gas grill and propane tanks?" asked Bloom.

"Outside. Oh, God she has a cat and a Quaker parakeet."

"Do you have a key to her back door?"

"You think the front door may be booby-trapped?"

"Who knows? Why should we smell gas in the house?"

"I have the key to the back door."

"Let's just see what's doing in the back. Come with me."

They walked between the detached houses and onto Ida's screened-in lanai.

"The grill is missing and so is the second propane tank," said Rachel.

"Does she keep the grill or grill tanks in the house?" asked Bloom.

"No. What do you want to do?"

"Does Ida have a security alarm?"

"She never uses it."

"What should we do regarding the pets?"

"Who knows if they're even in the house?"

"I doubt if Stine knows anything about the gas."

"Why do you say that?"

"Stine's goons do stuff on their own, and even though I think Stine is bad, I don't think he's mean."

"What about his goons?"

"I've seen how they protect him."

"So what do you say we do?"

"We go to your house and see if it's intact. Then I call Jones, the head goon."

Rachel's house was three-tenths of a mile away. Her car was intact and started right away." The doors were locked, and no gas was coming out of the mail slot.

"I'm glad things look normal here. Should we go inside?"

"Let me call Jones now," said Bloom, finding his number and calling him. Jones answered on the first ring.

"Yes, Dr. Bloom."

"I was at Ida's house and there's a gas smell coming from the mail slot in the front door."

"Yes."

"I have some questions I would please like you to answer."

"Since you said please, I will try to answer them. But first I would like you to answer a few of my questions."

"Sure."

"Did you know Ida was going to shoot Mr. Stine?"

"No."

"How were you able to arrive at the hospital within fifteen minutes of the helicopters?"

"Yesterday morning I got a call from Ida's sister Rachel telling me Ida was not at home and was without her phone, which was turned off. Rachel said she called Ida's main contacts, including her hair and nail salons, and couldn't find her. So she called me, and I called three or four news stations and found out nothing. I put on the TV and saw Mr. Stine was having a rally at 11:30 a.m. in Key Biscayne. We were afraid something might happen to her there, so we took I-95 south. When we were nearing Jackson Memorial Hospital, we learned from the news a shooting had just taken place, so we went to the hospital."

"You had no idea Ida had a gun and was proficient in using an AK-47?"

"Neither I nor Rachel."

"What about the note she had on the pad on her desk?"

"I wasn't in the house and Rachel didn't mention anything about a note."

"I saw some scribbling, but I didn't know what it meant," volunteered Rachel.

"Where did she keep the Kevlar jackets, rifle, and ammo?" asked Jones.

"She told me where when I saw her in the hospital this afternoon—in the back of the linen closet," said Bloom. "Can I ask my questions now?"

"You can ask as many as you want."

"If I open either Ida's front or back door, will there be an explosion? And what do I have to do to prevent the explosion? In addition, are Ida's pets still in the house? Last question, is Rachel's house safe for her to enter?"

"These are all good questions and I will try to answer them in a timely manner. Anything else you'd like to ask me?"

"Do you have any answers right now?"

"Yes. Call me and I'll tell you tomorrow."

"For the sake of the pets can you tell me if you've taken then out of the house?"

"Like I said, tomorrow is the day you might find out, or not."

"I must say, I expected a little more from you. Nonetheless, I'll try to resolve the issues without your help. And just to show you that despite your non-adult behavior, I will be helping you out. You will be very surprised (and not in a good way) when Mr. Stine finds out what you did. You see, despite what she represents and what she's done, Stine respects Ida. Let me give you some free advice, which you certainly don't deserve. You should tell him what you did and undo it before he finds out. Basically I'm saving your ass by taking care of the situation you created! He won't find out from me. But I will have to tell him should either of her pets gets sick or dies."

"Wait a minute!" screamed Jones. "Don't hang up!"

"How do we enter Ida's house? Is her sister's house safe to enter?"

"For Ida's house, break the window, detach the igniter at each door, and just pull out the igniter's plug."

"Thank you."

CHAPTER 98

JUST HAPPENED TO HEAR...

After Ida's ten-day stay at Jackson Memorial Hospital, Missy went there to bring her home.

While she was waiting in the nursing office, she said she saw two people who were being discharged that were having a rather interesting, amusing but serious conversation and were unaware she was there. She said she immediately began to record what they were saying.

"Care to listen to their conversation?"

"Are you going to tell me who they were?" asked Bloom.

"That won't be necessary. Here goes." Missy touched the "play" area on her phone.

"Is Clark the third going to continue taking care of your practice? You remember him, he's the one who purposely went into your room when you were septic and in isolation in order to decrease your health status and thereby increase his chances of becoming chief honcho?"

"I love your way with words, Ida. Are you planning another attack?"

"You mean because you didn't succumb?"

"You did do a number on my lung. I still have my hip to take care of."

"That's from those years in the Israeli army my using AK-47. You were standing when I saw my bullet hit your chest. So when you fell, you broke your hip. That was a bonus."

"You're a good enemy."

"You mean I'm worthwhile?"

"As an enemy."

"I am a Jew. As a Jew I'm worthwhile?"

"Yes. Would you now give me your bone marrow?"

"Nothing has changed. You're being released from the hospital. You don't need anyone's bone marrow."

"But if I need it at a later date?"

"What do you think? I owe you nothing. I didn't ask you to drop the charges against me."

"You know my people will get your marrow by one way or another."

"It'll have to be by another."

"Do you play golf?"

"As a matter of fact, I do."

"How are you at getting out of sand traps?"

"I don't know. I've never been in one."

"I don't want you to have to call 911."

"Like Mr. Gold? Did one of your buddies get his first kidney?"

"As a favor to your Dr. Bloom, I'm keeping him from losing his second one."

"Thank you. That should get you a Nobel Peace Prize."

"Are you always this charming?"

"I'm a charming individual. I'm only this way with neo-Nazis."

"I, too, was once a charming individual."

"Yes, you were, for a few minutes in Dunkin' Donuts, until you abandoned that injured Jewish boy."

"I mean in my much earlier life. I'd like to tell you about it."

"That's not gonna happen."

"Why not?"

"I don't want to hear about the boy you pushed onto the tracks of an oncoming train."

"That's all she wrote," said Missy, announcing the end of the recorded conversation.

"Sounds like Stine wants their relationship to continue," said Bloom, "but Ida's not interested."

"Did you just take a psychology tutorial?" asked Missy.

"Why, was there one missing?"

CHAPTER 99

WHY HAVE YOU BEEN SO NICE?

"Hi, Ida. Sorry I wasn't able to see you two days ago when you were discharged from the hospital," said Bloom.

"You were busy."

"How are you feeling?"

"My chest is a little sore. My esophagus appears to be healing. The bleeding seems to have stopped. Everything is a fog. Tell me again what happened at my house?"

"You had some gas leakage. Henchman Jones put your two patio propane gas tanks into your house and let the gas escape."

"What'd he do with Quacker and Purrer?"

"He left them in the house. I took them to a vet. Purrer was kind of sluggish and Quacker was not talking much. They're both doing better. Rachel is looking after them.

"That was from the gas?"

"Uh huh."

"I doubt Stine instructed them to do it."

"So do I."

"Did you tell Stine about it?"

"I haven't seen or spoken to him in a while."

"Jones did a bad thing. Stine needs to know about it."

"I'd be very surprised if Stine knew about it. Before I forget, my office called me this morning to tell me they received Sigmund's passport and fingerprints from Oskar Fuchs."

"What do you plan to do with them?"

"Match them up with those collected in the FBI's database to see if we can get a last name. Remember we learned that Sigmund was probably adopted by another family in Brooklyn with which Fuchs was unable to touch base. The fingerprints could be related to a crime or to a job application. We learned from Oskar that Sigmund was in a Brooklyn branch of the New York Foundling on Livingston Street between 1945 and 1947, but not under the name of Fuchs. Fingerprints don't significantly change as one gets older, so successful matching can occur at any age."

"I haven't thought about him in a while," replied Ida.

"We've all had a lot on our plates recently. I'm going to start the ball rolling today concerning the fingerprints. I don't expect immediate results, but I'm certain at one time or another, considering some of his past actions, we'll come up with something."

"I'd like you to mention Jones to Stine," repeated Ida. "And please let me know when you have."

"Right after my calls to the FBI, but that might take a while."

"Got you loud and clear. Bye."

Bloom got dressed and drove to the office, picked up the material sent by Oskar Fuchs, sat down at his desk, and spent the next two hours trying to access the FBI's Integrated Automated Fingerprint Identification System (IAFIS) for an eighty-nine-year-old German Holocaust survivor mother who had given up her son just before being sent to Auschwitz in 1940. He told them she had a copy of his fingerprints, and she was looking to reunite with him. Bloom was given some additional numbers and organizations to call as well as how and where he should send the material.

Then he called Stine, who was glad to hear from him. Stine said he was not aware of what was done to Ida's house and her pets. He said for some strange reason, considering what she represents and all the venom she's spewed at him, he likes her. "But don't tell her so," he added. Bloom then called Ida and told her he had spoken to Stine.

"And?" she asked.

Q: On page 320, Bloom tells Ida she mad
it to 90. If I'm reading that correctly, she
wouldn't be eighty-nine anymore... ?

"He said he didn't know about it. Time will tell. We'll see if and how much of Jones remains part of his goon squad."

Five minutes later Bloom received a call from his office asking him to call Stine.

"Mr. Stine, how can I help you?" asked Bloom after making the call.

"I should have asked you something when I had you on the phone," said Stine. "My butt has been itching for the past week."

"You're scheduled to see me in three days.

"I think I can wait. Did you mention anything to Ida about me liking her?"

"No. That's between you and me. Have you told her yourself?"

"No. But I think she knows that."

"It's amazing how you two could possibly connect."

"I don't think she would say we've connected."

"You're probably right."

"I think she'd still kill me if she got the chance."

"Again, you're probably right."

"Dr. Bloom, why have you been so nice to me?"

"Hippocratic oath for one thing. Hippocratic oath for another thing. Self-preservation for my family for a third thing. I try to separate our relationship from what you've done to Ida, to me and my family, and for what you stand for."

"That's the way my life turned out."

"It's a shame. That's my opinion."

CHAPTER 100

AWOL TAKE 2

"According to the *Philadelphia Inquirer*," said Bloom, "Our NNS is starting back this Tuesday on his first Goose-Stepping Philly marching tour since his left hip repair three weeks ago in Florida."

"I guess Neo-Nazi Stine decided not to go ahead with the bone marrow transplant," replied Missy.

"Susan said that even if Ida agreed to it, which she said she'd never do, Stine said he had gone through too much recently to go ahead with it."

"Is Ida planning a short trip to the City of Brotherly Love?" asked Missy.

"We'd better call Rachel and give her a heads up," said Bloom. "Do you think Ida and Sophie Bernshtein already have one?"

"Already have one what?"

"A heads up."

"I think both Ida and Stine and their cohorts know exactly what the other one is up to," said Missy. "I don't think I really want to know what's up her sleeve."

"We have to make sure she's safe. Do you think she's already in or on her way to Philly?"

"Nothing would surprise me."

"Whom should we call, Ida or Rachel?"

"Ida."

"Ida it is," said Bloom, dialing her number. "No answer after fifteen rings. I'm calling Rachel."

"Wait! What are you going to say to her?"

"I'm going to tell her I need to reach Ida to talk about one of the medications she's taking. That I've been unable to reach her. I'll ask her if she's away."

"Suppose she doesn't know where she is?"

"I'd ask her the last time she spoke with her."

"Suppose she says two days ago?"

"I'd ask her if she could be visiting a friend. If she says like who, I'd say Sophie Bernshtein, or ask her if she knows anyone in Philadelphia."

"Suppose she says other than William Stine? He's not there now. But he's supposed to be there sometime next week."

"I'd ask, 'How do you know about Stine?'"

Missy replied, as if she were Rachel, "He's always on Ida's radar."

Bloom continued with the imagined conversation, "How did *you* learn about Philly?"

"From Ida."

"Did she say anything about paying Stine a visit?"

"She hinted at it."

"What'd she say?"

"Something about completing the job."

"Does she have her AK-47 with her?"

"I can't discuss that with you."

"Why not?"

"That might make you an accessory."

"Was there anything else she said?"

"She said she thinks it's about 50-50 she'll be killed. I don't know why she told me that. She said this was her decision, and this would be the way she'd want to go out."

"And that's okay with you?"

"I don't want to talk about it."

"If she kills Stine, someone like Russell Clark III will fill the vacated position."

"There'll always be somebody. That's not the point. With Stine, it's personal! He killed two of her friends and tried to kill her multiple times. In Florida she had an advantage, not so in Philly. And I'm sure they're already onto her."

"This whole thing stinks."

"Yes, it does."

"Still, I would like to be kept in the loop."

Bloom then called Rachel and had almost verbatim the made-up conversation he just had with Missy, including to have Rachel agree to keep him in the loop. He told all this to Missy, including the fact that Ida may not have her phone.

"What are you going to do?" Missy asked.

"I don't know. I don't want her to die."

CHAPTER 101

IMPRISONED IN THE RITZ

"When are you goons going to release me?" asked Ida, looking out the window from the top floor of the Philly Ritz-Carlton onto 10th Avenue of the Arts.

"Sometime after tomorrow's march," replied Tess, her captor. "And never call me a goon!"

"What is your title? Goonness? Female goon?" asked Ida.

"I'm carrying a gun and I don't mind using it."

"I'm sorry. I don't mean to be rude," said Ida, sarcastically.

"You need to shut up," said Tess, pulling out her gun and pointing it at Ida.

"Okay, okay," replied Ida raising her hands.

"You'll be released tomorrow after the march is over. And you're not getting your gun back. You should be thankful President Stine put a woman in here with you. I don't know why he bothered. Why he thinks any man would want to fuck you is beyond me. How old are you?"

"Almost ninety."

"Have you ever been fucked?"

"No," she lied.

"Tonight will be the night you're fucked by a woman."

"I thought your leader didn't approve of homosexual activity."

"He doesn't. But we ain't gonna tell him," replied Tess, taking out her gun again.

We'll see about that, said Ida to herself, adjusting her left bra strap and slightly raising a small pistol in her bra.

At exactly ten o'clock, Tess called Ida into her room. Tess was naked, spread-eagle, and holding her ankles, pulling them back 180 degrees like someone anticipating deep tongue and/or deep penile penetration. Ida unbuttoned her blouse, turned around, took it off, removed her gun and straddled Tess, putting the muzzle of the gun into Tess's vagina.

"Feel that? That's my gun in your cunt!" shouted Ida, deciding that was the language she'd have to use with her. "Don't move or squirm a fucking inch. If I pull the trigger, you will never fuck again, you will never piss again, and you will never shit again. And don't move backward looking for your gun. It's not in your fucking nightstand," said Ida. "It's here," she added, showing Tess the gun that Tess had kept there. "I don't want to see your fucking face anymore. If you come out of this room, I will shoot you in your fucking face with your fucking gun. If you stay in this room, I won't tell President Stine about your motherfucking sexual fuckups."

Ida un-straddled Tess, taking the muzzle out of Tess's vagina, pointing it at her, then picked up her blouse and backed out of the room, closing the door behind her. She took the pull cords she had previously removed from the curtains, tied two of the cords to Tess's doorknob, unplugged and moved the refrigerator against Tess's door and anchored it so Tess couldn't get out of her room. She then unsuccessfully searched the suite again for her AK-47.

I have to make a decision, she said to herself. *I have two guns now instead of one but I'm missing my baby. Tess will definitely alert Stine of the situation and whatever advantage I had when he thought I was holed up in this room I've lost. He could cancel the march but probably wouldn't do that. Maybe I can get hold of another rifle. I can make some calls. Damn, all my numbers are in my phone. Without my baby, it'll be difficult and he'll probably be Kevlared to the hilt, and he and his goons will be doubly vigilant after Tess calls him. Maybe she'll be too embarrassed to tell him about losing her gun and being locked in her room. I doubt that. I better just get out of Dodge.*

She called Rachel from the lobby and said she was okay and on her way home.

CHAPTER 102

A STINE/STERN MEETING

"Dr. Bloom, William Stine's on line 2," said Cathy through the intercom. "He says it's personal."

"Yes, Mr. Stine," said Bloom picking up. "Whatcha got?"

"I've got a problem with one of your patients."

"Let me guess."

"I'm having to spend too much time, money, and energy keeping her out of harm's way. Because she's hell-bent on killing me, my men are chomping at the bit to kill her!"

"Mr. Stine, we're very appreciative of your efforts," replied Bloom, really wishing to say, "Sounds like you're now doing what she had been doing for so long, trying to keep you from killing her!"

"It can't continue," added Stine. "I've tried calling but have been unable to get through. I'd like to have a cease fire and sit down and talk with her. Is there any way you can help me?"

"I'd like to help. I'll see what I can do."

Bloom terminated the call with Stine, dialed Rachel's number and was told about Ida's Philadelphia ordeal. He learned Ida had gone to Philadelphia to kill Stine, who already had known about it and sent his men to keep her prisoner in her Ritz-Carlton room. She added that Ida managed to escape, but because her rifle had been taken from her and couldn't be replaced, she aborted the plan. Rachel also said Stine had reimbursed Ida for the hotel stay, the cost of the rifle and ammo, and the plane fare back to Ft. Lauderdale.

Bloom told Rachel that Stine wanted to speak with Ida to see if the situation could be resolved. "Honestly, I don't know how this can happen. I've got the impression that at this point in her life, killing Stine is worth the risk of giving up her own life."

"I'd say you're probably right," said Rachel. "But deciding a few days ago not to continue because she could not replace her rifle gives us some hope she may not be as committed as he's convinced she is."

"He's trying to get a cease fire for them to meet. He trusts Ida will keep her end of the bargain if she agrees. But I can't say I believe for sure that she'd comply. Do you think she'd agree to a cease fire?"

"Are you asking me to ask her?"

"Yes."

"I can do that. But I can tell you she'll never meet with him."

Ten minutes later Ida called Bloom's office.

"This'll never work," she said when Bloom got on the line.

"What won't work, the cease fire?" replied Bloom.

"That's the first thing."

"Why won't it work?"

"Maybe it will work, meaning that either I or Stine or both of us will kill the other within the first few seconds after we meet. I mean, that should resolve the issue."

"So basically you won't agree to a cease fire."

"Oh, I'll agree to it. I just won't follow it!"

"How's that going to happen? You'll both be patted down by two people, one from each team."

"Okay, so I won't agree to it."

"Ida, can I speak uninterrupted for a few minutes?"

Ida didn't reply.

After a silence of ten seconds Bloom laughed.

"We're both tough cookies," said Ida, also laughing. "Speak."

"Ida, you know I love you, don't you?"

"Yes. Speak already!"

"For some weird reason, Stine likes you. I'm sure you already know that. Although he, your sister, and I feel you're committed to wanting him dead, Stine doesn't want anything to happen to you, and it's not all related to your bone marrow. When you decided to abort your plan because you thought your chances for success were greatly diminished with your AK-47, your sister and I were hoping that might mean you may not be that hell-bent on seeing this through, and that your life did matter to you, like it matters to us.

"Stine was told by a number of people to have a bone marrow transplant because of his age. He has a donor, though it's not as good as you would be. The reasons he gave for not going ahead with it was that he said he had gone through enough from his gunshot wound and add-on hip surgery. Will he need to have it sometime in the future? We don't know. But as of now, it is off the table.

"Stine has been spending a lot of time, energy, and money keeping you safe from his entourage, who I know for a fact is eager to kill you, despite his orders not to harm you. Most of the money he spends to keep you safe comes out of pocket, including your Ritz-Carlton Hotel bill and flight back to Ft. Lauderdale. He dismissed Jones because of what he did to your house and to Purrer and Quacker—although, I have to say, Quacker is not a very good name for a Quaker parakeet. No comment, please.

"Although it is true that nothing substantial might come from a meeting with him, one never knows. Might there be someone in your organization that could do the 'job' for you? Is there something he could do to lessen the need to kill him? Is there anything in his early past that could have led him to the path he took? Considering your age and health, is your need to kill him something that has to be done, whatever the cost to you?

"It's always good, if you're able, to dialogue with your enemy. There should be more instances like this available in life. I know it sounds like you have an ideal situation as is, a sort of win-win situation, so you may not feel the need to change the present status, but I strongly disagree. Okay, your turn."

"I hate the guy and what he stands for. I feel it would be a supreme mitzvah if I killed or someone else killed him. He is a protégé of Hitler, the man who killed most of my family and supported barbaric experimentation that inflicted pain on me and my sister and in some part is responsible for me now being childless. Stine is responsible for many deaths and the perpetuation of the madman's philosophies. There's no way I want to sit in the same room with him and validate his life's work. Your turn."

"Suppose he could be turned around? I know that would be more difficult and more time-consuming. You'd actually have to work with him. Your turn."

"There's too much venom in me for that. It would be much more fun killing him. And there would be immediate gratification. No, I'm not interested in that. No more turns."

"Sorry. One more turn. He may accept your decision to not meet with him and continue protecting you or he may feel very slighted and not protect you anymore. It may be wiser to meet with him once and say face to face what you feel. Please run our chat by Rachel. Thanks."

Rachel called Bloom twenty minutes later to tell him that Ida was not going to meet with Stine, mentioning Bloom's salient points and Ida's responses.

CHAPTER 103

THE IAFIS REPORT

loom heard what sounded like "Dalai Yama" being yelled and got up from his desk and opened his office door. He saw Stine in his wheelchair accompanied by his aide David in the waiting area.

"Aretha said she'd be back in two minutes," said Stine.

"Are you having a problem?" asked Bloom, unaware he was seeing patients today.

"I need help removing the Band-Aid," said Stine. "I tried but I couldn't get it off. Even in the shower."

"Wasn't it to come off last week?"

"I had a dental emergency."

Everything okay?"

"A filling came out."

"Did you ask the dentist if he could remove the Band-Aid?"

"The dentist is a she."

"Okay," said Bloom laughing. "What was someone yelling a little while ago?" asked Bloom, turning his head toward the TV screen and seeing the Dalai Lama's picture.

"I'm back," announced Aretha, coming into the office.

"Were you in the office when we put a Band-Aid on Mr. Stine's butt?" asked Bloom. "I know Cathy was here."

"No, I wasn't."

"Just let me know if you speak with her while I'm in the office."

"Will do."

Bloom went into the exam room and came out two minutes later after depositing his gloves and the Band-Aid into the biohazard box.

"Dr. Bloom, IAFIS is on line 2," announced Aretha.

"Tell them I'll be with them in a minute. They probably can't do it or they need more information," Bloom told Aretha.

"This is Dr. Bloom," he said, picking up the line.

"Hello, Dr. Bloom. This is Susan from IAFIS. We've got the results for you, which we're sending to your office. Do you have pen and paper to jot some things down?"

"Sure. What do you have?"

"I have three names for you."

Three? Three names? Here goes nothing, thought Bloom, expecting no help from IAFIS.

"The first is Sigmund Fuchs F-U-C-H-S. The second is William Stein S-T-E-I-N. The third is William Stine S-T-I-N-E. The last two names are pronounced the same. All three are the same person."

Bloom was dumbfounded and asked the second and third names to be re-spelled, although he didn't know why he asked that. He sat back in his chair, took some deep breaths, and used the intercom to ask Cathy to remind him when it was ten minutes before the hour.

"Do you want me to get Missy on the line at that time?" asked Cathy, knowing ten minutes to the hour was when Missy was finished with her patient's session.

"Please."

"I heard you yell 'Wow!' Is everything okay?"

"Yes. These walls are paper thin. See if we can get them padded."

"Seriously?"

"No." Bloom sank back in his chair and waited for Missy's call. His head was abuzz with the new information and the possibilities that could ensue, and he thought the picture made sense—a lot of sense.

"Missy's on line 1," said Cathy twenty-five minutes later, startling him out of his reverie.

"How much time do you have?" asked Bloom picking up.

"An hour. My next patient rescheduled."

"I found Ida's son!" announced Bloom.

"Is it Stine?" blurted out Missy.

"We both thought it might be," answered Bloom. "Remember two weeks ago I told you some patient ate the last two Mallomars in my office?"

"Uh huh. You said it could have been Stine."

"It was. He told Cathy those were his all-time favorite cookies and that he grew up on them. She said the next day his goons brought in three boxes for the office."

"That was nice."

"Today Stine yelled 'Dalai Yama' when he saw His Holiness on the TV in my waiting area. He said he'd been calling him that for as long as he could remember. And Adele told Ida Sigmund used to call his pet llama 'Yama.'"

"That's funny. But neither of these things prove anything."

"This morning, I got a call from IAFIS."

"What's IAFIS?" asked Missy."

"The Integrated Automated Fingerprint Identification System. They analyzed Sigmund's fingerprints we got from Oskar Fuchs. Are you ready for this?"

"I'm ready."

"They said the fingerprints match three people."

"How can that be?"

"The people are Sigmund Fuchs, William S-t-e-i-n, and William S-t-i-n-e. He must have been adopted by the S-t-e-i-n-s after Oskar Fuchs."

"And we know he changed his name to Stine."

"Who should tell Ida? And should we tell Rachel first?"

"The information will be difficult for Ida to process no matter who gives it to her," said Missy. "Rachel may be the best person."

"Of course, especially since her recent rebuff of Stine's meeting proposal and cease fire. Do you think there could be a happy ending?"

"Considering how she felt while in Auschwitz about Sigmund being Hitler's son and the fact that after the war she said the orphanage was bombed and didn't go back for him, I think there will be a sad ending. Do you think she's better off not knowing?"

"Probably yes, but that doesn't factor in. Even with their natural animosity, there has developed some respect and a feeling of closeness toward one another."

"Mainly him for her," interrupted Missy.

"Yes, mainly him for her."

"Rachel Stern is on line 2," said Cathy.

"Ida is AWOL again," began Rachel once Bloom picked up. "I'm very worried this time! She's either not answering her phone, it's turned off, or it's not with her."

CHAPTER 104

SOMEONE NEEDS TO REACH IDA

"What timing!" Bloom remarked to Missy after telling her about the phone call he had just received from Rachel. "Ida may not have her phone with her."

"You'll need to find out if she can she still be reached," said Missy. "I can't believe this is happening now!"

A few seconds later Rachel called and said she was on her way to Ida's house.

"Rachel, before we go on a wild goose chase," began Bloom, "please speak with Ida's neighbors and call Sophie Bernshtein as well as Ida's friends. Also check the clock alarm settings and messages from the answering machine and check what's on her calendars and scratch pads. And check to see if she took her wallet and hearing aids, and also call her hair salon. Meanwhile I'll ask my office staff to see what they can dig up on William Stine's schedule—luncheon meetings, rallies, picture signings, neighborhood talks, community gatherings, whatever."

Bloom hung up with Rachel and got back on the line with Missy. "We didn't expect to have to tell Ida without first telling Stine or telling Stine without telling Ida, but we might have to," said Bloom.

"At least one of them should know," said Missy.

"Thankfully, I have Stine's phone number," added Bloom.

"As it could play out, why would either of them want to know?" asked Missy.

"What do you mean?"

"Ida finds out her son is a neo-Nazi and president of the American Nazi Party, and Stine finds out his birth mother is Jewish and he's no longer president of the Nazi Party."

"So you mean she may want to die not knowing he's her son?"

"Yes. And neither would Stine want to know his mother was Jewish. His first instinct might be to kill Ida and deny their relationship."

"There's no way that's going to happen. No way. Both of them will need help to resolve this. And I think they can wind up on the same page. A mother and her son and a son with his mother.

"What'll we do if we can't reach Ida and we feel we have to tell Stine, because he could now feel differently about not harming Ida, especially after what she recently told him about not wanting a cease fire or to meet with him? Remember she said it was okay to research her son to get a platelet donor for her or a bone marrow donor for Stine, but did not want to learn anything about her son."

"That was before she got involved with Adele, Gert, and Mr. and Mrs. Fuchs."

Meanwhile, Rachel called back saying neither Sophie Bernshtein nor anyone else she asked could locate Ida. Bloom's staff was unable to find a venue where Stine could be found, which created a waiting game for them all. Rachel said she had last spoken with Ida on the phone two days before.

"We should put a microchip into Ida so we know where she is at all times, like they're starting to do with pets," said Bloom, only half jokingly.

"I'm still at her house," said Rachel. "Her phone was here. Her wallet and hearing aids were not. Everything looked normal. Her pistol was not here, and if she replaced her AK-47, she took it with her."

"Was there anything else missing?"

"Yes. Purrer and Quacker."

"She took her pets?!"

"And their litter box and bird cage."

"Has she done that before?"

"Never. I'm sure it's because of what happened when she was hospitalized in Miami. She was terribly upset with herself for not taking them out of her house before she left for Philadelphia, and probably now since her last conversation with Stine, she wouldn't want to take that chance again."

"Is there a smell of gas in her house?"

"No."

"What about her medications?"

"She must have taken them."

"I know Bill from Bill's Bird Boutique in Davie, where Ida got Quacker, and the number of the vet she used. I'll call them. Can you get me the number of the pet store where she got the cat?"

"Yes, can do. Do we have a plan?"

"We're doing it! In a few days we'll start calling all the hospitals. But now, I need to tell you something. Are you sitting down? If not, please sit. Let me know when you're sitting."

"Is Ida all right?"

"It's not about Ida's health or whereabouts. Are you sitting?"

"I'm sitting. But Ida is alright?"

"Yes, she's alright."

"I just found out ten minutes ago—"

"Well, what is?"

"Auntie Rachel . . ."

"You found her son?"

"Yes."

"Well, who is it?"

"Are you still sitting?"

"Yes. Just tell me!"

"William Stine!"

"Blech!" uttered Rachel, throwing up. "Blech!" she continued.

"Rachel, are you alright?" yelled Bloom.

"Oh God! I just threw up," said Rachel still retching.

"Rachel, take some deep breaths."

"This has got to be the worst thing imaginable!" uttered Rachel, now hyperventilating and retching. "How'd you find out?" she asked, trying to catch her breath.

"Fingerprints."

"Through Oskar Fuchs?"

"Yes. I'm going to let you digest this for a while. Right now, just think about how it'll affect Ida. Missy and I have already discussed it."

"And?"

"You need to think about it. Since you're the one who will tell Ida—that is, you will decide to tell her or not. We'll all discuss it, but you will make the decision. Again, sorry. The question is what's in the best interest for Ida? Call us when you're ready to talk."

"It certainly makes sense about Stine," said Rachel calming down. "We knew he was adopted. His early history was sketchy. And his and Ida's DNA match. But I must say the possibility never crossed my mind even once."

"I know this is a lot to process right now, but we still need to find Ida."

They hung up and Bloom dialed the boutique's number, exchanging pleasantries with the owner Bill and learning that Ida had recently boarded Quacker there. He found the same situation with Purrer, when he called the pet store. He called Rachel back to tell her what he had found out.

"We've called all the hospitals within a hundred-mile radius," said Rachel. "She hasn't called any of us and has boarded her pets. There has to be something more we can do."

"There is," replied Bloom, debating over whether he should call Stine and ask him if he's sequestering Ida in some hotel like he did in Philly or if he's planning some event where Ida could be lying in wait.

"There is? What?" Rachel asked.

"I need to run something by Missy before I tell you. I'll see if I can reach her this morning," added Bloom, seeing it was 10:45, hanging up with Rachel. At 10:51 he called Missy.

"Watcha got there, Jamie?" she asked.

He told her his thought about calling Stine. "But if I do, that might put Ida in danger if now Stine was no longer wanting to keep her safe based on her response to not sitting down with him and not having a cease fire, but if he was keeping her confined, he'd be able to talk with her any time. But on the other hand, if he had been planning to harm her, he might change his mind. Maybe it's better not to say anything because that's probably what Ida would have wanted."

"Quite a soliloquy punctuated with a run-on sentence or two," replied Missy.

"I know. The bottom line, I think we'd best not talk to Stine yet."

"I agree."

Bloom hung up, thought some more, then called Rachel and told her they should wait a few more days to see if Ida resurfaces.

"Can there possibly be a good outcome from this info about Stine?" she asked.

"For whom?" asked Bloom. "If the info about Stine comes out, I would think most likely he will be removed from his post, either by himself or by his organization. But if acceptance with change occurs, he might get a good outcome. But who knows? He could wind up committing suicide, or first killing Ida."

"I'm talking about a good outcome for Ida!"

"If Stine dies by the hands of Ida, she would be happy. But if she later learns that Stine was her son, that would probably be bad."

"If Stine doesn't die, can Ida still be happy?"

"Again, if he changes and bonds with Ida—and Ida lets him—Ida might also change."

"I think the best thing would be for Stine to die and Ida to never learn Stine was her son," said Rachel

"I don't agree," said Bloom. "We need to see how the present episode plays out. The question is, do we intercede on Ida's behalf to keep her alive? I think we should wait."

"Je suis d'accord."

That evening at 7:34 p.m., Dr. Bloom received a call from Dr. Osmi Hernan from Jackson Memorial Hospital, telling him that his patient was in the surgical ICU.

"What is the patient's name?" asked Bloom.

"Ida Stern," answered Hernan. "She's a patient of yours, isn't she?"

"Yes. What's wrong with her?"

"Haven't you been watching her rescue on TV this evening?"

"Rescue from where?"

"From a collapsing painting scaffold on the seventeenth floor of a Miami high-rise."

"I'm sorry, did you say from a collapsing painting scaffold on the seventeenth floor?" repeated Bloom.

"Yes."

"What was she doing there? Never mind. What happened to her?"

"She's lost a fair amount of blood from a leg laceration."

"Is her leg intact?"

"Yes, the laceration was closed. There were no vascular injuries. Her leg is nice and warm."

"Has she gotten any blood?"

"She gotten some. We're trying to get more."

"Where'd you get the blood?"

"I'm not sure."

"Is she stable?"

"The bleeding's been stopped. As I said, we're still trying to get more blood."

"What's her BP?"

"80 over 60."

"What's her mental status?"

"She knows where she is. She knew your number."

"I'm not on staff here. But I teach here. I live in Broward County. I'll be there as soon as I can get there. Tell her I'm coming and I'll try to bring her sister."

"You don't have to come."

"Trust me, I do. Just to be on the safe side, if you have a HIPAA form, please have Ida sign it, giving me and her sister Rachel permission to speak with her medical and nursing staff."

CHAPTER 105

EMERGENCY SURGERY IS NEEDED

"Dr. Bloom, a new patient is on line 2," said Aretha. "He said his foreskin is stuck and he can't pull it back down over his penis. He's in a lot of pain. Your vasectomy patient rescheduled. Should I bring the patient with paraphimosis in right now?"

"Yes," replied Bloom. "Tell him not to eat or drink and have him come in right now. Also find out if someone can drive him here."

"Will do."

"How'd you know that word?" asked Bloom.

"Crossword puzzles," replied Aretha.

"I'm profoundly impressed."

"My husband had that condition."

"Too much information," replied Bloom chuckling. "After you do that, please get the Jackson Memorial Hospital surgical ICU on the phone. I'd like to speak with the nurse taking care of Ida Stern. Any patients waiting to be seen?"

"Yes. William Stine is here to speak with you. Should I send him in?"

"No! Not yet!"

Oh, God! Bloom thought. *I hope Rachel has her phone on.*

On the fourth ring, Rachel picked up.

"I've got a problem here. Stine's in my office. He wants to speak with me."

"Don't tell him."

"I didn't plan to. Did you tell Ida?"

"No, and I'm not going to."

"How's she doing? I didn't get a chance to speak with her doctor or nurse this morning."

"I haven't seen or spoken with Ida yet either."

"As far as you know, what happened yesterday?"

"She was on the scaffold with another person for the purpose of shooting someone who lived in that building."

"Whaaa?"

"Stine's building. I didn't know he lived there."

"Anything else?"

"She managed to get a shot off that grazed his neck as the scaffold was falling."

"She's unbelievable! Can we tell Stine that Ida said she'd no longer go after him?"

"Why would she have said that?"

"Then what should I tell him?"

"Tell him something!"

"Rachel!"

"Tell him we'll talk to her!"

"That won't be acceptable."

"Try it."

"Why don't we just tell the truth and let the chips fall where they may?"

"You are not going to tell him!"

"It was just a suggestion."

"It's not your choice to make."

"I hear you!"

"You'd better remember that."

"Should I tell him to talk to you?"

"Listen to what he has to say and get back to me."

"10-4!"

Bloom hung up and brought Stine into his office. He shook his hand and noticed a bandage on his neck.

"What happened yesterday?" asked Bloom.

"First, how is Ida doing?"

"I haven't yet spoken with her doctor or nurse."

"Did you see her last night?"

"Yes, in the ICU."

"How was she?"

"Her vital signs were starting to stabilize. We're still trying to get her more blood."

"What did you hear happened?"

"She was rescued from a malfunctioning scaffold on a Miami high-rise."

"What was she doing there?"

"I guess painting or cleaning windows."

Stine laughed.

"Did you cut yourself shaving?" asked Bloom.

"Only when I shave with my Smith & Wesson."

"What can I do for you?"

"It's obvious. I've never met such an obsessed person."

"Is that good or bad?"

"Both."

"I just spoke with Ida's sister."

"What did Rachel say?"

"She said she'll talk to Ida."

"Why can't I talk with Ida? Can you arrange it?"

"Why don't you sit down and talk with her?"

"Great idea!" replied Stine smiling. "Can you arrange that?"

"She'll probably want to bring Mr. Wesson and Mrs. Smith along with her."

"They're not invited."

"You know she doesn't want to sit down with you."

"Why not?"

"We're not going through that again."

"We need to."

"It ain't gonna happen."

"What do I have to do?"

"Are you serious?"

"I don't know. Somebody make me an offer."

"You make an offer. You need to talk with Rachel."

"I'd rather talk to you."

"Make an offer."

"You make an offer."

"I may make an offer that you can't refuse."

"I usually don't like those kinds of offers."

"Have you ever liked any?"

"Not that I can remember."

"Meanwhile, you should be safe while Ida is in the hospital."

"I'm never safe from her."

Bloom was going to send him off with a Mallomar but he didn't want to mention anything that might remind Stine of his younger days. They shook hands goodbye, and Bloom said he would call him shortly. After he left, Aretha got Rachel got on the phone.

When Rachel got on the line, Bloom said, "Stine has come and gone."

"And?" Rachel asked.

"He wants to sit down with Ida. I said that wasn't going to happen. Then he asked what he had to do to make it happen. I asked him if he was serious. Then he said he didn't know but wanted somebody to make him an offer. I told *him* to make an offer, or to talk to you. He said he'd rather talk to me and again asked someone to make him an offer. And I said I may make an offer he couldn't refuse—meaning that he should voluntarily give up his neo-Nazi position or we'd announce that Ida Stern (the Jew) is his mother and therefore he's Jewish, which would be the end of his reign. Of course, I didn't say that to him. But if he did, do you think she'd still need to have to kill him for what he's done?"

"I don't think it's a decision she could or would make now."

"Suppose he steps down with just the threat of disclosing their relationship?"

"That would mean they both would learn of the relationship."

"For this, they'd sit down together."

"I must say, this sounds very intriguing!" said Rachel. "I don't know if either of them would go for it. Wouldn't that be more likely to put Ida's life in danger?"

"Possibly. But we have the proof, and he also likes her."

"To give up one's life's work or to kill one's mother--."

"She only has five to ten more years of life to live."

"She has nine lives."

"And she's used up ten of them already."

"Sorry to interrupt, Dr. Bloom," said Aretha, "but the paraphimosis patient is in a lot of pain and is ready to be seen. He's in the second exam room with his wife."

"Thank you," Rachel, I have an emergency here. I'll call you after I take care of my patient."

Bloom hung up and went into the exam room and introduced himself to the patient and his wife. He took the patient's medical history and performed a physical examination, explaining the condition and the need to take care of the problem, not only to relieve his pain but to prevent injury to the penis, which could already be present.

"What kind of injury?" interrupted the wife.

"Gangrene of the penis with loss of a portion of it."

"How does it look now?"

"I don't see any gangrene now, but it's a matter of how long the blood supply of the penis has been compromised. The first thing I'd do is try to manipulate the foreskin off the shaft of the penis, back into it's normal anatomic position."

"Suppose you can't?"

"I'd have to do it surgically."

"In the office?"

"With local anesthetic."

"How successful is that?"

"I should be able to do it. If not, I'd have to do it in the OR."

"We don't have insurance."

"Something needs to be done regardless."

"How much would we have to pay you?"

"I can find out for you. But I really won't know until I do what I have to do. And we'd work with you regarding the payment. His health is the main issue here."

"Why's that?"

"This is an emergency. He needs to take care of this now!"

"We'd like to get another opinion."

"That's fine, Mrs. Johnson. We have two other urologists in this building. My office will give you their names and phone numbers. But please see them right now."

Bloom walked the couple into Aretha's office, who gave them the building's other two urologists' names and numbers, and he quietly told her not to charge the patient. The couple left the office and did not say anything to Aretha about paying for the office visit. Bloom spent the next twenty minutes documenting the office visit and recording a note for the chart, including the comment he made to the couple as they left to return to the office if they were unable to see another urologist.

A call to Jackson Memorial Hospital was put through and Bloom learned that Ida's blood pressure was still low but stable and, without further bleeding, she probably would be leaving the ICU tomorrow and possibly be discharged in two days. Bloom told Ida he'd see her this evening. With that in mind, Bloom got Stine's office chart and made a copy of his office photo and put it in his wallet. Then he called Bill's Bird Boutique and the pet store that boarded Purrer, learned her pets were doing well, and told them Ida would be picking them up in a few days.

He then called Rachel, left the news about Ida and her pets, and saw four more patients, then called Rachel again.

"I want to tell you a little about Stine, whom I've gotten to know over the past year or so. The first time I heard of him was when I was visiting Ida in the hospital and his picture appeared on her TV screen. She screamed 'Mamzer!' cleared her throat and spit on the screen. She explained the meaning of mamzer and did a soliloquy about William Stine, who he is, and the terrible things he'd done. I immediately disliked him, and she hadn't even been shot yet. At that time, he was one of the leaders of the Nordics Against Zionistic Inhabitation Party. My personal introduction to him was not good. He replaced one of my circumcision patients with another person of his choosing, and I was later forced to perform that same operation on another patient, when I was kidnapped, sedated, and held captive in a limo, where I did the surgery. When I refused to accept payment for my 'services,' one of his goons pulled a gun on me and threatened to harm my son Peter if I didn't comply. I finally met Stine when he became a patient. I must say I was quite surprised by his demeanor. He was funny, polite, had a great sense of humor, and was very appreciative of my care. He was hospitalized a number of times by me and was always pleasant and appreciative. I reported everything to my lawyer and put all that money I was forced to take into a special account. All this was going on before and after he shot Ida for being part of the group that tried to stop the Skokie march in June 1978.

"Even Ida spent a pleasant morning with him and thought he was charming, before she realized who he was and before the neo-Nazi showed his true colors. Over the past few months, we've blamed him for a number of things we were not able to substantiate, namely, sabotaging her ventilator and killing her platelet donor. Whether due to guilt, which I doubt, or more likely, an ulterior motive of obtaining her bone marrow, he sent Missy and me to Cincinnati to make sure Ida received proper medical care, managed to get her a private room in Health South after her stroke in a facility that never had private rooms, and was able to get her platelets on at least two occasions when she was bleeding out. A lot of the bad things he was blamed for may have been perpetuated by his goons, including threatening my family and gassing Ida's house and pets with propane. Most recently he showed admiration and, I might add, affection for her. He has seen her dedication to her cause, and he admires her for it. I think he might be amenable to some form of compromise and possibly even resign his position without being forced and have a relationship with her. I feel some change can or is taking place in him, although I know it can't erase the bad he's done. I shouldn't but I must say this—your sister's absence, though excusable to some degree in 1945, may have played a role in determining the path he took. I feel he might be amenable to some form of compromise, especially if he retires."

"I think you somehow have been brain-washed, and I'm sure Ida won't see things as you do. I certainly don't."

"You may be right. I'll see you at the hospital tonight."

"See you then."

Bloom saw the rest of the patients on his schedule, called the Johnsons and left a message, made hospital rounds, spoke with Missy, and went home. He changed, lowered the hoop on basketball backboard, shot baskets with Peter, hit a dozen golf balls into a net, swam a few laps in the pool, showered, and got dressed. He read *Rumpelstiltskin* to Lisa, had dinner with the family, and left for Jackson.

At the hospital he introduced himself to the blood bank supervisor and asked to see the technician who obtained the blood for Ida's platelet transfusion last evening.

"Was there a problem?" asked the supervisor.

"No, I just want to speak with him."

"Can I ask you why?"

"I would like to speak with him," repeated Boom.

"I ask again. Why?"

"Because the woman who received the platelets last night is a patient of mine and she is also immune to platelets resulting from previous transfusions and requires HLA platelets from a special donor."

"What does that have to do with the technician?"

"I would like to know if my patient got HLA platelets."

"She got HLA platelets."

"Great! I would still like to speak with the technician."

"What for?"

"My patient is still hypotensive and may need more blood. I would like to know who donated the HLA platelets just in case. Was it William Stine?"

"I can't say yes or no," replied the supervisor, nodding.

"Okay," answered Bloom, likewise nodding. Leaving the blood bank with a smile, he headed for the surgical ICU. He stopped at the nursing station, spoke with Ida's nurse, and looked at her chart and most recent labs. He approached Ida's bed just as Rachel was starting to leave. Seeing Bloom, she turned back around and started talking to Ida. Bloom smiled, thinking that Rachel turned back to Ida because she thought he might spill the beans without her there. "Hi Rachel," said Bloom, approaching her. Instead of saying out loud, *was it something I said that caused you to go back to Ida or was it something you thought I might say*, he mumbled it quietly to himself.

"What were you doing in the blood bank?" she asked.

"Just browsing."

Walking to the bedside, he reached down and gave Ida a small hug and then reached for her wrist and took her pulse. "Someone's making progress," he announced. "Your heart rate has come down nicely."

"I know," replied Ida. "I'm getting out of here tomorrow."

"How's your wound?"

"They checked the dressing a few minutes ago. It's dry. My pain is minimal."

"Did they get you out of bed?"

"It hurt a little getting me out. I didn't do any walking. I just sat in a chair."

"Do you have graduated compression stockings on your good leg?"

"I have something. Should I be on blood thinners?"

"Not yet. Do they dangle your legs every few hours?"

"Can you mention dangling and compression stockings to the nurse?"

"I will. Now, can you please tell me what went on here?"

"You mean why am I here?"

"Something like that. Let's start off with whose idea was this?"

"Mine."

"How did this come about?"

"First of all, he—that is, Stine—knows where I am at all times. I'm followed everywhere I go, and I mean everywhere. He has eight men that do that—though not all of them at the same time. I call them his *octagoons*. I've seen them when I'm trying on clothes in Bloomingdales, in the dentist's waiting room when I'm seeing the hygienist, when I see my gynecologist, when I'm at the refrigerated produce section in Costco, when I'm getting ammo for my AK-47, and when I go to the lady's room at Maggiano's. Get the point?"

Bloom nodded.

"When he gets out of his limo, he has two pairs of goons on each side of him, all the octagoons. He has unbelievable security in his high rise. I can't get in anywhere, including his garage. They knew I was up to something when they saw me dropping off my pets at Bill's and the pet store. From there I drove straight to the Miami Airport, valet parked my car, and 'took' an El Al flight to Tel Aviv," she said, putting the word "took" in air quotes when she said it. Then she made a gesture like a baseball umpire giving the safe sign, signifying that she didn't want to talk about this anymore now.

They chatted for a few more minutes. Bloom hugged Ida good-bye, left the unit with Rachel, spoke to the nurse about the compression stockings and leg dangling, and then took the elevator to the ground floor.

"Ida's getting more paranoid," said Rachel, walking Bloom to a tabled and treed outdoor sitting area.

"She comes by it honestly," replied Bloom. "I assume *you* know what happened?"

"I can tell you here. Have a seat. But first, I know you've told me you won't tell her about Stine. You have to know I've thought about it a lot. I don't want her to know her son was a neo-Nazi. Let her die killing him or him killing her."

"I told you it was your decision alone, and I would not interfere. But why can't she make the decision about him? He just saved her life."

"Who saved her life?"

"Stine saved her life."

"How so?"

"He gave her two units of platelets yesterday!"

"Is that why you were in the blood bank?"

"Yes, to find out how she was able to get platelets so soon. And this was after Ida grazed his neck with a bullet! She's probably planning her next assassination attempt as we speak. Tell her about Stine, and this craziness might stop. Listen, he knows she's Jewish. He admires her anyway. He respects her. He cares about her. He may even love her. Maybe he knows she's his mother. Who knows? Just my brain working overtime. Let nature take its course. Once he finds out, he'll probably resign his position."

"Or kill her!"

"Or kill her! Tell me about yesterday's failed assassination plot."

"About three months ago, Ida learned that Stine's high rise was having its windows washed sometime this month. She contacted the JDL and told them of her plan to kill William Stine in a Miami high rise where she would act alone and would take full responsibility for the kill. She said she only needed them to teach her to operate a window washing scaffold. She said she had rappelling training with paratroopers and AK and pistol training in the Israeli Army. When she met the scaffold man, who over the phone said he could help her, my sister said the guy snorted when he saw her.

"'You're a ninety-year-old nothing,' he bellowed. 'Get out of here.' Within a minute she had him face down on the floor with his hands handcuffed behind his back.

'Who the fuck are you, lady?' he asked.

'Someone you're going to teach how to work scaffolding,' she answered in a nonmenacing voice, removing the handcuffs and helping him back to his feet."

Rachel continued, "Initially assisting, then soloing on the last two jobs, she was proficient enough to be given the green light. She then went back to the JDL, who showed her how to appear to board a plane by giving her boarding pass to the airline gate agent but then exiting the jetway and airport before boarding, all while avoiding detection. That along with leaving her car at the airport and using taxis and renting cars allowed her the mobility to prepare for the event and have fewer concerns over being watched by Stine and his goons. How that played out and what happened on the scaffold you'll have to get from Ida. All I know is that she was in her harness and anchored to the scaffold, but the moment she fired her pistol the left support rope of the scaffold slipped, and in order to grab hold of the scaffold, she dropped the rope she was to use to rappel down from the fifteenth floor. I just happened to be watching *Eye Witness News*, and they had a closeup of her hanging onto the scaffold with her left hand. She was then able to grab the scaffold with her right hand and hooked both arms over the scaffold's bar. Her body was now at the level of the fourteenth-floor window. She said in a few minutes she could see a flurry of movement in the room on the fourteenth floor. It took them about twenty minutes to remove the glass intact from the window." Rachel recounted what Ida had told her about the rescue.

One of the fire rescue officials, standing about eight feet away from Ida on the fourteenth floor, asked her how she was doing.

"I'm looking for a strong rescuer, he doesn't have to be young," answered Ida.

"I'm Jim. Who are you, and what were you doing up there?"

"I'm Ida. I was just hanging out. Are you the one that's going to catch me?"

"Ida, don't you mean fetch?"

"Just don't say the word j-u-m-p."

"Are you really 89?" asked Jim laughing.

"I was 88 when I started this venture. Are you going to give me instructions?"

"As soon as I find out what they are."

"Are they getting the net ready?"

"You're not j-u-m-p-ing, are you?"

"Do you want to j-u-m-p together like in *Lethal Weapon?*"

"I saw that movie."

"But did you really *see* that movie?"

"What do you mean?"

"I'll tell you after you save me."

"We're going to do that right now," Jim said. "Bob, get me the ten-footer, please. I'll be needing the five-footer right after that."

"Your fishing rod is not long enough," said Ida, seeing the pole, "And you'll need to put some bait on that hook," she added now seeing the end of the pole.

Jim hooked the pole to the free end of the scaffold above where Ida was hanging and brought Ida to within three feet of him.

"I'm feeling a little dizzy and I'm nauseous," said Ida.

"Bob, take this pole and hold it exactly like I'm holding it."

"I've got it," Bob said.

Jim took the five-footer and brought Ida to the edge of the window frame. He noticed a large amount of blood draining from the drop cloth she'd been on.

"Jack, come here, take my pole and hold it exactly like I have it, and, Bob, get on the left of me and help me get her in here."

"I'm slipping," said Ida. "You need to get me now," she screamed as her grip on the scaffold bar was becoming tenuous.

"Bob, when I yell *now*, I want you to grab me around the waist and pull me backward to the floor," yelled Jim, reaching down and grabbing Ida around her waist. "Okay, *now!*" Bob grabbed Jim and quickly threw him to the floor pulling Ida onto Jim.

"It's been at sixty-three years since I've last spooned," said Ida turning around and kissing him on the cheek, remembering it was with her husband Meyer Berger in 1940, their last year together in Berlin.

"You're an amazing woman, Ida. I know about that 200-pound guy you took down and cuffed. Now let's see where your bleeding from," said Jim, getting out from under her.

"He was more like 250. You could've stayed there for another minute or two."

Jim laughed.

Ida thought about that man, the one who had instructed her on scaffolding. He had volunteered to be with her this night and was thrown from the scaffold and fortunately rappelled to safety. She was glad he was okay and hoped no one was aware he had even been up there with her.

"And, as promised," said Ida, "the scene where Riggs is jumping—I can say the jump word now—off the roof handcuffed to the supposed suicide victim, if you look carefully, you'll see that their hands are not actually joined when they jumped. I've never heard that mentioned by anyone, and millions of people have seen that movie."

Rachel concluded, "Most of what happened to Ida I got from her."

"Your sister is a remarkable woman," said Bloom.

"I just want her to be happy. I'm sorry. I can't take the chance of telling her."

"There's no way he could kill her. No way."

"She hates him. There's no way she could accept him."

"I don't agree. Yes, she hates him for what he's done and what he stands for. Given the new information, that could change. They need to talk."

"He'd be forced to give up his position."

"Which he could do, depending on Ida. If she kills him, which she could do at any moment, and then finds out Stine was her son, she could be devastated."

"She'd very easily rationalize his death."

"Remember a few days ago when Stine wanted to sit down and talk with Ida and we said no way?"

"Yes, I remember. You said that wasn't going to happen."

"And he asked, 'What do I have to do to make it happen?'"

"We never answered him."

"That's right. I think we should remind him and hear what he has to say. Maybe he was asking himself what *he* thinks he should do rather than what *we* think he should do."

"I'm not following."

"It's obvious that Ida's not going to stop what she's doing, and he's going to continue keeping her safe, but either of them could get killed in the process—Ida because of her age and the difficulty of her attacks and Stine by Ida because she is quite good at carrying out her plans. I think it's just a matter of time. Someone will need to change if that is to be avoided."

"They're zebras, not chameleons. Ida will continue to hunt Stine, and Stine will continue to hate and hunt Jews. How could either change?"

"Ida will have to stop trying to assassinate him."

"I doubt that. It's in her blood. What about Stine?"

"He must stop hating Jews. That's why they must learn about their common bond. Maybe he already thinks or knows he's her son but isn't ready to give up what he's earned. If he doesn't know, he must be told. The same for her. Then we'll see what happens. So let's tell them both."

"I'm not telling Ida. And you're not telling Stine!"

"Because you're afraid he'll have Ida killed if I tell him?"

"Yes."

"Did you ever think Stine already knows he's Ida's son, that maybe that's why he's been protective of her but silent about it because he wants to keep his position in the Nazi Party?"

"It's more likely he's just infatuated with her."

"Would that be reason enough? Maybe, but if it was infatuation and blood . . . Rachel, I hate sounding like a broken record . . ."

"Jamie, wait a minute. You love sounding like a broken record . . ."

"I wouldn't say love . . . okay, maybe I like sounding a little . . . Rachel, do me a favor . . . Missy is the voice of reason. Can you run it by her?"

CHAPTER 106

STERN/STINE MEETING ON DOCKET

"Dr. Bloom, Mrs. Johnson is here," said Aretha. "She'd like to thank you."

"Is she in the waiting area by herself?"

"Yes."

"I'll be right in."

Bloom walked into the waiting area and was greeted by Mrs. Johnson. "Bob had his surgery yesterday by the doctor on the second floor. He said he wouldn't do it in the office."

"It's much easier all the way around in the hospital. He should be fine. Dr. Smith's an excellent urologist."

"I gave your secretary some money."

"Thank you. Did Dr. Smith circumcise him?"

"Yes."

"Good."

"We appreciated your prompt evaluation and concern."

"I'm glad it was taken care of."

"Rachel's on the line," said Aretha, poking her head into the waiting area.

"I'll take it in my office," replied Bloom, saying goodbye to Mrs. Johnson and heading down the hall.

"Hi Rachel, how's your sis doing today?"

"She's leaving the ICU this afternoon."

"That's great!"

"I spoke with the voice of reason this morning. We both think you should be the one to communicate with Stine and tell him Ida is ready to meet."

"Thank you, Rachel."

"You haven't said anything to Ida, have you?"

"You mean about Stine?"

"Uh huh."

"No."

"Nor will you."

"Yes. Nor will I. Rachel, I gotta go. Talk to you later."

Bloom saw two patients, checked his emails, and asked Aretha to get William Stine on the phone.

"Mr. Stine is on line 2," said Aretha through the intercom.

"Hi, Mr. Stine, your long-awaited meeting with Ida is going to take place."

"That's great! I have things I must do. It'll have to wait a week."

"Seriously? Are you going somewhere?"

"If I was, you'd be the next-to-last person I'd tell," replied Stine, starting to laugh.

"Ida would be the last?" said Bloom.

"The very. Thanks, Dr. Bloom. You're a good man. I'll call you in a week."

"Until then," replied Bloom, hanging up.

Bloom then called Rachel and told her of his short conversation with Stine.

The week could not have passed soon enough for Bloom. He had two bladder, two prostate, and one testicular cancer surgery along with the associated lymph node biopsies with which to concern himself before the Stern/Stine meeting. The outcomes of the surgeries, he thought, would be more predictable than the meeting. He got through the week with one of the bladder cases being more difficult than usual, requiring him to call a GI surgeon into the OR when a frozen section showed the sigmoid colon to be involved despite no involvement seen on the CAT scan. It was good the patient had had a bowel prep in conjunction with the bladder surgery.

Meanwhile Ida, soon to be discharged from Jackson and realizing it would be some time before she'd be sufficiently recovered, combined with Stine's heightened vigil after duping him into believing she had actually flown to Israel, thought about the upcoming meeting as a way to further embark on her goal to kill Stine. This was with the full knowledge that Stine and company would be expecting her lessened condition to invigorate her into another attack against him. This meant, she thought, she'd have to hide a weapon in the agreed meeting venue and have sufficient time to accomplish her goal.

CHAPTER 107

THE LEADUP

"Hi Rachel," said Bloom. "Stine just called me and said he was ready to go ahead with the meeting. I'm waiting to hear from the CEO of University, who may let us use the hospital as a venue."

"That would be fine," said Rachel.

"What we need to do is listen to Stine's spiel. He'll probably tell us he can't continue to protect Ida, that her obsession to kill him will wind up killing her. And she will say she doesn't care if she gets killed. But I don't think he'll kill her or allow any of his goons to kill her. Anyway, that's his problem. We don't say anything about them being mother and son. Ida has to paint a picture of what she and her family went through. Mention all the suffering. How your mother was chewed to death by a German shepherd and your brother's eyes were burnt out because they found some Hebrew writing in his mattress. We've got to hit him hard with Holocaust details in order to shake his denial. Very hard. Ida is a person he knows and admires. She's a real person and has had these bad things happen to her, which he may think or thought never happened. Let her read to Stine what Spielberg wrote about her and you in his *Holocaust Chronicles*. Is there a tape we can play? And tell him what happened in Auschwitz. Remember he's the one that asked for this meeting. Let me ask you something. Do you think Ida might try to kill him during this meeting?"

"I wouldn't put it past her."

"I'm sure both of you will be checked for the presence of firearms. So will Stine and I."

"I assumed so."

"So make sure Ida doesn't bring any."

"I'll tell her, but Ida does what Ida does."

"He's allowing you to be with Ida during the meeting. I will be the moderator. Stine will speak first. Let him say whatever he wants. Don't interrupt him. There will be time for questions after you both speak. The audio portion of the meeting will be recorded. There will be no video recording. Make sure everything you want to get recorded is brought to the meeting. If we use the hospital, we'll be sitting in be the shape of an isosceles triangle with me at the apex and Ida and you at the end of one of the two equal legs and Stine at the end of the other. Are there any questions?"

"What does Stine really expect to get out of this?"

"I really don't know. I would imagine getting Ida to quell her obsession with killing him. I suspect it's keeping him from doing his work. I assume we'll find out if that's the case. Maybe it's also just to see Ida. Who knows?"

CHAPTER 108

THE MEETING IS OFF

"Dr. Bloom, this is your answering service. I just got a call from University Hospital that there's been a break in at the CEO's office and your meeting today has been canceled."

"What time is it?" asked Bloom, looking at his clock and seeing it's face was turned away from him.

"3:33 a.m."

"Did they leave a number?"

"They just said it was the hospital."

"Okay. Thanks," said Bloom, hanging up. He turned the clock around, saw that the alarm was set for 6:30 a.m. and put his head back on the pillow. He got up at 6:30, found there indeed had been a break-in, then checked his computer, waited until 7:30 and called Stine. Stine asked if they could come to Miami and have the meeting in his board room if he could secure it for some time this morning. Bloom said he thought they could but didn't know if it'd be okay with Ida since it might be too soon after her ordeal there. He said he'd run it by Ida and get back to him. Ida, after giving it much thought, agreed.

The meeting was set up for 11:30 a.m. Bloom was told that when he arrived, he was to wait in his car with the two women and call the number he was given.

Bloom arrived outside Stine's high rise at 11:05. Being Saturday, the traffic had been light. He called the number he was given and when one of the doormen came to his car, Bloom and his passengers took their papers and recorders and got out. He was told to lock the car and hand the doorman the key. The doorman gave the key to another doorman and took the three into the lobby and waited with them for an elevator. Ida was unhappy about not being able to hide a firearm in this venue, like she was able to do in the University board room bathroom. Nonetheless, she welcomed the opportunity to see the building in a different light, other than being taken down from the fourteenth floor in a service elevator on a gurney and put into a waiting ambulance. The doorman took them to the second-floor boardroom and waited with them.

The women were then taken through a metal detector, and a female security guard was called to bring the women into a ladies' room to get patted down.

The women were then brought out and waited for Stine and Bloom to do the same. Stine then met the two women who accepted his nod. The women wore dresses, the men sports jackets and shirts without ties. All were brought into the boardroom and seated, each given a pad, a pen, and a bottle of cold water.

Bloom introduced himself and the others, discussed the format and the ground rules, and told them to mention their name whenever they spoke. He said William Stine would speak first.

"I'm William Stine," began Stine. "I am thankful for the courtesy extended to me by Ida and Rachel Stern to speak to them today. Although we are long-standing enemies, I harbor no animosity toward either of them. As a matter of fact, I have a lot of admiration for Ida Stern, for acting true to her cause, and I applaud her efforts, which have brought us to the situation we are now facing. None of my opponents' allegations to do them bodily harm have been substantiated. I repeat. None. These allegations include shooting Ida Stern while she was driving on the Sawgrass Expressway, sabotaging her ventilator in the hospital, killing her platelet donor, and trying to do her bodily harm. On the contrary, I have secured for her—and actually had constructed—a private room in Health South to have her rehab after suffering a stroke, paid for Dr. Bloom and his wife to fly and stay in Cincinnati after Ida almost bled out, and donated my platelets on that and two other occasions when she needed blood. And I donated platelets just last week after she lacerated her leg when she shot at me from a building scaffold.

You may say that all the good I did was so that she would reciprocate and give me her bone marrow should I need it since we're nearly perfect blood matches—and that could be so—but so far even though I've been successfully treated for leukemia, I've never needed a bone marrow transplant. Could I need one going forward? Yes. My problem is that Ida is so hell-bent on killing me—she has tried at least three times—I spend all my time watching her and trying to figure out what she's up to, I have no time left for the other things I must do. Because of how I feel about her, I try to keep her safe. I have eight people whose main job is to follow her and protect her from harm. I am afraid that either they will not be successful in keeping her safe or they will 'accidentally' do her harm themselves. I had one of my men fired who, on his own, set a propane tank to blow up her house with two of her pets inside. Dr. Bloom found out about it and defused the situation. All I want is a cease fire."

"This is Dr. Bloom," said Bloom. "Are you finished, Mr. Stine?"

"This is Mr. Stine," said Stine. "Yes, and I thank them again."

"This is Dr. Bloom," said Bloom. "Ida Stern, you may speak."

"This is Ida Stern. Thank you, Dr. Bloom. It took a lot for me to consent to sit in the same room with William Stine, which I felt would grant him respectability despite all the horrific things he's done and what he represents. I felt it was important for me to say that before I started. I was born and raised in Berlin, and I never gave it much thought growing up that I was different from my own and extended families in that I was the only one of fifty or so family member with blue eyes and fair skin. I felt special.

"I became what would be considered today a physician's assistant for my future husband after finishing two years of dental school and not being allowed to continue my education because I was Jewish. I married in 1934 at age twenty. After five years of being unable to become pregnant, I was inseminated in a Berlin infertility clinic on October 13, 1939, by Joseh Mengele. Without my knowledge, he used Hitler's semen in place of my husband's and our son Sigmund was born.

"Around that time Jews were experiencing discrimination and persecution. Jewish stores and businesses were being boycotted. My husband's pediatric practice and his office was taken from him a year later. I got a job cleaning the house of a family whose sixteen-year-old daughter worked in an orphanage, while my husband found part-time work in his cousin's shoe store. Because we were no longer allowed to leave Germany and conditions for Jews were worsening, we decided it would be best for Sigmund to place him with the family for whom I worked. The family brought him to the orphanage where the sixteen-year-old watched over him. I saw him twice a day from a distance and was happy watching him bond with her. The day after the family said they were planning to adopt him, the fifty of us—our entire extended family— were herded into boxcars and deported to Auschwitz, and we never saw Sigmund again.

"Rachel and I were the only two in our family that survived Auschwitz. Our stay in the death camp was chronicled by Steven Spielberg, whose group interviewed hundreds of Holocaust survivors. Rachel will now play some excerpts from that interview." Rachel put on the recording saying Ida's and her names. After a few minutes she stopped that recording and played another, then shut the recorder off. "We frequently went on marches in the death camp," continued Ida, "and if possible, my mother, Rachel, my younger brother Simon, and I would try to stay near each other if we could. Because of our poor diet, severe diarrhea was a frequent problem and we'd cope with it as best we could. On one such march, the diarrhea was so bad that my mother stopped for a second to pull the bottom of her pants leg to the side to let the stool fall onto the ground instead of going into her shoe. I immediately gave a loud cough, warning her to continue walking, but it was too late. The German commandant had already sicced his German shepherd on her. She lay on the ground, bleeding from both carotid arteries. She exsanguinated and died in ten minutes. 'Du wiist der Nachste Sein?' (You will be next?) he asked me. 'Nein' (No), I answered shaking my head. That afternoon Rachel and I went to my mother's barrack and watched them hose down the wooden plank on which she slept. At the back of the plank Rachel saw a black object, which she picked up after the cleaner left. It was my mother's diary. Rachel started to read it and immediately put it down. 'You don't want to read this,' she said to me. I don't know why, but I picked it up and read the first page. It was dated February 3, 1912, the day my parents were married. 'Der langste Tag meines Lebens' was written on the top of the page. 'The longest day of my life.' Further down the page and continuing on the next was the reason Rachel put the book down. It said that my mother was raped on her wedding night by a person with blue eyes and fair skin. All those years that I had felt special because of my eyes and skin . . . I couldn't stop crying. I told Rachel I wanted to die. She stayed with me for three nights. I threw myself on the electrified barbed wire, but the electricity had not been turned on. I didn't even feel the cuts from the barbed wire. Six months later a book with Hebrew letters was found on the plank my brother slept on and both his eyes were burned out. After an hour, when his kicking and screaming was starting to subside, he was shot to death.

"Sometime later, Rachel and I were taken to the medical clinic sixty miles southwest of Auschwitz to Birkenau to see Dr. Josef Mengele. Like most of the women prisoners, we had stopped getting our periods shortly after coming to the camp, due to malnutrition and poor living conditions. Having had some medical knowledge, I learned from one of the nurses that we were two of four women who were given anesthetics and artificially inseminated that day and were going back to Auschwitz. I was told the other two were from Birkenau. Neither of us were told by Mengele what had been done. The nurses said we'd be returning to see the doctor in six weeks. In three weeks, we both began to have morning sickness. This was Rachel's first pregnancy. A week before my scheduled visit, I stood on my bed plank and jumped onto the point of it injuring my lower abdomen. Three days later I miscarried. Rachel jumped but at the last second put out her hands to break her fall and only hurt her hands. At our visit a week later, Mengele said he'd see me in a few months, but he never brought me back. Rachel was kept and was returned to the Krakow camp fourteen weeks later without her uterus and fetus. In 1945 we were liberated sometime between Hitler's death and the bombing of Japan. I can't talk anymore. I need a few minutes."

"Sure," replied Bloom. "Let me know when you can continue."

After a few breaths and a sip of water, she said, "This is Ida Stern. I am ready to continue."

"Go ahead, Ida," replied Bloom.

"I have some questions for Mr. Stine."

Stine nodded.

"You have heard me and should now understand why I'm hell-bent on killing you. Question number one. What do you want from me?"

"This is William Stine. The men who did that to you are dead."

"This is Ida Stern. You have taken Hitler's name, his date of birth, and his signature salute. You are him and all the men who followed him and harmed me and those I love."

"This is William Stine. I have not hurt you or your family."

"This is Ida Stern. You did not help the boy on the bike the day it snowed."

"This is William Stine. That's true. Lots of people didn't help. As far as I remember, not any or many others helped. But I didn't hurt him. Did he die?"

"No," replied Stern, "no thanks to you. Question number two. Are you a Holocaust denier?"

"Yes, I am. But I feel badly for what you went through."

"Why is that?"

"Because."

"Because why?"

"I'm not really sure myself. But there's something inside me that wants to protect you."

"How's that?"

"That just is. Can I ask you a question?

"Yes."

"After you were liberated, did you try to find Sigmund?"

"That was a very difficult time for me."

"Would you rather not talk about it?"

"I've put off talking about it for over fifty years."

"If you rather not do it now, it's alright with me."

"It's much easier not to talk about it. I have one more question for Mr. Stine."

"This is Mr. Stine. What is your question?"

"Are you an ableist?"

"Yes."

"For the record. Can we say that you discriminate against persons with disabilities and believe that these persons are imperfect and need fixing?"

"Yes."

"And is anti-Semitism part of your dogma?"

"Yes. Neo-Nazism was founded on these principles, but we don't strictly enforce it."

"What does that mean?"

"Strict enforcement is optional. Rules can have exceptions."

"You're the president of the American Nazi Party and you say rules have exceptions?"

"All rules have exceptions."

"Based on what?"

"Benefit to the organization."

"Would all neo-Nazis agree with you?"

"If they were honest."

"You might consider me a friend?"

"I wouldn't go that far. But I do harbor friendly feelings toward you."

"Even though I want to kill you?"

"I guess so. Do you ever have friendly feelings about me?"

"Never!"

"If you did, would you say so?"

"I'll never have friendly feelings about you."

"You did before you found out I was a neo-Nazi."

"I hated you the second I learned who you were. As an ableist, you might have had good feelings about someone and then you saw them walking with a limp and disliked them."

"That's true. I am cautious about accepting people. But I should add, if my relationship with them had blossomed or they became beneficial to me, I might have looked the other way. I'm being totally honest with you."

"I understand that."

"I've told you that you're a good enemy."

"Yes, you have. On more than one occasion."

"You're still going to kill me?" asked Stine.

"What do you think?"

"I think no."

"I'm sorry. Did you say you think so or no?"

"No."

"You're smarter than that. Yes, I'm still going to kill you."

"Okay. This is Dr. Bloom. "Are either of you capable of changing if the other can make an offer to change? And what can the other do to allow you to make a change? And what can you offer to allow your opponent to change his or her mind. What rules can each of you stretch and be comfortable with?"

"This is Ida. Since he's the one that's flexible with rules, let him offer. I'm not flexible. I can't offer anything."

"This is Dr. Bloom. This is to Ida. What can Mr. Stine offer that might allow you to change?"

"Renounce his presidency, leave the Party, and become a Holocaust sympathizer."

"All three of them?" asked Stine.

"And get circumcised," added Ida.

"And what about being castrated?" asked Stine.

"Yes, that too. I'd pay whomever does the circumcision to do that also."

"Ida, what could you do?" asked Bloom.

"If Dr. Bloom could teach me, I could do the castration," replied Ida.

"I meant to get Stine to change," said Bloom. "There should be light at the end of this tunnel," added Bloom.

"It's the train," announced Ida.

"You're talking," said Bloom. "That's good. Can we keep the cease fire and meet in a week?"

"No, I don't want to," said Ida without hesitation.

"Ida, as I see, you and Mr. Stine are talking," said Bloom. "How about it?"

"No, not even for you, Dr. Bloom. Not even for you. And no more meetings!"

CHAPTER 109

TIME TO TURN OVER THE DOWN CARDS

"Your sister's one tough customer," said Bloom, rehashing yesterday's meeting.

"She's confident, knows what she wants, and is not influenced by others," replied Rachel.

"Do you think she was being too hard on Stine?"

"No, not at all! All Holocaust survivors would have felt the same way as my sister," answered Rachel. "She said it all when she spoke. Hitler murdered her friends and entire family except for her and me and was responsible for her giving up her baby. Stine assumed Hitler's identity by taking his birth date, first name, espousing his dogma, and using his salute."

"Because of Ida, I basically hated the guy way before I met him," Bloom said. "Then, when I saw what he did to my practice and what his henchman was doing to my family, I hated him even more. Then I was forced to take him as a patient, and I saw another side of him. He knew Ida was also my patient and he began to treat her differently. You and Ida never saw it. The printout I got of him about his childhood, teen, and adult years showed a horrific person who was against all minority groups and had no problem taking a human life. All the bad things that were happening to Ida were assumed to be due to Stine and his minions. Like he said and I believe him, we were not able to find him responsible for any of the bad things that befell Ida. You made a comment to me that I was brainwashed and didn't see him for the animal he was. I'm sure you could say he's been okay to Ida and me because of her bone marrow match and because I've given and gotten him good medical care for his kidney stones and leukemia, that we're valuable to him in keeping him alive and well. Okay. I don't disagree with that, but I get to know sick people very well, and I see their appreciation for what we're doing for them. What I like about Stine is his ability to see that things are not all black and white. As an anti-Semite he could like a Jew under certain circumstances and as an ableist if he got to know and really liked someone through a relationship that developed via the phone, he might still like him if he learned the person was gay or was an amputee. I don't think Ida has that capability. I also was surprised by the dialog she engaged in. It seemed like she let her guard down. That's why I mentioned the light at the end of the tunnel."

"When did she let her guard down? She was serious about her demands, including having Stine circumcised."

"And castrated?"

"Yes! She wasn't trying to dialog or be amusing. She really hates him!"

"I think once he learns of their relationship, he'll move on it. Then it'll be up to Ida. I also think it's not likely she'd be able to. The bottom line is that with no cease fire in effect they're both at risk for injury or death, and we must tell them of their relationship. When we saw she was not going to budge, we should have told them yesterday they were mother and son. Tomorrow I'll tell Stine, and you'll tell Ida. Settled?"

"All right," sighed Rachel."

"We'll see where this goes," sighed Bloom. "We might be surprised."

"You know how I feel."

"Yes, Rachel. I know how you feel."

CHAPTER 110

BLOOM TO STINE

"Good morning, Mr. Stine," said Bloom, shaking Stine's hand and taking him into the consultation room. "We're going to be here for a little while. You'll be doing most of the listening."

"You said you had some information you wanted to share with me?"

"Yes."

"Couldn't we have done this over the phone?"

"We could have. Tell me if we should have when we're finished."

"Is Ida okay?"

"Yes. As a matter of fact, Rachel is having a similar conversation with Ida just about now."

"Couldn't it have been at the same time?"

"It is being done at the same time."

"You know what I mean," replied Stine smiling.

"Again, you can tell me when we're finished."

"It sounds so intriguing. Should I be worried?"

"No."

"Good."

"I'm going to speak for a while. The water's for me. Would you like some?"

"What about the tissues?" asked Stine, shaking his head no to the water.

"They're always there."

"I'm just a little nervous, that's all."

"I going to repeat some of what Ida said when she spoke a few days ago," started Bloom. "She said that in 1940 she and her husband gave up their son Sigmund because they didn't think he'd survive the Nazis. When Ida was in Birkenau and saw Dr. Mengele, he remembered her from the clinic in Berlin. He told her that he had twice inseminated her not with her husband's semen but the semen of Adolph Hitler. When the war was over, she never went back to look for her son. You remember the difficulty she had in answering your question?"

Stine nodded.

"After the war, Ida, like many of the Holocaust survivors, required psychiatric treatment. She told her psychiatrist she found that the orphanage had been bombed during the war. When her psychiatrist visited Berlin in the 1990s she put a note in Ida's chart that the orphanage was intact and never had been bombed. The psychiatrist subsequently died, and my wife received the doctor's records when Ida became her patient. In the records the doctor wrote that Ida never wanted to talk about her son. The question of her son came up again when you got leukemia."

"Me? What did my leukemia have to do with anything?"

"Because you and your minions were pestering—and I use the word in its most subdued or benign meaning—Ida and my family about getting her bone marrow. I thought that we should try to locate some of your family and Ida's son as a possible source of matchable DNA. Ida would only agree if we never mentioned her son's name or referred to him. I tried to get whatever information I could about you but hit a dead end. Then I got a printout of your illustrious record as a teenager and young adult from your rap sheets and neo-Nazi and multiple other groups' archives. That's how I knew about the Ferris wheel, the parachute jump, the Bronx Zoo, and the train 'accident'—and I don't mean the one with the platelet donor. These are all part of your public record. This is from many years ago, and as far as I'm concerned you are a different person. I'm finished with the bad stuff. Would you like us to rest for a second?"

"That was my life. You can go on."

"Trying to find Ida's son, I called the Berlin orphanage and got connected to their archives. They were able to get me in touch with a ninety-five-year-old German woman, Adele Bekker, who was rehabbing after a recent stroke. She had a story to tell that she's told to no one and wanted to tell it before she died. She said she started to work for Hitler in 1930. She said Hitler knew everything about Ida's pregnancy and postpartum care along with Ida's handing Sigmund over to the Albrechts prior to being taken to Auschwitz with her family. She said Hitler was happy with the adoption but was not happy how the Albrechts were raising Sigmund. She said that one day while Sigmund was in the park with his family's maid, Hitler had someone detonate a bomb in the Albrechts' house, killing the entire Albrecht family, and Sigmund was brought back to the orphanage. Bekker said she was embedded into the orphanage and was told to locate a suitable male orphan in the orphanage who was two years older than Sigmund and help them bond. She chose a boy named Edsel. After three months, Hitler instructed Bekker to remove the boys from the orphanage one night and bring them to his Berlin compound. With Adele as the caregiver for Sigmund, they hired another woman caregiver, Gert Strauss, for Edsel. Each day the two caregivers spoke for three hours in German and two in English and taught the boys German songs and how to draw the German planes and battleships. By the time the boys were almost three and five, Edsel could speak and read German and English and Sigmund could speak it. The caregivers loved the children and taught them to call Hitler papa and tell him they loved him. Adele says that raising Sigmund was the happiest time of her life. She and Gert loved their charges, and the children loved them in return. Hitler also loved the boys, especially his progeny, Sigmund. He loved when the boys talked about the German planes, battleships, and submarines and when he carried them on his shoulders around the compound. By the time the boys were past three and five, Hitler knew he was going to lose the war. So did Adele and Gert. When he called Pope Pius II and arranged for the boys to be taken by them to Rome by train and then by ship to New York to be adopted, the caregivers decided to leave Berlin with the boys and raise them away from Hitler and bring them back to Berlin when the war was over and unite them with Ida if she survived. When they realized that Hitler would never let them leave and if they did, he'd find them and kill the two women, they decided to go along with Hitler's plan. The boys enjoyed their train and boat trips and were adopted by

Karen and Oskar Fuchs, a German-American family in Brooklyn, one of the organizers of the Madison Square Garden German-American Bund event on February 20, 1939. The plan was for them to stay with the boys for six months and to use the million dollars Hitler gave them to be given to the family over time. The adopting mother turned out to be immature and jealous of Adele, who was told to leave after only three months. This was relayed to Hitler, who said Adele should leave and continue to periodically send them additional money. When the mother refused to take their calls and would not let the boys speak with Adele on the phone, Adele and Gert kept more than three quarters of the money. Within one and a half years of the adoption, the adoptive father, who was a writer and worked from home, was banned from the household for being a pedophile after Edsel was found touching the genitals of two of his classmates and naked photographs of the boys and Oskar were found in Oskar's closet. Shortly after that, Karen was diagnosed with breast cancer and died eighteen months later. Oskar was not allowed to care for the boys, and they were made wards of the state. For the next two years, the boys moved from one foster care facility to another. In retrospect, Oskar said he should have gotten in touch with Adele and Gert and either asked them bring the boys back to Germany since Oskar could still not care for them, or brought the two women to Brooklyn.

"Hitler died in April 1945, and shortly thereafter the U.S. bombed Japan, and the war ended. Six months after the war, Ida had not yet returned to the orphanage and she could not be located. The caregivers tried to regain contact with the boys. They were able to contact Oskar Fuchs, who still could not see the kids but was able to give the caregivers the number of the Flatbush Ave Foster Home in Brooklyn. They spoke with Nurse Helene Washington and learned the boys were there, but they refused to get on the phone with either Gert or Adele. Helene told Gert the boys were getting into trouble and were getting more difficult to control, especially Edsel, who had full control over Sigmund. They also learned that Sigmund was now Ziggy and Edsel was now Eddie.

They used Hitler's money to fly to LaGuardia Airport, took a cab to the foster home, and were greeted by the nurse.

Washington left the women and returned two minutes later with the boys and brought them into the room. She waited a few seconds to make sure there were no outbursts and closed the door behind her. The boys walked to the back of the room and faced the back wall. Since the caregivers thought Eddie would be the more likely one to speak, Gert spoke first.

"Eddie, do you know who I am?" she asked.

Eddie did not reply.

"Eddie, do you know my name?" She asked again.

Still no answer.

"You can say anything you want. Anything. I just want to hear your voice."

"Fuck you, Gert," he said.

"Fuck you, Gert," said Gert. "Anything else you'd like to say? Soon we'll be gone, Eddie. Don't lose this opportunity to say what you'd really like to say."

"I said what I wanted to say," said the almost eight-year-old.

"I taught you to express yourself better than that."

After a few seconds, Eddie spoke. "You abandoned us and left us with a faggot father and a useless mother."

"Eddie, that was not our plan," replied Gert. "You didn't belong to us. You were on loan to us. We had no control of your future. We thought we were leaving you with a good mommy and daddy. That's what we told the people who were not able to take care of you anymore. We now know the people who adopted you were not good for you. We came back because now we may have a say in your future."

"What's the use? This is what we'll always be."

"And what is that?"

"We're bad. We lie, we hurt, we steal, and we cheat. They say we have no regard for human life. And we can't change. You deserve better than us."

"We made you good once. We can make you good again."

As Gert started to move toward Eddie, he cried out, "Don't try to touch me or hold me. I will fight you with all my might. I'm taking Ziggy and we're leaving you now. You'd better not stop me. I have a knife in my pocket, and if you were anyone else I would have used it already."

"Okay Eddie," said Gert stopping in her tracks, "please allow Adele some time with Ziggy. Let them have their day."

"He doesn't even know who she is. He's never mentioned her name."

"Please take Ziggy to Adele."

Eddie lifted Ziggy and carried him to within five feet of Adele, with Ziggy still facing the back wall.

"Sigmund, have you ever seen me before?" asked Adele. When he didn't respond, Adele asked him what his favorite cookie was. When he didn't answer she opened her purse and took out a Mallomar and held it up. 'Do you know what this is?' she asked, holding it out to him. 'Is this still your favorite cookie?' He quickly turned around and lunged forward, grabbing the Mallomar and stuffing it in his mouth. 'And Sigmund, do you remember what you called your pet?'"

Stine, now crying, said, "Yama the llama."

By now Bloom had come around to the front of the desk carrying the box of tissues and put his arms around Stine. Stine took a tissue and began shaking and crying uncontrollably. Bloom held Stine until Stine stopped shaking and sat him back on his chair and went back to his side of the table.

"I'm sorry," said Stine, still shaking. He took a deep breath and sighed. "I didn't expect this. Is Ida learning the same thing?"

"She had a little more information than you going in, though not as much as she could have had. She might have figured out you were in the picture."

"She knows now?"

"She does or will know soon. I have a little more to tell you, mainly the corroborating evidence we got a few days ago."

"I'm listening."

"Before I get to that, there were a number of little things. Like how close your DNA matched up. It was uncanny. Then there was Sigmund's 'brother' Edsel and your brother Eddie that was two years older than you. Then there was confusion about where you were born. And your love of Mallomars, and you calling the Tibetan religious leader the Dalai *Yama*.

"The real evidence came from the IAFIS, the Integrated Automated Fingerprint Identification System used by the FBI, which was just recently created. When Adele and Gert took the boys to be adopted in 1942, Hitler supplied them with Sigmund's birth certificate, passport, and fingerprints, which they gave to Karen and Oskar Fuchs. I was able to get in touch with Oskar Fuchs, who still had your fingerprints. I got them from him and took them to IAFIS, who called me with the results a few days ago. Sigmund's prints matched with two others—William Stein and William Stine. Bill, you changed the spelling of your last name when you were 18, I remember."

"Yes, Dr. Bloom," he answered with a smile after being called Bill.

"Let me just finish up. The caregivers never saw, heard from, or heard about the boys again. I'd love to call Adele and tell her I've found you but I'm afraid it might lead to another stroke. Her love for you may have been the only love in her life, and you don't remember, but it was a very much a mutual love. Would you like to talk?"

"I'd like to talk to Ida."

"She's going to need time to digest this. I wouldn't push her. Rachel is supposed to call me after she speaks with her. Do you have someone you can talk to?"

"Basically only you.

"Would you like to talk to me now?"

"By law am I now Jewish?"

"I don't know. I'm not Jewish. You'd need to ask a rabbi."

"You're not Jewish? When did that happen?"

"Probably the day I was conceived."

"Isn't Bloom a Jewish name?"

"Not in my extended family."

"My life as it has been is just about over," continued Stine.

"Maybe it's just beginning."

"What do you mean? I don't think Ida would accept me no matter what I do."

"None of us know that. It may depend on what you do."

"What are my choices?"

"What would you want to happen and what could you do to make that happen?"

"Theoretically, as a Jew I could hate myself. Maybe I should see a psychologist."

"A psychologist might be able to help you. You may need someone that could help you accept yourself. Can I ask you something?"

"Sure."

"Why were you crying a little while ago?"

"Why do you ask?"

"To get some insight into what was going through your mind at that moment. What were you feeling when you yelled out 'Yama the Llama'?"

"That I was this kid."

"What were you feeling?"

"That I was this boy that was given so much love and had tremendous potential."

"But what were you *feeling*?"

"I felt happy because I was him and received so much love. Then I felt sad—about how I turned out."

"How should you have turned out?"

"Not aligned with the neo-Nazis."

"How'd you feel about being a neo-Nazi fifteen minutes ago?"

"I didn't know anything else."

"Again, how did you feel?"

"I didn't feel good about it, not with the Jewish people I now know."

"That's a start."

CHAPTER 111

RACHEL TO IDA

"Dr. Bloom, Rachel is on line 2."

"Hi, Rachel," replied Bloom, taking the call.

"How'd it go with Stine?" she asked.

"Stine's in a tizzie."

"I'm not surprised."

"Tell me about Ida."

"She said she always thought Stine might be a possibility."

"She did? What kind of reaction did she have?"

"She was disappointed it turned out this way."

"In what way?"

"Her son being a neo-Nazi with Hitler being his father. She wasn't too surprised. She was mainly just disappointed."

"Any regrets?"

"Yes. I guess not looking for him in 1945."

"Might that be a point of contention?"

"Yes."

"She'd admit to it?"

"Probably."

"Would you think she could have a relationship with Stine?"

"I don't know. I guess it depends."

"On what?"

"What he can give up."

"His presidency?"

"Among other things."

"Anti-Semitism? Ableism? Holocaust denying?"

"Probably."

"She'd have to stop hunting him."

"I would assume! Do you think they should meet?"

"Not yet. I think it's too soon. I guess it's really up to them. Bill has me and Ida has you. I wouldn't have them getting together right now. But again, it's up to them."

CHAPTER 112

THEIR FIRST DATE

"Who would have thunk it?" said Stine, pulling into the golf course parking lot and dropping off his clubs at the bag drop next to a set that was already there.

"Never in my wildest dreams," said the woman who was waiting for him. "Remember, we agreed, no gimmes or mulligans after we're off the driving range and practice putting green," she added.

"I'm playing from the white tees and you're from the reds and you're getting a stroke a hole, right?" said Stine.

"I didn't ask for a stroke a hole."

"You're not a 100 percent yet. I'll get a flag to put on our cart so we can drive close to the greens. It's late in the day and it rained up until an hour ago so there shouldn't be too many people playing. We should have plenty of time to talk."

"Not while I'm hitting or putting," she replied smiling.

They spent ten minutes warming up and proceeded to the first tee, a 400-yard par five. He drove 200 yards, she 150 yards, and both were on in three. They both two putted and parred the hole.

"You're amazing," said Stine.

"I used to play a lot."

"I didn't mean golf."

"You think too much of me."

"That I do."

"What about you? You've agreed to change your life around."

"I really have no choice. I'm going to resign my presidency and leave the party. I'll adjust if I have a relationship with you and Rachel."

"On what basis will you tell them you're leaving?"

"I'll tell them I've been advised by my physicians to step down because of the leukemia, that I'm going to need a bone marrow transplant and need to reduce the stress in my life."

"Or you could have killed me!"

"Maybe before. But not now. Matricide is not in my blood. But filicide is in yours."

"That's true. After I found out in Auschwitz that Hitler was your father, I was consumed by the thought of killing you. I went back to the orphanage in 1945, but there were no archives, and I had no way to find you. I just harbored the idea of you continuing the work of Hitler and the Nazis. And I was correct. I actually thought you could be my son, so I had to stop you."

"You abandoned me. You could have found me and put me on the right path. Adele didn't know what path I was on until 1946 when she went to New York to find me and take me back to Germany. But then I was already on the wrong path. Since Adele wasn't married and Oskar Fuchs was not willing to give me up, I stayed in New York, on the wrong path. You returned to Berlin in 1945 after you were liberated and could have found out about my relationship with Adele and the amazing care she gave me, along with the difficulty Karen and Oskar Fuchs were having, and you could have gone to New York to remove me from that environment. I was definitely redeemable at that time."

"At that time, I wouldn't have been looking to redeem you. Instead, I would have been looking to kill you."

"You would have actually killed me?"

"Yes. Just as killing you became my obsession when I knew you as William Stine. You have no idea of how preoccupied I've been, thinking about killing you."

"Are you still preoccupied?"

"No. But you need to let me win."

"My God. What you've had to go through to try to kill me!"

"Bill, do you have a God?"

"Just for these few seconds. Wouldn't you have had tremendous guilt feelings?"

"I would have rationalized it," replied Ida, beginning to get defensive. "And what would you know about guilt feelings?" she added. "The boy you ran away from that needed your help on that snowy day and all those you killed as a teenager and as an adult … and those on the Sawgrass and railroad tracks," mumbled Ida starting to get out of the golf cart.

"Ida, I don't believe you're saying this?" said Stine teary-eyed, reaching for her, but she was already out of the cart and was running toward the parking lot.

"Don't follow me," she yelled. "I have a gun in my purse, and I swear I'll shoot you. You and I are a big mistake. Take my clubs to my car and go away. The next time I see you I will kill you. That's a promise."

CHAPTER 113

IDA AGREES TO COUNSELING

"I knew it was too good to be true," Bloom told Missy after detailing his recent conversation with Stine.

"That issue had been festering for almost sixty years," said Missy.

"It sounded like Ida just snapped, bringing up things that were thought to have been resolved. She threatened to kill him the next time she saw him."

"It sounded like Stine was willing to accept her outburst and unfair fighting tactics and was almost ready to excuse it."

"That's the way I saw it. Ida doesn't look like a person who readily takes things back."

"Have you spoken with Rachel?" asked Missy.

"I think it's best you speak with her."

"I agree. I'll give it another twenty-four hours."

"Good."

The following day Missy called Rachel.

"Ida is still sleeping," said Rachel.

"Did you see her before she went to sleep?"

"She called me when she got home yesterday."

"Did you see her?"

"No. She said she was going to bed."

"Have you spoken with her?"

"No. She must have shut her phone off."

"Call me after you speak with her."

"What happened yesterday between Ida and Stine?"

"You need to get Ida's take on it before we talk."

"Is there anything you want to tell me now?"

"No."

The women hung up, and Missy called Bloom and told him that Ida went to sleep without talking to Rachel. Three hours later, Rachel called Missy.

"Ida is up," started Rachel. "Sigmund is Ida's powder keg. Ida shouldn't have brought him up then, not on their first meeting."

"You're absolutely right," agreed Missy. "Does Ida know that?"

"Yes. And she said so."

"Did she tell you what she said as she was leaving Stine?"

"She said she had a gun, and she'd use it the next time she saw him."

"Did she say anything about the way she behaved?"

"Yes, she said she was sorry. She also said she thought Sigmund would forever cast a pall over any relationship she had with Stine."

The next day Missy called Rachel.

"I've got a very good geriatric psychiatrist for Ida to see," said Missy. "I spoke with him today. He has a large Holocaust survivor practice and is willing to see Ida and possibly take her as a patient. I would strongly advise her to meet with him."

"Where is his office?" asked Rachel.

"It's in West Palm Beach. Do you want me to talk to Ida?"

"Yes. She's here. Should I put her on?"

Missy spoke with Ida, who agreed to meet with the doctor and was given his number and address.

"Please call him now," urged Missy. "If for whatever reason you don't want to call him now, please let me know now. It's really important for you to see him."

"I'll definitely call him," Ida replied, reassuring Missy.

"Thanks. Please let me know after you've made an appointment with him."

"Will do."

"Have you spoken with Stine?"

"He's Bill now. I called him last night. We hope we're doable."

"That'll take work. Does Bill have any friends?"

"No close ones. He considers Dr. Bloom a friend."

"Did he say anything about seeing a doctor?"

"A psychologist or psychiatrist?"

"Yes, or a spiritual leader?"

"I doubt he has one."

"How are you feeling?"

"Better now. I wasn't happy with my outburst, or before my outburst for that matter. I definitely need help. I hope your doctor will help me. I can't believe Bill was able to get over it."

"He cares about you.'

"Yes. It seems like he always has."

CHAPTER 114

UNABLE TO WALK AFTER SURGERY

"Dr. Bloom, Bill Stine is on line 1," said Aretha through the intercom.

"Hi Bill, que pasa?" asked Bloom.

"Doing okay," replied Stine. "I've been a lot more tired than usual. I have something I want to run by you."

"I've been more tired myself. Maybe we're playing too much golf. Bill, what did you want to run by me?"

"I've been thinking of giving up my position as president of the Nazi Party.

"That would be a great thing to do! What are you going to tell them?"

"I'd just tell the truth, that I was just reunited with my birth mother, a Jewish Holocaust survivor, who had given me up in 1939 to a gentile family so I would not be killed by Hitler's Nazis. What do you think?"

"I wouldn't do that now. You should definitely discuss that with your psychiatrist."

"One of the first things he told me to do was to check with IAFIS and verify their result. I did. He told me to go slowly with the changes I wanted to make."

"There you go."

"I don't think I'd ever want to go back to my former life."

"You should tell your psychiatrist what you'd like to do."

"I'm seeing him in two days. I've also thought about getting circumcised. Is that a painful operation?"

"I couldn't walk for a year after I had mine."

"When was that?"

"A number of years ago."

"Really? You couldn't walk for a year?"

"It took that long before I was able to walk."

"That sounds terrible. I don't think I'm gonna have the operation." Bloom laughed.

"What's so funny?" asked Stine.

Bloom just continued to laugh.

"Why are you laughing?"

Bloom started to choke because he was laughing so hard.

"I don't know what's so funny!"

Bloom was now coughing, laughing, and choking. Because he was unable to stop doing those three things, he was unable to get any words out.

Stine waved his arms in front of Bloom, hoping he'd stop and tell him what was so funny, but Bloom even got louder and added shaking to his repertoire. Finally Bloom stopped his one-man show, but when he started to speak, he started his act anew. Now Stine was starting to laugh although he didn't know why. Finally Bloom stopped his show and started to tell him why he was unable to walk for a year, but again started his routine and ended up just blurting out, "Because I was only a day old when I was circumcised!"

Stine now joined Bloom in the laughter. Afterward he asked Bloom, "Were you really circumcised?"

"Yes. My uncle was a urologist and told my parents he thought I should be circumcised. So whenever an adult comes to see me and is looking to be circumcised and asks me how uncomfortable he'll be after the operation, I go through my routine."

"Does anyone not have the surgery?"

"No, they all have it."

"Should I also mention the circumcision to my psychiatrist?"

"Honestly, I think it's too soon in your new relationship to be thinking about it."

"You were circumcised on day two."

"I had no say in it. My parents made the decision based on my uncle's advice. My feeling is that the circumcised penis is less likely to develop cancer and that a circumcised penis is less likely to give a woman cervical cancer. I would think more about spiritual changes in becoming a Jew rather than the physical changes. I certainly would get in touch with a Jewish spiritual leader."

"You seem to know a lot about the Jewish people."

"More than half my patient population is Jewish. I have many Jewish friends, and I've been to many Jewish weddings, bar mitzvahs, and funerals."

"If down the road I was to have a circumcision, you would do it, wouldn't you?"

"No," answered Bloom. "I wouldn't."

"No? Why not?"

"You know or should know why not." Bloom waited a few seconds then continued. "You used me and my surgical skills to eliminate your competitors for the presidency of the American Nazi Party. And the time for your contrition has long passed."

"I know that. I'm truly sorry for what I did to you and your family. I truly am. I was a different person then. I didn't deserve your care and everything you did for me."

"I took an oath when I became a doctor to do my best for everyone and anyone. This was while my family and I were under threat from you and your minions."

"I realize that."

"It's kind of ironic that you are now thinking of having me do the exact surgery you had me inflict on others."

"I shouldn't have made you do that to others."

"I will find another urologist for you when the time comes for your circumcision."

"I understand. I hope you and your family will play an important part in my new family."

"I'm not abandoning you. Please call me after you see your psychiatrist."

"I will. Thanks."

CHAPTER 115

RELAPSE

"Bill should have called me two days ago," said Bloom as he grabbed his towel and followed Missy out of the hot tub.

"You spoke to Ida today, didn't you?" asked Missy.

"I did, but I didn't ask her."

"On purpose?"

"I guess so."

"Why not?"

"My conversation with Bill did not end as well as it could have."

"You said it was a conversation you needed to have."

"Yes, I did need to have it!"

"You said you thought you should not have said anything about no longer taking care of him urologically."

"I didn't say urologically. It was only pertaining to circumcisions, and it was for down the road."

"Down the road meant not for the moment. You were being honest about the future."

"I thought I was. Is it too late to call him? Of course it is! I forgot, for you anyone at any time is too late to call."

"Except him," answered Missy. "He's a night owl. Call him."

Bloom dried himself well enough to get into the house and laughed that he had just toweled off to take a shower. He then called Bill.

"You're still tired like before?" asked Bloom when Bill got on the line.

"It's much worse and I just got a nosebleed—first time ever."

"Can you be at my office at 8:30 tomorrow morning?"

"Sure. What do you think?"

"It needs to be checked out."

"Should I call my regular doctor?"

"Just come in tomorrow."

"Okay. I'll see you at 8:30. Thanks."

"What's going on?" asked Missy, hearing the tail end of their conversation.

"His leukemia may be back."

"Because he had a nosebleed?"

"And the worsening of something or other."

"Don't you think he should see Winger?"

"He's not due to see her. I'll have the blood result in ten minutes. He can see her if it's positive or see his primary if it's negative."

Stine showed up at the office at 8:15, sat on the floor with his back against the office door and waited. Within five minutes he was asleep. Bloom showed up ten minutes later, saw Stine's pallor and took his pulse. He noted he was febrile and tachycardic and had some blood around his left nostril. He went into the office through the staff door, grabbed an examining room pillow, told Cathy that Stine was sleeping against the door outside and asked her to meet him inside the front door and he would tell her when to open the door. Bloom left through the staff door with the pillow, put it behind Stine's head and told Cathy to slowly open the patient door. Stine's upper body and head were let down on the office floor. Cathy got the office wheelchair and they woke him up and helped him into it. Together they wheeled him across the crosswalk into the ER entrance. Bloom spoke with the ER doctor and told Stine the doctor would be examining him shortly. He said the blood test had been ordered and he'd see him a little later. Bloom washed his hands and went back to the office, dictated a note on Stine for the hospital record and called Dr. Winger's office. He then called Ida and gave her a head's up on Stine.

"Nothing yet, but a couple of things disturbed me," said Bloom to Ida. "He was pale, feverish, lethargic, and had some nasal bleeding. I'll see him after I see my first patient. I'll tell him I've spoken with you and will give him and you his results when they're available."

Bloom saw his patient and spoke with the ex-congresswoman who had bladder exstrophy that was treated in Raleigh, North Carolina. She thanked Bloom and said she was doing well. Her bladder biopsy was negative and she and her husband decided not to do the reconstructive surgery. She said when they came down to Florida next winter, they would like to take Bloom and his wife out for dinner.

"Did you get the DQ Blizzard I recommended?" asked Bloom.

"We always follow our doctor's advice," replied Alameda Dixon. "The 410 calories for the mini chocolate brownie extreme blizzard was worth it."

"That's my favorite," said Bloom. "I limit myself to only one a week."

"Thank God we don't have a DQ within 50 miles of our home."

Bloom laughed.

"Thanks for calling me," said Bloom, hanging up and writing a brief note in her chart.

"The hospital is on line 2," said Cathy through the intercom.

"This is Dr. Bloom."

"Hi, Dr. Bloom. This is Meryl in the ER. Your patient William Stine has a recurrence of his AML. We've already called Dr. Winger."

"Does the patient know? If not, don't tell him. I'll be there in ten minutes."

"I think he knows."

"Okay."

Bloom returned to the ER, spoke with the ER physician and went to see Stine.

"I heard the ER doctor tell the nurse to call Dr. Winger," said Stine. "I assumed it was about me. Was I correct? My leukemia came back?"

"Yes."

"You suspected that. What's next?"

"That's up to Dr. Winger."

"Will I need a bone marrow transplant?"

"Not initially. But really, I don't know what needs to be done at this time."

"Is Dr. Winger going to see me?"

"She's been called. I'll see if she's responded. Hold on."

Bloom walked over to the nursing station and asked to see Nurse Meryl.

"I'm Nurse Meryl," replied the first person he saw. "You're Dr. Bloom?"

"Yes, Ma'am. Have you heard from Dr. Winger?"

"No. Dr. Winger has not returned the call. Do you want me to call her?"

"No thanks. I'll call her when I get back to the office. Is he febrile and is his U/A back yet?"

"His temp is 101 and his U/A, chest X-ray, and KUB are pending. Are you going to admit him?"

"Dr. Winger probably will."

"Nice meeting you, Dr. Bloom."

"Same here," answered Bloom. He wrote a note in Stine's chart and called Dr. Winger, who was with a patient. He went back to his office, called Ida, brought her up to date, and told her he had reconsidered and would continue being Bill's urologist for all aspects of urology.

CHAPTER 116

DITTO PREVIOUS TREATMENT

Bloom finished the vasectomy and learned that Stine had a minimally obstructing three-millimeter kidney stone in the distal right ureter and remembered Stine's back pain was on the left. He went back to the hospital, looked at the ultrasound, reexamined Stine, looked at the urine report and concluded that he would not concern himself with the kidney stone at this moment. He wrote a note in Stine's chart and told him he had reconsidered and would continue to take care of him for all urological matters.

He then spoke with Dr. Winger and learned that Stine was to be started on the same regimen that got him his remission and that he would need a follow-up bone marrow transplant. Bloom ordered a urine culture and for the urines to be strained for stones and for him to be notified if Mr. Stine had worsening of his right back pain or developed pain on the left.

He then called Ida and got her up to speed regarding Bill. She called Bloom fifteen minutes later, after hearing from Bill that Bloom was still Bill's urologist for all urologic conditions. Bloom said he had changed his mind because he felt much better when he learned the two circumcisions he performed were totally arranged by Jones and that Stine had only found about them after the fact.

Bloom saw two consults and hurried to the office to see a new patient who had not been able to urinate since early yesterday evening.

The patient had previous prostate surgery in New York with resulting urethral strictures that required dilatations. Using filiforms and followers, he was able to dilate the stricture and insert a catheter. Aretha told him that Stine had just passed the kidney stone and that a KUB was being done to show the stone was no longer present.

CHAPTER 117

TRANSPLANT ON THE DOCKET

Like he had with his first inductive phase of AML treatment, Stine had an episode of sepsis during this one, requiring and responding to a different antibiotic regimen than the first, and then had an uneventful consolidation phase. His bone marrow showed nine percent blast cells. The repeat biopsy showed a further clearing of the cancerous cells, and his and other oncologists advised him to proceed with the bone marrow transplant, which Ida now agreed to. He had broken ties with President Russell Clark, the new leader of the American Nazi Party, and the racial and anti-Semitic epithets that he had hurled for all of his adult life were now being hurled at him by others around the globe, including some in his immediate circles. His illness precluded proceeding with his plan for an elective circumcision at the present time, even if done under local anesthesia, to which he acquiesced after listening to Dr. Bloom, his psychologist, and his local rabbis.

Both Ida and Rachel (especially Rachel) were amazed how quickly the trio had bonded, considering the bitter animosity and outright disdain the women had had to overcome. They were surprised by Stine's apparent genuine remorse for the past things he admitted to having done. They wondered at whether a person could change so quickly. On the other hand, Stine's admiration and regard for Ida was readily apparent and was believed to be authentic, especially considering the work he left behind and his wanting to proceed with his circumcision. Stine had many questions regarding the bone marrow transplant process, but his main concern was what Ida would have to go through. He was reasonably assured that it would be a painless process, done under general anesthesia, which might result in some minor back soreness for a few days, and that whatever marrow was taken from her would be replaced by natural processes in a few weeks. Although he knew the survival rate for a sixty-two-year-old going through this was less than 50 percent, his new outlook on life and desire to share his remaining time with his new family made him anxious to move forward with the chemo and get on with the transplant. A repeat bone marrow biopsy one week later revealed no malignant cells present. According to Dr. Winger, there would be no benefit in waiting to do the bone marrow transplant. Ida will need to be cleared for general anesthesia. Stine, because of his age and recent chemotherapy, will undergo a reduced intensity conditioning regimen consisting of total body irradiation and Cytoxan chemotherapy to wipe out his marrow, stop the growth of abnormal cells, produce space in his marrow for Ida's implant, and help prevent his rejection of the donated stem cells. Ida was told she'd have no pain during the procedure but may have some back pain afterward that would be relieved by mild analgesics and that what was taken from her would be replaced by her own body within a few weeks. Stine was told he might have some GI side effects, swelling of his salivary glands, and hair loss. He was also told that he'd be in the hospital for three months and be receiving antibiotics, antifungals, and immunosuppressants and would be allowed masked and gowned visitors in his room.

As planned, Stine scheduled his irradiation and chemo for three days later and Ida for the bone marrow portion the following day, assuming she was cleared by her cardiologist. The next day Ida was cleared, and all systems were go for two days from then.

CHAPTER 118

X-RAY AND CHEMO PRELUDE

tine, Ida, and Rachel spent the next two days holed up in Ida's house and went to the radiation oncologist and chemotherapist together. The X-ray machine looked like a monster from a science fiction movie. It was huge, scary-looking, and made a creaking noise. It also moved and rotated. It made all of them nervous. The planning session took almost two hours. Stine's jewelry, watch, and glasses were taken from him. He was told to lie down on the machine's couch. His body parts were measured and the amount of radiation they would receive was monitored by attaching diodes to them. Gel pads were placed between his legs and over his neck and chest, and he was tied down to the couch. The machine was turned on, and after fifteen minutes the machine rotated 180 degrees to simulate irradiating the other half of his body. He was told about the myriad side effects he might have from the X-rays, among them bleeding from the nose and gums, fibrosis of his lungs, and cataracts.

They went for lunch and then spent an hour with the chemotherapist, who explained the Cytoxan chemotherapy he was to receive over the next three days along with its possible side effects.

All this for much less than a fifty percent cure rate, but he never told Ida or Rachel that fact. *And to think,* Stine said to himself, *I'm never going to feel as good as I am feeling today.* Did it make any sense for him to go through with it and subject Ida to her part of this "experiment," as he called it? He promised he'd have this discussion with them when they got home. When they did get home Stine said he had something to talk with them about. After he was finished—actually before he was finished—they interrupted him and said they knew about that statistic but didn't think he knew it and they weren't going to tell him, though they didn't believe the statistic and neither should he. So it was settled. Ida drove Stine to the hospital two days later and stayed with him until he was strapped onto the couch. She stayed with him for two days of X-rays and Cytoxan therapy and went home to get ready for the next day's marrow letting.

CHAPTER 119

NO, NO, NO!

At 6:05 a.m. Bloom got a call from Rachel telling him that Ida was not at home when she came to pick her up, and that her front door was open, her car was in the driveway, and her wallet and cell phone were on the kitchen table. He looked at the clock on the nightstand and realized that Peter should still be asleep. Nonetheless, he checked to make sure Peter was in his bed and not yet at his bus stop, a reasonable response, thought Bloom, considering his past dealings with Stine's henchman Jones and Ida now being missing. He decided he'd call Stine at 7:00 if he hadn't heard from him or Rachel by then.

At 6:50 Rachel called back with nothing further to report other than that Ida had taken her medicines with her and that Quacker and Purrer were still in the house. Bloom told her he'd speak with Stine and let her know if he found out anything. Ten minutes later Rachel called Bloom back and told him the hospital had called her and said that Ida did not show up and wanted to know if she'll be there soon. At that point, Rachel told the hospital that she thought Ida may be missing.

At 7:30 Bloom called Rachel and learned nothing new. Bloom asked her if she had gotten any strange calls and she said she had not. He did not think Stine was getting irradiated at this moment, so he put a call through to him. Stine picked up immediately.

"Ida's not here yet," began Bloom. "And she's not answering her phone," he added.

"I know Ida is missing," said Stine. "I just got off the phone with Jones, the guy I fired a few months ago. He wants money."

"How is Ida?"

"I think okay."

"What can I do?"

"Nothing right this second. I have the money. I just have to get it to him."

"Can that be done today?"

"Yes. Jones is vindictive. But he's usually reasonable. It depends on how reasonable he is after he gets the money."

"How much is he demanding?"

"I'd rather not say. It's a fairly large amount."

"Can I tell Rachel what's going on?"

"Yes, please tell her. And tell her Ida is okay. I should be finished with my irradiation by the time my bank opens. Tell her I'll call her as soon as I can."

"How are you doing with the chemo?"

"My mouth's a little dry. I keep hydrating. It's not a problem."

"You've always been a very good patient."

"It doesn't help being a bad one. Time to get onto the couch," added Stine, seeing the X-ray transport team coming into his room.

"Good luck," said Bloom.

"You're a mensch," said Stine.

"Is that the first time you've called someone a mensch?"

"I've always thought you were one, but I didn't know the word yet."

"And so are you," replied Bloom chuckling.

After the final of three irradiation courses was completed, Stine was brought back to his room. The only glitch in today's treatment was at the halfway mark when Stine was rotated 180 degrees. A wave of nausea overcame him, which required the couch to go back to the ninety-degree mark and a cold compress was applied to his head. As soon as he got back to his room he called his friend, the president of the First National Bank of Miami, and using the bank name, account number, and routing number Jones had given him, wired five million dollars to Jones's off-shore account. The original three million price was bumped to four, and then five when Stine insisted she be brought to the hospital today.

At 4:30 p.m. Stine got a call from the bank president that the account number to where the money was to be wired was incorrect and the transfer was not made. By the time Stine got the correct number, he was told the transfer would have to wait until the next day.

CHAPTER 120

GUNFIGHT IN CORAL SPRINGS

The elevator on the sixth floor opened and Jones, another goon, and Ida got out. The hood that had been placed on Ida in her house was removed just before she exited the elevator. The three of them, with Ida in the middle, turned right and stopped at room 610. Ida purposely dropped her purse and nonchalantly looked back to the left as she picked it up, noting the exit sign some sixty yards away. Turning back to the right she noted construction was taking place on the remaining right side of the sixth floor. There was no exit sign seen on the right end. She thought escaping via the left was definitely the order of the day, probably of the night. A paid ransom followed by her death seemed in the cards for her. The latter would have been acceptable a short time ago, but not now. Jones used a keycard to open the door, and when he checked the adjoining room door to make sure it was locked, Ida realized they must be in some kind of hotel. Her room had no phones, TV, or mini bar, but had a large bathroom with a Jacuzzi tub. Before they left her there, they both essentially violated her in looking for a concealed phone and gun. She knew now that they would have to kill her. Throughout the day and night, using a cup and her ear to the wall, she listened for sounds coming from the 608 and 612 rooms, and hearing none, assumed these rooms were empty. She was happy to see some utensils that would allow her to pick the lock to the adjoining room and also some tools in the cabinets that would help her hot-wire a car, a skill she learned through her stints in the Israeli Army. She was also happy she could find a way to lock the bathroom door from outside the bathroom, which would give her extra time to distance herself from Jones and his goon.

The daytime hours could not pass fast enough. Jones was stationed at her door and there was always someone with him as she heard talking throughout the day. Jones brought her food into the room and took out what was left over. She knew she had to get everyone that was outside her door to come to her bathroom door for her to escape.

She had gone over her plan several times. She so wanted to get a message to Bill, but had no phone and no access to one. But she thought that by now he had been in contact with Jones, and he knew she was at least alive and a ransom plan had been established. She knew Bill would pay it. She also knew Bill had some men that were still loyal to him and that after this episode Jones would suffer the consequences of her abduction and the men's violation of her should Bill find out.

At 10:00 p.m. Ida took her meds except for the blood thinner and remembered she had to be NPO for the next day's bone marrow letting. She got her handbag ready and checked the penlight she kept in there. She set her vibratory watch alarm for 3:05 a.m. for her 3:15 planned departure and shut off all but the hallway light and put her head on the pillow. At 3:05 she was awakened by her alarm. At 3:10 she opened her half of the adjoining door to 608 and using the fork and knife and hallway light, opened the other half of the adjoining door. She put on her shower, turned the heat up to maximum, waited for five minutes, closed the bathroom door, now locked from the outside, put her utensils into the bag with her tools and meds, and screamed help as loud as she could three times, then grabbed her handbag, went into 608, closed both halves of the adjoining doors and waited at the 608 door to the hallway, listening for the hallway door to 610 to open. When it did, she counted to ten, opened 608's door, then closed it and ran to the exit door at the end of the hallway. She took the stairs to the ground floor and out the building's side door. She was happy no alarms had gone off and didn't think she'd been seen. She ran past four dumpsters and onto a sidewalk, which brought her to the back of the building. She purposely started running away from the building, taking the wrong way down a one-way street that led toward the building so that anyone looking for her by car would not initially see her. She didn't know how much time she had before Jones would know she was missing. She was glad he allowed her to keep her running shoes on and had planned to run for at least ten minutes and thus put at least a mile's distance between herself and Jones before she'd look for an unlocked car to hot wire. She was happy she had run a half marathon within the past three months.

When Ida did not open the bathroom door, Jones dialed the operator and asked for a maintenance person to be sent to the room to open the locked bathroom door. After five minutes and no maintenance person yet showing up, Jones took out his gun and shot the door's hardware. Still not able to open the door he shot the door three more times. When he finally opened the bathroom door and found the room empty, he checked the rest of the 610 room, opened the adjoining door to 608, shot open the 608 half of the door, and looked through the 608 room.

Following the mile run, Ida crossed the intersection and began looking for an unlocked car. At the end of the second block, she spotted an open 1990 VW. She took out the wire cutter, screwdriver, and penlight and removed the plastic cover around the steering column to reach the ignition switch and removed the screws under the steering wheel. This enabled her to find the wiring harness for the ignition switch. She located, cut, and stripped the positive battery, starter, and ignition wires. Then she twisted the battery and ignition wires and heard the ignition turn on. She touched the starter motor cable to the positive battery cable and the car started up. This coincided with a spark of light going on inside the car as the VW was being passed by Jones, who spotted Ida crouched down on the driver's side and slammed on his brakes just as Ida put her car in gear and turned the wheel in the direction of the oncoming traffic. Before Jones could turn the car around, Ida floored the VW gas pedal, turned right at the next corner, drove three short blocks, and turned left without seeing Jones's car in her rearview mirror. When she reached Commercial Boulevard, she smiled and turned right, crossed over the turnpike, then turned left on University Drive and took the back way to the Coral Springs Radiation Center. She ran to the nurses' desk, asked to use the phone, and dialed Bill's number.

"Ida?" shouted Bill.

"Sorry I took so long to get here," she replied.

"Where are you?"

"I'm here at the Radiation Center. Oh no, they've followed me. I've gotta run!" she yelled, hanging up and running toward the back of the building and spotting a security guard.

"There's a man with a gun," shouted Ida, running behind a dumpster and taking the stairs down to the laundry. She climbed into the fourth open industrial-sized washer and hid between the wet sheets and towels.

"Wait!" yelled Stine to no avail. He disconnected the call and dialed 911, telling the sergeant who he was and what was about to happen.

He unhooked his IV fluid bag and found comfort and safety in the bottom of a linen closet in an empty room on the floor below after first securing his IV fluid bag on a shelf above in a pile of washcloths and face towels. Stine and Ida both heard solitary shots and the scurrying of people above and below them. This was followed by periods of silence, then more scurrying and rapid rounds of gunfire, mixed with sirens, horns blowing, and ambulances. This continued for another forty minutes. Then everything stopped. Neither knew whether or not it was safe to come out, so they stayed hidden for another hour.

Stine dialed 911 and told the dispatcher where he was and asked if it was safe for him to come out of hiding. When he was told it was, he asked the dispatcher to send someone to the radiation center and go to each floor and announce, "The eagle has landed!" Fifteen minutes later Stine heard the four words and slowly stood up grabbed his fluid bag, waited for those words to be said on his floor, walked out of the closet, and found a Broward County police officer waiting. He asked him if he had seen an elderly female who was not in hospital clothing, but the officer said he knew nothing of her. That's good, Stine thought.

"How many people were shot?" he asked the officer.

"Four," he was told. "One hospital security guard, one police officer, and two others."

"Any killed?" asked Stine.

"All of them. Were you the one that called 911?"

"Yes."

"You saw what was happening?"

"No. I was in a room on this floor. Listen. I need to find my mother. I'll tell you everything after we find her. She's hiding somewhere in this facility. She may not have a phone with her. If she does, it's probably not hers. Her name is Ida Stern. Can you please get me a wheelchair?"

The officer got a wheelchair with an attached IV pole and transported Stine with his IV bag to an elevator. "Have you checked all the floors?" asked Stine.

"I've checked the lobby and the upper floors. Nothing so far."

"Can we check what's below the main floor?"

"There's a parking area and a laundry."

They went to the lowest floor and got out. The officer checked the thirty or so cars in the parking area and returned to Stine.

They went to the laundry area. The ten washing machines were open and each was sitting in front of an open dryer.

"Ida, I'm here!" shouted Stine. "You're safe now!"

"I'm in washer number 4," yelled Ida. "I'm cold and wet."

"I've got a dry towel," cried Stine ecstatic to hear her voice, music to his ears.

CHAPTER 121

IT HAPPENED

The early morning crime scene where four people died—hospital security guard Leon Ainsley, James Jones and his goon, and Broward County Officer Marvin McTate—should have shut down the hospital. But since the patient had already received three days of pre-transplant irradiation and antibiotics, the hospital deemed it necessary to proceed immediately with the transplant, and a quart and a half of the best matched bone marrow was taken from the patient's mother, Ida Stern, and transplanted to her son, William Stine, later that day.

EPILOGUE

William Stine (now Sigmund Berger) spent the next four months at the hospital, with Ida Stern (now Ida Berger) and Rachel Stern at his bedside each day. By day 24, engraftment began when Ida's donated cells made their way to Sigmund's marrow and began making new blood cells. Although he had a few bouts of mucosal lining infections in his mouth and GI tract (mucositis), there was no graft failure or graft-versus-host disease. Through Ida and Rachel, Sigmund made a list of 65 relatives and Jewish friends who Ida and Rachel knew from Berlin, representing a small portion of the 60,000 Jews who were deported from Berlin to death camps in Germany, Czechloslavakia (Theresienstadt), and Poland. Through the internet and the National Holocaust Archives in Asia, Australia, Europe, and North and South America, Bloom was able to learn that seven were still alive.

He was able to obtain the addresses of Marie Knoop, Adele Bekker, and Gert Strauss and told all three of them he would like to meet with them. Shortly after discharge, Sigmund was circumcised by Bloom and had all of his swastika tattoos removed. With the tattoo ink removed from his buttocks, a scar consistent with the scar received in infancy was now apparent.

Six months later, the three traveled to Canada, Germany, Israel, Queens, Brooklyn, and Manhattan.

GLOSSARY OF ABBREVIATIONS

ACLU	American Civil Liberties Union
ADA	American Disabilities Act
ADL	American Defamation League
AMA	Against Medical Advice
BCG	Bacillus Camette-Guerin (bladder cancer therapy)
CBC	Complete Blood Count
CBI	Continuous Bladder Irrigation
CPT	Current Procedural Technology
CT	Computerized Technology scan
CVA	Cerebrovascular Accident (a stroke)
ER	Emergency Room
Epi	Epinephrine
H&H	Hematocrit and hemoglobin
Hasid	Member of a pious orthodox Jewish sect
HIPAA	Health Insurance Portability and Accountability Act (patient health privacy act)
HLA	Antibodies produced by the immune system in response to foreign antigens
ICU	Intensive Care Unit
IVP	Intravenous Pyelogram (a kidney X-ray)
Joules	Unit of work energy given to shock someone back into normal sinous rhythm
KUB	An X-ray of the kidneys, ureter, and bladder
MGB	A sports coupe made by British Motor Corp
MI	Myocardial Infarction (heart attack)
NPO	Nil pers os (a Latin phrase that translates to "nothing by mouth"; a medical order given to prevent a patient from eating anything)

OR	Operating Room
PSA	Prostate-Specific Antigen (used to diagnose prostate cancer)
SMA17	A specific panel of blood tests
TBC	To Be Confirmed
V-Fib	Abnormal heart rate that requires immediate treatment
WBCs	White Blood Cells

ABOUT THE AUTHOR

Warren Streisand is a retired physician living with his wife in South Florida. He has spent the last fifty years practicing urology and mentoring medical residents from the University of Miami's Miller School of Medicine. He enjoys fishing, golfing, and playing competitive pickleball.